AF424447

VISIONS OF SNAPDRAGON

THE SEER'S BLESSING: BOOK 1

Jana Sun

Copyright © 2023 by Jana Sun

All rights reserved.

No part of this publication may be reproduced, distributed, or transmitted in any form or by any means, including photocopying, recording, or other electronic or mechanical methods, without the prior written permission of the publisher, except as permitted by U.S. copyright law. For permission requests, contact Jana Sun at www.janasun.com.

The story, all names, characters, and incidents portrayed in this production are fictitious. No identification with actual persons (living or deceased), places, buildings, and products is intended or should be inferred.

Book Cover by Etheric Designs

1st edition 2023

Contents

Chapter One

JACK

Wine drunk, I went scrying barefoot under a full moon during an unusually warm November night, with only my cat tethering me to the physical world. The ground was still too cold, making my toes ache but not enough to walk back inside. The night breeze caressed my face, cooling the flush in my cheeks. I'd made better choices in my time, but the energy was right. My crystal ball glittered in the moonlight. The sky was black and clear; I could count as many stars in the sky as there were in the crystal in my hands. There was magic in the wind.

I knew better than to scry alone, but the magic pulled me, the moon called me, and the wine made me too brave.

The energy of the universe hummed in my chest, blood pumping through my temples. Everything was aligning. I felt it. The moon glowed, and I felt the atoms of my being aligning to its energy. This was right. My visions weren't always precise–sometimes I had to listen a little closer or squint to make out the details, but not tonight. Letting myself fall deeper into the magic, I could hear a name.

Dei—

My fat cat, Puddin, meowed loudly, piercing through the magic to pull my feet back to the earth. She had white fur with gray spots that shone in the moonlight. She was massive from all the fluff and too many treats, and she glowed, watching me and flicking her fluffy tail. I should have made a stronger anchor when wandering this far into the magic. Tethering a soul to the mortal plane was a lot of responsibility for a creature that cares more about her dinner than making sure I'm there to open the can.

"Oh, Jack, what are you doing, girl?" I said under my breath.

Puddin rubbed against my leg, and I felt the earth under me more. I felt the dirt on the soles of my feet, the softness of it, the wetness of the grass. I tasted the wine on my lips and I knew I'd feel that in the morning.

What was that name? It was slipping through my fingers already. Even with Puddin demanding some attention, I wasn't ready to let go of my circle and drop the magic. The magic was still there, still wanting my attention too, and I needed to listen to it.

Tell me your name again, please, I pleaded with the vision.

Usually, my visions were quick, easy. I'd get everything I needed to know within a few seconds, processed a few seconds later, and back to my normal self within fifteen total. Usually.

Tonight wasn't a usually kind of night.

Energy surged against me—two figures. Male. Dark green energy and black energy. Not hostile. Not to me anyway. They reeked of death and sandalwood, and I could have sworn that I knew them.

The black energy clouded my mind, and it choked me. I was suffocating from the weight of it in my chest. I was holding my breath as a bubble formed between my ribs and—

It popped, and the dark green presence forced its way to the forefront of my mind.

Green was more normal-ish. Uncommon, but human. An alchemist, a witch. Magic. I felt their auras, their essence passing through me, wrapping tightly around my heart. The green one matched my own aura; green like the earth, like life. His–and it was definitely a he–was a deep, forest green. The darker the hue, the stronger the magic. Mine wasn't that dark and I was decent at magic. I made my living with it, but his aura was the color of the earth at night. His magic would be astounding in person.

I couldn't see their faces, but I felt them, and that was enough for the moment.

"I'll find you," a voice whispered in my ear. Metaphysical ear. I wasn't fully back in my body and I was too drunk to know where my parts started and where the crystal ended.

And then, the vision truly hit.

This was the not-so-fun part of being a psychic. Sometimes, a vision would hit me like a brick, and I prayed that I wasn't operating a vehicle, holding anything remotely weapon-like, or otherwise doing something that landed me in the emergency room. Again. Most of the time, I could go through the whole vision while still being upright and no one would be the wiser.

I sat down, the evening dew seeping through my jeans and chilling my over-warm skin, and let the vision run its course. I always tried to ground my human senses while the vision like this took over. This time of year, the nights smelled like winter had already arrived–crisp air, almost too sharp in your chest, and pine.

My eyes were cloudy, hazy, and the vision bloomed fully in my mind. The figures felt familiar, and I stayed tapped into their energy. They walked shoulder to shoulder, Green bigger than Black, but only slightly. It was air-less around Black, like the pressure of a thunderstorm, and the suffocating feeling came back. Green moved easily, hastily. They were only outlines, but I'd know them instantly if I saw them on the street.

Puddin nibbled at my toes and I snapped back to the present. Coming back from a big vision made me a bit nauseous. Sorta like that pre-puke feeling from light food poisoning. The citrine pendant against my heart gently pulsed, sending heat through me to combat the chill. Magic wasn't innate to humans, not really. We tapped into the natural magic of the earth, but we needed some help. Something to channel it, like a pendant. Or a crystal ball–which was also good for my psychic reading and magical artifacts shop.

"Jack, are you back here?" My best friend, Mari, called out.

"Here," I yelled back. My voice was always quieter than hers, even though I wasn't a quiet person. Mari commanded attention whenever she entered a space. She was already barefoot, stepping lightly through the patchy grass of my backyard. Being the corner lot had its advantages; having a large patch of earth to cast with was a blessing, even if it was full of crabgrass. My backyard had enough space for my gardens and planter boxes too. I had four official planter boxes, a good dozen other flower pots, a trellis for climbing plants, and a large garden arch near the gate to the front yard. The six-foot stark white privacy fence acted as a physical and magical perimeter; Mari and I had been laying protection spells around this place for years. This space was our sanctuary.

"Moon's clear tonight," she said. I replied with a hmm, and she plopped down next to me in the dirt. Her pants were going to be wet too, but they were already covered in paint stains and clay. Mari had a small dresser in my apartment full of extra clothes, and I had a flash of her digging through the bottom drawer for her old, ugly yoga pants that she should have tossed out ages ago. I passed her the bottle of wine and like the classy ladies we were, she took a swig.

"Good night to scry," I said.

"Figured you'd be out here, but I was thinking you'd call before you went into the looking glass."

"I had Puddin with me."

"And she's lovely, but a stronger pull would have been smarter."

Mari would never outright say you're an idiot. She got the point across with a shoulder bump. We'd been in each other's lives since we were born. When her mama passed away, there was no question where she would go: with us. Now she lived in another apartment complex just down the road but we were never apart for long. Mari wanted space, wanted to stand on her feet, and even though those were also words she would never say, she wanted freedom. I bumped her back.

"I saw an alchemist and something else," I told her. Alchemists made the magical artifacts we needed to cast any type of magic; a witch was the common term for an alchemist. We're both alchemists. Mari made objects, I made ingestible magic. It sounded like drugs because it's a little bit like drugs. Everything I made was legal. But it wasn't too hard to guess which products sold better than others.

"Something?"

"I think so." Guilt tugged at my heart; he wasn't a something. He was a someone.

"Hrm, anyone we know?"

I chewed on the inside of my cheek. "I think he could blow us out of the water."

"Damn, should we be worried?" Neither one of us brought up the last vision I had, and I was grateful for it. Puddin curled up in my lap, all twenty-five pounds of her, and her soft purr rumbled through me. Thinking about that other energy was like itching a bug bite; the more I dug at it, the more I had to. It—he?—was dying and my heart ached. What was that name?

"I made you some new bracelets for the shop," Mari said, the thin bangles on her wrists jingling as she moved. She specialized in jewelry. Beads, crystals, and gems on hemp or braided wire. They were lovely, and a hit with my customers. All of the magic we sold was ordinary enough that it couldn't harm a fly: gentle healing spells, spices and tea mixes to calm the nerves from all natural items. Magic was more ordinary than most thought; it's the science we know and the things we couldn't explain. My shop specialized in both.

"Can't wait to see them," I said, standing up to grab Mari's hand and tug her to her feet.

"We're gonna talk about that other vision and whatever else you're tryin' to hide once you're sober, by the way." I felt the raised eyebrow without having to see it. Her hair was in long, thin braids tonight that jingled when she moved.

"Uggghhhhhhhh."

"Groan all you want. I'm still calling Peony in the morning." Peony, bless her, was my older sister. She worried like she's paid to do it and single-handedly kept at least three antacid companies in business. She's our contract queen; nothing legally or magically binding happened without her seal of approval. Peony was the only one in the family that didn't make a living from magic. She had quite possibly the most life-draining job on the planet: she's a lawyer. Peony and I could connect our magic to amplify my visions, but she said it gave her heartburn. Really, my visions gave Peony the heebie-jeebies, and she didn't want to know about her future, or anyone else's.

She lived in NoVa, northern Virginia, but came down once a month to visit. I hated to admit how much I missed her when she wasn't here, but Cape Margaret was too small for the life she wanted for herself.

"Nachos?" I asked, desperate to distract Mari from dragging Peony down a whole two weeks before her planned trip.

"Duh, I already ordered delivery. Should be here any minute." Mari had her own set of keys to my place and let us inside. We bypassed the first floor, which was my store, and went up the stairs leading up to the home portion of the building. The front porch and door opened directly into the store, but the back entrance had a small mud-room and the stairs hidden away. Puddin hustled back to the house with the promise of nachos. She probably shouldn't eat half of the things on them but it's hard to tell a cat that can float and teleport no. She showed up on my doorstep about five years ago, mewing to come in and then promptly teleported on to my kitchen counter and started nibbling on my chicken salad sandwich. I saw the aura of magic around her and when she looked at me, I heard her tell me that this was her home now too.

Mari jogged back down the stairs when the doorbell rang. I hoped she tipped the driver a little extra for the late night run; it was well past midnight. Mari and Puddin had already torn into the pile of nachos by the time I realized they were unpacked. I closed my casting circle too quickly, dropping it faster than I had wanted to, and the magic from the vision lingered. It had more to say to me, but wasn't ready. I couldn't tell if it was the wine, the intensity of the moon, or the vision itself, but I wasn't hungry. My cat and best friend parked themselves at the breakfast bar, a trail of Mari's things on the floor right behind them. Nachos and toppings were everywhere on the small nook, and I settled on my old couch. My stomach churned and I wrapped my favorite shawl around my shoulders. Mama had infused it with jasmine and–

Sandalwood.

The voice from the vision was back. My eyes were clouded, and the choking, heavy energy drowned out the rest of my senses.

"Blossom."

Definitely wasn't the wine.

CHAPTER TWO

JACK

The smell of espresso woke me. I didn't remember really dragging myself to bed; the night was a bit of haze. The magic from the vision still rattled through me, and I was groggy. Coffee sounded divine. Peony and Mari sat in the kitchen with their favorite cups in hand.

Peony.

Peony was here.

When–

Puddin materialized on the table, brushing noses with Peony, fluffy white tail flicking back and forth, waiting for me to say something about her being on the table. I didn't. She was perilously close to knocking Peony's pink "fuck around and find out," flower mug off the table. Mari lifted her cup to her lips, taking another sip. The little foxes on the badly rendered version of Monet's *Water Lilies* peeked out around her fingers. It was truly the ugliest coffee mug ever created.

My small four-person round table felt full with them sitting there. Their energies were stronger than normal today, and I was already planning on making myself a double shot. It took me another beat to realize that Peony was *here*, sipping away at her coffee, way ahead of her scheduled visit. I glared at Mari and she glared back.

"Darling, you look like you've been dead for three days," Peony said. She looked effortlessly pretty. Very boho lawyer. Everything about Peony was pink. Her oversized pink glasses sat low on her little button nose with her strawberry blond hair with soft pink streaks piled in a messy bun. Flowy pink skirt and slouchy cream sweater with her favorite necklaces: one for each of us. They sat at varying lengths, a Jack-in-the-pulpit flower for me, a peony for her, and then a marigold for Mari. All of us had flowers relating to our names, and she wore small gold coins etched with each flower.

Peony would joke that she and I had the same face, only hers knew how to be a face better than mine, and it was a little true. Peony's smiles were always perfect, sharp and sassy or sweet and genuine, she was always photo ready. I wasn't; I was Peony without the makeup, and I preferred it that way.

"You're here early. Did Mari call you?"

"No, you did. I felt you pass out, so I drove down last night. I got here a couple hours ago and let myself in. What happened?" Straight to the point, as always.

"She was out scrying after a bottle of red." She winked at me.

"Mari!"

"Jack–"

"I can explain–"

"Meeeow!" Puddin yeowed and we all stilled to look at her. *Let her speak*, she shot through us. Puddin could and would speak aloud when she wanted, but jolting us with a bit of magic never got old for her.

"Go on before we get the claws," Mari jingled as she spoke. Her hair always had beads or sequins. Today she had her tight curls in space buns on her head with gold bobbles in them. I knew the braids wouldn't last long. Mari was my opposite in every way–her dark skin was always annoyingly flawless to my fair but suntanned freckled skin. Her dark curls to my pin-straight auburn. Dark brown eyes to hazel. I wasn't a troll or anything, but it was hard to stand next to Mari and not feel a bit trollish. Mari had her mom's pale blue sweater on, and she picked at the hem of her right sleeve. It would be threadbare if she didn't stop but of course there was no stopping her.

"I couldn't pass up a super moon like that," I said. I buzzed around the kitchen, my back to them, so I didn't have to see their worried faces. Neither of them really approved of scrying–it wasn't forbidden magic, or any nonsense like that, but looking into the Veil meant being willing to leave the plane you're planted on. They weren't on board for that, but I was.

"And that's the only reason you went wine scrying?" Peony asked. I felt the edges of magic in her words, like a little itch in the back of your throat. Peony could gently suggest that you go jump off a bridge, and you'd ask which one.

I added the sugar in my favorite mug, just clear glass, a softly curved golden handle. The coffee dripped into the mug, and I held my breath until Peony's magic forced a couple of words out.

"Well, mostly."

"What did you see?" Mari asked.

"Me, I think." I squeaked more than I had intended. I was a fairly renowned psychic. I sold readings and even helped solve a few crimes, but I've never seen my own future until last week. It came in flashes, much sharper than a normal vision, like someone opening and snapping a book closed in my mind. I looked green, which wasn't that weird because all witches looked kinda green in visions, but I was overgrown. My face wrinkled with the texture of leaves, vines twining in my hair, moss on skin. I felt neglected and alone. I didn't leave my shop or apartment for three days after the vision. The woman in the visions had the same set of eyes as me, but the sharpness of her nose, the pointy bow of her lips was harsher than I ever looked. I was rounder, softer than this woman. My almost-face kept popping back up when I'd look in the mirror or see my reflection in a crystal. It happened so fast that it felt surreal, but the rage in her eyes from each flash left me shaking. I needed the gravity of the moon to ground me further so I could dig deeper into my magic to see what these visions meant.

I told them the details quickly and neither of them said a word: she cried, she screamed, she looked straight at me with nothing but burning, searing rage. So much magic surrounded her, it was like she had no *body,* just energy. She'd touch her face, confused, reach for me and I'd snap back. She was falling; constantly falling. The vision felt groundless, like I was hovering above her, and she hovered near me, and she just kept dropping. I kept dropping, and snapping back before we crashed.

It wasn't the strangest or even the darkest vision I'd ever had, but being the star of it unnerved me. I liked not seeing my future. Truth be told, I never saw the appeal in wanting to know. Why ruin the surprise of your life? Why try to alter what the Fates had written for you?

Now I knew why I was content to live in ignorance.

I never wanted to be that pointed or sharp. I breathed in the scent of the coffee, bold and strong, and envisioned those same traits for myself. I'd do anything to avoid that rage from the visions.

"We're doing a spell tonight. The moon will be high enough still and you're stuck in the vision. I can practically smell it on you. You stay upstairs today and rest. Mari and I will run the shop." Peony spoke in absolutes—I will rest, they will run the shop. End of discussion.

"Speaking of, I'll go down and open up. It's already ten." Mari dug through my kitchen junk drawer for the spare keys to the store and till. She bumped her knuckles with Peony, gave my arm a quick little squeeze and headed downstairs. Puddin blinked out, presumably to take her sacred place on the window to watch and entice customers to come in.

"Thanks," I said. My instinct to fight them and insist I was *fiiiine* had taken the day off. I wasn't fine. I was hungover from too much merlot and too many visions.

"Goddess above, she's going quietly. I'm making chicken and dumplings." Peony was a godawful cook, but that was the one thing she could make, and it signaled to everyone that she had entered Crisis Mode. I grimaced; Crisis Mode was like having an overbearing sister who was also a pissed off grizzly bear. I let my hair down from my lifeless pony tail and even my hair smelled hung over. I needed a shower.

"Jack?" she said. She stood up to inspect me, to look for the pieces of magic that still had its grip around my throat or in my mind, and see how she could ease them.

"I'm good, really. Just a little hung over."

"You're lying, but that can wait. Shower. Sleep. I don't know how deep you went scrying, but you need to recover, that much is clear."

I didn't protest once again, and hugged my sister. She smoothed my hair, tucking it behind my ear.

"Yeah, shower first."

"Rude."

"I'm gonna start making some dumplings. I'll go help Mari in a bit."

I nodded; things were going to be okay. Her dumplings were my favorite thing, and Peony being here meant that things would be fine. I fought my instincts to go down to the shop, and instead headed for the shower.

MARI

There were already three customers hovering by the door by the time I hurried down to unlock and open Visions and Trinkets. Jack had a good head for business. When she was eighteen, Jack took over this shop. Her mama was made too much from wind to stay still, and once Jack announced her plans, she let herself take flight. It suited Jack. She had become an odd pillar of Cape Margaret. People came from the other Seven Cities on the eastern coast of Virginia to see her. Locals either tried too hard to befriend her or avoided her completely. Awkward as hell to me, but Jack was oblivious to their stares. Her future sight kept her eyes focused so forward she didn't see what happened on the day to day. Seeing Jack so confused and unsure made something in my gut twist; Jack wasn't prone to uncertainty. She lived her life easily, joyfully–watching her hide the images in her mind was a first for us.

Although Jack was a great business owner, she was a bit flighty, and that's why I have a set of keys to her home and business. And why I do her taxes.

"Excuse me, how much are the peace charms?" an older woman asked. I scanned over her, felt a wave of sadness hit me–her husband had passed recently–and gently guided her to the healing crystals. I couldn't predict the future any more than a horoscope, but my magic could read a crowd. Gut feelings, knowledge that rooted deep in my core, came from magic. My gift was my standard alchemy; my creations were stronger than Jack's or Peony's, and more focused. I understood the energy of all things, and that helped when pairing them together to make artifacts. But it also made any other kind of magic harder for me. Basic elemental spells, locating spells, healing spells–all hit or miss for me. Usually miss, but that's what practice was for.

"I think these are more what you're looking for, honey. Time heals all wounds, but a little bit of rhodolite and amethyst never hurt." I touched her hand and felt her sadness well up, ready to burst. I pushed a wave of warm, soft magic into her; I didn't know what this kind of magic was, but I could ease some pain with the warm, firelight of magic that burned in my chest. Her eyes shot up to me, the bubble of sadness suddenly lessening, and she squeezed my hand.

"Yes, um, that sounds lovely."

The other customers bought some tea and some pot and left quietly. Jack was also famous–*infamous?*–for being the nicest "drug dealer" in town. The weed she sold was all natural and cut with lots of other herbs, but she mixed each blend so uniquely that the high came more from the blend of magic than the weed itself. Her regulars tended to smell like they'd bathed in a spice rack.

The shop was divided into three spaces: the main shop where customers sifted through the crystals and packaged spells, her reading room that was all decked out in psychic kitschy decor, and her workroom where we made the charms and spells that she would sell. I stayed mostly in the main shop area. The energy that pulsed from Jack's crystal ball in the reading room was heady and made my skin itch.

The main shop area had lilac walls, with several metal and wood book-shelves along the walls. There were two large tables pushed against each other, covered in soft, light blue and green fabrics that each of us had added magic to. Peony added truth to them, so the customers would always find what they needed. I added warmth so they would find comfort, and Jack added wisdom so they would understand how the crystals and spells were intended to be used. Everything about the place hummed with magic, so much so that even the magic-less could feel it. The tables were metal and wood too, just like the bookshelves. Jack had arranged glass bowls of random designs and textures on the bowls. They ranged in size too, but the arrangement never made sense to me. I wanted them to be orderly; largest to smallest, colors in order. Jack said that the crystals needed to be arranged *just so*, but never explained what the "so" was. The hand-made signs were done by Peony, who, despite being a lawyer, had the prettiest handwriting out of all of us.

Once the shop was empty, Peony came down. She didn't love playing hostess in the store, but her and Jack could be twins when they wanted to be if you weren't paying attention. Their vibe was the same, one was just considerably more high strung and had pinker hair.

"Dumplings are going," she said.

"Good, that'll calm her down a bit," I said.

Peony trailed her fingers over the bowls of charms, adding another layer of magic. Always adding, Peony left soft traces of herself everywhere. When my mom died, Peony would sit on the bed their mom, Jazzy, had done up for me. She'd run her fingers over the seams of the quilts my mom made, adding a little extra magic, adding something to capture the smell of my mom's perfume forever in its fibers.

"Is she gonna have to raise the prices on those?" I asked. Peony smiled, and we both laughed.

"Just adding a bit of truth to them," she said.

"Guess that means they'll be on clearance soon."

"People don't like the truth?"

"Only their version of it." We eyed each other; our familiar dance of sarcasm. Peony played the older, wiser sister card very well. On Jack. I was wise enough for the both of us, and she knew it. Her grin was the wild, ferocious one that she never let loose around Jack. Even though we were edging up to our thirties, Peony still saw Jack as the baby sister, the one that needed to be protected instead of brought into the jokes. "Why are you here, P? Early, I mean."

"I told you, I felt something was wrong with Jack, so I came."

"Something's been wrong for a good two weeks now."

Peony sighed, barely audible enough for it to be a sigh. Peony Hawthorne certainly never *huffed* but she was pushing it.

"Something's off, Mari. I don't know what. Jack's visions are getting more intense, and it's hitting me too. I'm noticing that my magic gets a little wonky when she has one."

"Like a surge?"

"Or an ebb. Sometimes I'm asking a simple question, no magic at all, and getting some dark confessions. Other times, I'm *trying* to cast, and just, nothing. Something is seriously off, and I'm here to shore up the defenses."

"Off how? Like we need to add more cameras to catch a break in?"

"Marigold, I would not drive four hours in the middle of the night to help you set up cameras. I don't know what it is, and I'd prefer to keep it that way. I'm adding a few extra layers to her crystal ball and necklace too. And whatever artifact you want me to touch up for you." Peony was already at the windows, tracing the outline of the frames, a spell on her lips. She drew the sigils for iron and strength on the glass.

"For me?"

"When has a Jack problem *ever* just been a Jack problem?" I thought back through the years. There were the freaks and creeps that came with running a drug-adjacent store. Then there were the animals that sought her out like she was a real life fairy princess. Peony and I nodded, both instantly remembering the *bear* that escaped from the zoo, only to be found on Jack's doorstep, waiting for a belly rub. Then there were the unhinged folks, demanding that she not only read their futures but alter them. We couldn't forget about the lady that insisted she was an alien, either—

I felt a headache coming on.

"I'll give you my wand."

"A wand, really?"

"Girl, you love a good cliche as much as the next witch." She laughed, her glasses slipping down her nose, and rolled her eyes at me. No one uses wands, but the look on her face was worth the lame joke.

I handed her my amber bracelet and the amber around my neck. I pulled magic from amber more easily than any other stone. Everyone has a certain affinity for something, and amber was mine. Peony wrapped her fingers around the stones, being sure she touched each one. A light blue glow came from her hands, so I knew the spell was serious.

"Peony?"

"Just to be safe."

JACK

Green, green moss. My skin itched. I scrubbed my fingers through my hair, digging at my scalp. It felt gritty. My fingernails were brown with dirt. The moss was everywhere, I was overgrown again, magic tugging at my core, pulling to the earth again.

No, no, no, no, no. This isn't real. It's a vision. Just a vision. Breathe. Everything is fine. More than fine. It's great. Peachy.

I'm talking to myself.

Come back down, Jack, back to yourself.

I rolled over in my bed—was I just dreaming?—and stretched. The magic crackled through my body, and I shuttered. I hated having visions when I was asleep. The natural magic of dreams and my future sight mixed easily, and it made reality too far away for me to parse out at times.

My room was a soft, pale green. Almost too pale to even be called green. I had plants upon plants; hanging ivy, a rack of succulents, a large spider plant. They seemed more lively, attuned. Like they had turned toward me instead of looking at the sun. My bedroom was similar to the main floor of Visions and Trinkets; I liked the vibes to be similar so even when I was resting, my magic was comfortable. My long, antique floor mirror was in the corner, the armoire door ajar enough for the mirror to face me.

My face stared back at me. Covered in moss and vines and leafy viscera–

I screamed. The girl–*was that me?*–faded so fast that I thought I hallucinated her. Was I dreaming? I jumped out of bed, and inspected the mirror. Nothing. Just me. No one looked back, but I saw it. Her. I saw her watching me, sharp eyes and anger. Why was she so angry with me? *That's not me*, I reminded myself.

The scream, gasp, whatever sound that erupted from me was already out, and the cavalry was storming up to my room. Puddin beat the girls, teleporting and landing right at my feet. She wove herself between my legs, her little paw gently resting on the top of my foot. I reached down and scooped her up, rubbing my face in her white fur. *I'm alive*, I reminded myself, that's not me, that's not me–

The sigil for endings flashed in my mind, and all at once the dread hit me like a brick wall. Peony and Mari stood in the doorway, not wanting to interrupt a vision or startle me. I closed the cabinet door of the floor mirror, seeing only my reflection in it.

"I think I'm gonna die," I croaked out.

Not on my watch, Puddin's voice echoed through my mind and she extended her claws just enough for me to feel them.

"Jack, your citrine," Mari said.

I glanced down at my necklace, the stone laying right across my heart, had a gentle green glow. It was the same color as the moss, and I felt the impression of words in my mind. ***Not your magic. Not yours!***

"This is precisely why I'm here early, Mari." Peony said, tapping her foot. "Jack, give me your necklace, I'm going to layer some more magic into it. I've already added a couple layers to your crystal ball."

"Peony–"

"No objections. I'm staying until we know what the hell is going on." The conversation was over; I gave her the necklace, feeling naked without it. Puddin settled on my bed, purring loudly, and I desperately wanted to curl back up with her.

"Come join me in the shop when you're up to it. You need a distraction." Mari waved and headed back down, letting me have some space.

Peony stood in my room for a couple more beats, waiting for some sign that I wasn't about to collapse. I smiled weakly, and she returned to her post in the kitchen, manning the dumplings.

Chapter Three

JACK

I had two readings scheduled for the afternoon. Mari had excused herself and left the shop; she wanted to go crystal hunting, and I needed the peace. Both Mari and Peony decided that they would stay with me tonight, so I savored the quiet of my store before anyone disrupted it. My house was only a one bed, one bath apartment. I had air beds tucked in my closet, and when Peony would stay, she would just pull the trundle out from my bed and sleep in my room with me. But this time, they wanted to be in the living room, air beds taking up too much space, blankets and pillows and overnight bags everywhere. Mari and Peony were just as much like sisters as we were. But whenever they colluded in private—in my living room—it usually meant one thing: they were convinced yet again that I needed monitoring. They fussed over me like a mother hen, pecking at each other and then at me. The pecking was mostly unnecessary too. They hovered. If I didn't love them so dearly, I'd have strangled them both.

Anytime they helped in my shop, I spent the next day undoing whatever they decided to rearrange to begin with—another form of their hovering. Mari tidied up my crystal display. She thought I needed to sort them more traditionally, which was the most bizarre thing about Mari. She was never a fan of anything traditional, until it came to my crystal racks. Match similar energies and goals. I made a rainbow instead, mostly; I found putting all the same vibes together lessened their overall intensity. Put a healing stone with one for strength and it boosted them both. Peony organized my desk around the till. It took me twenty minutes to find my day planner that she had filed in my filing cabinet under *S* for *scheduler*. Who even calls it that? The downstairs espresso machine was left untouched by them, thank the goddess, and I made myself a latte.

The morning passed quietly with all the cleaning and fixing. The soft mood music I played was cliche, but I loved it. Soft piano or upbeat spa music. My shop was simply laid out. There were racks along two opposing walls, tables by the windows, and the largest display in the center. Like my bedroom, I had hanging ivy and potted plants everywhere. The crystal racks were in the center, my crystal, glass bowls adding an extra glint from the lighting, with packaged spells and charms on the wall racks. I had books for basic, simple magic that regular humans could access on the rack closest to the door. Teas near the front counter. Trinkets and bobbles and cute figurines lined the rest of the racks. If I didn't use a very, very light wind spell in the shop daily, it would be covered in dust.

About six years ago, I closed the shop down for three weeks and did some major renovations; I knocked out the front walls by the porch and turned them into huge windows with window seats. The front of the shop faced the sun, and light poured through the windows each day, keeping the gloom of winter away even during the height of the season. The small dogwood trees in my front yard had turned their signature pinky-red, and despite my freakout earlier, the calm that came with fall settled in me.

I loved autumn in Cape Margaret. We didn't have the intensity of colors like in the northeast, but we had enough. The waves got choppier and the air still smelled of salt. I only had a sliver of an ocean view but it was enough.

With the crystal display sorted out, I curled up on one of the window seats. They had decorative pillows, all psychic and nature themed, with a few little trinkets and a basket of fall decor on each. I switched up the items in the window seats regularly, but it had been several weeks since I had wanted to change them. Fall was my favorite season; the changing of the weather felt like magic, and the taste of it on my lips always made me smile.

I sipped my latte and snuggled into the large yellow leaf pillow as the wind suddenly howled, pushing more forcefully than normal against my dogwood trees. The windows rattled, the front door creaked, and the hair on my arms stood up. Noreaster? I checked the weather on my phone, but the app predicted nothing but sunny, clear skies. The wind didn't stop, so I hurried to my table for readings, and went for my crystal ball. All jokes aside, they really were perfect for scrying and meditating. The reflective surface was easy to get lost in, the sparkle of each little gleam of light, the darkness inside the ball itself like a nebula. It didn't come that way—I bought it online when I turned eighteen and my mama, Peony, Mari, and I all layered magic into it. It had a decade of magic sealed in it. This ball was so in tune with me; I could feel it call to me when there was something it needed me to know. I named it Harold, but only Puddin knew that. And now it was calling for me.

I side eyed Harold. I felt its magic stir, a neon sign practically blinking for me to take a look. Puddin manifested in my lap and I jumped. If cats could raise an eyebrow, that was the look she gave me. The wind made one of the tree limbs crack, sharp and loud like a whip, and we both went back to the window. It hung uselessly from the tree, still barely connected. The flowers had shaken themselves loose too, falling like little pink raindrops.

"Wonder what that means," I said to my cat. She meowed at me, deciding to be a regular house cat instead of a magical being. "You're no help!"

The bell of my front door jingled and I glanced at the time. It was 2:05 PM, and my first reading of the day was five minutes late.

"Sorry I'm late! There was like a freak storm or something. Did you see your poor tree! Ugh, I know a great landscaper if you need some help with it," she said. Kaylee Smitherton smiled and wiggled. She was in constant motion, shifting her weight from foot to foot, flipping her hair, playing with the keychain on her purse. I let her energy and essence wash over me for a second and felt the reason she had come to see me. Kaylee was pregnant. She wanted to know if everything would be okay.

"Thanks, but I think I can handle the tree. I have to say Kaylee, you're glowing," I winked at her, and she absolutely beamed at me.

"Really? That's um, what I wanted to ask you," she said, hands pulling on strands of her ponytail.

"Why don't we get settled? I'll make you some tea. I think some purity tea would be good for you today, no caffeine, just lots of love."

I brewed one of my tea blends, and Kaylee calmed down a bit. She reached for my crystal ball but then stopped herself. Kaylee had been coming to me for a while now, and she knew I didn't like people touching Harold, but I understood why it was tempting. I placed the cup in front of her, and she inhaled the scent. She stilled a little more.

"So um, I'm um, pregnant. It's like really early still, but I just wanna know if everything is okay." Her hands went instinctively to her tummy, and my heart warmed for her. I made a show of looking deep, deep, deeeeep into the crystal ball, churning my hands around it like I was summoning something from within. As much as people wanted a true reading, they were also paying for the experience of magic. A little razzle dazzle helped sell more readings, and as much as I loved being a professional psychic, some months were tighter than others. The holidays were always the leanest months of the year for me. Not that I minded; I did well for myself, and I loved my life, but a little extra showmanship tended to help spread the word of my oh-wisen-ways.

"Hmm, ah, yes, how lovely. This baby is growing happily. Avoid apples though, she doesn't like them. You'll get heartburn."

"She!"

"Oh yes, you're going to have a lovely, perfect little girl. She's already quite content. I sense that you might be a little anemic, be sure you mention that to your doctor. I've got some teas I can recommend for you, as well. And a rose quartz too."

"I just picked up my iron pills! You're so gifted, Jack!"

The rest of the reading went easily; we chatted about this and that, I assured her again the baby would be okay, and Kaylee left with four different tea blends and a couple of crystals. I charged the rose quartz a little more for her. Kaylee was a sweet girl and my favorite type of client.

As she left, Harold flashed again and I turned to look at it. The magic from the moon scrying sparked alive again, glittering and reflecting every star in the sky. Sometimes when I'd put too much magic into the ball, it would work like a little projector, showing me pieces of my visions for all to see. It was a neat trick, and not one that I ever did intentionally, but I didn't stay on that train of thought too long. A sentient, magical cat was enough for me; I didn't want to think about all of the feelings my crystal ball had too.

An outline of a man shone. A familiar wave hit me again, and I remembered the green and black energies when I was scrying. I traced my fingers along the edges of the outline; the magic didn't fade or ripple. The man seemed to notice, or feel the touch, and shifted a little. If it had eyes, I would swear he was looking for me. Puddin tapped the crystal ball, studying it and the outline faded. She stared at me and I groaned.

"Yes, yes, I'll call the girls."

Puddin kept glaring.

"Fine! I'll call Mama too." Puddin purred and disappeared. I could already feel them circling and ready to hover even more. Peony would be making enough dumplings to feed an army. I watched out the window as the broken limb of my tree swung slowly back and forth, back and forth. The branch finally snapped, and the limb hit the ground. It felt like an omen, and not a good one.

PEONY

I saw him for a second when Jack came to me. The outline of a man. I didn't see any other details. Sometimes, when Jack would talk about her visions, our magic would mix and I could see them too, but just for a moment. Little flashes. I don't think I'd have realized it *was* a man unless she had told me. I couldn't see the future like her and Jack had only just scratched the surface of what she could do. The well of power in her ran so deep, and she didn't realize how much of the spark in her was actually just pure magic. I couldn't say that I wasn't a little jealous of her strength and the way that magic poured out of her, but mostly I was terrified. The magic was waking up, and more than anything, I just didn't want to lose her to it.

Jack picked at the chicken and dumplings. I heard her stomach growl, but she didn't take a bite. Just picked a little more. I tried to keep her apartment as tidy as possible so even though Mari and I were camped out, it didn't feel as invasive. That was a me problem–I was *invasive*. It came with the territory of my truth magic, but I didn't *want* to be a bother.

"You're not a bother, Peony," she said.

"Now who's invasive? Going through my thoughts," I replied. I took a bite, and mentally patted myself on the back. These dumplings were damn good.

"The tree was an omen," she said. The last time Jack scried during a full moon with a bottle of red, she told me that she was an envoy for the Seer, goddess of fate. She cackled as she said the words, too drunk to mean them, but the hair on my neck stood up, and the words echoed through me as truth. The morning came and her words were forgotten, but I remembered. Mama had told me a few years ago that Jack would one day need me to refocus her eyes when they became clouded. The storm was rolling in. She finally ate a dumpling and the knot of tension in her shoulders relaxed just a smidge.

"You eat. I wanna see this tree."

"Tell Mama I said hi," she said.

Having a psychic as your little sister was a pain in the ass sometimes. I excused myself and went down to the garden, and to the front yard. The limb was huge and it had snapped too cleanly. It looked deliberate. It looked like magic.

I called our mother.

She answered on the first ring. "Peony? What's wrong?"

"Mama," I said.

"Where are you? And Jack?" Jack wasn't short for anything; not Jackie or Jaqueline. She was just Jack. Mama had named us both for flowers because they were the greatest beauty and most naturally powerful magic on earth. A peony for me so I would be pretty but honorable. But with Jack, she walked by some Jack-in-the-pulpits, and she knew that her baby would be a powerful alchemist; the curve of its petal with the strong blackish streaks reminded her of a queen wrapped in furs. The bright red berries they produced symbolized the brightness of her magic.

"We're both at Jack's place."

"See you tomorrow morning, Peony."

Jazzy Hawthorne was coming to town. Heaven help us.

I dug through my bag and popped two berry flavored antacids. I leaned too heavily against Jack's white privacy fence, and heard it creak. Mama was the only one that could stress me out more than Jack, mostly because I saw her as my future state, when I finally snapped and decided the law could take a hike. At this rate, it would be sometime next week.

JACK

I paced the small area of my kitchen. I had anxious sweats and my heart beat too heavily in my chest. Mama was coming. Mari was back from whatever errands she didn't want to discuss and was already at the counter making coffee. It was nearly 4pm; I was going to be up all night. She bought some biscotti, and I was on my third one.

So, here's the thing. I loved my mother. Dearly. Every fall she left Cape Margaret to commune with the Spirit Realm—Sanctum—and came back by Christmas. I had no idea where she went for this communion and I didn't ask. She was a spectacular alchemist. A lovely person. And she really was a good mother too.

It's just. She was a lot. My mom could read me like no one else—not even Mari.

I *hated* it. Was this how everyone else felt about me?

"Because you've been in a state for weeks and I'm concerned. Mama can cast something to at least make you feel a little better—"

"You bring bagels when you're concerned, Peony. You don't have to call in the armada." She sat at the breakfast nook, picking at her biscotti. Mari sipped my coffee and avoided eye contact. She shrugged her shoulders, pretending to appear indifferent and that she wasn't eavesdropping.

"Oh my goddess, you traitor. This was *your* idea!"

Puddin sent me a thought, *well child it's not like you have much of a chance solving it on your own.*

"Et tu, Puddin?"

I'm a cat. Stop quoting your terrible human literature to me.

"How long do I have before Mama gets here?"

"A few days at most? I don't think she's flying, but she's somewhere in northwest Canada?" Peony said. I paused, taking that tidbit in and my mouth hung open. Of course Peony would know where Mama goes every year. My blood pressure went up a couple of notches–degrees? This was why I'm not a nurse–and I chugged my too hot espresso.

"Smart," Mari mumbled, and I threw the biscotti at her. "I need to source some more amber before we do any heavy spells."

That made both me and Peony stop. Amber was Mari's stone; she wore a few pieces of it, but when she wanted to really concentrate on a spell, she needed a new piece of amber. Every alchemist connected to one stone or crystal more than other. Mine was citrine. Peony's gem of choice was a moonstone or a pearl; her magic was rooted deeply with the moon and with water.

"What kind of spell are we gonna be casting that you need some new amber?" I asked. Her magic was strong but a little unpredictable. She could craft and layer magic like no other alchemist I'd ever known, but Mari didn't need amber for that–she just poured herself into whatever she was creating. Amber stones were powerful in and of themselves; having something trapped within it made the magic even stronger. Mari picked at her fingernails. Her cuticles were generally a mess but she had been better lately. I saw a dot of blood well up on her right thumb. She had bitten it too hard. Puddin read my mind, literally, and swatted at Mari. The damn cat was nearly a better psychic than me. Nearly.

Whatever helps you sleep. Puddin flicked her tail, challenging me. I knew better than to push her. She'd mercilessly attack at night when I was asleep. This wasn't a battle my toes were willing to fight.

"I don't know yet but I don't wanna be unprepared," Mari said. Her voice trailed off, already ready to start chewing on another finger.

Peony spoke up then, "I think we need to speak our intention. Like, we need to know what the hell is happening in your brain and why you're suddenly seeing yourself. That's weird."

"I'm not sure that it's actually me," I said, wanting that to be true.

"Alrighty Misses Hawthorne and Hawthorne, I've got some research to do," Mari said.

"Back to the crystal markets?"

"Yep, I didn't have much luck last time. Nothing good to find. I'm going to Abuela." We nodded and knew that Mari would be gone for the rest of the day. Abuela could be hard to find, and Mari always took her time when she saw her.

Mari was off moments later, and I looked at the mess my house had become with the girls staying. Peony said it would take Mama a few days to arrive, so really she would be here in the morning. I had a lot of cleaning to do.

"I'm putting you to work. My house is a disaster." Peony mock saluted and started tidying.

MARI

Underground crystal markets sound more sinister than they are. Alchemists, witches, magic casters—whatever they called themselves—needed a place to procure their items. This was my world.

Jack sold items of low magical value to the masses and more specifically, the regular, non-magical people. I was a trader; buy, sell, craft, and trade artifacts. Jack made a living as a respectable shopkeep, Peony was our fancy lawyer, but I roamed the markets, kept my ear to the earth, and tracked the magic that needed finding. I was my mother's daughter. She'd bring me to dig through the markets as a child, and after she was gone, I'd find pieces of her in the goods that I found.

The markets moved around a lot, and there were some regs that would find us and sift through the artifacts. You can always tell though; only a dumbass alchemist would giggle at an enchanted rabbit's foot or ask the gold quality of a necklace or charm. The best finds were always the accidental ones; the items from regular vendors that had no idea they were peddling something powerful.

A few of my favorite vendors had set up in the parking lot of an old thrift store. The store had seen better days; it was run down, boarded up windows, and probably abandoned. It was mostly dark by the time I arrived, but there were enough lights to make it feel less sketchy.

They hung wind chimes from their tent. Framed tarot cards and tacky animal prints were lined up against the bottom of the tent, ready for perusal from the regs. The ancient woman that owned the gem tent smiled at me with all five of her teeth. She was equally adorable and terrifying, and seeing her smile at me made my heart swell.

"Marigold! Haven't seen you in a few moons!"

"I've missed you too, Abuela." I have no idea what her name was. Every time I saw her, she had business cards out–props to comfort the masses–with a different name on them each time. This time she was Ethel May Casas. Her name was most assuredly *not* Ethel May. The beads in her hair jangled too softly, her too bright skirts swished too much, and the flowers sewn into her blouse were too accidental to be accidental. I had to hand it to her; *Ethel May* could put on a show. She looked like this as far as I could remember–somewhere between ninety-five and dust–when I met her at a market as a child. *Call me Abuela, child, no need to be so formal with the ma'am's and missus.* And that was that. She knew my mother, and I'd spend summer nights and winter weekends with her. They both taught me the craft of true alchemy–transferring magic into a non-magical object–and

Abuela was the one that figured out amber would be my stone of choice. I spent even more days and weeks with her too, once my mother passed.

"You're too skinny, Marigold," she fussed, pulling me in for a hug and pinching the skin of my inner arm.

"I'm eating fine, you know I don't turn down something good." I winked at her. Business time.

"Mmhmm, and have I got something for you. I happened upon some amber. The best I've seen in ages."

"You *happened* upon it?"

"Well, there mighta been a whisper on the wind that my girl would need it, so I listened. I always take care of my Marigold," Abuela said, all smiles but her eyes were sharp. I didn't know the depth of magic, but nothing ever got past her. She always said the wind was her guide but I didn't know what that meant either.

"What did this wind tell you?"

"Child, it's a real good thing you're pretty because heaven almighty *knows* you can be dense as a box of rocks. Plain, ole road rocks." She reached out and pinched me again.

"Hey!"

"You don't go *asking* what the winds tell you. You listen and prepare an arsenal."

"An arsenal? What—"

"Plain, ole rocks!" Abuela shushed me and dragged me behind her tent. She pulled out five amber stones, one with a huge, perfectly preserved maple leaf in it. My hands itched to touch it. People buzzed around us, the markets finally coming to life, but I was zoned into that large amber stone. These markets came alive at sun-up or sun-down, and rarely any time between. The waning light caught on the amber, and I felt my eyes go wide.

"Abuela, that's beautiful," I said, my words trailing off. It wasn't often that magic could enthrall me but I was caught. I couldn't look away. She covered it with her skirt.

"A darkness is coming. Your girl is standing at ground zero, and you gotta be a shield." Abuela's eyes had turned golden, true gold, the magic in her bubbling up in every pore. Her words thudded through my chest, like she was screaming through a megaphone. My ears were ringing. I tried to play the words back, to listen to what she said instead of just hearing *loud*.

"Doesn't she need her own shield then too?" The gold faded in her eyes so she could look at me like I was simple. She waited, giving me a moment to catch up with her.

There was no catching up. We were having two different conversations, on two different pages in two totally different books. And I was having a hard time thinking about anything other than that amber.

"You can't hold a shield when you've got both hands on a sword. Your girl is the sword. So you take these gems and keep them tight. Layer the magic, don't you go rushing it." Abuela patted my cheek, sass gone and just affection lingering between us. "Take some of my empanadas too. I made them this morning. I knew you'd be too skinny," she said.

Abuela wrapped the amber in a silk cloth and tied the ends shut. Some stones needed to be held gently, some needed to be wrapped or covered to make them stable. This amber was about the size of my palm; the leaf in it was smaller, but perfectly preserved.

"Thank you," I said as I kissed her cheek. Her hand was all steel on my arm. It took me back to when I'd tried to touch her rose gold chains as a child. Three interlocking chains, tied together at various points. She always had them around her neck; it was the only constant piece of her appearance. Abuela said that the magic was not for a young one to touch, and the bruise she left from a pinch was enough to convince me of such. She squeezed a little harder, my arm aching, to bring me back to the present.

"You call me if there's something you can't handle, you hear me?"

"I don't have your phone num–"

"You tell the winds you need your Abuela, you box of rocks." Three more kisses to my cheeks and forehead and I was shooed away, my bag heavier from the stones and a heaping basket on empanadas.

JACK

"Snapdragon," I heard in my head as I dumped my laundry on the floor of the living room. A man's voice. Sweet. Sensual? Maybe an accent. There was no actual sound, more like the impression of what the sound should be. The memory of it, and a familiar one. I'd never heard this voice, but I knew this energy.

Sometimes, I'd hear a voice echo in my mind, and I'd need half a second to decide if I was just talking to myself or hearing someone else. It's one of the creepier side effects of my magic. Usually it's innocent, passing by some stranger and I'll catch a snippet of their thoughts. They're typically harmless. Awkward mostly. But this voice wasn't just passing through, it was reaching out. For me. *To* me.

That's not even my name; and I was sure the voice I heard was calling a name. It's Jack. Nothing special or unusual, just Jack; maybe it was a little odd for a woman, but no more unusual than Peony. Thank the goddess Mama didn't name me something horrid, like *Petunia*.

"Snapdragon, where are you?" He searched as he reached for me. The energy was so dark and heartbroken. The voice replayed again and again–*where are you, where are you, where are you*– until I finally responded.

"That's not me," I said out loud, "I'm sorry."

"But... who are you?" The voice faded and a wash of sadness from it flooded me. My citrine pendant burned against my chest, and I winced. I yanked it up away from my skin but not fast enough. There was a small burn, nothing hospital inducing, but another spot to add to the others. I told myself it was like having another freckle, but one that stung. I held the necklace up, the citrine swaying but looking a little darker.

Mari came in at that moment, huge ass purse in tow as always and plopped it on the couch. I was on the floor pulling clothes into my lap to start folding when she slid down next to me. "Were you trying to hypnotize yourself? Seems like yet another stellar idea." Her voice oozed sarcasm, and I didn't even try to control my groaning. Mari grabbed a towel and folded it. I folded a t-shirt. I washed everything together, clothes, undies, and towels. This was a pain point for Peony, but considering *I* was the psychic, and nothing had ever gone wrong with my laundry, I wasn't changing my laundry habits.

"It burned me," I said. I made the words as even-keeled as possible. Mari and Peony both had been a little excitable lately, so I wanted to tread lightly.

"Your necklace?"

"Yep."

"And you're not concerned?"

"Well, it wasn't a *bad* burn–"

"Jackie."

"It's nothing–"

"Who were you talking to?" The question caught me off guard. I dropped the shirt I was folding in my lap and sighed.

"I don't even know," I said. It was the truth; how do you explain that you're talking to an impression of a voice?

"We're gonna figure this all out, hun. Don't worry." Mari rubbed my shoulder, and the contact made me want to cry. I bet that voice needed a hug too. "Wait here, let me show you something."

Mari stood up and went to dig through her purse. She pulled out a brown paper bag and unpacked it. Amber. She had found Abuela and gotten some new stones. I could feel them before she had finished unpacking them. These stones were intense; the magic that filled them was darker and stronger than what Mari was comfortable casting.

"What did she tell you about those stones? Something is off with them, Mari. I don't like it." I grabbed the stone from her, and my vision started to fade. Black and white dots danced in my eyes, and I was spinning. Something was wrong with that amber.

"What? I haven't even started casting anything."

"Don't touch it!" I yelled. The magic seeped through my body and I was sick with it. What the hell was going on with this amber? My knees locked, my cheeks were damp, and Mari's hands had latched onto my arms and I was going down, down, down–

THROUGH THE VEIL

The human woman that favored my magic cried and cried and cried. Humans really do enjoy that amount of emotion; constant tears, constant wallowing. The link I held was threadbare and so, so thin. It had taken centuries to rebuild this much of a link, and it was so fragile. My staff floated before me, the crystal at its apex glowing like a star, a nebula.

The throne room was empty, as it always was now. As I commanded it to be. I sat on his throne–*my* throne–and glanced at the walls of the royal hall. The tapestries were as threadbare as my hold on world links. The emptiness without the court was perfect and terrible. Everything was duller without the King, even the sunlight couldn't warm me, but I didn't allow those thoughts to linger. He was gone.

The King's voice was still made of honey and wine, and it sedated me. Like it always did; moons in my eyes, flowers blooming in my palms, blossoming always, always, *always* for him. I pushed myself back into the throne, the scent of sandalwood and aged sap filling my nose, and my wine goblet shattered.

No. Do not remember. Do not miss.
A Priestess needs no man. A Queen needs no one at all.

JACK

My clock stopped because of course something else would go wrong. It sat in the kitchen and had three caterpillars in a field of flowers on it. I made it when we were all in middle school, and it was actually pretty hideous, but the memory wasn't. This was significant–it was *enchanted*. It was the first thing I ever crafted from alchemy. So it never stopped. It was always on time, even for daylight savings. My head still pounded from whatever had knocked me out. Mari had me laying on the couch, fanning me slowly with a washcloth.

The clock on my phone had also stopped. I got up and looked around the rest of the house. I liked clocks; I liked the ticking and the tocking, the faces, the hands. They were lovely reminders of the present, and I needed that.

The grandfather clock near the living room window had stopped.

And the one in my bathroom, another caterpillar disaster. Mari was still fanning, even though I was clearly standing a few feet away from the couch. She was moving slowly. Really slowly. A voice grated in my mind, **"Stop looking for me!"**

I twitched. The voice was familiar, I thought. It was feminine and shrill, a bit, but so damn familiar. It was irritating, like I was listening to someone speak the words of a popular song but then couldn't remember the tune.

Puddin popped back into the kitchen and screeched so loud I swore I saw the sound waves, and then we were back in motion. Time skipped ahead, the clock hands spinning fast to catch up to where they belong. The greener version of me flashed in my mind again; she was smiling, and it was an awful smile.

Mari and I plopped on the couch and Puddin floated over. She mewed softly while she twirled in the air. Some type of healing spell wrapped around my heart and weaved between my ribs and the rest of my bones.

Peony and my mom chose that moment to come in; my cat dancing in the air with Mari and I held tightly in a spell. They both pinched their noses together in the same manner and I sighed. A deep, guttural sigh that only a mother–and mini mother–could induce.

"We're doing a cleansing. Now," Mama said.

"Oh shit balls," I muttered.

Chapter Four

JACK

There were several types of cleansing spells: literal cleansing, like using a cheat code on the dishes or taking a shower, or spiritual cleansing, which was great after a loss or a trauma.

Then there was alchemical cleansing. A witches' cleansing. Whatever word was used, it absolutely *sucked*. It's a bit like setting your magic on fire and hoping for the best. *Best* being that nothing actually gets burned. The last cleansing I was in, I wore oven mitts. Everyone laughed but guess who still has all of her finger prints? With Mama fussing around the house, instructing everyone to move my furniture, roll up that carpet, sweep the floor–we all knew what kind of cleansing she wanted to do.

"We need an anchor," Peony said. Mama and Puddin eyed each other. They nodded, mewed, and huffed at each other until their eyes locked onto Harold, my crystal ball.

"Noooooope!" I yelled. Aside from being a priceless magical artifact and a delightful, inanimate friend, Harold was crucial for my business. No one wanted to visit a psychic that waved her hands around a candy dish to see the future.

"Well other than your cat, it's got the most magic in town," Mari said. I felt a small surge of pride; Harold was exquisite. Which was *precisely* why I didn't want it on the cleansing block.

"I can literally see the wheels spinning and the smoke coming out of your ears," Peony said.

"Girls." All of us–except Puddin of course–stopped bickering and sat on my couch, which was now shoved up against the breakfast nook, shoulder to shoulder like when we were teens all over again. Mama wasn't overbearing or stern. She's fun and free spirited, until our safety was involved and then she turned dark, too serious, rising to her full height as a witch. The air around her was electric. No games. No playing. Time to cast.

Jazzy Hawthorne was a force. She didn't like the term alchemist, even though it was more proper. She didn't hide her magic at all, and when confronted with any criticism or scorn, she'd crack a *slightly* unhinged smile asking, *"What else would you expect of a witch?"*

Alchemists came in several varieties. Some could create and enhance items, like me and Mari. Some could work excellent spells and used magic words, like Peony. Some could do both and more, like my cat.

I didn't know the depth of Mama's magic, but I felt the well it lived in. Magic ran so deep in her, I wondered if her magic would ever run out or weaken. I prayed that when she finally does die, she will make it to Obius, the magic realm, instead of the spirit realm. Her soul didn't need eternal rest; she needed eternal magic. A pang of envy came with that thought. Wouldn't anyone blessed with magic want to live in magic eternally? Maybe if she made it there, I could too.

"No. You won't." The woman's voice from before rang out. My body shook and the pressure from her voice squeezed my lungs and throat. My lips and tongue moved on their own, and the words rang out again. I clawed at my throat, feeling someone's words caught in it.

"Mama, her eyes–"

"Move girls, now!" Jazzy shouted.

Mari and Peony stood up, and I suddenly did not want to be alone on this couch. I wanted them with me, shoulder to shoulder, listening to Mama's spells. My lips moved again, more words in my throat, and they were already tumbling out.

"No. You. Won't."

Everyone stopped moving, even Mama, and looked at me. Peony's hand shot straight up to her mouth, never breaking eye contact. My eyes felt *weird* now that I thought about them. Wider? Less focused, wandering. I saw my nose from my left eye.

The auras around everyone were so vivid. Everyone was green, except Puddin but that was to be expected. She was golden, of course. Mama's aura was such a dark green, nearly black. The energies I saw before–one dark green and one black–came back to me then. The dark green one in the vision was even darker than Mama. That sent a chill through me.

"Snapdragon, listen. Please." The male voice was back and he was begging, desperate.

I tried to will her to listen too but she wouldn't. I'd never had two voices in my mind, chatting away, without me being part of the conversation. They pulsed in my mind, and I wasn't sure if any of the words were coming out of my own mouth or not. I felt so very far away from my body just there; was I having a vision?

"Never." The woman's grating voice boomed through me.

"Who is she talking to?" Mari asked. Her voice cracked and I saw her with only one of my eyes; the other was elsewhere, in a misty, cold forest.

Where was this place? Where was my body? How could I have forgotten that already?

Then Peony shouted spells: healing, banishing, and orders to speak only truths. "Say your true name! Release her! Light of lights descend on–"

My face jerked toward her, lips parting in a smile, my hand reaching for her face. I was too keenly aware of my body now. *And why couldn't I control my arms?*

Possession was nine-tenths of the law. Wasn't that a thing? Seemed like a thing. My body moved and smiled and talked on its own, without my say on the matter.

I wasn't in control. I was barely even a passenger. I felt the vines snake through my brain, and it itched.

Hysteria was a bitch, I'll say that. That one was *all* me. Air melted in my lungs. My rib cage did its cave-in thing where it threatened to puncture a vital organ but nah it's all part of the panic act. Panic at the me-o! I could control my panic though, yessiree, I could do that and calm down and let my rational mind regain control. Rationality wasn't my strongest point though. Panic I was good at. Really good.

Nope. Think horrible thoughts.

Dead kittens. Pollution. Global warming. The ice is melting and that's bad. Really really bad for penguins. Oh, god, they have those teeth that go through their whole fucking mouth. Vortex of masticating terror.

Oh, Fates above, why me?

A fury of claws hit my nose and I snapped out of it, my eyes shooting together making me dizzy, Peony's face was suddenly fully back in my view. She was scared, magic tightly wound in her, ready to fire. I was scared, but the peanut gallery that was chatting and taking my mind and body for a spin had retreated, and that was enough for me at this particular moment.

"Cleansing spell, now!" I shouted, and Peony hit me with the strongest spell I've seen from her.

MARI

Jack's eyes weren't exactly focused. They sorta went in different directions. One straight ahead, the other drifting slightly to the right, slightly at me. Peony had cast something on Jack to start the cleaning and to hold her. Jack looked like she was playing freeze tag; her body frozen awkwardly, eyes darting around, panic winding through her and then through the rest of us. We needed to cleanse. We needed a safe place to do it. We needed a True Circle.

There's only a handful of spells I can truly cast. A True Circle was one of them. It requires at least three alchemists to cast. Everything in threes. Three casters. Three drops of blood. Three crystals. Three candles. Three in all things. It was the perfect number; the number of balance. I rummaged through the pouch for the last of my new amber stones that Jack hadn't condemned, the stones now grimy and weak, and started to enchant them. I tried to add my magic to them, layer by layer. Intent was important with all magic, but especially when you're doing real alchemy–blending and combining magic into an object.

I pictured a channel, a current. Slow and flowing. Unending. Gently winding, yielding to the grain of the earth, bending with it, not against it. Calm waters.

The amber cracked, forming hairline cracks through it, radiating from the center. My magic had been as soft as a feather. I didn't crack stones. I wasn't an amateur.

"Mari," Jack said, her eyes still not totally back to normal. Puddin's eyes sparkled blue with magic, gathering the candles and arranging them, and with a meow the candles were lit.

"I know, I know, it's weird. When was the last time I cracked a gem?" My voice cracked just like the amber, and I shook myself out, trying to get rid of that juju. The last stone I had cracked was a quartz. I was fourteen, maybe? Middle school age. It shattered from all of the magic I forced into it. I had a little funeral for the quartz. I'd have another one for the amber too.

With the circle drawn around her, Peony let Jack out of the holding spell. Jack reached for the amber, and I handed it to her. She touched the cracks on the amber and the entire stone turned to dust. Everyone paused to stare at the pile, while I couldn't help but run my fingers through it.

"I don't know what I did," Jack said, her hands shooting up protesting innocence. I didn't know what she had done either. She wasn't casting. I felt no magic from her, just the lingering aftereffects of whatever kind of crazy was playing in her head.

"Later," Jazzy hissed. She was already back to working on the Circle. Peony passed me a knife, and I cut the tip of my finger. Three drops of blood from each of us. I started to pass it to Jack, but Peony stopped me.

"Not until we cleanse her," she said quietly. Jack's eyes went large, then she faced away from us. Jack had always been her anchor. She was everyone's anchor.

"Am I going to be your anchor?" I asked. Peony nodded. Jazzy stood at the head of the Circle. She led the spell. Jazzy began to cast, and Jack trembled. She visibly gagged and coughed. Jazzy wasn't playing with this spell. I just hoped that she didn't hurt Jack in the process.

THE OUTLINED MAN

"We've gotta find her," I said. "I'm not gonna be able to even walk for much longer."

"I know, D, and we will. What else can you tell me about her? What did she say when you connected?" Falcon asked. He squeezed a stress ball, passing it from hand to hand. Falcon was always in motion. It was exhausting. He re-tied the worn bandana on his right arm. It covered a tattoo of scales, out of balance. The stones weighed the left scale down. He tightened his ponytail. Constant. Motion.

It was mid-afternoon, and we were still in the same crappy hotel room that we'd been in for three days. I couldn't stand being in this gray, lifeless room for any longer. I laid back on the bed, staring at the gray, lifeless ceiling, and sighed.

"Not much. She just kept telling me that she isn't Snapdragon."

"And you're sure she is?"

"I'd bet my heart on it." Their faces were different, but so lovely. The magic was the same. Blessed by the Seer; no human would have that magic. I needed her to rebind the pieces of my heart—to see them, to find them. I needed Snapdragon back in my arms again, no matter what her human form looked like. She'd somehow made it to Earth, and she was so close to me now. My fingers trembled when I thought about the silky feel of her vines, velvety leaves and petals.

Fated to love are the King and the Priestess, always at arms' length, never hand and hand. The last reading she ever spoke to me, her words thick with tears, and it had replayed in my head thousands and thousands of times.

"Oh that's rich, dude. You've only got, what? Like half a piece of your heart left?"

If I'm lucky, I thought. My chest ached. It had been too many years with only slivers of a heart to keep me alive enough to function. I'd lived too long, and I needed my heart.

I needed Snapdragon.

JACK

My magic was screwed up. It felt foreign in my veins. I kept getting flash-es of things. Mari, Peony, people I've seen in town. Everything flashed in front of my eyes so quickly I was spinning. I saw fields and fields of snapdragons. Reds and pinks and whites and yellows. They shone. Some-one–Mama?–pushed on my shoulders and had me sitting down in the center of the True Circle. They chanted.

Goddesses of Magic, Flesh, and Spirit, hear us.

Fates of Time, guide us.

Hold us tight,

Show us light,

Let us all be cleansed.

Light and pain exploded in my chest. It traveled down my arms, through my belly, through my legs in shockwaves. So hot it froze me. I twitched and spasmed and could not control any of it. Mari brushed her fingers against my forehead and they sorta stuck to me; I was sweating.

The spell worked fast. All of us were being cleansed, but no one else laid flat out on the floor. When did I lay down?

"I don't think it worked," Peony said.

My vision came back slowly, the ever-familiar dots floating away until I could see again. The ceiling. I sat up cautiously, my head still swimming, and scanned my apartment, my home. Nearly every glass was shattered. Picture frames on the floor. Glass everywhere. It was in my hair. I touched my forehead, and it was bleeding. My hair clung to my face. I laid back down on the old wood floor, because everything was spinning, and puking wouldn't make this mess any better. Why was everything so *loud*?

Mama kneeled to inspect me. I probably needed a good inspection. Blood pounded in my ears and I took inventory of my home.

Aside from the shattered glass, my books were on the floor. A few teacups. My favorite one with a frog had a chip around the mouth of it; it was laying on the floor a couple feet away from me

Don't cry. Don't cry. Nope. Get that shit under control, Jack.

A tear escaped and Mama wiped it before I could pretend it didn't happen. Mari and Peony hovered.

"Honey, why did you block the spell?" Peony asked. She interlaced her fingers with mine, her magic flowing into me, calming me. Wait–

"What?"

Chapter Five

JACK

Harold survived the spell. My perfect crystal ball sat at my coffee table, on the plush purple pillow Mari made me for Christmas a couple years back. No one wanted to talk about the bomb that went off in my house, so we all just started cleaning. No one wanted me to help clean either, so I sat at the breakfast nook with Harold in my lap and watched as everyone buzzed around me. Puddin tried to sit on some of my broken figurines to hide them. A frog with a leaf umbrella. Another frog wearing a pink polka dotted hat.

I reached for my necklace, but had forgotten that I had taken it off before I started folding the clothes. Those were all over the house now too; at least I hadn't gotten too far into the folding. So much of my home was shattered. Black dots pricked at my eyes and the room became cloudy. No, misty. I breathed in and let the magic take over as I drifted into the vision, I was back in that misty forest, and then–

Flashes. Heat. The smell of sandalwood–

The man came back into view. I saw his aura this time; still dark, nearly black but some yellow shone through, just like the color of my citrine necklace. He was still just an outline, but from that outline I could see the shape of his shoulders, his longish hair, and that he was lean and tall. So tall that the vision made me mistrust his height as real. The girls came to me; I heard their footfalls, too human to be anywhere in this misty forest, fussing over me–always fussing–trying to guide me back to a chair but I pushed their hands off. I needed to focus. I needed to see him. His voice was clearer this time. This forest was his, and his words were loud.

"Tell me your name."

"Why?"

"So I can find you. Snapdragon, I'll find you."

"But that's not my name."

"It was...a long time ago."

MARI

Sometimes when Jack had a vision her eyes rolled back or crossed. This time, one rolled back. The other looked squarely across the room. I hated her visions. Jack's eyes always felt dead, like those weird frog figurines of hers. She doesn't even like real frogs. We're down to seven frogs now. How was she going to survive this? Making a run to the local home decor store for creepy frog figurines wasn't at the top of my to do list.

She was having another vision now, and the crystal ball in her hands glowed gold. Something deep in Jack's magic was activating, changing. She was slipping more easily into the visions, more often. Peony and I were heading to her, but the crystal ball shone brighter, and we stopped. Another frog figurine rattled off of the bar and broke. There goes another one.

PEONY

Oh goddess. Another frog. She got this one from an ex, so maybe it's a blessing. The magic was cleansing her home from negativity. Frog statuettes must have *loads* of dark energy.

As Jack floated away in whatever vision she saw, I picked up the pieces of another figurine. I could fix this–with a little glue and a little magic, I could put the pieces back together. Jack's eyes were unfocused, but shimmering with magic. I don't think I could fix whatever was happening in her mind.

JACK

"Don't go! I've never been able to speak during a vision. Why can you hear me?"

"A vision? My flower, we are soul linked. You can always reach me."

"Who are you?"

"You already know my name."

"But I don't–"

He was slipping away and I was slipping back, and the wrongness of that settled through my chest. I didn't want him to slip away; I just wanted to see his face.

THE OUTLINED MAN

"She's online," Falcon said. "Four point seven outta five stars. Visions and Trinkets, 'a shop dedicated to providing legitimate psychic readings and high quality crystals, spells, and herbal supplements.' So like, weed?"

Falcon and I sat in yet another dingy hotel room. He lived in them; I didn't ask how he constantly paid for them, and he didn't supply any answers. His work paid well, his clients paid well, and he lived freely. We had just delivered some middling quality amethysts to a young guy in his early twenties. He had little glasses, little eyes, little nose. Everything about him shouted smallness, and I hoped the magic of those basic stones brought him to life. He handed Falcon a wad of bills, and the deal was done. We had stopped for fried chicken and sodas, and the room stank of it.

"What's her *name*?" I asked, scrubbing my hand over my face. I needed to shave. I always needed to shave; my human face perpetually grew hair, no matter what I tried to stave it off. Falcon's face was clearer. He insisted it was just genetics, but it was still infuriating. Our skin tones were similar, sort of a tanned, olive-like color. Falcon was a little tanner where the sun met his skin, but not by much. He drummed his greasy fingers on a napkin next to his computer.

"Jack Hawthorne."

"Jack?"

"Yep. Look, here's a picture of her on the About Me page."

I touched the computer screen. Jack's hair was more human colored, light brownish instead of the forest green I knew. Where Jack had freckles, *she* had leafy tendrils. Maybe this was what she would look like in this realm. The human realm. They were different, but I could see the broad strokes of their faces; the soul truly does stay the same through however many lifetimes it cycles through.

I've been here for centuries and it still didn't feel like home. It never would. Obius would always be home even though I'd never be welcome there again. I pictured the misty forest outside of Trellis Castle, where Jack was reaching out with her magic. She knew the forest, and she knew I would be dreaming of it. I was always dreaming of Obius.

Link breaker.

Destroyer.

Shatterer.

"Diego? Bro, you gotta stop this dissociating crap. It's weird." Falcon bumped his shoulder against me, and the worry lines around his eyes were pronounced. He never just said his piece. Falcon carried so many burdens he didn't need, but couldn't figure out how to set any of them down or which ones will lighten his load the most. I was his favorite of the weights he hung around his shoulders.

"Huh? Sorry."

"I know she's cute, but don't be weird about it."

"Where's her store at?"

"Some place called Cape Margaret. Virginia. Twelve, fourteen hour drive? I don't know, I'll look up some directions. I haven't been back that way since uh, well, that weekend." *That weekend* was Falcon pretending not to get his heart broken. Or his nose. The woman he met in Virginia was small, petite, and very skilled with her fists.

"I remember her turning us down and kicking your ass, yes."

"It was just a misunderstanding," Falcon murmured. His eyes were far away but he smiled that sunny smile of his. Too much teeth, and didn't reach his eyes. The topic was closed. Falcon slammed his laptop shut, stuffed it in his bag, and grabbed his keys.

"Start packing," he said.

Be there soon, Jack.

"Don't forget my chicken," Falcon called; he was already heading out the door.

MARI

When Jack's house was finally clean, it was well past midnight. I didn't bother to look at the time, because I was already tired and depressed without the confirmation that it was two AM. The spell had a shockwave effect on her shop below too. I volunteered to put it back in order. She had been out of it after the spell and I needed a break. There was too much magic in the air and I couldn't breathe.

Once I was sure Jack was asleep, I left. She had Peony and her mom and Puddin. Honestly with that cat, she didn't need much else. My emotions were fired up and that meant mayhem for my magic. I wasn't cold and collected like Peony, or dreamy like Jack. My magic burned hot through me, just like my emotions, and when one was off, so was the other.

My apartment was only two blocks away, a bit further from the ocean and closer to the farmer's market. It was enough space away from them. I didn't want to be *away* per se, just enough space for us to be separate people. Jack had the tendency to absorb everyone and everything around her without trying. I skipped taking the stairs and rode the old elevator up to the third floor. I let myself in, and I dropped my keys and bag on the counter and watered my plants.

And then I cried.

My magic felt so weak. I couldn't reach for it. I couldn't feel it. The cleansing had cleared out the magic in my chest, and I felt naked without it.

The amber I got from Abuela felt weaker now too. I drew magic from crystals, like every alchemist, but I couldn't wear them constantly. It suffocated me with magic. Peony tried convincing me that meant that I was in tune with myself enough to know what my limits were, but all I heard was that I *had* limits, unlike them.

I tried a grounding spell. Barefoot. No metal on me. I wrapped myself in my grandmother's old wool cardigan and reached for my magic again.

Her cardigan was handmade about sixty years ago. It was green, the color of magic in my eyes, and felt like home. I didn't have a blood sister like Jack and Peony had each other; they were my family but I didn't have any blood on this earth now. And my mother had already departed for the spirit realm. My dad–sperm donor–flitted in and out of my life, and stayed mostly out. Which was better for everyone involved. Sometimes during a full moon, Jack would contact my mother's spirit. It's hard, it took tons of magic, and she'd usually be out of it for a few days after. I don't ever ask her to, but she still would. Jack missed her too; or at least I felt like she did.

I shifted my focus inward, letting my mother's words tug deep at the corners of my heart.

Find the magic in your veins. Feel it. Pull it to the surface, and cast it free.

Sparks flew around my finger tips, one catching on a piece of junk mail on the table. Nothing else happened; I wanted to cast a simple spell, a light. Jack called them fairy lights. The spark flickered again, and I stamped it out with my hands.

My magic was gone.

PUDDIN

The roads between the realms had shifted again. The alignment was wrong. Not that there was much left to align, but the threads that held it all together were messed up. My girl was restless, pacing, talking to herself like a crazy human with a twitch. She didn't cause this shift, but damn if she ain't magnifying it. I'd even need to save my magic now; casting too much could gain too much attention from something in another realm, looking for a place to hop though. Jack went scrying on the wrong night, with the links too close and open just enough for someone to notice her. She was hard to miss; not in all my years had I heard of a human receiving a blessing from a goddess.

Jack finally settled on her couch, and I curled up in her lap. Her fingers immediately combed through my fur, ruffling my ears softly, and I purred. Humans love a cat's purr, and I go overboard. I practically vibrated because it soothed her so much. I never thought I'd actually tolerate–much less *love*–a human, but here we were. The Seer was strong in this girl, but I loved her because of her, not just because of the blessing the Seer had placed on her.

"You're the best cat," she said.

I know, I said back. She laughed. We booped our noses, and she hugged me. Oh my girl.

JACK

I needed to open the shop. I had three readings scheduled today and a new shipment of herbs would be arriving. I needed to pick flowers from my garden and ready them for winter. I had too much shit to do to be sitting on my couch doing nothing. Visions and Trinkets was my everything; I had put so much into my business over the years and no random crisis from me would be enough to interfere with that. Puddin laid in my lap, so warm and comforting. She purred and cuddled more than normal. I didn't need my magic to know she was trying extra hard to make me feel better. Mari cleaned up the chaos so I could open it today. Her handwritten note and silky scarf on the kitchen counter made the morning easier. With my mind going so fast, visions hitting me left and right, I needed softness; the world was easier to come back to when it was cushioned. Every item in my apartment spoke to comfort and softness, like my lilac colored, crushed corduroy couch and my light blue, overstuffed chairs.

I kissed Puddin and gently scooped her up to bring into the shop with me. There was a staircase just outside the front door that led me down to the shop. I waved my hand, flicking a little magic to open the lock and pushed the door open.

Mari had rearranged the displays again. They were closer to how I liked them, but still not right. I reminded myself how much I appreciated all their help after I detonated in my living room. I'd be finding glass shards for the next week or more, but they helped me get everything cleaned up so I could walk without cutting myself. At least there wasn't any broken glass here. The crystals were undamaged, and aside from things hastily stuffed back on the shelves and tables, the shop was intact. The back door chimed, and Mama and Peony came in.

"Jack, you look well," Mama said. I hadn't washed my hair in two days and wore a hoodie. I couldn't remember the last time I washed it either. *Well* was a stretch.

"Hey hey," I said. I had to be sunny for her. Mama struggled with any dark emotions. If I was sad, she was devastated. If I was mad, she was hellfire incarnate. So I projected only good things. Smiles. Lightness.

She could read right through me, but still. I wasn't a quitter. One day, I'd feel like absolute dog shit and she would be none the wiser. It's just not today.

"Jack–" Peony started. I held my hands up in surrender.

"I'm not fine, but I'm not arguing with y'all about it. I've got appointments booked all day."

"Let us help," Mama said.

"There's no escaping you, is there?"

"Not a chance in any realm, darling," she said, hugging me tightly. I needed a mom-hug. Mama was a world class healer; she pretended it wasn't true, but I was sure she had healed more than one terminal prognosis in her time. Her magic tenderly wrapped around me, and it snaked through me, just like the vine-like magic did before, but this time it was comforting. I sighed into her; at least she knew how I liked my crystal display.

"Fine start with the crystals. They're not aligned for proper–"

"Already on it. The vibrations are all wrong. I'll do a rainbow configuration," she said. Peony had taken to straightening all of the teas and herbal supplements on my shelves. She distinctly didn't touch the relaxation teas.

Peony didn't disapprove of weed but she wasn't a fan, and she left magic traces everywhere; no one wants to be confessing their secrets when they're trying to chill out.

The teas made me feel too dull for my magic. I needed to be in control. I needed to stay as clear headed as possible for my readings to be accurate. Any time I mixed anything with my magic, it never ended well. Like wine scrying.

Magic buzzed and hummed through me still; the cleansing didn't work. I was cloudy and foggy, not fully in control of the magic that rumbled around in my body. I touched the citrine pendant that laid across my heart, and the magic settled again. Other than Harold, I hadn't used any other magical artifact in years. Peony and Mama were quiet, working around me, careful not to infringe on my personal bubble or make any sudden movements.

"So we're *not* talking about how I've fucked up everyone's magic?" I finally snapped.

"*It wasn't you, meow. The ties between the realms are shifting again.*" Puddin meowed so they knew that she was addressing everyone. I translated. She floated up to the checkout counter and sat squarely in a bowl of crystals.

"Shifting? How weak have the links gotten?" Mama asked the cat. It was always weird to see one of us–other than me, I mean–talk directly to Puddin like she was human.

"*Paper thin, but there's more openings. It's like they are trying to be rebuilt.*"

"What do you mean rebuilt?" I asked.

"*The links weren't stable, Jack, you knew this. Someone's trying to put them back together, I think. That's why your magic is acting oddly. There's a shift in our link to it.*" Puddin flicked her tail back and forth.

"Is your magic okay?" I asked her.

She only purred louder, floating up so everyone could see her little display of power, and then perched lightly on my shoulder. Even though she was a cat, I knew she had more magic than me and less fucks about using it against people. Or anything else, really. Her outlook and attitude were truly life goals for me. Peony rolled her eyes, and as Mama was about to ask Puddin something else, a customer came in.

I automatically switched to shopkeeper mode. Serene smile, setting my eyes just past them when I said a soft and sweet hello, looking equally ethereal and wise. I'd practiced this face in front of a mirror until I knew how to hold myself just so.

My business was real. The products were real. My readings were real. But reality doesn't *sell*. The regs didn't want magic; they wanted the idea of it. So I sold both. Enough real magic that they felt it–most just thought it's the placebo effect, but they still get the benefits of whatever item they bought. Then I put on the psychic persona to give them the experience that they wanted. The magic cat staring and being generally creepy also helped. Puddin would meow like she's dying to add to the ambiance during an intense reading. Mama waved a little goodbye, and I knew she was heading upstairs. I prayed that she was going to clean up the kitchen some more and make some food.

"Can I help you?"

"Oh I'm just browsing."

"Of course. Love potions are on the middle shelf by the window, sweet pea. Heartbreak teas are on this shelf next to me and peace crystals are on the table by the back window. They need sunlight," I said

"How–"

"It's a vibe," I said. The girl nodded at me. She was eighteen-ish. Her mascara and eyeliner were a couple days old. The messy bun on her head was too messy to be on purpose, and her leggings had at least two stains on them. I didn't need magic to guess what she was looking for.

Black dots floated at the edges of my eyes. Oh no, not now. Not in front of a customer.

A vision.

Sometimes they come on easy like this, sometimes they hit me like a truck. The haze came in slowly, and I eased myself toward the back to follow Mama. I needed to find a place to be still, and alone, and away from customers.

I felt that dark green energy again. And the black energy. My mind swirled, disconnecting from this reality and mixing with my magic forcefully. I stumbled, reaching blindly for the door handle, and yanked it open harder than I meant.

"Peony, can you help her if she needs anything? Prices are on the bottom. I'll be right back," I called, already out the door, hoping my words were loud enough for her to hear but not too loud to sound crazy.

"Sure," she said breezily, icily. She wanted to help, but she heard the pleading in my voice to keep things as normal as possible. Puddin used magic to push me gently up the stairs. My knees locked again, and I grabbed onto the railing, I'd be lost to it any second–

The outlined man turned. His eyes were on me even though I couldn't see them, scanning me. I shifted. His energy was black, black, black.

It engulfed me. I felt it pouring out of my mouth and nose and ears and my cheeks were wet, was it coming out of my eyes now too?

He was so close. There was such a heaviness in this energy that my bones ached from the weight. He was everywhere.

Black

Black

Black

"Jack, come back to me," he whispered. *Was he here? I couldn't move, I couldn't breathe–*

Puddin had propped herself between my head and one of the steps. I reconnected to my body slowly; remembering his words and remembering that I was here, in my stairwell, alive and corporeal.

"He knows my name," I said to no one.

DIEGO

She answered. I called to her and she *answered*. I knew it; our soul link was still alive! I knew it was Snapdragon. Falcon cruised down the highway. We were still a good day's drive out. He had his beachy music playing with the windows cracked. His hair had escaped the pony tail and was everywhere. It whipped me a couple times.

I didn't care. I was less than a day away from Snapdragon.

"Calm down bro," he yelled. He had to so I could hear him.

"I'm fine," I yelled back.

"You got like a third of a heart at best. Chill out. Get too excited and you'll kick the bucket before we ever make it there." I couldn't stay calm; my love, my priestess, my everbloom was in this blessed realm and she was alive.

JACK

He. Knew. My. Name.

DIEGO

I'd know her anywhere, in any realm. She's perfect, even as a human. I'd bring her flowers to braid in her hair since she couldn't grow them any longer.

JACK

Don't panic. It's not like he knew what I looked like.

DIEGO

I bet that picture didn't capture her true beauty.

JACK

But he knew my naaaaame! He didn't say my last name. How many people named Jack were there online? At least a million. Maybe even a billion. Would searching "Jack" even turn up people?

DIEGO

I wondered why she didn't keep her name. Jack Hawthorne. Snapdragon wasn't any stranger than Falcon. She had a second name, like most humans too. It was nice. I liked it.

JACK

Peony assured me that she would handle my customers and come get me before my first reading today. I crawled into my bed as the dots floated back, and I flowed back to a vision. That awful energy was there; the blackness. I was sick already. I saw a car interior. Sixties beach tunes on the radio. Wind blowing through the windows. I was in the backseat, watching.

The dark green energy drove the car. Some type of SUV. Older but the radio was replaced; too many lights to be standard. The black energy sat in the passenger seat. I still couldn't see their faces. His fingers drummed on the top of the window sill. They were golden, bronzed. Natural, not from a bottle. I felt his face but couldn't see it. I wanted so badly to touch him, and that realization was awkward. I'd never wanted to touch a vision, but the smell of sandalwood, earthy and alive, made him so real. The feel of the old cloth car seats under my fingers and wind whipping through my hair; it was all so real, like I was riding with them.

Then a heaviness hit me as I saw myself reaching for him, for the man with the blackhole of energy, and I pulled back.

"Don't go," he said.

"You knew I was here?"

"I'd know you anywhere." I felt his smile, and the warmth of it blossomed through my chest, down through my fingers, down through my stomach, to my core. He was telling the truth; this man knew everything about me. The vision faded away, and I didn't pretend that I wasn't reaching for him. The blackness of his energy, suffocating and thick, but I was so drawn to the sadness that edged around it. To his sadness. My fingers brushed against the outline of his energy as I slipped away, and I felt something shatter in my heart.

"Don't go," he said again, but I was already gone.

PUDDIN

For the love of all that's holy, why did Jack figure out astral projection as her magic was going haywire? I sat on her bed, by her stomach, and watched over her. I used whatever was left in my magical reserves and made a circle around her, protection from whatever watched her from the other realms.

"Stop wandering from your mortal body." I scolded her and swatted her hand. She yelped and had that adorable look on her face like a lost kitten. It took a couple of beats for her to remember where she was, what happened,

and then when tears filled her eyes, I climbed on her chest and gave her a little privacy with her thoughts. Once she collected herself, I explained what she had just done.

"Those aren't visions, girl. You're projecting your soul to Goddess only knows where. You can't just go around using astral projection without any protection! You can get lost like that. Stop it."

"I'm doing WHAT," she said, sitting fully upright, eyes suddenly wild. The citrine around her neck was glowing molten gold again, and I purred louder to soothe the storm in her heart.

"Oh, Goddess, give me patience."

FALCON

D looked extra weak. I don't know what he was casting but he was straining his already weak ass heart; the spell he used was intense, and the other energy that filled my car made me uneasy, but I played dumb. Diego wouldn't tell me he was chatting with his apparently-not-dead girlfriend no matter how I asked the question. He'd been alive for at least a couple hundred years with a shattered heart in his chest. Magic kept his blood pumping, but with the links acting all wonky, he wouldn't be able to cast enough to *keep* it pumping.

I floored it. He wouldn't stop talking to this girl even if it killed him, and it would.

CHAPTER SIX

PEONY

There was a reason that Jack ran her shop and I was a lawyer. My job was to annoy people. On purpose. I got paid to be a bitch. It worked out great for me. Peony, Peony, sweet as can be. Until it was time to work. I liked the puzzle that was the law. I liked digging into a story and tearing it apart until the truth was laid bare. I *liked* having an opponent to go toe to toe with.

But now I was smiling and being sweet and selling some peppermint tea that Jack had brewed and infused with magic in her small, sweet garden. It suited her; where Jack saw a rainbow, I saw the puddles. This was why I was the lawyer.

She wouldn't be able to do her readings today and according to her schedule, she was booked for weeks. Her business was thriving. Cancellations and rescheduling never went well with clients, but sometimes it was unavoidable. Today was avoidable. I could do the readings for her. I have zero psychic ability, but I can coax the truth out of anyone and I'm good enough with body language to guess vaguely enough to make the customers leave happy.

So, here I was, sitting across from Jack's client in her little reading room, peering into a crystal ball hopped up on more magic than coursed through my veins, and praying I got at least a few things right. The reading room was less a *room* and more of a *section* that Jack had walled off the area with large bookshelves. She added more carpets, more baubles and chimes, to really set the stage of visiting a psychic. The tapestry of a moon goddess that hung behind her reading chair felt regal even though she bought it online for about twelve bucks. The client, a man, probably mid to late twenties, sat quietly. Men were less likely to call on a psychic for life advice, but it happened. Usually something with a career. *Was the wife cheating? Am I going to make more money?*

This man was not looking for any of those things.

"You're a legit psychic, right?" He cocked an eyebrow at me, all easy smiles, and not buying any of the bullshit show I was putting on for him.

"Yes," I said cautiously. Alchemists don't just spread the word about magic, but we don't deny it to the person actively paying us either. He sized me up, his eyes assessing every movement and a little thrill shot through me when his eyes stayed an extra second on my lips.

"My magic... it's fading. I think I'm losing it."

I stopped moving, stopped the act completely and took my time looking him over. He *did* have magic. Now that I was looking for it, I could see it. The truth surrounded his words when he spoke. He was an alchemist.

"You're an alchemist?"

"Yeah, this was going to be my first reading with Jack but uh, where is she?"

"Indisposed."

"Is her magic gone too?"

"What! No, of course not!"

His shoulders slumped forward a little, he pulled on his knuckles, not quite meeting my eyes before he spoke again, "Why is mine gone? What did I do wrong? I don't know what happened, I was just casting some basic–"

"Why did you schedule a reading with Jack if you have magic already?" I cut him off. He wanted answers that I couldn't give, and I wanted that faraway look on his face to disappear.

"Uh, because I can't see the future. I'm an herbalist. Sometimes she buys some of my teas." He did look familiar. More like a stock photo than someone I'd met. A gorgeous stock photo. Sandy brown hair and soft brown eyes. Tanned from the sun, like most people are in Cape Margaret. Light blue tank top even though it's November. I didn't need to look at his feet to know he was wearing flip flops.

"What's your name?" he asked.

"I'm Peony. Jack's sister."

"Ah, the lawyer. She's mentioned you. Why are you doing my reading?" He reclined in his chair; the purple velvet and scalloped edges of the chair didn't even clash with him. His energy fit right in with the vibe of Jack's shop.

"Because Jack isn't feeling well so I'm helping her out."

"Wow, must be a family gift, huh?" I nodded, not willing to commit a lie outloud. Words had power, and I knew this more than most. I glanced at Jack's calendar on the bookshelf next to me. Her large, bubbly handwriting told me his name: Sherwin P. Without the hokey act, I didn't know what to do with my hands, so I tucked them under my knees. Hands were very telling if you knew what to look for in them.

He caught me looking at the book and laughed. "Shit, you can't do readings, can you?"

"Umm, I'm not as good as Jack but–"

"You're covering for her. I got it." He winked at me. He *winked*. His magazine cover good looks and cheekbones were laser focused on me. I pushed my glasses up on my nose–any reason to break eye contact–and smiled.

"What were you coming to ask her?"

"Honestly, if I was ever gonna meet a girl but then my magic crapped out, so I figured I'd ask about that first." His eyes sparkled. This man all but glittered; how did I not immediately see his magic?

"I'm not enthralled, if that's what you were hoping for," I said dryly, the little white lie slipping from my lips without a second thought. I chewed on the inside of my cheek to keep myself from smiling. He caught it anyway. Sherwin had a hearty laugh and my cheeks tinged. So maybe I liked the laugh and the face it came from. Sherwin leaned forward, elbows on the reading table, his hands so very close to mine, and I sucked in a quick breath–

"You busy later?"

"Probably, but call me."

Sherwin laughed again and reached for my phone. He tapped in his phone number and added a kissy emoji next to his name. Cute. He winked again–ohh, this man was *dangerous*–and waved goodbye. My cheeks were still warm.

DIEGO

Falcon got a call for a lead on a piece of my heart. He knew a seeker that could find anything, and she finally called him. It'd been months. Seekers were the magic hoarders; they knew where and how to find things, and having one on speed dial made alchemy faster. It helped Falcon work his odd jobs faster too. He was also a seeker, but acted as a protector or a treasure hunter more often than not. I think he preferred those jobs. He was a magical problem solver, and my problem was unsolvable. He loved me instantly.

We had to make a detour from Snapdragon–Jack–to see this seeker of his. Falcon and I spent more time in this run down SUV of his than anywhere else. We've cruised up and down the East Coast of America, driven coast to coast, and on everything in between. He made the days a little less lonesome and a lot more entertaining, but with this latest shift between the realms, I was running out of time. My heart was getting weaker and weaker, and soon, I wouldn't have enough magic left in it to keep me alive.

My heart was fractured when I had shattered the link between the realms as a punishment from the Goddesses. After I broke the ties between the worlds, the Judge also locked me in the human realm. My heart was in nine pieces. I'd been living with a ninth of my heart for almost six hundred years. Never dying. Never being fully alive. Living as a husk of my former self.

I don't regret it; not even for a second.

Snapdragon's visions were never wrong, and she saw so much destruction. I couldn't just let Trellis, my homeland, be decimated. She told me in detail how the city would burn, how the humans would trample the forests and kill anything in their path. She told me how she would die–

Falcon's words floated in and out of my thoughts, but I wasn't listening. I thought of her face; green like a summer leaf, in full bloom. She was exquisite; all tree nymphs were lovely, but Snapdragon was ethereal. Perhaps it was the Seer's blessing that made her so beautiful, but whatever the reason there was no denying it. It had been so long since I had seen her... I was worried that I couldn't remember the details of her soul any longer. And somewhere, Snapdragon was waiting and alive here. How long had she been alone, waiting for me to find her?

The human realm, Earth, was dull to me. The colors felt flat, even when the humans insisted they were alive and vivid. Humans were mostly flat too, but sometimes I'd happen across one that made me feel a little more alive, like Falcon.

I was tired. Falcon placed his hand on my leg, bringing me back to him. He had parked at some take out restaurant, worry etched around his eyes. Those little lines on his face were the only giveaway for his age; he had to be closer to forty, but like most things about Falcon, it was hard to pin down.

"Where is she? Your seeker?" I asked.

"She said she's not far from Jack actually. Williamsburg? Never been. There's an old flea market there and she's set up a stall."

"An alchemists' market?"

"Yep. Even if she doesn't have your heart piece, she might have something else to help."

"What's her name?"

"Not a clue," he lied so easily–his tell was that he smiled too wide. "It changes every time I've seen her, but I've always called her Nana."

MARI

I drove around to my normal haunts to look for the markets, with no luck. Abuela must be set up on the other side of the water. If there was one unchanging truth about living in the Seven Cities of Virginia it was this: the tunnel was always backed up. No one knew how to drive through it. You will never be on time if you depend on the tunnel traffic to move at a normal pace.

I shot a text to Jack that I was heading to the markets in Williamsburg. Abuela would be there. She needed to be by the ocean to stay connected to her magic, or she needed to be rooted in something old, historical. It's why there were so many alchemists in Virginia; this country wasn't *old*, but it'll do in a pinch, and being closer to the Native tribes always helped. They had more sense of how the Earth was alive. Jack replied with a few heart emojis and a "***be safe.***"

Peachy. She only sent that when her visions were unclear and something was up. At least her magic was still working. After striking out at the waterfront in Norfolk, I buckled in and prepped myself for the tunnel battle.

The only magic I could rely on was my GPS at this point.

One hour and thirty-seven minutes.

Just peachy.

FALCON

My coffee order was called, and Diego grabbed them for us. I needed a few minutes in the sunlight before hopping back behind the wheel, so we sat outside of the little cafe. The markets wouldn't open for another half hour; we had time to kill. My contact has known me since I was an infant, but D didn't need to know that. He was the closest thing to a best friend I've ever had, but he was still a job. A job that's lasted over five years, but still.

I called her Nana. My parents died when I was young. I don't know how old I was, and I don't remember them. But I remembered Nana.

She took me in and raised me off and on with my Auntie Alora. Nana taught me the basics of magic. She showed me how to be an alchemist, and how to listen to the magic of the earth to find my way, anywhere I went.

Now I helped other alchemists and creatures when they needed to be saved or found or protected. Nana always said I had the heart of a hero who was blessed by the Judge.

I didn't know about all that, but I knew right and wrong. And I had the magic to make sure that anyone that needed me stayed on the right side of things.

"You're quiet," Diego said. He swished around his iced coffee, mixing the cream in more. Always iced. It could be thirty below, and he'd still ask for ice.

"Thinking."

"Do you think she's really found a piece of my heart?"

"Dunno. What's it even look like? It's not like, a bleeding organ or anything right?"

"It's a sunstone." Diego trailed off and we got back in the car. Nana should be almost all set up for the day once we arrived.

MARI

Can you die from sitting in traffic? How long would that take? There's–*shockingly*–a back up in the tunnel. Again. Always.

Only a fourteen mile back up. I banged my head against the headrest. Only.

ABUELA

The winds blew from the east, and it caught in my skirts, wrapping around my old bones. All of my darlings were coming to see me today. Best to keep them separate. The shattered one would be here too. Falcon had gone and got himself in a right old mess. Worse than death, an undying that never ends. He should have just *died*.

I righted the stack of prints that the winds blew over. The winds were happy that the shattered one still walked, but I wasn't.

Perhaps it would be better if they did get to meet my Marigold; even I won't undo what the Fates have written.

And, it would happen sooner or later.

My stall looked rightfully shabby with little hints of chicness to make my goods appeal to the humans. They so loved to pretend they had magic. Flexing my fingers, straightening out the fake twists and knots so they looked young again felt good–it was always nice to remember how they used to be. I dropped the spell as other vendors set up the stalls; my hands shriveling up back to look like an old woman's hands once again. The winds sighed against me, a little gust curling through my crooked-again fingers.

Best prepare some extra empanadas before the children arrived.

MARI

Two wretched hours later, I made it to Williamsburg. There was a crash in the tunnel. Construction on I-64. There'd been construction happening on I-64 since before I was born, at least.

There was an old flea market that set up shop in a strip mall that's seen better days. A laundromat, check cashing service, and what might have been a hardware store faded into the bleak exterior. The flea market had booths set up outside; this place was too sketchy for even seasoned artifact hunters. It was my favorite market.

Abuela was always outside. I listened for her wind chimes, the signature of her booth. She had a couple of ladies that usually set up booths with her, but today she was solo. She picked a good spot, shaded by a tree, but still within view of the parking lot. I felt a hint of the magic of her charm spells before I got out of the car. A little charm spell here and there never hurt to attract a customer or three.

But today it was an actual flea market, not one in disguise for the regs. She didn't have her crystals out. Or the tarot cards. No wands either. Today she just had beaded jewelry on her tables, with some prints lined up against the front of the stall. The colors in the beads and drawings were pretty, but there was no magic in them.

Or maybe I just couldn't feel it anymore.

Abuela's face split into a huge grin, her arms held out wide to me. My chest tightened, and I broke out into a run to her. Her hug was the closest thing to my mom's hugs; Jazzy was great, but she hugged me like I was ready to break.

"There, there child. What's got you shaken so bad? Tell me," she said. Abuela stroked my hair. I took it down from my buns and pulled it all back into some larger braids. She yanked on one to get my attention.

"Well? Don't take all day to tell me what's on your heart. I'm old," she laughed. I laughed. Then the flood gates opened and I cried. Abuela held me closer, pushing little sparks of warm, loving magic into my back.

"My m-m-magic," I sobbed.

"What's wrong with it?"

"It's *gone*," I cried harder. Abuela shooed a customer away and told them to come back in ten minutes. She patted my cheeks, dried my tears with the end of her sea green cardigan, and squeezed my hands.

"Child, your magic is fine. The link between our realm and the source of all magic has fractured again. It's been weak for centuries, but it's breaking down further. Ain't nothing wrong with your magic, it's the world itself. So now we need to right it. I'm working on that today. For now, let me heal your heart. Everything about your spirit is bruised, and I don't like it."

"But–"

"Your girl is struggling too, hmm? She's floating too far for her own good."

"Yeah," I squeaked out.

Every little thing *always* came back to Jack. I shouldn't be hateful like this, but my magic was gone. Hers was wonky, but still working. Abuela lifted my chin, forcing my eyes up and she tsked at me.

"Don't be dark hearted. Your magic is there, child."

"I broke all of the amber."

"I bet you did, all bruised up like that. I have more with me. I made another one for you. But you need to be in a better head space and with your emotions in check. I think you need some time in the forest. You need to pray."

"Abuela–"

"I know you're not trying to question me now, girl. You are pure gold, you hear me, and you need to shine yourself. Now take these stones and go. Find some trees and earth. Recharge. Center. Stop worrying about Jack. Your time is coming. Be ready." She hugged me again too tight around the neck and I felt choked. She slipped her turquoise medallion off and held it to my forehead.

She said nothing. Abuela stared into me and I was visible. Fully visible to anyone that bothered to look. Bone tired. Afraid I'd never feel magic in my heart again. Still missing my mom. Wanting to be with my best friend and feeling safe with her.

And then, it sparked in my chest and slowly wound its way through my arms and legs and through my head. My nerves all tingled, electricity and energy lighting me up from the inside out. It settled in my core, and I could have cried again. It was *back*. Abuela ran her old, soft fingers over my forehead, my eyelids, my nose, and drew little circles on my cheeks.

"I've revived your spark. Don't let darkness stamp it out again. Always pray to the light, always face it. Go pray, my Marigold."

Abuela had spoken and she was done giving out wisdom. She passed me a tote bag full of food and a small Tupperware container with amber in it.

"Pray first. Don't go diving in for that amber. Heal yourself before any darkness tries to settle again."

She kissed my cheeks, hands, and the pulse in each wrist. I wiped the tears away, electricity still surging in my veins and just hugged her again. She always smelled like old-timey soap, baby powder, and fresh, fresh linens. I breathed her in and Abuela chuckled in my ears. She kissed me once more and released me.

"You are pure gold, my girl. Don't you ever forget that. Jack isn't the only one the Goddesses have smiled on. Be strong, Marigold, and listen to that heart of yours."

I was alive again.

FALCON

Nana hugged a pretty Black girl, looking over her shoulder and directly at me. I stopped. Nana was telling me to wait, to hang back. I had parked my truck at the end of the parking lot, far away from the other vendors, and away from Nana. The markets were at an old flea market this time. I remember my aunt bringing me here a few times to sift through some comics and old coins. She loved flea markets, and dragging me to them all over the states instilled a love of travel in me. And a love of the search for something magical.

The girl buried her face in Nana's old shoulders. A small pang of jealousy thudded through me and I brushed it off. Nana wasn't mine. There had been a steady stream of kids that she had loved over the years, but this was the first time I'd ever seen *her*. I'd remember a girl like that. She was *young*. Or maybe I was just getting old now. She clung to Nana's sweater so tightly, I saw the color of her knuckles change even from this distance.

This girl was magic, regardless of her power level. Nana kissed her gently, the girl cried, and her true magic flashed like a beacon to me. She shone like gold–rare and beautiful.

When I was really young, Nana had told me that I could see magic in others. Like an aura, but always green, the color of magic. The girl's aura was grass green. Summer grass. Vibrant and bright and alive. They said the darker the hue the stronger the magic, but that's not really right. It's more like the intensity of it; how deeply magic has buried itself into you. My aura was a dark, dark green. Like a forest at night. Some shades didn't have power because they were designed to be gentle. Healers were all shades of green but always pale and soft. Herbalists were sea green. Every type of magic had its own hue, but this girl was the color of creation and birth and life. She glowed and shimmered–it was the kind of magic a guy could get drunk on.

Diego's aura was black. He was pure magic, and it damn sure doesn't exist in this realm. Shouldn't exist, anyway. There were a few creatures on this side that originated from the Obius, the Magic Realm, but over the centuries they've adapted. They existed, but only on the fringes of the human worlds. The normies called them vampires, werewolves, ghouls, and demons. None of those things were quite right either–probably? Maybe? I wasn't an expert on magical hellions, despite my chosen career.

D was teetering on the *not existing*. He walked on auto pilot, trained himself to follow me and stop when I did, with his eyes blank. He'd utter an affirmative *uh-huh* or *yeah*, but that was it. He didn't talk when he got like this; too drained to operate, but able to carry out enough normal human bodily functions to appear alive.

It creeped me out sometimes, with those dead fish eyes, but he was alive. Barely.

I slowed my pace, allowing him an extra second or two to figure out where I was so he could follow. Nana wrapped up her talk with the girl and once she was out of eye sight, she motioned for us to come over.

"Earth to D, it's time," I said, gently tapping his arm. Diego twitched and he was back, fully in his human body. I wondered what he looked like in his true form, whatever that was. When I asked, he just laughed and told me that he just looked like himself.

"Okay," Diego said. His voice was hoarse, like he hadn't spoken in years when it had only been about twenty minutes. Nana was chuckling with a customer, an older woman ready to buy half of her inventory. Nana bought these things online for nothing and sold them at three times the cost. One bracelet paid the cost of the entire haul and shipping. *Smarter not harder, boy. You think my old hands can sew like this without getting a cramp?*

The older woman passed a few bills into Nana's hands and took her bag of definitely-handmade-by-someone-else beads, smiling all the way to her car. Nana's eyes sparkled and she tucked the money into her neon orange fanny pack.

"Falcon," she said. There was so much warmth in her voice that it choked me up. It always did; Nana sounded like home. Aside from my aunt, Nana was my only family. And I only saw Aunt Alora on Christmas or if someone was dying. Usually me.

"Nana, I brought a friend."

"You brought a disaster is what you got. Honey, are you even alive?" She shifted her weight, poking a hip out, arms akimbo and full of grandmotherly sass. Fae or not, he didn't stand a chance against this woman.

"Mostly," Diego said. He held out a hand to her and Nana shook it. She recoiled, a snarl on her lips. Sparks flew from their hands, and her eyes whipped around to see if any customers saw it. I froze. Nana stepped in front me, putting space between me and Diego, rising to her full height—which wasn't much, she was at least a foot shorter than me—and magic pooled in her eyes. Golden and full of power.

"Falcon, do you know who this is?" I flinched at her tone. She was completely neutral, asking simply if I knew what I had gotten myself into. Of course I knew; I walked into trouble with my eyes wide open.

"Yes, he's my best friend. He needs help." Diego had taken a couple steps back—good man, there was a reason he'd survived this many centuries on his own—and I moved back to his side.

"He needs to serve out his judgment." Green flashed in her eyes, lighting up the already brightness of her magic, her voice dropped low, Diego now incensed, stood taller—

"My judg—"

"You heard me," she said, voice so frosty I had chills, "Falcon, why did you bring this beast to me?" My body and mouth and mind were working at different speeds, and I stuttered out a few unintelligible sounds. *Beast?* Diego was so gentle even butterflies flocked to him. Nothing about him could ever be *beastly*.

"Because I don't want him to die," I said. They both looked at me. Nana's worn features, the lines on her face more pronounced because she was frowning. Diego's handsome, half-dead face etched with fury but finally looking alive. He tucked his hands behind his back, guarding, always guarding, and inclined his head just *so*. There was something regal in the smallest parts of him, the parts he hasn't been able to fully erase even after so many years in this realm.

I wished I had known him then.

I've been traveling with Diego for about five years now. I'd never brought him to Nana. He saved my ass a few times, burning through what little magic he had to keep himself alive. Diego had inched closer to me, he had dropped his shoulder, hands now at his sides.

Diego was ready to fight. I patted him on the back too hard, too jovially, plastering my signature fake ass smile and he relaxed again. Back to decorum and grace. He shifted his moods and faces and everything so, so fast. The tension drained out of him almost immediately and he was back to being my chill best friend.

"Nana, please. He's only got like a tiny piece of his heart. He fractured–"

"Shattered. He *shattered* it. He shattered *everything*," she spat. Literally. She spat on his shoe and the fires of a fight picked up again between them.

"Falcon, it's okay, let's go," Diego said, turning away from her. A mistake. She *hated* when someone turned away from her before she was done speaking. She wasn't done speaking. I swooped her hands up, tucking them in the crook of my arm–I could play this part so well, the grandson, the handsome devil, the charmer–and kissed her knuckles.

"Hang on D, she said she has something for me." Nana paused, pulling herself free and going to the fanny pack.

"Tell me something, shatterer. Do you regret the damage you've done?"

"No," he said earnestly. I wanted to groan. I wanted to smack him. Diego couldn't read a situation any better than he could a map. Spoiler: we do not ever rely on his navigational skills. He didn't stand down. They glared at each other. He let a little of his magic slip and damn, did I feel it. Between him and Nana pretending not to swing their magical dicks, I got overloaded. One of my many talents was that I could be an amp, a power boost. I boosted everyone around me, making their magic even better. Or worse, honestly.

"No?" she asked, her husky, angry laugh stuck in her throat. Well I guess it didn't matter that he was dying at this point, because she was going to kill him. I could feel it.

"I was lied to. I just wanted to save her, and then... this happened. I didn't know until later what really happened."

"Hrmph," she said. Nana walked around Diego, casting a truth spell–they always stank to me, like hard boiled eggs–and she demanded he tell her everything. The spell bounced off of him, something we *definitely* needed to talk about later, but he took a deep breath and just told her the truth anyway.

"I'd break every bond ever created by magic if it would have saved Snapdragon. She was my heart, and when she died, so did I," Diego said so matter of factly. It was his facts, his truth. He'd burn the world over if it meant his girl would be alive; and for a minute I was thankful that he was so sure that she *was* alive. I had my doubts. He was mentally chatting with someone, but deciding this chick was the solution to a centuries-long problem had me skeptical at best.

"Then you'll need this," she said. She handed us each an enchanted stone. An emerald for me. Rose quartz for him. "You need purity and vitality."

"I thought you found a piece of his heart?"

"I did, but you're already on the way to her."

"Her?" we said in unison. No, no, no, no, don't say the psychic. Don't say—

"Jack Hawthorne," Nana said. She hugged me, put a small emerald dagger in my hands, and turned for the sack of food she prepped. I never left Nana empty handed. Diego bowed this time, low and mighty, and it was so awkward it was perfect? So Diego. So fucking weird.

"Thank you," Diego said.

"Don't you hurt that girl," she said, turning away from us. The conversation was done now; we were dismissed. I hugged her again—just one more moment to remember home.

"I love you," I said to her, so soft I doubted she could hear me.

"Do the right thing, Falcon. I know you will. Just listen, and you'll know the right thing."

CHAPTER SEVEN

JACK

Pine and dew and earth filled my nose, bringing me to life. Was I awake? I couldn't tell. Vines snaked across my face, around my neck. Leaves and twigs scratched against my arms, and little thorny plants with stickers dug into me. Every time I breathed, I swallowed some dirt. Pink, yellow, red, and white snapdragons sprouted and bloomed all over me. Where was I? My body was enormous, like I was the earth itself, and every nerve was another blade of glass.

I was dreaming.

"You're blooming."

I searched for his voice—the outlined man, I knew it was him, I just knew. This world was hazy and full of life, but none that I could touch. I felt him next to me. The air was warmer right behind me, like he was standing inches away, like he was there just to reach for me. Wet grass and mulch and the smell of animals flooded my senses. Something like a fox brushed against my leg–when did I have legs again?–and I realized then that I felt wooden. That I *was* wooden. His voice drifted on the wind and brushed against my face. He touched me like a lover would, and my insides warmed.

"Your flowers are so lovely." He was next to me; his energy was warm instead of full of sorrow, and I felt him smoothing the ruffled edges of my flower petals, almost like he was running his fingers in my hair.

The touch faded, and he was gone. He was here, wasn't he?

"Where are you!" I yelled.

"Here."

There. His outline was mostly human, but he had small horns that curled toward the back of his head. Antlers? That felt like the right word. He seemed tall, maybe too tall to be a human. Everything was distorted.

I was watching through a large stained glass window with the Goddesses' images. The Goddesses bathed in golden light; larger than life, larger than any stained glass I'd ever seen before. I peered in, the room below made of stone with ivy creeping in, grand and ancient, but still so lively.

A woman in emerald green robes, fitting snugly across her chest and hips, flaring at the knees snapped into existence, like Puddin did when she teleported. Her hair was made fully of vines, small flowers woven through them like a crown. Her ivy colored skin complimented the gown she wore. Even in the distance, I could see that her eyes were green.

She had a crystal ball just like Harold, on a wooden staff with flowers and bones dangling from it. The staff floated next to her as she strode across the hall. The clacking of her shoes rang out, and I shivered. She walked like the world was beneath her and judging from the power circling her, she might be right.

She was terrifying.

The horned man was so far from her, like there was a veil between the three of us. He looked between us, back and forth. He stared at her for a fraction of a second longer, just enough for me to notice. He always turned back to me though. *Please don't look away*, I heard myself saying.

Jealousy pulsed through me. Her magic turned everything green around me, blacking out my senses, then the vines tightened around my throat and I just couldn't *breathe*, thorns stabbed at my side–

"This is not your world."

Her voice thundered and the world shook.

"Jack, Jack, Jack! Wake up! Come back!" Puddin's gravelly voice reminded me that I wasn't in my body, that I was floating in the ether, looking in on another world.

"Jack!" she screeched again, and I felt myself fading. Like when the visions took over, black dots floating in my eyes, my neck was aching, and I was gone.

I flung myself out of bed, clawing my neck, it *hurt*, everything hurt–

"What the hell is happening?" I said. Puddin was next me, pawing at my leg. I was in a tangle of sheets and blankets on the floor. Why did I need so many damn blankets? My feet were twisted up in an old, ugly comforter. A drop of blood splattered on my bare leg and panic ratcheted up through me.

Why was I bleeding?

"You soul walked yourself into some hell hole. I told you, you can't just *do* that. You need to let us know. You need to be grounded!" she purr-yelled at me.

"I can't control it!"

"Then you better learn before you get yourself killed!"

Mama stood in the doorway, white as a ghost. She dug her hands into the pockets of her sweater, but I saw how she tugged too hard on them. The sweater strained down, and guilt quickly replaced all of my panic. Another drop landed on my leg.

"Where did you go?" she asked.

"I don't know. It wasn't here. It was like a forest and then I saw some stained glass windows, maybe a tower. I could smell trees and rain. I saw her again," I whispered.

"Her?" Mama and Puddin' said in unison.

"The woman in my visions that has anger issues. She's something else." I didn't want to talk about how terrifyingly beautiful she was, or how she looked like she was made up of tree bark and vines, or how everything about her was green and creepy.

"Let's just start with dressing that wound, hmm? We can talk about the vision later," Mama said. I nodded, not willing to fight, but there would be no *later*. She wrapped her hands around my neck, and her fingers were so cold, but as she casted her healing spell my nerves tingled. She was closing the wound. I wanted to see what happened, but it was probably better that I didn't. I wasn't great with blood. When she let go, her hands were red with it, and my stomach churned.

"You're safe, baby girl. It wasn't bad, it just looks a little rough. Shouldn't leave a scar." Mama's fingers trailed over where the cut was, and I savored the extra few seconds of mom-love.

"What time is it? I need to open the shop–"

"Close it today. You're still shaking," Mama said. She was, as always, right. I tucked my hands between my knees. I was still tangled up in my sheets, and Mama was on the floor with me. She smoothed my hair, and I felt it sticking to my face. The sheets were sticky and clingy with sweat and I squirmed against them. Mama pulled the blankets back slowly and the heat trapped under them flooded out leaving me chilly. She rubbed her hands down my legs, massaging feeling back into them like she used to do when I first started getting visions.

"I'll keep the shop closed. Uggghhh," I groaned into the hideous comforter. Peony tried to take up sewing several years ago, and after destroying the inner workings of the machine twice, she finally gave it up. Not even magic could save that sewing machine. The comforter was supposed to be a quilt. There were patches of several different fabrics, all in shades of pink or filled with some kind of flower. The edges were chewed up. The squares were more rectangle-ish and were only straight if you squinted. It was lumpy too, but no one really ever figured out *how* Peony made it lumpy. I twisted my fingers in it, balling up my fists with the lumpy, ugly thing and felt comforted. It was probably Mama's magic, but the comforter needed the win more than her.

"I can reschedule your appointments, Jack," she said. Puddin plopped in my lap, purring fiercely to drown out the thoughts in my head.

"Thanks, Mama."

I tried not to think about the appointments. I'd need to stay open longer and schedule more readings over the next months to make up for the loss. My shop did well, but canceling business was never a good idea. The holidays were coming, and that meant I'd get a good uptick in sales, but my readings would decrease. People didn't have time for an hour long reading when they had fifteen other errands to run. The sales should keep the lights on, at least. Being a one-woman show was great until I was sick or needed time off or started losing my mind.

Like now.

Astral projection. Puddin used that term a few times and it sounded a little hokey even to me, a psychic. Soul walking, spirit walking. It didn't happen. Humans didn't do that. We were locked in our human bodies until death. So, I was either dead–unlikely, judging from my pulse rate lately–or going bonkers. The only time I'd ever gotten injured from a vision was when it hit, and I couldn't get to someplace safe to let it pass. Like when I drove my car into a lamppost. Or when I was seven, and didn't realize what was happening and walked into a metal door at school.

I hopped in the shower. Puddin wasn't pleased that I moved her, but I needed to clear my head. Mama had disappeared into the shop, and I savored the droning of the shower and the steam in my lungs.

I saw the rest of the marks once I took my shirt off. They looked feral, and it made me remember the shrillness of her voice when she saw me. I wasn't bleeding, at least. My neck had ugly, red gouges on it. A few on my collarbone. They were scratches from my own hands. Skin and blood were under my nails, so I scrubbed them more in my loofah. I still felt the vines wrapped around me. The shower stall filled with steam, and I finally could breathe.

My bathroom was the fanciest part of my apartment. I had a separate tub and shower, and standing under the rainfall shower counting each color tile eased the tightness in my chest. The shower had small, hexagon shaped tiles in blues, greens, and whites. The pattern was random but it always looked like the ocean scattered on my walls. Water beat down on my shoulders, forcing my muscles to unwind and I breathed in the steam. *It wasn't real, mostly.*

The claw foot tub was large and stark white with golden feet and stood out brightly even through the steam covered glass walls. Sunlight made the whole room sparkle. I had soft, plush cream-colored rugs and incense and candles. It was my favorite space, even more than my reading room. I cut the water off and stood there, just willing myself to move. Water dripped on my feet, so I dried off and wrapped my drippy hair in a towel and grabbed my fluffy robe.

My apartment buzzed with energy; I felt each one of my people hurriedly cleaning whatever mess I made from this latest vision. Dream. Soul walking. I pictured Mama gently coaxing everyone to *not talk about it, don't look at her neck, it's fine, everything is fine.*

Mari was back; I'd recognize the thud of her gigantic purse anywhere. I glanced out of the window to see Peony, straightening my little porch.

She pulled out her phone a few times and smiled. New guy. Had to be. She leaned against the railing, and for once, she was really smiling. Peony tucked her phone away, and went back to pretending to sweep. Puddin blinked next to me.

"Yeah, everyone's here," I said.

She purred a little louder in response, floating up so we could talk eye to eye. "How's your neck?"

"Red."

"Knock knock," Mari said, coming into the bathroom with me. She'd been crying. It was easy to tell, no magic needed. Mari wore her emotions as accessories; she didn't wear them on her sleeves. You'd never see her cry, but you could see the aftermath if you looked closely. An extra bangle. Five hair gems instead of two or three. Softer clothes. And her god-awful sandals that she should have thrown away years ago.

Mari had six bangles on today. Sandals with plush socks were a check. She had woven some extra small beads through her braids.

Emotion level: Critical.

Mari sat on the lid of the toilet and picked at her fingers.

"What's happened?"

"My magic. I think I'm losing it, Jackie." Her lip quivered and then the floodgates opened. She sobbed, and I wrapped my arms around her so fast that I smacked my chin against her shoulder. Mari was the only person to ever call me Jackie. And only under extreme duress or annoyance. It was our code word if we ever got kidnapped or something. Jackie for me. Full name–Marigold–for her.

"What do you mean?" My skin was covered in goosebumps. Mari picked at her nails more and her fingers were a mess again. I knelt down next to her, and held her hands. She squeezed them, not able to meet my eyes. I got a quick flash of a thought–*I don't want you to see me like this*–and then it was gone.

"I c-c-can't cast right. I had to go to Abuela and get more amber because I screwed them all up. *All of them!* And she did something, some spell, and I felt the spark come back, but it's still not *right*."

"Mine's screwed up too. Ever since we did that cleansing. I think I screwed it up–"

"I couldn't cast at all, Jackie. Nothing. Now I can, but it feels all wrong." She exploded up and paced the small space of the bathroom. I tried to reach for her, but Mari pulled away, her chewed up fingers back at her lips.

"Marigold–"

"Abuela said that you're a sword and I need to be your shield. She said that something is coming and we have to be ready but I don't got any magic!" The sobs ripped through her words again, and I gently pulled her hands away. Two fingers were bleeding. I tried to replicate the spell that Mama used on me, but with limited success. Mari wasn't any calmer, and I was tired.

"When did she say that?" I let go of Mari to watch her face. She hadn't meant to tell me that. Mari was protective of her time with Abuela. I'd met her a few times, but she was Mari's mother's friend. Abuela was her sometimes babysitter as a kid and bonus grandmother. She'd be anyone's grandmother if they asked, but Mari was extra special to her. Our magic was so different that Mari needed someone else to help teach her how to use it. She needed someone that wasn't us. Someone that was another connection to her mother, Daisy.

"It was around the cleansing. When I got the amber."

"What did she mean about me being a sword?"

"I don't know." I guided her to sit again, and laid my head in her lap, kneeling on the rug in front of her. Mari picked at the threads on the towel around my hair.

"The visions are getting stronger," I whispered.

"Girl, what happened to you? You look chewed up worse than my hands."

"Me." I sat up and rolled the collar of my robe down so she could really see the scratches. They were still red.

"Jackie..."

"I did it when I, um, soul walked. 'Astral projection.' That's what Puddin said anyway. But, like, that doesn't happen so I must be going crazy. Like really crazy. But it can't be astral projection because I can't *do* that, and I also didn't try to strangle myself, and I think I might be dying?" Mari inspected me, looking at my hands and neck and eyeing my face.

"We need to shore up our defenses, Jackie. I'm talking wall spells. I'm not reliable right now–"

"Nonsense."

"I'm serious. Until I get my shit in line, I don't think I should be casting."

"I'm gonna make you some tea to recenter your spirit. You're scattered."

"I think I'm past scattered, girl." Mari wiped away her tears. She dabbed at her makeup. She did anything to not look back at me.

"We're gonna fix it. It's gonna be fine."

"Lying to your best friend ain't cool," she said. She laughed a little, and I was so grateful for the sound of it. Mari wasn't a crier.

"We need a drink. Something stronger than the tea," I said. Then she really laughed. Mari was still messing with her makeup and poked herself in the eye. She muttered a slew of curses, all while still laughing.

"Isn't it like ten in the morning?"

"We're past judging at this point. I'll pour."

"Amen to that, but go put some clothes on first." Mari tugged at the tie on my fuzzy bathrobe.

"Oh, right."

DIEGO

The visit with Falcon's adoptive grandmother was a bust. She gave us each an artifact to fortify us and an earful to me, but that was it. And the empanadas, which were incredible. But she didn't have one of my heart pieces, so while the little boost would help, I wasn't any closer to being fully alive than I was a few hours ago.

Falcon tried to shield me but I saw her hand him something green. Probably nothing I wanted to know about. He didn't offer up any details and I didn't ask. Falcon enjoyed his privacy, what little of it he had, and I was happy to oblige him.

I dreamt of Obius. We don't call it the magic realm; it was just home. I couldn't even remember how many years it'd been since I was home, but I missed it.

Tonight, I dreamt of it.

I saw Jack in my dream, and it felt real. The forests were confused but fascinated with her. Tiny, fae birds chittered and chattered about her presence. Flower children and seedlings gossiped. Everyone was buzzing and excited and alive. She was there, taking in all of the sights and sounds, letting it all seep into herself. She was blossoming. I stayed close, watching but out of the way, out of her reach. The world was hazy, and I couldn't touch anything, my hands passing through the trees and the leaves like I was nothing. Because here, I *was* nothing.

The full ache in my chest turned sharp. Remembering and dreaming were worse than forgetting. I'd forget everything if I could. Anything to make existing in this magicless husk of a world more tolerable. Falcon drove in silence, turned off his music, and just drove. He hummed a little here and there, but mostly the car was silent. It let my thoughts wander too wildly.

"Glad you're getting some sleep," he said.

"How long was I out?"

"A while. Just rest, man. You still look mostly dead."

She was beautiful though, for a human. They all seemed so small to me, even Falcon who was considered large. Humans don't like to assess each other just by their might. I've found only the lower evolved ones focus on the physical might. They like to add in the human essence. They don't care if a male is the biggest so much as if he's the most *male*. They've changed over the years too; humans now enjoy their jokes and laughter, where before they cowered before their gods. I liked this world more than the ones before it.

Still, Jack seemed small even by human standards. Her bones appeared so breakable, like if I held her hand it would snap. They get more brittle with age too; Nana would snap if I squeezed her hand at all.

I only grew more dense with age. Details were getting harder to remember. What shade of green was Snapdragon's luscious skin? How long were her vines? How strong were her bones? I struggled to remember where her flowers would bloom, the shapes of her feet, and the scent of her hair. I'd been earthbound for so long, I couldn't remember the sunrise in Trellis.

The stillness of the car lulled me back to sleep. When I started to dream of Obius again, Jack called for me. She was frantic, searching. I tried to assure her that I was here, that I was nearby. Everything in me wanted to hold this woman, this human, that I'd never met. In all my years on the earth, I'd never connected with a woman here. Who could compare to Snapdragon?

Jack's voice rang out again, she was lost in the forest, and I wanted to help her. I wasn't allowed back in Obius, not even to dream of it, but I was here. Everything was so different, so wilted and foreign. Tree beings, fae birds and squirrels, flower children, and saplings all flocked to Jack, trying to tear her apart. She didn't belong here.

Neither did I.

JACK

My phone was ringing off the hook. Do people even still say that? It was blowing up. Angry clients. Potential clients. The holidays were coming and my unsettling visions wouldn't be enough of a reason to cancel more business. It's hard to maintain a professional image when there's no running water or electricity. Which was a bit dramatic–my business was thriving, really. Steady influx of clients for readings, and the natural state of the world being in constant crisis had people looking to the divine for answers.

I did the rough math in my head–thriving or not, I'd need to do five to six readings a day plus whatever I managed to sell to keep the shop closed for a week.

Great Goddesses, I needed the week off. I looked like shit. I felt like shit. And my magic was temperamental at best these days. It loved trying to kill me, and was less helpful on any other front.

The door chimed and I smiled, adjusting my scarf so it covered the ugly red marks on my neck. Mama's magic helped, but they were still visible. A couple of teenagers came in. Probably looking for love potions, tarot cards, or weed. It was almost always the weed. Marijuana was a beautiful and magically stable plant. It held and took so much magic that I stored my excess spells in my garden.

The girls looked around fifteenish. They giggled at the potions, touched the crystals lightly, and smiled goofy, braces filled smiles. I tried to do a quick scan of them, but nothing came. Mari greeted them–when had she come down?–and then came over to sit with me.

"I can handle things if you need some more rest," she whispered.

"I can't get a read on them," I said. Mari pulled my citrine necklace out of her pocket and handed it to me. She had been doing some spell work; her magic radiated from it. The strength of the necklace had changed and grown, and it was apparent as soon as I touched it.

I slipped it around my neck and everything came into focus so brightly and keenly; I cracked a few teacups when I looked at them.

"Breathe it out girl. It's got some heavy magic in it."

"I thought you said your magic was wonky."

"Not today it seems."

The teens were now panicked, seeing me suddenly look alive and watching things start to crack and break around the shop. I smiled at them. It was so clear. My mind went calm and the aura of every magical item and person shone.

They wanted friendship bracelets to secure and bind them together. The taller of the girls has magic but she doesn't know it yet. They held each other's hands tightly. I wondered when they would realize the love there was more than friendship. Their lives played out in my mind; together, constantly and happily. Prom dates. Traveling somewhere with mountains. The taller girl had a few unfortunate haircuts. There was so much joy between them. I saw the end of their lives, hands still tightly held but with old, worn faces. Still so much in love.

"My dear, the bracelets are here. I think some jasper, pink agate, and a few quartzes would suit you two."

"We wanted some friendship bracelets," the shorter girl said. "Are those good for friendship?"

"And for love," I said. The shorter girl blushed a little and the taller one grinned.

"We'll take two of each!"

They left happily, bracelets on their wrists, hands interlocked. Mari chuckled, seeing everything in them that I could see too. She cleaned up the glass vase I cracked, and grabbed the two tea cups that would need some repairs. They were just decorations for the store, but another *thing* breaking made me angry. My magic was so volatile now that I was ruining the things around me.

"What did you do to the necklace?"

"Nothing crazy, I just layered the magic. Jazzy and Puddin added magic to it too. I wanted it to be as strong as your crystal ball so you could carry it with you," she said. The thought of needing that much magic at a moment's notice seemed silly; we lived in a beach town, not a warzone.

"Why?"

Mari shifted the broken cups in her arms so she could properly shrug, "Just wanted to cover all the bases." She fished the superglue out of the junk drawer from my reading room, and I studied the necklace. It wasn't as strong as Harold, but it was damn close. The magic settled into me and I felt like I could fly.

DIEGO

We checked into another hotel. According to the directions, Jack was less than a mile away. Even with the boost from Nana, I was too weak to cast a finding spell. Luckily, human technology could find her for me. Falcon hid his eyes behind his aviator sunglasses, but the tightness of his face, the overly friendly smile, with his silence told me he hated every second of being here. Falcon tried desperately to hide in plain sight and he was good at it, but his silence spoke the truth of his feelings: he didn't like this idea to find Jack. I didn't know why he was so against finding her. Because I would be healed? Because I might have my hopes up for nothing?

Because he thinks I'll just leave?

Falcon wasn't my blood, but he was my family now. Still, I tried not to think too hard about what it'd be like to be whole again, and fully alive. I doubted I would ever get to walk through the trees in Trellis or stand in the Great Hall of Trellis Castle. I'd never see the roses bloom in the courtyard, or see my people, or dance to Trellian pipes for the Harvest season. My throat clenched.

Falcon plopped his bag down on the bed closest to the door—he always wanted to be near an exit—so I took the bed closer to the window. It was still light out; the afternoon sun was starting to set, but the night was young. I could still go to her today.

JACK

Four hours later, I was still buzzing from the new magic Mari layered into my necklace. The stone was small and irregular, and honestly not that pretty, but it was a powerhouse. I tuned into the stone, feeling out the different layers of magic. I saw Peony's magic and Mama's in it too; they'd all added to it over the years.

Mari's alchemy was masterful. She layered it with precision and didn't leave traces of herself in the stone. I knew it was magic from how clean and precise it was. She was skilled as a surgeon with her alchemy. It left me in awe. I was amped up, and it was hard to dial the magic back.

Vision after vision hit me—any and everyone that came into the shop, or walked by, or if I thought of them. I saw their thoughts, the next portion of their day. Sometimes when I dialed into someone too much, I started to see how they would die before I shut down my magic and closed myself off from them.

I might have been a bit overwhelmed.

Humans needed anchors, or artifacts, to draw their magic from, to focus and guide it. The artifacts were just a channel for me; having such a powerful stone around my neck made everything look ultra HD. I saw colors even finer, noticed sounds from farther away, felt the emotions of everyone passing by. I connected to the essence of the earth, and felt its magic coursing under my feet.

After about another hour, I took it off. I'd been wearing it for years, but Mari had completely transformed it. Colors dimmed and life looked and felt duller but I could complete a thought without hearing snippets from every other living being near me. Without the necklace, my store looked so drab. Was this how it was seen by my customers? Old, colorless, and boring? So many of the pieces that made it perfect were damaged from the cleaning spell that everything felt lifeless.

But.

It couldn't *hurt* to keep it on. I'd get used to the extra thoughts, or better yet, learn to turn them off when I wanted. My magic was too unstable and unpredictable with all of the visions and soul walking. I needed the grounding. The citrine was perfect, really. Not pretty, but still perfect. The vibe from the added magic meshed so easily in my mind, and I missed how vibrant the world was when I had it on. I slipped it back over my head, let the magic unwind through me, and let the world hum to life again.

PEONY

Okay. So Sherwin was cute. He used too many emojis, but that wasn't enough of a reason to drop a guy. Especially when you were nearing your mid-thirties and the landscape was *barren.*

He was picking me up for a coffee later from Jack's place. She knew something was up but didn't ask, and I didn't tell her anything. Sherwin rolled up in an old red station wagon that was covered with surf stickers and a well-worn roof rack. There wasn't a fancy piece on this car and it suited him. It was honest, and I loved it. Sherwin rolled to a stop, the window down with his hair windswept, and I couldn't hide my grin. He pushed his aviator sunglasses down so I could see his eyes. I wanted to push them back up just to have a reason to touch his face.

However, a little magic to check his intentions wouldn't hurt anyone.

"Hi," I said, adding just a little magic to it. Jack and Mari were better about this; not using their magic to influence things. It was harder when

your words and magic were so intertwined. Intention was key with magic
and language. Of course I'd want someone to answer me honestly!

"Hi, yourself," he said. His eyes traveled the length of my body, paused
at my mouth, and a wolfish grin spread across his face. Heat shot through
my belly, and I got into his car.

Sometimes I got more honesty than I wanted.

FALCON

Jack Hawthorne's shop, Visions and Trinkets, was a fifteen minute walk
from our hotel according to the directions I pulled up on my laptop. I
scrolled through the pictures, trying to feel out what we were getting into.
It was on a corner lot. A hot pink and yellow concoction of a house that
would have been hideous in any other location but it fit here. The buildings
were old but brightly colored like every beach town.

I stayed very still on my bed, while Diego paced. His energy rarely took
up any space but this hotel room was suffocatingly small with his emotional
spikes. I stared out the window and could catch a glimpse of the water.
The ocean here did seem more alive than usual. The magic rolled with the
waves, and I felt the energy with every wave break even in my hotel room.
Standing on the beach itself was gonna be a contact high.

I ordered room service and forced Diego to stop pacing and staring out
the window like a lost puppy.

He was itching to see her. Ever since he saw that picture, something
jolted in him and he was fixated.

My gut said this was all wrong.

That *she* was wrong.

This chick wasn't the solution for Diego. She wouldn't be able to piece
his heart back together. My thoughts kept drifting back to the emerald

green knife that Nana gave me. The right thing. Do the right thing. As if I knew what the hell that was.

JACK

With Mari's help, I made it through the rest of the day. The shop closed at its normal five PM, and I hadn't moved off of my couch since then. When the dots prickling around my eyes started again, I leaned back into the overstuffed arm of the couch and let the vision take over. I was comfortable and safe and ready to let it tell me its story.

I saw the man again, in the same forest. The same location from my dream.

He stood at the tree line. His horns brushed against the branches. How big was that tree? Everything was distorted.

Little birds—people?—fluttered around me. They had little human-ish faces. Rounded heads but with beaks. Wings with small little hands at the tips.

Don't look too close, girl. This isn't your world.

"Glad you finally see that!"

The voice boomed, and I flinched but didn't move. She wasn't here. She was somewhere else, watching, and pissed off about me being here. I wasn't *there* though. The angry woman and I were both watching, both looking, but from different vantage points. The horned man was too far away for me to see any details, but I felt like he was looking at me. He didn't hear her rage, he didn't flinch from her voice; he only had eyes for me.

He had hidden behind one of the trees, head whipping around searching. I knew he was searching for me. I wanted it to be me.

I ran toward him.

The ground was soft. Too much rain. The leaves didn't crunch beneath my feet. The sticks and brush only bent instead of snapping.

Taking in a deep breath, the magic of this world filled me, and I commanded it now. The man realized I was coming for him and he ran toward me. Something was awkward about his gait but I couldn't place what. His steps were too long, too slow to be moving as quickly as he did. My heart raced. He was coming for me.

The details of his body, his face were blurred. The vision faded as he got closer and closer. A tear welled in my eye and when I was back in my reality, my arms were wide open, reaching for him.

I forced myself to think about what else I saw, not just this man that called to me, but where I was, what I felt, and smelled, and could touch with my fingers. With my pendant on, I saw that the trees weren't green but several different colors; my brain just told me they should be green, so they were. Purples, blues, and yellows. The leaves shimmered all the colors of the rainbow. This forest *was* a rainbow. The bird-people-things were mostly reds and oranges. Squirrel-adjacent critters were yellow and gold with purple, violent eyes. They would kill me if I offended them.

The citrine was warm against my skin; not too hot, but enough for me to take notice. It wanted to be noticed. Flashes of him came back in waves, but the man was gone. His energy, *black black black*, was gone. He felt like a black hole when I could see him, and now everything was lighter.

My heart sank. The black hole felt like it had moved into me. The weight of his sorrow seeped into my pores. What goddess awful thing could cause pain like that? My lungs ached from trying to breathe through it. The vision–that wasn't right, it wasn't the future, I saw–edged back into my eyes but I pushed it away. Everything in my body ached, and when I thought about it too closely, I missed him. The tears came back, and this time there was no fighting it.

DIEGO

My spirit wandered to the space between the realms while I was sleeping. This used too much magic but sometimes I couldn't control it. My human body would need to rest, to heal, but my spirit needed magic, so it would wander.

Jack was here. I didn't really know where *here* was, but we were walking through a memory, my memory. This in-between space didn't exist in any realm except in dreams.

The forest outside of Trellis Castle materialized. Trees in Obius were green, of course, but they were more than that. Light filtered through their leaves and branches in all colors. A walk through the trees at moonrise would be like walking through shades of blues and purples. Sunrise brought the colors of the sun with it, and the leaves would turn red and yellow and orange. The trees of Obius were a living rainbow. I loved the trees. I couldn't touch anything but I still felt the tree bark in my memories.

Jack walked through Obius like she was born there; her feet touched the grass so lightly, like she had never been bound to the earth. The creatures were awed by her presence and buzzed and chittered around her, curious and gossiping. Everyone was excited that this human was here, and I wanted to climb to the treetops, shouting her arrival. This could be her world, and I wanted that for her as much I wanted it to be mine again.

The banners of Trellis danced above the castle and my heart clenched. I was full here, whole. I didn't feel broken or lost. Trellis pulled at my every molecule and with each passing breeze, the feel of the wind on my face lessened.

Because this was only a dream.

Maybe I was the one that was excited.

She saw me behind a tree and took off in my direction. This wasn't how we were supposed to meet. Not here. Not in this in-between realm where I am even less of a being than I was in her world.

I had to run, but as I started to move, I was running to her.

Wake up, wake up, wake up! I willed myself to wake up. She was getting closer and closer, and I wanted to stop just so she could catch me.

"Bro, wake up, can you hear me?" Falcon's voice was so far away. "Come on D, come back."

My body was being shaken. It took several tries, but when I finally got my eyes open, Falcon was staring right through me. I tried to smile but everything felt stiff and he chuckled.

"You lookin' rough, D. What happened?"

"I think I was remembering Obius, but Jack was there."

"Weird."

"Yeah," I said. My hands were shaky, my breath was shaky, and my chest ached. It would hurt less if there was a knife sticking out of me than just this emptiness.

"Go on," he sighed. "Tell me what's on your mind."

"I think I need to go see her. Today. Now."

Falcon paced through our room, tossing a stress ball up, catching it, switching hands, again and again. Constant. Motion. I knew he was weighing all the options and trying to figure out how to convince me this was a bad idea. It probably was, but I was going to see her with or without his blessing.

Jack kept calling me, and her call forced my spirit to stand at the edge of the realms while my human body lay catatonic on the hotel bed. And I couldn't keep doing that.

My chest heaved, and I struggled to breathe. She called again.

"Come back, please. Tell me your name." Jack's voice felt like flower petals brushing against my skin.

I will soon.

"Where are you?"

I'm in your city. Cape Margaret. I'll find you–

"I'll be here."

Jack's voice echoed louder and louder, the featherlight touch of flower petals turning to thorns in my very conscious brain, and I just sank into the bed. I wasn't dreaming, or remembering, or wandering. I was awake and I heard her loud and clear. Falcon was shaking me again. He looked panicked, angry. It took a few minutes before I could feel my hands and feet, but when I could, I sat up. My head weighed a ton and I just sank back on the bed.

"Oh for fuck's sake, *fine,* we're gonna go see her first thing tomorrow. Take a sleeping pill. You need to fucking sleep before you accidentally kill yourself."

Chapter Eight

MARI

Jack and I prepared for visitors. After her last round of visions or spirit walking or whatever, Puddin and I decided that all of us needed to reconnect and get Jack back to center. She was wandering too much, her eyes were too clouded, and it scared all of us. Me most of all.

We were high with magic. The amber grounded and recentered me. I was connected back to the earth again. Power radiated off of Jack, and while the citrine helped, it was like she had come alive. Like I'd never seen her before, and now she was shining.

Jack and I walked barefoot through her garden, barefoot through her house, barefoot through the shop. We stood holding hands in the center of the garden where we had made a stone circle connected to each other and to the earth. The weather had cooled off immensely in the last couple days, and my toes ached from the cold but we *needed* this. I needed this. A light drizzle started and the sun set and the fire crackled in her outdoor hearth–

The elements were aligned. We were in lock and step together.

It was perfect with just the two of us.

Jazzy and Peony were drowning, overwhelming forces. Jack shrank around them, wanting to be smaller and easier and everything they wanted. I did too, but I wasn't expected to be their perfect little flower. I wasn't *theirs*. Peony was my balance too, but my feet always stayed true even when she wasn't there to hold me steady.

Jack was always there; she was the other half of my heart, and standing in the circle made that realization hit harder. Jack would always be a part of them, a part of us, a part of the earth. They wanted her to be small because seeing everything she was sat too heavy in their minds.

But she wasn't small. The magic that was unfolding in her was grand and old. This was what Abuela meant–she was a sword, made for magic and life.

I would always be her shield.

"Let's cast a circle. Full circle. It's not a full moon anymore, but it'll be fine. Get the sage?" Jack said. I was already on my way to her outdoor kitchen. I had a bucket of blessed and enchanted dirt. We had prayed over it, Jack mixed in a blend of spices for power, and I kneaded it together, sealing it with focus.

Protection.

We needed to be protected.

The two energies Jack had felt were coming and we needed to be ready.

JACK

Mari moved with practiced efficiency. We'd cast this circle a thousand times. It was the first one we ever got right without Peony setting the intention for us. This was our circle: the Full Circle. Once the circle was drawn, it glowed.

That was first.

We watched the glow fade back into the line of the circle, and we stepped inside. Heart to heart, Mari and I connected the circle to ourselves.

Her amber and my citrine brimmed with magic. I worried that we'd overpower the circle or that something would happen again–

No.

Intention was everything. If I thought something would go wrong, it would.

"Get your head straight Jackie. I'm ready to cast if you are."

"Let's do it."

I lifted my right hand, Mari lifted her left. We touched the tip of each finger, one at a time, slowly until all five fingers touched and we pressed our palms together.

To protect my–our–home.

Then we did the same thing with our other hands.

To guard our hearts.

Next, we stepped forward, the insoles of our feet touching.

Guide our feet to the light.

The spell swelled in my chest, burning brighter than it ever had before. Mari gasped and her eyes darted around wildly, her hands stiffening, so I gripped her hand tighter, keeping her bound to the spell to let the circle close. We drew three circles in our minds. One around us. One around my property, just inside my fence line. And one over the threshold of my shop, the main entrance to my house. Everything in threes. Always.

Black and white danced at the corners of my eyes.

"Jackie, no, no, no, stay with me. Don't slip away–"

But I was slipping. The magic pulled me, and a vision hit. I hit the earth, the smell of lavender and Mari's perfume the last things I remembered before I lost my tie to this world.

I saw the energies again, the green and black ones. I knew them now. The black one was the same from the Magic Realm, the man I could never reach. The green had popped up in my mind often enough that it didn't frighten me anymore. He wasn't a threat; he was a friend.

They were coming toward me, but I knew that too. They would be here soon.

It was the woman that scared the shit out of me. She popped up randomly; I'd be following the energies, looking for him, and she would appear. Angry, cruel. Her face staring back at me, knowing there was nothing good, nothing worth saving in her. The hatred in her lit every part of her being, twisting every feature into something unrecognizable and nightmarish.

She wanted me dead.

She wanted everything dead.

I heard Mari shouting for me, trying to get me to come back and be present with her, but not yet. I needed to see more of this woman. The forest wasn't here this time. Just stone walls. Empty stone walls inside an empty castle.

What made you this way?

The rainbow forest flashed in my mind. Images hit in quick succession, and I struggled to understand them all. An altar. The horned man and the vine laced woman.

She had a golden dress, the details too bright to look at head on. There were thousands of creatures staring at her. The horned man was too far away, he rushed toward her but he wouldn't reach her in time. A man with black wings stood next to her with a knife. It was dark green, and dripped with green blood. I smelled it.

She stumbled back, the golden dress now slowly turning green. She looked at the horned man and screamed.

He broke through the crowds, trying desperately to get to her.

He was too late. I heard his voice whispering more to himself than to anyone else, ***"It's not real, it's not real, it's just a nightmare. You're safe with me."*** I wondered where he was and if those words brought him any comfort. They didn't for me.

Mari pushed the hair out of my face, the circle still glowing around us. She helped me sit up, and I watched the rainbow forest fade from the light of the circle. As the lights from the trees dimmed, my heart sank. The forest was surreal and I wanted to touch the leaves and learn the pattern of every tree.

"Did you see that?"

"The trees or the woman getting stabbed playing out like a hologram in the circle?"

"Right."

The circle's glow was dimming; we had fully lost our focus, and needed to close it properly. Mari stood, light at the ends of her finger tips, and she drew another circle around us to close it.

"Were my fingers glowing? Because it looked like they were glowing." She cracked her knuckles, sending little sparks around us.

"That shift in the realms was no joke." My heart was beating a mile a minute. I took a few deep breaths, counting the seconds to get my lungs regulated again. In for three, out for three.

"For fucking real. I'm putting you to bed. This spell's got me all weak. No more visions. Center yourself and then go to bed. I need to crash. Will you be okay?"

"Yep," I said. It felt like a lie, but it was well intentioned. I had no control over my visions, and even less control than normal now. Mari really did seem out of it. The Full Circle had too much magic and I felt like I had been electrocuted. Mari looked the same. She bumped my shoulder and headed back into the house for her shoes.

After she left, I stayed in the circle. Puddin watched from my bedroom window. Mari had closed the circle, but the magic was still there, waiting to be revived.

So I did.

The visions came back. The rainbow forest. The altar. The knife. The horned man. He was still so far away. I focused on him, forcing the magic to zoom in like I would with a picture on my phone. The outline was more 3D, but still blurred. I couldn't see his face. I dropped the circle, maybe too quickly, and it disappeared. He disappeared.

I poured myself into bed and prayed for a dreamless night.

FALCON

I'd run out of excuses to keep us at the hotel. *Let's rest. Let's think of our approach. Let's reconsider the whole damn thing and leave before this Jack girl fucks up our whole world.* How would she be able to *fix* Diego when Nana couldn't? Diego reluctantly agreed to wait until morning to track this chick down, and morning had come.

We both noticed that magical energy surge as the sun set last night. It had to be her. My normally still and stoic travel buddy paced and paced and paced. He ran his hands through his longish hair–a mannerism I'm sure he learned from his soap operas–and continued to pace. He watched the window, watched the sun sink in the sky.

Diego said she had called him and it forced his spirit to wander again. He convinced himself that this girl would solve his problem. *But Falcon, she will fix my heart. She will help me rebind the links I shattered because I'm naive. She's the answer.*

She was very likely going to tell us to fuck off. That's what I would do. Two randos approach me and beg, *please miss, heal my* literal *broken heart?*

It was like a bad pick up line.

Magic or not, her survival instincts would tell her to walk away from the giant men waving red flags. That's what I was; the reddest flag anyone had ever seen. And this girl wasn't dumb. She had a whole business hustling people out of their money for her "psychic vibes." Diego flipped through the TV channels, stopping on his favorite soap. He mimicked the doctor's hair flip, and I groaned.

A greasy burger and a bag of cheese doodles wouldn't fix the heartbreak when she lets him down.

Nothing can fix that.

I just really hoped it wouldn't kill him.

DIEGO

Falcon asked me three times to reconsider going to her. I didn't have a choice. Jack would keep calling, pulling me to the space between the realms until we were together or my heart failed completely.

I was going to die either way.

He drove as slow as he could. Falcon never followed the speed limits, but today he did. His GPS said it would take seven minutes to get to her shop. We'd been in the car for twenty.

"I just got a bad feeling about this chick. Something ain't right, D. I can just feel it."

"How long do you think I have left? It's been centuries. I've got one fragment of my heart left, and every time she calls me I use too much magic and I can't stop it. What choice do I have, Falcon?" I wanted to slam my fist on the dashboard, but I was too tired. My words were as weak as I felt, and I didn't have enough fight in me to convince him of anything.

I let that hang in the air. Falcon blew out a sigh, and turned down the next street. I saw her house, the pink and yellow one from the picture on the GPS, and my heart raced. As much as it could, anyway. Her house sat at the end of the street corner.

JACK

I jolted awake, confused about where I was, and how I'd gotten there. Last night came back slowly: the Full Circle, the nightmare visions that I was sure weren't real, the color of her golden gown and the green glint of the knife. I needed coffee.

Mari was already in my kitchen working on making lattes. I didn't have the heart to tell her that I needed an espresso IV drip today, instead of a frothy treat. She jumped when she heard me. Puddin poked her head up. Something itched at the back of my mind; something was wrong. It nagged and nagged at me.

"Jackie?"

"Shh, hang on," I said, squeezing my eyes closed, searching for whatever my mind was trying to tell me. It faded too quickly and I couldn't remember. I needed to remember. My apartment felt so closed up. The walls were closing in, there just wasn't enough *space* in here.

The door, the door, the door.

It was closed.

It shouldn't be closed. The door needed to be open. *All* of the doors needed to be open.

I have to be open. I started with the windows. My skin was on fire; my nerves were tingling, and I had to *move*. My hair was slipping from its bun, and the sensation of hair on my neck made me itch. I shook it out and tied it up. Even my hair was tingling.

"It's like forty degrees outside, what are you doing opening the windows?"

I broke into a run for the front door of the shop, flying down the stairs as fast as my feet would move. I had to keep it open. Then the back door. The door to every room in my house—

"Jackie." Mari followed me down to the shop, the crystals glowing gently around her and vividly near Puddin. I had tracked dirt and muck all through the store from last night, but the cleaning had to wait.

"My girl, what are you thinking?" Puddin purred.

"Jack? Jack Hawthorne?" a male voice said.

I knew his voice, and I felt his energy. He knocked quietly on the oak door, sending magic through the room, but not entering. His black, black energy, like a void pulling me toward him. I squeezed my eyes shut. This wasn't how I was supposed to see him. Not in this world, that would hide his horns and feathers. Not in this realm that he wasn't made for. Not in my shop while I was sleep rumpled, and a barefoot mess. Mari and Puddin searched my face, looking for a cue on how to respond.

No no no no, no tears Jack. Get. Your. Shit. Together.

I huffed and sniffled and blew out a breath until my lungs stopped heaving. He was here. There was no avoiding it. His energy filled the whole room—thick and heady, reeking of sandalwood—and he was still standing in the door frame.

"Jack?" He stared at me. The girls stared at him. Them. Green energy was here now too, hanging back on the porch and trying to observe as he shifted back and forth, sending little shock waves of energy to me. How did no one else feel that?

My eyes were still closed.

He touched my arm so softly, I thought I imagined it but I could hear his heart beating so slowly and irregularly. Was he nervous? His breath was a little ragged. I still hadn't turned around. He squeezed my arm.

"Jack?"

"Yep, that's me," my voice sounded steady, and I was grateful for that.

His voice wasn't steady. I heard the tremble. Was he afraid? That made me turn.

He was... human. Human looking at least. He dropped his hand, realizing it had been there too long and tucked it behind his back. A soft gray-black sweater. Dark wash jeans. Dark, olive skin. Black hair with a little curl that fell just to his ears and a little stubble. His nose was a tad crooked, but only if you stared.

Like I was. Like I was doing right now.

His eyes were dark, dark brown. I'd never understood what molten eyes were until this moment. His eyes churned with magic, dark like the energy that radiated from him.

He stared back at me.

Rightness flowed through me. His magic, my magic, the energy in my shop was charged and alive and *right*. He stood just inches from me, and the scent of sandalwood was strong. He smelled like the earth, like life. I held my hand out, and he took it.

"It's you," I said. His mouth quirked a little, just the barest hint of a smile. His lips were soft and full and perfectly sized–

"It's me," he said. "Hello."

"Hi." He squeezed my hand a little, and I broke into a smile too. He was real.

He was beautiful. Not handsome. He was that too, but there was a beauty to him that was surreal. *He* was surreal: not of this realm. He looked like someone you'd see in a magazine, perfectly refined and buffed and touched up until he existed in a world that most people would never see.

I brought his hand to my chest, to my heart. He didn't protest, and I listened for whatever his magic would tell me. My heart beats slowly and irregularly now, in time with him. It hurt a little, feeling so off from my normal. I listened, trying to hear it and whatever else his heart would tell now that he was here, standing in front of me, holding my hand. *Deign.*

"My name is Diego," he said like he had announced that someone had died. In a way, someone had.

I studied his face.

He smiled again.

I smiled.

I kept his hand tucked against my chest, "No, your name is Deign."

Green Energy man finally stepped through my door step. "Who the fuck are you?" Green Energy said at last, quietly. It was venomous and utterly ineffective.

"Who the fuck are *you?*" Mari shot back, instantly between us and Green Energy.

Who the fuck cares, Puddin whispered to me.

"His name is Falcon. He's my best friend. He's an alchemist too," Deign said. *Diego* said. Diego was his name here. Not Deign.

"He's rude," Mari said. They sized each other up, and Falcon flashed a thousand watt smile. Mari didn't smile. She cocked an eyebrow, looked back at me, and I shrugged. He sized her up too, taking in the sights of my shop, distinctly not looking at me. Falcon had long black hair, past his shoulders, tied in a low ponytail. He had a long, good looking nose, sharp cheekbones, and an easy smile. While Diego looked sophisticated and put together, Falcon was rough and ready. Bandanas tied on each arm. Short sleeve shirt even though the wind was cold. Falcon was effortlessly cool, and I didn't trust any part of his smiles.

Harmless but desperately wanting not to be.

"Not rude, just apprehensive," Falcon said. He smiled again, too wide for my taste. I dropped Diego's hand and nearly lost balance; letting go of him was like dropping an anchor, and I had to urge to jump in the water to follow it. But I needed to see Falcon's aura more clearly. It was brilliantly, vibrantly forest green. His magic was stronger than mine and Mari's combined. He looked thirty-something; a bit older than me but far more experienced with his magic. I held my hand out for him to shake and he took it, but we both noticed the pause. Falcon had more guards built around himself than I ever knew existed.

"Cat got your tongue, Falcon?" I said, trying to lighten the mood. Puddin whipped her tail back and forth.

"Not yet, but I haven't been here long." He glanced over at Puddin and her little cat lips turned up in a smile.

"I wanted to hire you," Diego said. He pulled at his fingers, like he was trying to crack the joints. It made my fingers ache.

"Hire me? For what? I'm just a psychic. Did you want a reading?" The stoop of his shoulders held more sorrow than seemed possible, and I drank in the details of him. Peony said I was macabre, but sometimes I found sadness to be lovely. And Diego was lovely. Sadness and regret poured out of every fiber from him. He stood very close to me still, trying not to take up space despite his size. Diego was a head taller than me. He inclined his head just slightly, Mari had shifted, now standing close enough to me that I could feel everything she thought without trying. This citrine was something else, but Diego's thoughts were still hidden away.

There's so much bullshit coming from him I might actually puke. He cute though. I traced her look and she was staring at Falcon. She wasn't wrong.

"It's a long story," Diego's voice was so quiet, I thought I might have been the only one that heard him. Diego met my eyes and my breath caught in my throat.

"Go ahead, D. These ladies aren't falling for any charms I've thrown out, so the truth is all we got now." Falcon chuckled and pulled a chair from my reading table and sat. He reclined a bit, trying too hard to be at ease. Everything about him was too poised. The more I watched Falcon, the more alarm bells went off in my head. He was very good at hiding right in front of you.

"You call that charm?" Mari said.

"I've been told the mysterious thing is sexy," he said. Falcon winked, making bedroom eyes at Mari, wiggling his fingers in a playful wave. She snorted with laughter.

"Maybe work on your approach," she said. *Damn he is cute. I hate it.* Everyone had sorta forgotten that Diego was in the room. He moved a bit, shifting his weight from foot to foot and fidgeting and my attention snapped back to him. How did he just *fade* like that?

"I'll spare you the backstory. My heart is broken," he said as flatly as if he had told me that it would rain today.

We all waited for him to explain.

He didn't.

A beat passed. Another one. Then another. Falcon scrubbed a hand over his face.

"Bro," he said.

"Oh right, ah, I meant that quite literally. It's been fractured. Shattered. I only have one piece of it left and it's, it's not really quite working–" he stifled a laugh. It was such a human gesture that caught me off guard.

"That is not how a heart works," Mari said.

"Beg pardon?" Diego said.

"Hearts are organs. They don't just shatter, and if they did, you'd need surgery, not a psychic."

"Oh, yes. About that. Ah, it's not exactly a...How do I put this...? A human one."

This time we all went quiet. Diego pulled on his fingers again. Falcon rubbed his hands over his face. I let my magic slip and probe at him; nothing really came to me, but I did get some impressions of their relationship. Falcon had the same exasperated and affectionate vibe toward Diego most of the time.

"Do you have horns?" I asked, the words tumbling out of my mouth before I could stop them. It felt intrusive, like I was asking if he could prove his humanness. I was in his personal bubble, and Diego made no effort to step away. His eyes widened a hair, but otherwise he was still. Puddin had floated over, asserting her magical self into the conversation. She curled around my shoulders, but her weight was suffocating instead of comforting. Everyone but Diego stiffened. Falcon had leaned forward, attack mode activated and ready to pounce. Sore spot located–he wasn't a fan of Puddin. I gently plopped Puddin on the closest table.

Diego's aura radiated even more sadness. It was morose. Undeniable. Drowning. All consuming. Black. Black. Black–

"Not currently, as you can see." He titled his head a bit, proving to me that he was hornless. My hands were reaching for his hair, but I stopped myself.

"But you did," Mari said, deadpan, not allowing the conversation to lull again.

"Ah, yes, yes, I did. They were, well, horns. I quite liked them." There was a light in his dark, dark eyes then. I desperately wanted him to tell me every detail about the horns. Anything to ease the sorrow in him.

"How did you know about his horns?" Falcon said. His voice had turned to ice. To steel. He was standing now, suddenly right at Diego's side, and too close to me for my liking. Green aura now blazing bright. Falcon was an attack dog and Diego held the reins. He moved soundlessly and fast as anything.

"I saw them in a vision. I saw y'all driving here too. The sixties are a classic," I said to Falcon. "I couldn't see your face though," I said to Diego. He nodded.

"I know, I remember."

"You knew I was there?"

"Yes."

"But how?"

"I told you. I'd know you anywhere, Snapdragon." The hardness around him softened when he spoke her name, the woman made of vines and leaves. Diego's shoulders had dropped a little, he wasn't standing at full attention, but his attention was laser focused on me. Diego licked his bottom lip as his eyes scanned my face, stopping at my lips. I didn't need to mirror to know my cheeks were flushed. He didn't blink, didn't change focus. Heat rushed through me like I had casted something perfectly. His magic brushed against me and my lips parted just a smidge, just a fraction–

"I've missed you," he whispered against my ear.

"Me?" I squeaked out.

"What did you call her?" Puddin growled. Her words were out loud, in English. They were rumbly with her cat-like voice, but clear. She floated, energy sparking off of her, hackles raised.

"Puddin! What are you doing!" I scolded.

"Tell me what you are," she said.

"Just a man," Diego said.

"Don't lie to me."

"I don't know the human word, or even if there is one. Here I'm just a man." It wasn't true; he was less than a man. He was a husk and realization hit me hard. I was looking at the ghost of who he was.

"Why do you call her Snapdragon? Her name is Jack." This time he smiled. It was radiant and bright. Regal.

"Names are funny things. Sometimes they change."

MARI

Bad vibes. Bad, bad, *baaaad* vibes coming from these two.

Jack reached for my hand, and we wrapped ourselves together. A customer came in, and I felt Jack silently groan. It was time for a reading. She wouldn't turn them away so she slipped behind me to greet her customer.

"Garden. Now," I said. They followed obediently.

"Was that cat... flying?" the woman said.

"No, of course not. She was just sitting on a shelf," Jack lied easily. Puddin had parked her ass firmly on a desk, hopped down, and ran out the back door to the garden.

"Oh, I see..." the woman trailed off. Jack led her to her reading desk and everyone else followed me outside.

Diego immediately wandered through the garden, not touching anything, but wanting to. Jack's gardens were organized chaos, much like the rest of her life. Falcon moved as far away from me as he could, which was fine with me. He made me antsy. They both did, but Falcon had the look of a man that would stab you for stepping on his shoe. I blocked the door to the shop. They could wander all they wanted out here. I wouldn't let them cause a scene for Jack.

JACK

I couldn't believe I forgot to cancel an appointment. I thought all of them had been canceled. Didn't someone do that? Wasn't someone on top of that for me because I'm helpless and unable to do anything? Wasn't that the narrative we were rolling with lately?

Take the bitterness down a notch, girl. Do the reading. Make some extra cash and not stress about paying the bills on time. Maybe even sell a few extra charms. She looked suggestable. I reached for her name; normally I'd have my calendar nearby and I wouldn't need to use some magic to get it, but today wasn't a normal day. I glanced at the door to the backyard, to my garden.

Lily. Her name was Lily.

"Lily, please come take a seat. Here, flip through this deck and just start thinking about what we need to focus on today."

"I know what I'd like to ask." She looked to be in her thirties. Fine lines around her light blue eyes. Soft blonde hair braided tightly against her head. She had workout clothes on, and her pink cheeks meant she'd been to the gym. Lily wanted to ask me about love.

"Okay," I breathed out a little too hard, a little too tired for a client to see. My hands were restless and sparking with magic. I redid my bun again, tying it with ribbon. Less secure but looked the part. I waved a hand over Harold, and it glowed a bit. Lily sat back in her chair, startled. I dialed my magic down; everything was still amped up and buzzing through me. Diego was *right there* and I was stuck *here*–

"It's okay, I'm just connecting with my crystal. What did you want guidance on today?"

"I just want to know if, um, someone will notice me. If he'll see me, and then maybe things will go from there?" She tugged at her braid, threading it through her fingers again and again. I'm glad this appointment didn't get canceled. Her energy was timid and sweet, and her energy was easy to handle. It was calming.

"Let's see what we see?" I did the hand waving and ohh-ing and and humming. Lily laughed a little and tried to stop herself. I winked at her and let the magic do its work.

I saw two men. One white dude, standard issue. He looked kinda like a bro, but a nice bro. A decent bro. A bro's bro. I liked him. He definitely saw Lily, but I didn't get romance from him. Lots of love, but not the kind she was looking for. There was a slim, tall Black man too. He had great energy, the life of the party. He absolutely saw her. She was all he could see, really. The man's eyes were practically little hearts.

I told her as much, and at first she looked... upset.

"Lily?"

"So you're saying that Jake doesn't love me?"

"Jake is the bro?"

"Uhh, yeah. I mean I wouldn't call him that–"

"He loves you, but as his best friend. That's it. He might be gay? Maybe ask him about a party a few weeks ago." She looked deflated, but I wouldn't lie to her.

"Oh."

"But the other guy, there's potential there."

"Thomas."

"I didn't see their names, but if that's what makes sense to you, then yes, Thomas." Disappointment kept rolling off her in waves, and I squeezed her hand to comfort her. Thomas was the catch of this girl's life if she would stop obsessing over the bro. She needed to let go of that, and be open to this possible life with Thomas. Her life felt so short, so abrupt. Thomas would be perfect for her.

MARI

The guys loomed over me in the garden. Maybe something about being inside a building shielded their full heights, because these assholes were *huge*. I'm not a short woman–a good 5'8 at least, and they towered over me. They both had to be well over six feet tall, so I squared my shoulders and lifted my chin.

Puddin floated beside me, lightly perching on my shoulder like some kind of weird ass magical cat-parrot. I steered them away from our circle, and back to some benches near the herb garden.

"What happened to your heart?" I asked.

"It was shattered, and then I had to leave Obius." Puddin's nails dug into me and I tried not to wince. This guy was trying to sell me on a literal heartbreak.

"Shattered? Honey, we've all been through a break up," I said. Falcon laughed–one huff of laughter that was so full of sarcasm, I wanted to groan.

"Probably not like this," Diego said. He sat on the bench, taking in the sight of Jack's garden. It was a hodgepodge of everything, and mostly a mess. Jack insisted that the garden was well balanced and that the vibes were right, but it looked like a mess to me. "This garden is quite nice," he said.

"I'll pass your compliments on to the landscaper." He got up then, walking over to our circle. It glowed as he got closer, and then I heard thunder.

In November. In the damn morning.

Falcon was up and already next to him, pulling him away from the circle.

I heard a crack then, panic lacing through me like something had hit me and I just hadn't noticed yet. These last few days felt like I was living in a horror movie, with jump scares at every turn. Falcon checked Diego over, but he was striding back to the house.

"Something isn't right," Diego said softly.

JACK

Lily leaned back. She shifted from side to side. Her eye twitched. I waited. Sometimes people just wanted me to just lie and tell them what they wanted to hear, but I didn't do that. My magic wasn't a show, and it wasn't a fraud. I wouldn't lie about what I saw, period. Lily just needed a minute.

Then her head jerked to the side.

Like.

Sideways.

I jumped back out of my chair and stumbled against the shelf of crystals and books.

"Lily? What the–"

Then her head flipped around to the *other* side and I think I screamed, knocking over my chair as I scrambled away.

Her fingers were bent backwards. Joints pointing unnaturally at herself. Lily's eyes had turned red and only one was focused on me. The other had rolled back in her head. I saw that her life was abrupt, but I didn't get the vibe that that meant *today, right this minute.* Her wrist snapped, the sound echoing in my head.

"Mari!" I screamed.

MARI

Jack, bless her heart, had a perfect horror movie scream. It had the right amount of drama, screech, shriek, and terror. In short: it made everyone within ear-range promptly move their asses.

All of us bolted towards the back door, towards Jack.

Puddin teleported in and beat us all. She hovered between Jack and her client.

The client with her head on backwards, folding herself all up pretzel-like.

"What the fuck," Falcon whispered. He and Diego tried to shield me, push me behind them. I shouldered my way past them and started pulling magic from my amber. I'd never used magic as a weapon before, but there's a first time for everything.

"It's a possessed soul," Diego said. He was already moving toward Jack, and I didn't have time to stop him.

"A what?" I asked. The girl noticed our presence and angled towards us. I shivered.

Jack's client–Lily, according to Jack's cries–had to be dead. No head can sit on a body in that direction and still be alive.

And yet.

Lily jerked forward, and I focused the magic down my arm, sharp and hot like fire as it tore through my fingers and burst at her. And the rest of the shop. Fire exploded and Lily fell back, smoking and sparking.

"What did you do!" Falcon shouted, and he was stomping on whatever was left of Lily.

There was so much fire. What did I do? The magic came out so fast and the fire wasn't slowing down–

"Hit the deck! We've gotta get the fire out!" Falcon shouted.

"Sprinklers! Stop it before the alarm trips!" Jack shouted. I hopped over the checkout counter and looked for her fire extinguisher. Diego had wrapped his arms around Jack and lifted her out of the shop. He grabbed her in one fluid motion, like he already had been holding her before deciding to flee. She struggled a bit, trying to get back to us, but he didn't let go. They were out the back door in seconds.

Falcon and I worked on putting out the flames.

Then the alarm went off.

Falcon sighed, the sprinklers already starting to descend and turn on.

"I knew this day was gonna suck," he muttered. He pulled out a green knife, sliced his hand open without so much as a grimace, and chanted something under his breath. The air was suddenly stale and it dried out my throat. The water droplets from the sprinklers stopped. The flames stood still.

I was still.

Falcon walked through the store, chanted something else and the fire died out completely from Lily's body. He poked the body with his boot. He used two fingers, drew a circle and some other shape in the air, and then the body folded in on itself. Again and again and again. Once Lily had folded into the size of a paperback book, he heaved it up and carried it outside. The mix of exasperation and *ick* formed on his face made his eyes come alive, like this was truly his default state. I wondered briefly what the hell he dabbled in that folding a woman up into a book didn't ring every alarm bell known to man.

I couldn't move yet.

"Oh, sorry," he said. Falcon whispered, "Close," and air rushed back in my lungs. I nearly collapsed from it but he waited next to me, making sure I didn't fall with his free hand on my arm. "I know you don't believe any shit that comes out of my mouth, but I really am sorry you saw that."

"What kind of magic was *that!*"

"Uhh, bad magic. The kind I shouldn't be using."

"How can you even–?"

"Long story. Buy me dinner before I spill all my secrets first." Falcon winked at me, full of warmth. Genuineness shone through him. Falcon hadn't let go of me yet, and I slowly worked out of his grasp. Magic still pulsed off of him and it made my knees a little weak. He felt like a nuclear reactor.

We stood there in silence for a couple of minutes. The shop was trashed. I picked up one of the bowls that hadn't broken and set it back on the counter. The main display was in ruins. The tables were still standing, mostly, but the fire and the sprinklers and whatever else happened in the last ten minutes had wiped it out.

"I'm sorry about the shop," he said.

"I think that's more on me than you."

"I mean, yeah. But still." Falcon laughed a little and picked up a couple more bowls. Some of them had chipped, but I think the majority of them would be fine. I had some little baskets I could give Jack to help replace the damaged bowls.

"Do you need help with, um, her?" Falcon had the book-like form of Lily still in his arms. I didn't look right at it. It hurt to look at–it was an abomination but also seeing a human compacted like that made my stomach drop.

"Nah, heavier than she looks, but I've got it. Her."

"What're you gonna do with her?" I crossed my arms. Uncrossed them. I didn't know what to do with myself.

"Best we not talk about that, honestly. Are you hurt? I tried to shield you from the spell, but sometimes it's kinda hard to control."

"I'm okay. Physically. I feel like I'm gonna need some therapy to process all that, but hey, it's fine."

"Maybe just repress it. Works well for me." Falcon grinned and my knees went a little weak again. He didn't need magic to be charming, that's for sure. How frustrating.

"Should we go get Jack and Diego?" I asked.

He shrugged. "I'm not really itching to see D making goo-goo eyes at her." This time I laughed. Falcon lifted Lily and nodded towards the door. "Let's get this over with."

JACK

Diego cradled me close to his chest. The scent of his skin washed over me, and he held me so gently. His arms were secure around me but not tight. He restrained his strength and just acted as a buffer between me and whatever was happening in my shop. There was a very faint, irregular beat in his chest. Visions and Trinkets was going to be destroyed. I heard the alarm. The sprinklers would have turned on and flooded the place within minutes. Thinking of how many products that were going to be water damaged made my stomach churn. Somehow I doubted a murder by fireball would be covered under my business insurance. Diego leaned his head on the top of mine, and I clung to him. It was easy to do. I fit easily in his arms, and it felt like I'd been next to him for years. I didn't know if the familiarity came from all of the visions, but this was right.

Do. Not. Cry.

"Falcon has it under control," Diego said. His voice was softer than when I'd hear him in a vision. He was softer. He rubbed little circles on my back. One arm had wrapped around my shoulders, the other under my legs. I was encased in him. He held me like a bride, and the thought shook me. Don't be jumping the gun, crazy.

"He has a fire bombed shop under control? Awesome."

"Will you help me?" He sat me down on one of the path stones in my garden. Diego sat on the bench next to me, and he was nearly at eye level with me. He must have practiced that sad, puppy look in a mirror. It was horrendously cute.

"With your heart?"

"Yes," he said. His words were crisp, like each syllable deserved equal attention. It was a little odd, but it suited him. It was another reminder that this was not his native language, his natural world.

"I really don't know what I can do."

"I just need you to be you. I need you to see."

"I don't understand."

Diego cupped my face then, standing and glancing down at me. He was real. This man I saw in my visions, with his horns and feathers, was real and standing right in front of me. I pulled his hands down and really looked at them. His hands were a little calloused. His fingers were long, but not oddly so. The veins in the backs of his hands all looked normal, human. Was he just an illusion?

"How are you real?" I asked him.

"Should I be offended?" he laughed. So human.

"I mean–"

"You know why I'm here," he said. I searched his face. He was telling me the truth. He really thought I knew.

"I really don't."

"Because of the links. The Goddesses sent me to wander the Earth with a shattered heart. Alive enough to live, broken enough for that to feel like hell." He ran one of his hands through his hair and the locks fell back into place like they were little soldiers lining up at attention. His hair was gorgeous. He was gorgeous. I touched his face this time; the stubble on his jawline was rough and it grounded me more in his realness.

"You heard me calling you?"

"Loud and clear."

"And you think that I can help you find the pieces of your heart because I'm a psychic?"

"I think that you, Jack Hawthorne, can help me because your true name is Snapdragon, Emerald Priestess of Trellis, She who is blessed by the Seer." The hair on my arms stood up. I knew this name, I knew those words, and I knew without a doubt that whoever he was looking for, it wasn't me.

"Diego, I'm so sorry, but that's not my name."

"But you've been blessed by the Seer, and a human has never received Her blessing–" He took a step back, and the void in him that dragged me closer to him felt so massive. His energy had shifted again and I was going to drown in it. The betrayal that flashed through his eyes burned bright and for a second, I could imagine the depth of his magic before he became so much less than he once was.

It was terrifying.

He tried to rein it all back in, to be as small as possible, but his energy still lashed out around him. I grabbed his hands and he flinched.

"I may not be Snapdragon, but I will still try to help you."

"But–"

Mari and Falcon took that moment to come outside, and I remembered the chaos that was happening in my shop. Where was the smoke? Or the flames? There should have been something.

Mari broke into a run to come check on me, and Diego quickly stepped away. He had shrunken his wild energy as much as he could, and the life in his eyes was gone again. Guilt tugged in the back of my throat–I caused the life to drain from him again.

"Girl, that dude is, like, *crazy* strong. I don't know what kind of magic Falcon is working, but it was scary. He like, *stopped time* or some shit, Jackie. Water droplets suspended in midair. It was some real sci-fi shit. It took him no effort at all. Girl, we have to go. These two are *dangerous*." Mari's hands shook. Her whole body was shaking.

"I can't," I said. And it knew it was true; I couldn't leave Diego. The sadness in him had infected me now. I felt the depths of it. I saw the little prisms of who he was and how everything had shattered in him. Mari stayed silent, waiting for me to elaborate on my declaration. "He's gonna die," I said weakly.

Diego stood by my trellis with the climbing ivy. It was near the gate to the front yard, and he just stood there with his hands in his pockets. At ease, or at least pretending. Relaxed. Dying.

"Girl, we're all gonna die. That doesn't make him special!"

"She's got a point," Diego said loudly enough so we could hear. His voice carried if he wanted it to.

"Why should she help you?" Mari puffed herself up and marched over to them, but she was still tiny comparatively. Her tall, lean frame was about as intimidating as a kitten. A regular kitten; not a Puddin. Puddin scared the bejesus out of everyone.

"Because she's the only one in this realm that can. Jack, you've been blessed by the Seer, and I need your help." Diego inclined his head, like he was bowing before a queen. Heat pooled in my belly, and it was a different kind of magic. Diego was lowkey sexy, but I tucked that thought away for another time.

"That's cute. She's been blessed by *the* Seer? As in oh ye Goddess of old?" Mari huffed.

"Yes," Diego said simply.

"I really don't think that's–"

"Jack, where do you think your magic comes from? Future sight is only bestowed by the Seer. No one else has your visions. No one else could find the pieces of my heart, no matter how hard they tried."

This was the *alive* version of Diego. He had energy flowing out of him and it pushed against my chest. I scanned him again, trying to really take in the details of his face, his hands, his shoulders. Looking for anything that could be a tell that he was lying.

I found nothing.

His mind was blank. I couldn't pull anything from his thoughts, and Falcon's mind was on lock-down. His warding spells were beyond top notch.

Falcon bounced back and forth, like a tightly wound coil, and watching him made me anxious. What had he done in my shop? Mari chewed on her cuticles again. Maybe he wasn't as harmless as I thought.

"Blessed one–"

"Bro, don't make it weird," Falcon said.

FALCON

It was honestly *astonishing* how this dumbass has stayed alive for *centuries* when his true gift was inserting his foot so far in his fucking mouth that his toes could scratch a kidney.

"I think I just need a minute to process this," Jack said.

"The Seer is one of the old gods. The original gods," I said. The cat flicked her tail, staring. That cat gave me the creeps.

"Yes, we knew this, and...?" Mari said. I liked this girl. She was a briar patch. Pretty and prickly. The amber stone in her hand glowed with her magic. I needed to watch my mouth before she set something else on fire, like me.

"The blessing just means that Jack has a lot of magic, and we need someone that can help us find pieces of his heart before he kicks the bucket. The human one. Pretty sure he's already died in the other realms at least once."

"Only once. And it was a half-death," Diego said. He picked at one of the plants near him. It looked like weed to me, but I wasn't a botanist. The leaves turned brown once he let go of it. Jack's eyes shot wide open and it was the first real reaction I'd seen from her.

"I've never heard of the Goddesses blessing anyone. Is that a thing?" Jack asked. Her slightly red rimmed eyes didn't match the neutral expression on her face. An almost smile, calm eyes, muscles relaxed. Fake as fuck.

"You can see the future, your cat flies, and this one here can set shit on fire. The blessing is where you draw the line to suspend your reality? Seriously?" I was harsher than I meant to be. This wasn't helping our case. Diego shot me a look that would have killed me in his realm, I was sure.

"Darling girl, we should talk," Puddin the cat said. She spoke. Human words. Out loud. I'd get over it eventually. Diego, unfazed, nodded and motioned for me to follow him.

That was that. His fate now lies in the paws of a flying cat.

JACK

"Why do you think I showed up on your doorstep? Out of every human in this world, why did I stop here?" She floated up to eye level, perched on my shoulder, and snuggled into my face. She's been in my life for nearly a decade; Puddin helped me open my shop, survive two boyfriends, and guided my magic. A fairy godmother in feline form.

"Because this is where you're supposed to be," I said.

"Yes, it is."

People didn't have the type of magic that I did, not really. Future sight was rare, even among the strongest of alchemists, and those that claimed it were spotty fortune tellers at best. I wasn't spotty; future sight was my gift. I sat next to my small herb garden in the backyard of my building. Four planter boxes filled with herbs, and two small cannabis plants. The brick of the planter boxes, and even the building, needed to be repainted. My house, like all others near the beach, was vibrant. Pink flamingo. Sunny yellow.

Pieces of visions filtered to me so quickly I couldn't see them clearly; they were just little snippets of my dreams lately. I saw Diego more clearly now, still a little blurred, but not just an outline. I felt the truth in Puddin's words. This was why she came here, to the human realm, to me.

"I have to help him, don't I?"

"Yes darling, I think you do."

A spark of yellowish green hovered at his chest. It was his heart, and I saw how little was left and how weak it had become. Diego was at the end of the stone path that ran through the center of my garden and my eyes focused solely on him. I saw the aura of his magic, black black black, but imagined what it once was. I pictured him surrounded by gold, bright and warm. Mari tugged at me and gestured to the house.

"Let's go inside. I wanna see the state of my shop and Mari can make some tea," I said. Falcon's eyes were cool and assessing; he waited for Diego to move, and once he did, Falcon followed.

"Thanks for volunteering me," she muttered.

THROUGH THE VEIL

I'd send soul after soul after soul if that's what it took. That limp, small human broke so quickly before she could take down the False Priestess.

He will not succeed. He will not return here, and that charlatan of a woman would not pretend to be me.

My staff flickered; the magic here was dying too, like everything else. The tower felt darker these days too. Did the sun decide it wouldn't shine for me now? The throne room was meant for Deign, for kings. It was golden, not green. The banners of Trellis hung limply on the walls. The tapestries had lost so much of their shine too. When Deign left, he took the color from this realm with him.

Four fae-birds flew past me, and I trapped them midair.

Small, but full of magic. Gifted with flight and focus and drive, they were perfect.

Their necks cracked so easily. The spirit left their eyes and floated up through their small, crushed throats. I swung my staff around them, sharpening each soul into a spear that could pierce the veil. If the sun wouldn't shine, I would shine for the Trellians. Magic burned in my staff, ready to light up the sky. I aimed my staff to the heavens, and fired the little souls upward.

"Find the Shatterer. Find the false Priestess. Kill them."

Chapter Nine

DIEGO

Trellis was full of life. The trees swayed, the fae flowers danced. Their petal skirts blew with the breeze as they twirled around the dance floor. Dancers stepped in time with the music. Everyone was happy. Flower dancers were always beautiful but today they were divine. The tulips and lilies paired perfectly with snapdragons and violets. Stems and petals and hands and arms collided with precision.

Snapdragon reached for me, and I pulled her vines to my mouth to kiss each finger. Her petals rippled with each kiss.

I think that Bloom Festival was the last time I saw her smile.

JACK

"You look faraway," I said.

Diego was physically on my couch but mentally not in this realm. His eyes were hyper focused on something on the coffee table, maybe a book. I couldn't tell what he was looking at exactly. Falcon excused himself to take care of a *situation* and checked and double checked and checked again that Diego would be okay for a few hours, and then left.

The situation was Lily. Mari assured me that there was nothing that could lead back to the shop, but I was shaken. She also insisted that she would be going with Falcon to make sure this didn't blow back on us. I wondered how I could hold some type of ceremony for her, since there wasn't anything else I could do for her.

"Just remembering," Diego said eventually.

"Care to share?" I nudged his coffee cup toward him, and he leaned forward to reach it. Our hands touched for a second, his eyes flashed up, and they were brilliantly gold.

"Thinking about the Bloom Festival. It's a celebration of the changing seasons."

"That sounds really nice."

"It's my favorite time of year. A lot of the people in Trellis hibernate in the colder months, so the forest comes alive again. We hold a festival that lasts four days and celebrate the return of life."

"Sounds like quite the party."

"It is." The dark brown of his eyes had lightened completely and now they were solid, glittering gold. The memories must be wonderful if they bring him alive like this.

"How did your heart get broken?" I asked.

Diego's cheeks flushed, and it was the most human thing I've seen him do. He moved awkwardly, like he was a robot or a puppet. Sometimes too stiff, sometimes too floppy. His dark hair had little curls that bounced when he moved, like they had a mind of their own. They probably did.

"I made a mistake. I thought–I thought that someone I loved was in danger. And I was told that our kingdom was in danger. So I just–I acted. I had to. I couldn't just–" His arm jerked a little and he knocked the coffee mug over. It spilled all over the table and the carpet, with the mug chipping. Another thing broken.

"I'm sorry–"

"Slow down, Diego," I said. I picked up the mug and went to the kitchen to grab a paper towel. He followed and brought the rest of the roll back to the couch with him. He scrubbed at the carpet, trying to erase more than a little stain. His eyes were dark brown again.

"I was tricked." His nostrils flared; another human tick. He was good at pretending. Diego whispered an apology.

"How?"

"It's been almost six centuries, and I still don't know. Her visions told us that she was going to die, and then the kingdom would fall. Then the next one, and the next, until none of the Fae survived. They told us the humans would decimate our world, and that they'd start with her," his voice shook as he spoke. Diego raked a hand through his hair, and everything about him was suddenly so fragile. He *was* broken.

"Who was she?" I asked.

He paused. Not just his words, but himself. He became a statue, and then just as suddenly back alive again.

"Babe," he said softly. He chuckled, "*Babe*. I think that's one of my favorite human words. It sounds so charming, doesn't it? I don't think there's a word quite like it in Fae."

"Deign?" His eyes snapped up to mine almost instantaneously. They flashed gold, bright, vibrant gold and alive again. As pretty as his dark brown eyes were, the gold was better. It was the color of his true eyes.

"You. I think she's you."

DIEGO

Snapdragon held court today. She sat on her throne; the smaller one, not the Seer's holy seat. She should have been in the holy throne, but she respected tradition. It had been so many years since the Seer sat there, years since She had been in our realm. But we had our Emerald Priestess and it was all we needed. She was all I needed.

She listened to each plea, each subject needing guidance. The royal court visited her. The peasants. The animals. Emissaries from the other realms, on occasion.

Gods, I adored her.

She caught my eye, shyly glancing at her shoulder as she made a small snapdragon flower bloom there. She was obscene when she wanted to be; flirting in court. I stood at the entrance of the throne room. The Seer's Tower had three main towers. The east tower, where the Seer lived. The central tower which housed the throne room, reading rooms, alchemy spaces, the chapel to pray, and where people can come together. It was the gathering space between the races and the monarchs. The west tower was for her. Her room sat at the top of the tower, windows facing the Great River Treis. The twin moons could be seen on clear nights.

Only a priestess or her disciples could enter the west tower.

I'd been in Snapdragon's bed chambers many times. More than I could count.

"Your Grace, you're lurking," she said to me. I stood to my full height, and everyone bowed.

I hated the bowing. Meet my eyes, see my face. I was not so high above that I did not meet the eyes of those I served. We were in the central tower, as our people came and went, each one smiled and glanced between the two of us. Our love story was always the subject of gossip, and I usually didn't mind.

The rumors, although we always denied them, were completely true. Everyone knew it. Some days that made life even harder.

The walls here had portraits of all the kings past; their wives or husbands next to their right, their priestess to their left. Snapdragon's emerald image hung to the left of my painting. I wanted her to my right, too.

"Observing. You're quite busy today, Mistress."

"The moons are full. I should be scrying. There's too much uncertainty, and people are worried." Snapdragon's staff always hovered near her. She used magic to hold it there so her hands would be free. "Please, excuse us. I need to discuss my visions with the King." The room emptied quickly. I held out my hand, and Snapdragon slipped hers into mine. I squeezed her, and her vines wrapped around my arm, tightening almost too much.

"You're afraid," I said.

"Deign, I think I'm going to die."

JACK

Diego kept his distance from me. The air was charged—no magic, just being in the same space, my space, with him staring at me like I was a ghost. My vision blurred, and I knew what was coming. He did too. The little smile that tugged at the corners of his mouth was knowing and familiar.

I was still kneeling to clean up the coffee, and a vision hit. I rocked back on my heels, letting my weight and the heaviness of the magic roll me until I was leaning against one of my chairs. Flashes of the rainbow forest came and went. More strange creatures.

Diego was standing in the center of a rounded room. Light brown horns curled against his head. He wore a long, sleeveless vest that was emerald green. There was gold stitching all over it, but what caught my eye was the bright blue feathers down his arms. They started around his elbows and ended at his wrists, just along the outer part of his arm.

His face wasn't blurred anymore.

It was the same face that spilled my coffee and held me like I was as fragile as the mug he chipped. Exactly the same. Where Diego on Earth had a little stubble, Deign in this realm had very light fuzz. The rest of him looked the same too, just the horns and feathers–and his heart–were missing.

It felt like the truest parts of him had been erased on Earth.

The woman with vines and flowers for hair stood just off to the side, smiling wide. She was dressed in green, the same shade as her skin, and she stared adoringly at Diego. The room was filled with people cheering. I wondered if this was a normal day for him, or if this was the festival he mentioned.

"Long live the King! Long live the Emerald Priestess!"

"King Deign!"

"Priestess Snapdragon!"

The hall was filled with their cheers, and as if by saying his name, more of Diego came into focus. I saw the golden crown resting between his horns. There was a much smaller crown on Snapdragon's head.

This was another memory.

"Diego," I whispered.

Everything stopped. The music, the people, the cheering. Silence echoed around, my breathing amplified in the quiet.

Snapdragon's head whipped in my direction. Her eyes were red, blood red, glowing with fury, and she stared right at me. Diego wasn't moving either. Just Snapdragon. She hissed and my ears ached.

"I'll kill you, False One."

Her voice bounced off of the walls of the hall, reverberating through me. I jumped from the sound and was already floating back to my body on Earth, back to the safety of my home.

Diego was on the floor next me, watching.

"Jack, can you hear me?"

"Hmm," I muttered. Diego pushed the hair out of my face, and I realized then what an unshowered mess I must have been.

"Astral projection is quite dangerous. It shouldn't be used lightly. Depending on how strong you cast, depends on how much of you goes with your spirit."

"I thought I was seeing a memory," I said.

"You were, probably. Astral projection can go in any direction in time that you want, Priestess." I pushed myself off the floor and into the chair. Diego sat back on the couch, leaning forward on his knees, in case he needed to catch me again.

"When I saw Snapdragon, she noticed me. She looked straight at me and called me False One." I left out the murdery part. Diego was clearly still attached to her, and I didn't want him to mistrust me.

"She... spoke to you?"

"Loud and clear, yep."

"And she called you 'False One'?"

"Also yep." I pulled my hair out of the bun. I shook it out, trying to redeem it somehow, and pulled it back into a bun. It was limp on my head, which matched the rest of me.

Diego sat there a few more minutes, watching me. I let him. I didn't have anything to say, and I didn't have the energy for small talk.

He rubbed a hand against his chin, and shook his head. "I think I should go."

"But what about Falcon–"

"I can walk."

"Diego–"

"Please. I think I need some time to think. Is it alright if I come back to see you?"

"Yes, of course."

I stopped myself from saying *please come back, please don't go yet*, and Diego smiled. I got butterflies.

My heart skipped a beat. His smile felt like a secret that he was willing to share with me, and when he walked out the door, the room felt bare.

CHAPTER TEN

PEONY

My date with Sherwin had started with a coffee, then dinner at a little hole-in-the-wall place, and now I was sitting in his lap on a bench "downtown." Cape Margaret didn't have a "downtown" per se; it was more like a four square block with taller buildings and more modern architecture. More 2010s instead of 1980s.

His hands snaked up my back to the base of my skull, tugging at the hair there. He kissed me like I was going to disappear, each kiss so gentle, like I would crumble if he pressed his lips to me a little harder.

I kissed him back, opening my mouth, waiting for him to respond. Sherwin nibbled at my bottom lip, so soft. He was soft and gentle, and I was going to snap him in half if he didn't pick up the pace a little.

He broke the kiss, and I nuzzled at his nose.

"What's wrong?" I asked.

"I think your sister is calling you." My phone had six missed calls and eleven text messages. All from Jack. I groaned, and he laughed, and found a spot to nibble on behind my ear.

"Oh for *fuck's sake!*"

"Maybe next time," he said, planting one more kiss on my neck. Sherwin's hands were so warm, even with the temperature dropping. The chill reminded me that fall was ending. I leaned forward, pressing myself to his chest and he sighed.

"You're infuriatingly cute," I grumbled. I picked up my phone and rebuttoned my blouse. Time to be the Big Sister. The lawyer. The fixer. Whatever problem Jack had stepped into, I'd be there to clean up the carnage.

Mari picked up Jack's phone and quickly recapped what happened in the *hours* that I had left her alone. Guys from the visions showed up. Murder. Destruction. Burying what was left of a body. Jack pretending she doesn't have a thing for one of said guys.

Sherwin squeezed the back of my neck, and I blew out a sigh.

"Go kick ass," he said.

"We will continue this once I've put the fires out."

"Yes, ma'am."

He was *infuriatingly* cute.

JACK

Diego had been gone for about five minutes before Falcon and Mari came back, with Diego in tow. I doubted he made it down to the street before he ran into them.

"Long time no see," I said. He huffed out a laugh.

"Mm, feels like ages." His voice was all softness again.

"Situation has been resolved," Falcon said. Mari dropped her massive bag back on the floor and Falcon flinched at the noise.

"Falcon likes to pretend he's the star of an action movie," Diego laughed.

"Only action he's gonna see," Mari muttered. I elbowed her. "Also, I called Peony."

"*Ugh*. You know she's gonna overreact."

"She called your mama too." I groaned from the depths of hell, the bottom of my diaphragm, until it shook my core. Diego and Falcon didn't say anything, but just stared at each other.

"Maybe we should go–"

My front door flung open then. Mama and Peony burst through like they were ready for battle. Mama had magic at the ready. Peony stepped in front, stamped one foot, and demanded, "The truth. *Now*."

Her magic reverberated through the house, shaking everything that wasn't nailed down. Another froggy rattled off the kitchen counter and shattered. The power of Peony's magic was tangled in her words. She compelled the truth from people without really trying, but when she did force the truth with her magic, it spilled out in spades.

"I ate the last slice of pizza, meeeow."

"He's got a *fine* ass but he *needs* to stop talking." Mari jingled and adjusted her bracelets, not looking at anyone.

"I think I'm going to die," I whispered. The words had clawed up my throat and out before I could control them.

Even though seeing Diego lessened the overwhelming feeling of death that hovered around my head, I couldn't shake it. My magic was changing, I was changing, and it didn't feel survivable.

"She's a fucking walking disaster," Falcon said eyeing me.

"I shattered the link between the realms, and I'd do it again if it would save her," Diego said. His voice hardened with every word until everyone stopped speaking to watch him. I opened my mouth to speak and quickly shut it again; Peony's spell had already forced a truth out of me, and I fought against saying anything more.

"All of that and no one wants to mention the *murder?*" Peony thundered. Mama cocked an eyebrow but said nothing. I'd rather she give a tongue lashing than stay quiet. Quiet was worse. Quiet was dangerous.

"It was hardly a murder," Falcon said. I couldn't believe he was dumb enough to speak.

"Please elaborate, and start with your name. Full name," Peony had entered lawyer mode, and I imagined Falcon in an orange jumpsuit.

"Possessed soul. Something got into her before she arrived at the shop. It took over her body and it killed her. I just helped clean up the mess so your *darling sister* here wouldn't be traumatized," he said.

"How do you know she's my sister?"

"Seriously? Look in a mirror. You two and the old chick all look alike. Hi Mom," Falcon said, waving at Mama. She grinned.

"Wait, a possessed soul?" I remembered Diego saying that before he whisked me out of the shop. I still hadn't been back *in* the shop.

"Happens every so often, but it's becoming more common. The shift between the realms shook again, and the lost souls are getting antsy," Falcon said.

"I felt the shift too," Mama said.

"Not surprising, considering your daughter prolly caused a lot of it," Falcon said.

"What! I haven't done anything!"

"Maybe not on purpose, I can't tell yet. But that magic of yours is some intense shit," he said. Falcon eyed me, the distrust blatant on his face.

"What is your issue with me?" I closed the distance between us getting up in his face.

"My issue—"

"–is irrelevant," Diego finished. His eyes sharpened and Falcon threw his hands up and rolled his eyes.

"What do you mean you shattered the link between the worlds? And who are you? Why are you in my sister's house?" Peony asked. Magic flashed in her eyes, and for a second I pitied them. She wasn't focused on Mari and me anymore, so we moved out of the line of fire.

"I was lied to. I just... did what I thought was right. I couldn't let my home be destroyed. I couldn't let her die," Diego rambled, rubbing his hands on his thighs, then through his hair. Peony pushed her glasses up on her nose and waited for him to elaborate. He didn't.

"But how did you break it?" Puddin asked. Her tail whipped violently, angrily.

"I... it's hard to explain–"

"No, it's not," she spat back.

"It's a spell. Only members of my family can cast it. It's a part of my bloodline. I just performed the spell on a grander level." He crossed his arms, trying to conceal even more of his emotions. He didn't need to. I felt every fiber of his sadness, and to everyone else he was completely neutral. Falcon watched him closely, quiet and taking everything in.

"I know who you are," Puddin growled. Her voice was hard to understand, more of a growl than a word, and the hiss that followed was scathing. Her hackles were raised and she wouldn't let me pet her to calm her down.

"What have you done?" Mama choked out. There was a tear forming in her eye. Peony held her hands, still full of magic.

"This happened centuries ago," Diego said softly.

"Why is it only just affecting our magic now?" Mari asked.

Then, it clicked. It *was* me. It was my magic, the night I went wine scrying when the visions really intensified. They started a couple weeks before, but they were only flashes then. After I went scrying in that full moon, my magic felt more connected. I felt like I was finally awake.

Diego was watching me put the pieces together. That shy, little smile was back.

"Because of me," I said.

"Yes, Priestess, because of you." A chill shot through me like I had been hit with Peony's truth magic again. Priestess. Magic gathered in my chest, and Diego was beaming at me. My necklace warmed against my skin.

Yep. This was right. A Priestess. Rightness followed through my body and I realized that everyone else was gaping at me too. I blew out a sigh, trying to release some of the magic building in my chest. The citrine pendant was warming up again, and when I touched it I saw flashes. Emotions from my family, memories from Diego, and lots of nothing from Falcon. He was a blank wall and was trying very hard to stay that way. Black dots floated at the corners of my eyes. I knew what this meant.

"I'm getting a vision," I said.

"We'll be here," Mama said.

"Yes," Diego said.

"No," Mari and Peony said together, their shared anxiety blaring through me. They didn't want me to be vulnerable, unprotected. But Diego wasn't a threat; I knew that in my heart.

"No, it's okay, stay," I said. Diego nodded and that was that.

CHAPTER ELEVEN

JACK

I was dreaming again. Or maybe I'd left my body. I couldn't tell the difference anymore. I felt the stars brush against my skin as I moved weightlessly through time. Everything around me was black starlight and softness. Colors bloomed in my eyes, until they shifted into the spaces between the trees and the bricks of the castle. I focused in, my vision getting sharper and clearer until I saw them.

Deign and Snapdragon. They were dancing, I think. I was only supposed to look forward in time, but now I could look back–and I was doing that more and more. The past was beautiful when you got to be a spectator. The hall they were in was fit for royalty, for Deign. Snapdragon twirled with a staff that floated next to her. Soft streams of blues and greens and purples from her staff wrapped around her, with her as she moved. The hall was gilded, like Versailles. Everything was either gold or silver. The walls, the floors, everything. White and soft, pale pink flowers littered the ground with partygoers walking gently over them. Snapdragon twirled and twirled. The streams of magic trailed around her with her emerald, sparkling gown flowing and dancing with her.

She was casting a spell.

As I glanced around the hall, I realized it wasn't as empty as I thought at first; there were bodies everywhere. Dead ones.

Deign had a crown on his head that sat between his horns. I could see his face so clearly now. The olive skin and dark hair. His nose was straighter here. The crown was made of branches, adorned with small blue flowers and little white gems. He held a jeweled sphere; light caught it in every direction. It reminded me of the way light filtered through the rainbow forest. He held it at arm's length, until it began to really shimmer.

Snapdragon danced; the lights now wrapping around each of the bodies, with small golden orbs coming from them. The hall filled with them. There had to be at least a hundred souls here. She stopped dancing and chanting. The staff stopped too, fully upright in front of her. Snapdragon held her hands out wide, palms up, and then grabbed the staff and swung it like a scythe in a circle.

"Rest, be at peace. Return to Sanctum to be born again."

Deign's hands cupped his sphere, and said, "I open the door for you to return home. Be at peace."

The outline of a door sparked into being and the sphere moved to where a door knob should be. Deign's sphere floated above his hand, and he held it close to the door until it opened. The souls slowly went through the passageway, presumably to Sanctum.

Trellis–Deign's home, the name came back to me all at once–was full of light, like the sun was meant to shine here and only here. Even at night, the twin moons glowed and filled the sky. Trellis felt like a place of life.

Sanctum did not. Through the doorway, I saw only darkness. Not even a star shone here. It was dank, cold, dreadful. This was where a soul goes to rest? I turned away, forcing myself not to look at its chilling darkness.

"My flower, don't look into Sanctum," Deign said. That made my heart skip; he was talking to me. His voice was the same but then Snapdragon turned and leaned into him. A pang of jealousy hit, and I wrapped my arms around myself. Of course he was speaking to her.

The souls progressed, and they clung to each other. The temperature in the grand hall kept dropping. I shivered too.

"Your Grace, there is a presence here. It means no harm, but it does not belong." Snapdragon's voice was so sweet. It was quiet and feminine. Nothing at all like the rage filled demonic shriek that I was used to.

"Is it from Sanctum?" Deign said. His voice rose with alarm, and I watched as each muscle tensed. He pulled his golden cloak tighter around her.

"No, no, my king. I think it's a human."

"How did a human–"

Snapdragon turned to me; I was hovering from above, watching. Her eyes met mine and she jumped.

"Demon!" she screamed. She was truly terrified. I could see her shaking, with her vines wrapping around herself. Deign swiftly pushed her behind himself and held the orb up. It fired lightning, electricity, sparks of fire directly at me.

I flinched.

When I opened my eyes, I was back in my living room. Someone had guided me to the couch. I had to ground my senses again. Touch the fabric of the couch, soft and plush. Breathe in the scent of coffee and the cinnamon candles, earthy and spicy and warm.. Count the frogs, what was left of them–only eight.

Once I had regained control of my body, I told myself to breathe until my lungs remembered how to do it on their own. Falcon stood like a sentry next to Deign–*Diego*–just as he had done for Snapdragon.

Diego looked at me then, and that void of sadness I felt from him, from his black, black, black energy surged through me as if his lightning bolts had hit me. He sank into the cushion of my couch, trying his best to be invisible.

DIEGO

Jack plunged through my past and through me. My heart ached; I couldn't handle another bout of her magic. Not until I had more of my heart to keep me going.

"Jack, how are you doing that?" I asked, and my voice was thick and cracking. I knew the intensity of her magic was because of the blessing, but knowing that she couldn't control it had me worried.

"It just comes to me," she said.

"Perhaps you can take your necklace off for a bit? I think its strength is allowing you to access the depth of your power as a priestess."

"I'm sorry, but I can't."

Ah, lovely. She'd kill me before she could repair my heart. I glanced at Falcon, *what do I do?* He nudged my foot. If I were in Trellis, I'd be kneeling before her. Even a king kneels before a Priestess. She may not rule the lands, but her words were final.

I kneeled. Even I knew this was awkward, but I did it anyway. Her vision clung to her still and she smelled like moss. *Trellis.* She threaded her fingers through mine–she reached for me–and magic buzzed through us both. Her eyes turned green. I felt alive for a minute.

"How do I fix your heart?"

JACK

Diego forced my magic to ignite when I touched him. All of the sleeping magic, the wells of power I didn't know I had, blossomed. But only when in direct contact with Diego. The citrine necklace was like a jump starter too, but it was wild and I had no control. It wasn't like that when I touched Diego; I was laser focused then.

Mari's fascination with Falcon's backside was not something she wanted to share, and yet, here I was with that knowledge. She had a completely valid point, but I was sure she didn't want to share that.

Peony's thoughts were scattered, unlike her. A man—my herbalist—flashed through her mind. Good for her. Bad timing, but good for her.

Puddin's thoughts were not in English or humanish, or anything of this world. Her thoughts were the language of runes and sigils, and I did not let myself dig any deeper at that.

I called my crystal ball, and it came—that was a new trick. It floated up from the shop and into my house. I wasn't really sure *how* it got into the house, maybe it could teleport now too—but it hovered right in front me. I knew Harold wasn't *alive,* but I felt like it was proud of itself. I scooped up Harold to scry.

Breathing out magic to center myself, Harold shimmered. I opened my mind to the endless nebula of magic and energy in the crystal ball, letting myself be lost to the endless mirrors in it—

"Jack, no," Diego said. He let go of my hands so he could cover the crystal ball. No one ever touched it, and the heat of his hands on the smooth surface felt like they were resting gently around my neck. "Stay here. The answers are not in the past. They're here with me. Please." But I let myself drift anyways.

THROUGH THE VEIL

Her magic was intensifying. The shift had pushed our realms closer than they had been in centuries; this was likely the closest they have been since–

Deign was with her. I knew it in my bones. His magic was forever etched inside of me, and it filled whatever room, space, realm he inhabited. They were practically on top of each other. Constantly. Their magics blended and fused so brightly, it sparked here in our sky.

I don't know what caused the shift. Perhaps the links were trying to completely fall apart, like a rickety bridge finally giving way. I had to rebind them before our magic was gone completely.

Another surge, another flash of her magic.

Was she showing off now? Showcasing the power that I could barely call? The throne room was empty again, as it always was. My golden cage sat by one of the large windows, and I plucked a handful of fae birds from it. I needed magic. I needed energy. I needed a few souls to sharpen and send through the links. I crushed them in my hands, the souls filtering out easily and forged them into little spears. The souls wouldn't survive traveling the path to the Earth, but I didn't mind. Deign was there. She was there.

They needed to remember me.

FALCON

This chick freaked me the hell out. Like, scale of one to ten? She's a twelve. Between the freaky ass eyes and the magic that tore a hole in time for her to take a look-see, she was *terrifying*. And I was the only one that seemed to realize this.

"How is Jack going to just *find* your heart if you've been looking for it for centuries?" the sister asked, waving her hand at us like we were an annoyance. We were. Peony Hawthorne, according to the mighty internet, was a pretty badass trial lawyer. She would be a force to deal with, and absolutely who I'd call if I was legally fucked. Assuming she didn't want to kill me–a common problem for me.

"I have a spell she can use, but I need someone that is linked directly to the Seer to cast it. I'm not; I don't have an ounce of Seer magic in me. I've tried. I've looked for so-called psychics and fortune tellers, bone readers, sigil workers. Not one of them has been real or had enough Seer magic to cast the spell," Diego said. He was doing his statue thing again. He was too rigid, like he was half in rigor all the time.

"You need a priestess," the cat said. I jumped when she spoke. I'd get used to it. The cat freaked me out almost as much as Jack.

"I need a priestess. And they aren't exactly common in this realm."

"There's a reason for that," the mother said. She was an attractive woman, pushing sixty, at least, but you'd never know unless you stared. Or were me. I'm good at that–guessing ages. D was about thirty-six in earth years. Fuck only knows how old he actually was. He couldn't even remember. The sister was thirty-three, but claimed to be younger. She's got good skin, it worked for her. Jack and Mari were twenty-nine though Mari was closer to thirty. And the cat was about as old as Diego, which was also freaky.

Everyone in this crew was a *freak*.

"What's the reason?" Jack asked. The crystal ball hovered around her head, which *again*, freaky. Magic was my bread and butter. I didn't get creeped out often, but something about Jack crawled under my skin. The scale tattoo on my left arm was out of balance again. It shifted, letting me know if I was on the right path or not. Balance was the key; only I didn't know what would set the scales right again.

"The Goddesses each own a realm," Diego said.

"And–"

"The Seer is the Goddess of Obius. She does not belong on Earth, and she certainly should not be passing Her blessing to anyone here," he said.

"I feel like this is a bad thing," I added. Mari turned to me, half-staring, half-scowling. Maybe that was just her face.

"You're a real smart one, huh?" she said. I flashed a smile, and she rolled her eyes. I liked this girl.

"It... certainly would garner some attention," Diego said.

"Like, *look at me I shattered the realms* kind of attention?" I asked.

"Sort of," he deadpanned. Jack leaned back on the couch, not saying anything. She was smart; Jack hustled people out of their money with her readings, so she could read a room. I appreciated that, but I didn't want her hustling us. Especially D.

"What kind of attention?" Peony asked.

"Well, I'd wager a guess that the twisted soul that showed up on the doorstep was something of a sign," I said. Peony closed her eyes, took a deep breath, and fished a bottle of antacids out of her bag.

"Can I get one of those?"

"No." She popped two and swallowed without even chewing them. Absolutely savage.

"Wasn't that your fault?" Mari asked.

"Nah, I follow them, they don't follow me. See, sweetheart, I'm actually the good guy in all this crap." I grinned again, caught the hint of a blush on her cheeks, and tucked that memory away.

"And I'm a fairy princess," she said.

"Day's still young, never know what can happen." I winked at her, the blush deepened, and Jack snorted. She recovered quickly, but I realized that my wards had slipped for a second and she likely got a good scan of my noggin.

Then, as if the universe heard me, something smashed through Jack's living room window. We all jumped, except for Diego of course, and I realized what it was: another twisted and broken soul, but this one had been weaponized. It looked like a little spear before it started crumbling away.

"Oh fuck, *kill it!*"

More of them arrived. Glass had rained down in her house, the girls jumping away and Jack standing still. Adrenaline pumped through me and so did my magic. They reeked of sulfur and musk. Jack's living room was filling up with the weird ass spears. I stomped on one, readying magic to protect the girls so Diego and I could handle this mess. Jack's crystal ball lit up the room and the light caught my eye. She was standing, the ball floating between her eyes. Her eyes were green. I dove the hell out of the way.

JACK

Harold hovered between my hands, magic sparking from it. The... *creatures* had shattered my windows. They were pouring in but they looked like pieces of a larger arrow, instead of fully formed arrows. They were broken souls that had been shattered. Anger filled my lungs. Who could twist a soul like this? And *why?*

Diego tried to shield me, but when he wrapped his arms around me, magic came pouring out of me–too quick, too strong and I stumbled. Diego flew across the room–did I do that to him? He crashed against the breakfast nook, knocking out the barstools. One fell on him, hitting his head.

I raised my hands, Harold floating between them, and the screaming arrows stilled. The light within them dulled just a little, enough for me to see that they had faces and beaks.

They were fae birds.

They held there, suspended in my magic. The words came bubbling up; I'd heard them before and not long ago. The sigil of death and endings appeared in my mind, and Harold started to trace it in the air. The crystal ball shone with magic, and I swayed in time with it.

"Rest, be at peace. Return to Sanctum to be born again."

Diego was behind me now, a solid wall of a man, his arms beside mine as he slowly guided our hands together to grab the crystal ball. The magic shifted from gold to blue to finally emerald green. The arrows clanged on the floor. They were thicker, heavier than they looked, and the sound thundered around us. A small orb of light struggled to rise from them, and I touched one. The little orb shook a bit, then regained its silvery glow. The spell had taken the wind out of my lungs, and I leaned back into Diego accidentally. He smelled like sandalwood and fresh cut grass and dewy mornings. The scruff of his five o'clock shadow brushed against my hair.

The little orb floated up and up and up. We watched it pass through a window, and up through the sky.

"Well, if there was ever a doubt that you were a Priestess, that spell put it to rest right along with those souls," Diego said.

"What do you mean?" Mama asked.

"A Priestess has two jobs. One, she guides people to walk their chosen path with her visions. She warns and guides as needed. And two, when someone dies, she sends their soul to rest in Sanctum. Only a Priestess can cast that spell. It's the truest blessing of the Seer," Diego explained. I didn't move out of his arms, and he didn't push me away. Diego felt heavier suddenly, and his lovely brown eyes had turned ashen gray. I helped him to sit back down and he struggled to breathe. He glanced at my crystal, then his head slumped down. The magic was suffocating his weak heart.

"Mama–"

"I'm here, already casting; he's okay, darling." Her words were laced with magic, and I felt myself calming too.

PEONY

Jack pulled soul after soul and sent them to heaven. Or Sanctum, whatever. The heartless man leaned heavily on her, as she got him to the floor. He struggled to breathe, and the tiny light I saw in his eyes was softer.

The man, Diego, had soft, black curls that lost their shape. His hair curled around his ears, with a five o'clock shadow starting on his chin. Jack tended to him like a wounded animal. I'd never seen her move so tenderly. Diego didn't shy away from her, but he looked uncomfortable.

I was uncomfortable.

The longer I took in all of the details of his face, the more I realized how many other details about him were missing. His human face was attractive, but he was incomplete. Where were the creases in his face? The lines around his eyes or mouth? He was almost airbrushed, like his skin lacked texture. Lovely at a glance, unsettling to look at. Jack caught me staring, and I knew she felt it too. This man was truly broken.

"You know a spell that will save your life?" I asked him.

"Sort of. I need the pieces of my heart first."

"Then what happens?"

"I don't know."

"You damn well better find out."

Jack beamed at me; I was always on her side, and seeing her so invested in this man had me invested too.

Chapter Twelve

MARI

Jazzy forced everyone to regroup and to leave. I bolted. She sent Falcon and Diego home. The rest of them stayed at Jack's to clean up and board up a window and probably shower. And cry. Knowing Jack, she'd need a helluva cry to sort through all of *that*.

I needed one too. Once I was safely behind the wards of my own apartment, I peeled out of my clothes, and ran a bath. I needed the heat of the water to sink into my bones. I was *weary* and it had nothing to do with the weather.

Seeing souls depart dead beings left me shaken badly. It was too intimate to watch. I didn't have the right to watch the final moments of those souls, and I felt like a voyeur.

I sent a text to Jack, another **BBS, love you.** She immediately sent back a few hearts, all green as always. I wanted her to know that I needed to be MIA for a bit. I sank into the bath and shivered from the heat. My tub wasn't as large as Jack's, but it was big enough. I mostly fit, my knees poking out of the water if I sank enough to wet my hair. I had a phone holder on my shower walls, and it buzzed. Jack bought it for me one day because I mentioned how I wanted to listen to music in the shower. But that was like her–she'd listen to your words, or sometimes your thoughts, and show up with a gift.

Peony's texts lit up my phone, but I left her on read.

What the actual fuck mari

I was gone for like a day!

Who are those guys?????

Are they single? Lololol. I'm joking!

Mama and the cat are pulling out some old magic, idk what they're looking for but i don't like it

My phone dinged a few more times and I cursed under the water. I didn't know the number, but reached for it and checked the messages anyway.

Meet me @ 32nd and Riviera

11pm

Don't tell the girls

Nope. No siree. No way I was meeting some random ass texter at eleven o'clock at night near the damn boardwalk. That's how you get mugged. Riviera Street? Hell. *No.* Scarier folks than the dead what-cha-ma-call-its from Jack's place hung out on Riviera for shits and giggles. I left that number on read too.

Two hours later, too much Chinese take out, and a couple of internal crises later, I was putting on my damn scarf and coat. I kicked myself as I left my apartment for even getting out of the tub. At least I'd be walking off the crab rangoon calories. I pulled my scarf a little higher up on my face. November was cold by the water, and if they found my ass dead in the morning, at least they'd know I didn't die of exposure.

DIEGO

Falcon swore it would be a waste of time, but I knew Mari would show up. She was too curious and she didn't trust me; of course she'd come. We picked this spot because it was close to our hotel. I wanted to be close by in case Jack's magic acted up and I lost control again. My body was still weak, and I didn't want Falcon to have to haul me too far if I was out of it.

Even wrapped up in a coat and hoodie–*looking like some kind of perve*, according to Falcon–this whole realm was too cold for my liking. I spent about a century in only sunny countries, trying to get my body to remember what warmth truly felt like. It never worked, but feeling the sun on my face was the closest thing to Obius I'd found on earth. At night, my bones ached and my joints stiffened. We joked that rigor was setting in every time the sun goes down, but there was truth in it. Each sunrise, my body moved a little slower. My reflexes were not as fast. Aging, as the humans say. Decaying was what they meant. My neck stiffened more in the cold, and I envied Falcon's ability to hop back and forth, forcing the blood to keep moving in his veins.

I heard the jingles of Mari's beads and bracelets before I saw her; at least I still had my hearing. She stepped into the light, standing fully under the lamp post next to me. She had a hood up, but I doubted that Falcon would call *her* a pervert.

The locket was in a velvet pouch; I'd made this so many years ago, but I kept it close even when I got banished to the Earth. The chain probably needed to be mended. I'd rubbed it between my fingers so many times, that the links were rounded and smooth.

"What do you want?" she snarled.

"Your help."

MARI

Standing in the elevator in my building, I flipped the necklace around in my hands, inspecting it. It was pretty, I supposed. Not my taste, but I saw the appeal. It looked like someone with really tiny fingers crafted it and drew the design in gold. I put it back in the little pouch it came in. It felt fragile and old. I didn't want to handle it too much, and looking at it felt like I was looking too much at him. Diego had handed it over to me, and left quickly before he could change his mind.

Once I got in my apartment, I kicked my shoes off, tossed my coat and scarf on the counter, and went straight to bed. I kept my phone off and felt no shame in it. The world would still be ending tomorrow, and I didn't need to face another day as shitty as I felt today. I felt safe behind the drafty door of my apartment, closed up in the place that was mine alone. I'd painted the walls blue and added yellow accents everywhere because they were my Mama's favorite colors. My soft blue-nearly-white bedroom felt like I was wrapped up in clouds, and as I sank into my bed, Mama's perfume still lingered everywhere in my house, and it made sleeping easier. I tossed my phone on my dresser and snuggled into my pile of blankets.

JACK

No one wanted to talk about the accidental soul resting spells I casted. Including me. We sat in my living room, not speaking. Puddin purred in my lap. My trusty crystal ball still had too much of a glow for my liking, but I was ignoring that too. For once, I didn't want to go scrying, and having some distance from it helped me feel like a vision wasn't about to mug me. I wanted space from my magic. Diego was like a lightning rod in a storm of magic. I'd been electrocuted and everything in me was raw.

Peony and Mama disappeared to clean my shop again. It hadn't been a full twenty-four hours since the *last* emergency cleaning. The broken window would be an insurance claim; I didn't have the extra cash to get that fixed immediately. I called and started the process. I skipped the parts about *bizarre sort-of dead fae creatures* breaking the windows and went with some kids playing a prank and threw a big rock through the window. I snapped a couple pictures, hauled in one of my smaller garden rocks to really sell the story, and promised the adjuster that I would call and make a police report. Forty-five minutes later, the adjuster had cut a check for my window, and I could breathe a little easier. I went down to the shop, knowing I couldn't avoid them any more; Peony helped me board it up.

"You okay?" she asked.

"Yep. Fine. All good."

"Jack, you can tell me what's going on." She didn't mean to, but magic laced through her words, and the truth bubbled up in my chest–

"I can't let him die."

"Honey, you aren't a surgeon. You don't have to work a miracle on him."

Yes, I do. I refused to let the words out. I played with the citrine, letting the truth that clawed its way up my throat out into the necklace. She held her hands up in surrender.

"Sorry, I wasn't trying to force it out of you."

"I know," I whispered. And I *did* know that, but the guilt from Peony still washed over me, and without trying, I felt all of her emotions. Her worry about my safety. Her wariness about Diego. Disdain towards Falcon. Annoyance with Mari for not telling her more or telling her any faster. The general dread that came with having the dumpster fire of a sister like me. Peony examined the plyboard, making sure it was up to her standard–whatever that was, watching her do any sort of manual labor was oddly terrifying. It was left over from a repair I did to my shed last spring. Peony hammered in the last nail on the plyboard, and I slipped away to the garden for air.

It felt lifeless to me. My plants were still blooming, thanks to my magic and some of Sherwin's fertilizer blends. But still. It was cold and dank, and it smelled more like decay than it did life.

I escaped the garden and my family to go to my bathroom, my sanctuary. I locked the door and started the shower. It took no time at all to steam up the small space, and I savored it.

The citrine necklace laying against my heart felt warmer. Threading my fingers through the chain, I wrapped the pendant in my palm and focused on it. Cataloging each edge. Pushing each little point and nub of the stone against my finger tips. I brought it to my lips and kissed the perfect yellow stone. It didn't react to Diego's magic, but my crystal ball did. I did.

The water of the shower pounded against my back; I changed the setting from sweet perfect rain to meat tenderizer. My back and shoulders and even my butt were in knots. Diego's face came to mind, and I remembered the little smile he tried so hard to conceal. Did he even remember the last time he really smiled? The citrine warmed more in my hand, but remembering the smile on his face from my vision warmed me through. I *had* to see him smile. In real time, where I could touch or run my fingers against his lips–

"Jack?"

I groaned. Mama knocked on the door, magicking the lock open. The room felt cooler already. I groaned again. Louder.

"Yes?"

"I wanted to apologize." She stopped, and for a second I saw everything that she had wanted to tell me but never could have.

She knew about the blessing. She knew, and she kept it a secret, locking the knowledge behind every ward she could ever find to keep it from me. The guilt that she carried.

"Can we do this another day? I'm not mad," I lied. I was angry that she knew I was blessed by the Seer. She knew so much about my magic, and I knew so little. My visions never had anything to tell me about my own life, but my mother could have.

"You're really not upset with me?"

"I don't like that you didn't tell me, but I get why you wouldn't tell a child they've got that kind of mojo. But I'm nearly thirty, so you know what, it's fine."

"Darling–" I shushed her and complained about being naked, and she left my little sanctuary. I regretted the moment I stepped out of the shower, but my robe was soft and warm.

The citrine glowed, and I leaned into the energy, letting it revive my spirit. I saw a grainy image of Diego, before his life on earth. His horns curled against his head, and he was smiling. Every time I saw him now in a vision, I saw joy in him. It'd been centuries since he smiled like that.

"–right?"

"Hmm?"

"You don't have to do anything for those men. They're strangers with magic much stronger than ours. You have to be careful."

"Mama, I can't explain it, but I believe him. And not only that, I *want* to help him."

"Well, we should probably start honing on your sigil workings then. Can't be having a Priestess with sloppy spell-work."

I grinned and some of the heaviness from her dissipated. "And this is something that you're well versed in, I take it?"

"Of course darling, why wouldn't I be?" Mama winked at me, and all of the anger left me. Well, most of it. Mama kissed the top of my head and let me finally get dressed. Not five minutes after she left, Peony burst into the bathroom, a cut above her eyebrow bleeding heavily, eyes glowing silver.

"There's more of them!"

She was already running back out, and I heard the destruction from the shop beneath me. Refusing to face another not-dead creature in a towel,

I shrugged into my bathrobe and a pair of undies and tied it *tight.* By the time I made it downstairs, Peony was swinging a baseball bat around the shop, trying to stop the flow of twisted, angry souls.

Mama cast barrier spells and healing spells around us, her magic like a hug. This was how Mama shined; she couldn't see the future or force the truth from someone's lips or even accidentally set someone on fire, but she was a healer. *The* healer. Whatever else she could do, protection was her true power.

Puddin hissed, slapping at the partially-boarded up window. All of Peony's work was destroyed. A swarm of flying insects–beetles maybe–flooded through the window, crashed into it, already dead but still moving. The glimmers of their souls were soft, like little sparkles, but I saw them. Little red and pink lights from them. Birds dropped from the sky, thudding on the roof and landing on the front porch. Blue and white sparks; souls that were desperately clinging to the being that they inhabited. Peony destroyed a display of crystals. Snakes crawled through the open door, three dead cats, and a... hand? I didn't look too closely. The sparkle from the souls caught my attention more and forced my focus on them.

"*Do something!*" Peony shrieked. Puddin floated in the air, readying some type of spell, and Mama pulled out my letter opener from the drawer of my checkout counter and sliced her hand. Every dead thing stopped mid movement and stared at her.

The cut in her hand sparkled; I saw a glimpse of her soul then.

"Jazzy, stop it right now. I don't know how you're tapping that link, but *let it go,*" Puddin growled. The creatures swarmed her and bounced off of a bubble of magic surrounding her. They screamed and moaned and buzzed, rage pouring out of every one, and I felt sick.

She drew a sigil in the air; it looked familiar, but I couldn't place it.

I called Harold to me. It still glowed from the last spell, and the residual magic thrummed through me.

"Wait, let her try–" Peony said.

"I can't hold this spell for much longer," Jazzy said.

"Now Jack! Do it *now!*" Puddin yelled.

The ball hovered in front of me, and I did my showman arm movements like I would for a customer. It wasn't an act this time. Each movement, each motion brought the magic to me, pooling it in the crystal ball. All of the creatures, and the hand, turned back to me.

"Darling, no–"

"Rest, be at peace. Return to Sanctum to be born again." I pushed as much of my magic into the spell as I could; it bubbled up in my chest like I would explode and then–

Nothing happened.

The creatures and bits turned their focus back to Mama and her well of magic that made the room feel dark. She winked at me, smiled at Peony and Puddin, and then dropped the spell.

"I'll be okay, darling," Mama's voice played through my mind. I forced my body into motion to go to her but it didn't matter. The cut on her hand was blinding white, and the creatures all shriveled up. The spell was choking the souls out of them and out of existence.

This was death magic.

This was *wrong*.

"Mama, stop!

She didn't stop. Her eyes turned white. The blood from her hand had turned completely black, and my knees wobbled. She destroyed every twisted soul in the shop, destroyed the wretched little bodies they inhabited, and turned them all to dust. The light faded from each creature, even the hand, and my heart ached. I could taste the death in the air and my throat closed in on itself.

This was wrong. Those souls needed to be put to rest.

Mama looked like a demon. The smile on her face was wicked, and I didn't recognize her.

"Darling, if you could be so kind as to siphon some of this magic from me and into that crystal ball of yours, that would be lovely." Her words were strained. She sounded as dead as the creatures were currently. Her words were gravelly and uneven.

Harold was hovering by me, already glowing and ready for the task.

"I don't think I want that darkness in my crystal," I whispered. Mama's eyes were wild. The sickly grin was still there, and Peony gently squeezed my arm.

"Jack," she whispered.

I waved my hand and the crystal glowed. The magic fell out of Mama like a waterfall of energy, and the crystal took it all in, not once faltering from all of that horrible magic. Peony was already holding onto Mama, keeping her upright, and I was inspecting Harold. It was fine. The crystal was neutral like always, powerful and beautiful, and utterly fine.

"That crystal ball of yours is something special," Mama said.

"Where did you learn that magic?" I asked.

"Jack, Peony, my loves," Mama rubbed the backs of her fingers down my cheek, her other hand wrapped around Peony's waist. "I've always taught you that there is as much light as there is dark in this world. I'm a healer, but how many injuries do you think I *naturally* happened upon?"

She smiled again, less cruel, less wild, but the weight of her words sank in. Whatever guards and walls she had spelled around her mind were slowly coming down, and she let me see more and more of her magic. That well in her was bottomless.

"It's been a while since I've used any spells that intensive. I'm going to go back to the mountains. Peony, keep her out of trouble," Mama said.

"What? You can't just *leave*–" Peony let go of her, staring in disbelief.

"I have to. I'll be back, but for now, I have to–"

"Purge," I said. Her head snapped up, and our eyes met. I was right; Mama had to purge the rest of that hideous magic, and she refused to do it around us.

"Heal," she said.

I hugged her. I was furious, but I hugged her. I never wanted to see this side of her again, and I hugged her tighter.

"I'm sorry," she whispered. Puddin wound herself around my legs, trying to bolster my resolve.

"That magic is dangerous. Promise me you won't use it again," I said.

"I promise." Mama kissed my temple and then kissed Peony. She snapped her fingers, and her bag appeared in the shop, packed and zipped, with her purse sitting on top. She blew kisses over her shoulder and headed for the door.

"You're leaving, just like that?" Peony asked.

"Yes, Darling, but I'll be back."

And just like that, she was gone. I thought about all the times she would disappear for a season and come back stronger than ever, how her magic never seemed to wane, how she seemed to be so full of life even though she was aging.

"Is this what she does when she leaves every year?" I asked Peony.

"I don't know. I didn't know that she could... do whatever that was. I thought she was just meditating and partying, honestly."

"Well, I guess now we know. Do you have any cleaning spells? My shop reeks of death." It really did; the dust and whatever else was left from the spell was stuck in my nose and lungs, and I felt sick with it. I focused on my breathing, trying to will my hands to stop shaking, and get the rest of my body on board without having a panic attack. Mama's wicked grin replayed over and over in my mind, and my stomach hurt.

"Not really. Burn some incense, I'll grab a broom."

DIEGO

We made it back to our hotel room, and I crashed. Even before my eyes were fully closed, I was remembering and dreaming of home.

We sat in the courtyard together. My mother sat in a large yellowish-green tulip chair. Small insect fae people buzzed around her, and she laughed with them. My mother was the prior queen, but because I had never married, my people still looked to her as the queen. I loved it; she was much wiser than me, definitely much smarter, and never afraid to speak her mind. She was everything I wanted to be in a leader, one day.

Snapdragon sat on her feet by a small tree. She pretended that she was praying, but I saw the tears forming in her eyes. Mother tapped me with her hoof, pushing me to go check on her. So wise, so pushy.

"Mistress?"

"Your Grace, I'm sorry to disturb you." Snapdragon blinked quickly, pretending that the sun had caught her instead of me.

"Snapdragon, what's wrong? We're alone, I'm not 'Your Grace' right now," I moved the vines out of her face, tucking them behind her ears. She flinched at my touch.

"I keep having the same vision. The humans are coming, Deign. I don't know why, but they will be at our doorstep soon. They will burn the forests until we give them what they want."

"What do they want?"

"Me," her voice trailed off, and she turned away. Snapdragon got up quickly, went over to my mother and bowed. She left quickly, fleeing to her tower where I could not follow, at least not until the castle was asleep.

"Something is wrong with that girl," Mother said.

"Hm?"

"Be careful. The trees won't bloom around her anymore, son. Pay attention to the trees. They will always tell you the truth." She patted my hand,

straightened the crown on my horns. I hated wearing it, but it was tradition, and everyone in this court loved a good tradition. Except me.

"She's just afraid of the visions she's having. She thinks war is coming."

"Yes, son, I know."

The warmth of her hand raced through me so much that it startled me awake. The sun was up. How long had I been asleep? My mother's face faded, and I was already forgetting her.

"Glad you're awake," Falcon said. His voice was soft and he had his hand on a knife he thought I didn't know about.

"What's wrong?"

"Something's up. A big ole blast of magic was coming from Jack's place. I think we need to lay low a little before we show back up. You need to shave too."

"Should we go check on them?"

"Yeah, but I wanna hang back first." Falcon was already up and moving, so I took that as my cue to do the same.

Chapter Thirteen

JACK

Mari arrived about an hour after I called her in tears. Peony and I clung to each other like the world would open and swallow us whole too. Mama'll be back, I reminded myself. She was just retreating to wherever she went to recharge and dispel that crap. I still wasn't happy that Harold had taken it all in, but it had been hours since Mama poofed out and it was still as neutral as it ever was. Peony closed the shop–again–and we retreated back upstairs to my house. I was a lump on my couch, sitting where Diego had, and the scent of sandalwood was still there. I breathed deep, letting his scent soothe my frazzled nerves. And it *was* soothing. Everything about Diego was soothing, now that I could really see him.

I wondered if I soothed him too.

Mari moved about the kitchen automatically. She was in crisis mode. Mari made tea; our collective favorite spicy, fragrant chai. It was a home blend that I made myself. She added the sugar for mine, poured milk in

Peony's, and hers over ice. Mari plopped on my couch next to me. The three of us hugged each other for what felt like hours until we couldn't stand the silence any longer.

"She's going to be fine," I finally said, and I meant it. Aside from the scary death magic and that unnerving, demonic-like grin on her face, this was standard procedure for her: blow in like a tornado, blow out like one.

"I still don't *like* it. And I sure as hell don't like that magic," Peony said. A chill shot through me, and I nodded.

The ice had melted in Mari's tea.

"Anyone wish we could just wiggle our noses and magically clean the shop?" Peony said.

I blew out a sigh, "I'm sure the insurance company would prefer that."

"Little bit more than just a broken window now, huh? Do I even want to know?" Mari asked.

"No," we said in unison. Peony had gotten a decent amount of the death dust out, but no amount of incense was going to clear out that grimy death feeling. I knew because I had already tried eight different ones.

"Yeeeeeeep," I sighed so deeply my bones felt it, "I think I'm just gonna have to do it myself."

"Insurance is more complicated than practicing law," Peony said. We laughed, and I laid my head on Peony's shoulder and held Mari's hand. This was my family, my life. The only things left intact now were them. Everything around me was wrecked and ruined and missing. A couple tears rolled down my cheeks again, and Mari wiped them with her thumb.

"Diego called me to meet him last night," Mari said. She released my hand to pick at her nails. Peony finally broke and popped up to reheat her tea. She needed space. Peony was my rock but she was just as cuddly as one. She showed her love with words and actions; a hug could only last so long for her. I wanted to reach for her like a child clinging to their mother when she walked out of my immediate range of vision, so she stayed close but with enough space she didn't suffocate.

"He wanted me to make an artifact. Which is like, weird, because Falcon could do it in his sleep. He's a way better witch than me."

"What kind of artifact?" Peony asked, taking a long sip of the tea. The steam fogged her glasses. Peony could drink lava without breaking a sweat.

"It's a locket. Like, old school. He wants me to layer it with my magic."

"Creepy." Peony stated. She took another big swig of the chai and the worry lines around her eyes eased. It was a spell; I added calming spells to all of my teas, but the chai had a more potent relaxation spell in it. Peony... looked a little high. Her glasses had slipped down to the end of her nose, and she didn't immediately fix them.

"Do you have the locket?" I asked. It bothered me that Diego would entrust something so precious to her. Lockets were for lovers. Or mothers. And Mari was holding one that Diego had kept.

She nodded, hopped up, and started digging through her bag. Mari's purses only came in one size: mountainous. Mari's bag doubled as a weapon, pharmacy, closet, and roadside assistance. I'd found a wrench in there more than once. Her daily purse was big enough for me to pack for a weekend trip, maybe longer. I started in on my tea, because this would take a while.

"Girl–"

"I cleaned it out two weeks ago. Hush."

"Okay," I laughed. Mari dug through the bag; her entire arm to her shoulder was in it at this point. She could have a portal to Obius in there and no one would be shocked.

"Here," she handed me a small velvet bag. It hummed; not quite a song, but a beat. A refrain? Something. I took the locket out and ran my fingers over it. Rose gold, or something like it. It was roundish, like someone had drawn the circle instead of crafting it precisely. A pink snapdragon flower pressed into the cover, with soft rose gold leaves and vines around it. The chain looked like a few thin vines that were woven and braided together.

He made this. He made this for her.

I knew it as soon as I held it in my hands, felt its magic and love, and felt my heart break. It would have taken ages for Diego to make it; it was so intricate and delicate. I rubbed each little detail on it, and I wanted to wear it. I wanted to feel its weight against my chest and wanted to feel it warm to my skin. I wanted to be even closer to Diego.

I didn't wear it, but I did hold it up to my heart. The locket hummed, and the more I listened, the more I knew the tune. I heard it in a vision before. Diego held her gently, swaying in time with the beat, their arms interlocked and fingers twined together like they couldn't possibly stand being mere inches apart.

"Diego said that he needed my magic because I had some of the strongest protection spells he's seen. Which is flattering, but not true. I'm not sure what to make of it," Mari said.

I handed her the locket, and once she put it away, the humming didn't stop. Diego wanted her magic so it would be forever linked to me. The rightness of that knowledge flowed through me. He wanted this locket to accept me, so he started by introducing it to my world.

He wanted me to have it.

Wishful thinking on your part, I chastised myself.

"Actually, can I see it one more time?" I asked. Mari gave it back automatically, and the humming got louder. Neither Mari nor Peony seemed to react to the sound. They couldn't hear it, or feel it. I pushed a little of my magic into the locket, threading the chain again through my fingers. It heated up, like every other artifact I've infused with magic. Practicing alchemy was as simple as breathing for me; especially when I was drawn to a piece.

I was head over heels for this locket. I'd never seen anything so intricate. The details were like a labyrinth. I couldn't find the clasp to open it, and I *needed* to see what was inside. The little snapdragon petals still felt velvety even though they were sealed with resin. I pushed a little more of my magic, the purest bits of myself that I could summon, and the locket popped open. I jumped a little.

The humming wasn't a *hum*.

It was a beat.

The locket was beating. I dropped it hastily on the coffee table, and curled my knees under me. The beating kept going.

The girls buzzed around my house, doing this and that, and I couldn't focus on anything else other than this locket now. I got up and opened a window. The beating got louder.

I stripped my bedding and threw it all in the wash—color sorting be damned.

The locket kept beating.

I put the dishes from the dishwasher away.

The locket kept beating.

I wiped down the counters.

The locket kept beating.

"I can't believe I didn't get his phone number," I muttered. The locket would not stop humming, and I was going to chuck the damn thing out the window if it didn't stop. Beautiful craftsmanship and lovey dovey crap can only increase my tolerance for this incessant humming so much. And lordy knows, *I was hitting my limits.*

"Girl, is that why you're working like a woman possessed? I have his number. He texted me to give me the locket, remember?"

I stopped pacing; how long had I been pacing? My ankles ached. The sun had set. What the *hell*? It just would not stop humming. Beating. Whatever. Mari stood up and grabbed my shoulders. I stopped pacing.

"You're going to walk a hole in the floor. Go sit down. I ordered pizza. Should be here in like twenty minutes," Peony said. The floor was fine, but I wasn't. That sound was like an itch in my brain, deep where I'd never be able to reach it.

Dun dun dun dun dun dun dun d–

Puddin meowed, and I scooped her up. She was nuzzled up against my neck, purring her little kitten heart out. The purring sorta, almost drowned out the beating. Almost.

"Also while you were walking out that little meltdown of yours, I texted Diego and Falcon. They'll be here in time for pizza," Mari said.

"Wait, what?"

"Did someone say pizza?" Falcon had opened the front door to my apartment–which I know I locked. After having fifty or so twisted and dying souls break through my shop, I locked every damn thing I could. Not that it seemed to *stop* them but it felt like something.

"I'd like a slice if there is enough," Diego said quietly. His body took up a lot of physical space, but no emotional space in a room. Diego was a large man but once he dropped whatever mask he clung to, the sadness in him acted like a black hole. It sucked and pulled at every cell. I ached if I allowed myself to notice it too long, but even that was starting to lessen now that he was here. Falcon was the opposite; he took up a lot of physical *and* emotional space. Falcon was a bonfire on a dry night. He burned bright, but one spark would burn everything down. Falcon hovered near the door, blocking the exit. Everything about him screamed, *"I am relaxed, I am zen, I am peaceful and not a threat,"* and it was a very, very good lie. Every interaction I had with him, I chipped a little more of the perfectly poised façade and saw the animal behind it.

Diego's steps moved in time with the locket's beating. It pulsed inside my head. No one else reacted, not even Diego. We stared at each other, the humming and beating and breathing all thundering in my ears. The rise and fall of Diego's chest was just out of sync, and I twitched. My skin tingled and itched, like an itch inside of your ear where you can't quite reach it.

"Looking real feral there, Jack," Falcon said smoothly. His face was so wide and his eyes so hard I twitched again.

"Dude, I am *so* over your attitude. It's not like I wanted you two to show up on my damn doorstep and then *destroy my whole fucking store!*" I was yelling, it was too loud, and holy fuck *will this god forsaken beating ever stop!* My fingers were twitchy. My nerves were on fire; I felt the electricity sizzle through every tendril in my skin, and my head was busting.

"You look like you're about to go all savage on us. What's happening?" he said. Falcon dropped his arms; he had them folded, tucked tightly to his chest; another layer of safety.

"How do y'all not *hear* that? Oh my god, I'm gonna lose my mind. *Make this damn locket stop!*" I screamed. I dug at my ears and hid my head. It was so loud. Painfully loud. I didn't remember sitting down. I couldn't remember where I was, but the floor was there. I nearly curled up in the fetal position, but pride kept me flat on the floor instead.

"What beating?" Diego asked. His voice had zero emotion in it. He sounded robotic. Dead. He was on the floor with me. He held my hand, rubbing little circles on the backs, trying to coax me out. His eyes were so dead, so lifeless. Looking at him took my breath away.

"From the locket," I said. Was I still yelling? I couldn't tell. Peony shooed him away and knelt next to me, stroking my hair, weaving some type of calming magic into me. It didn't work.

"Mari said you gave it to her, and then I looked at it, and I might have added a little magic to it and now I'm going to tear my damn hair out if *it doesn't stop humming.*"

Everyone stared at me. I couldn't *see* them staring because the beating pulsed black spots in my eyes, but the hair on the back of my neck prickled. I was going to black out.

"Why did you use alchemy on my locket?" Diego asked. His voice was still robotic. Emotionless. Dead. Dead. Dead.

"I don't know, it just felt right and now–"

"Give it to me," he said. It was a whisper. A whisper of a whisper. It rang out so clearly because the humming had stopped. The beating was gone and I was painfully aware of him breathing. His breaths were too far apart, too shallow. *No Jack, don't touch him.* I stopped that thought from going any further. He was next to me. So close.

He's not yours to touch. I chewed on my lip and tucked my hands under my legs.

Mari grabbed the locket before Diego could take it from me, "Not until you back the fuck up."

Diego's eyes turned murderous for a second, confused and angry. His whole aura changed, personifying the darkness I saw in him more than he had before. I touched him then–just his hands. I wrapped my fingers around them, and the rage seeped out of him. His eyes shot around the room, until they finally landed on me.

The beating came back with a vengeance. I was drowning in the noise. I think I winced or whined because Diego's hands were on my face, trying to soothe whatever pain he saw there. I summoned the locket; I called, it came, floating obediently like my crystal ball had.

I looped it around Diego's neck, letting my hands brush against his hair, his chin, his neck, and I wrapped my arms around his neck too. His skin was so cold. The locket kept beating, and it warmed him. It warmed me. I couldn't force myself to let him go, and now his arms were wrapped back around me.

Please make the beating stop, help him. Heal him. Magic blossomed in my chest and I felt it seeping out of me and into Diego. He sucked in a deep breath, but didn't let go of me.

"Jack," he whispered. His voice was so small, so soft. I pushed my face into him, the scruff of his beard nuzzling my cheek.

"You're safe, I'm here."

He breathed. I breathed.

The beating stopped.

DIEGO

Jack added some intense magic to the locket. My chest was heavier. The nerve endings in my fingers burned. My bones creaked, and I felt them. Muscles and skin and blood–

I was alive.

"You did it," I said. My voice was louder. I could speak louder.

"I did?"

"I think you added a piece of my heart back." I touched my chest again, and smiled. I felt it beating.

JACK

Diego examined his hands, like he just realized he had them. He moved each finger slowly, the knuckles cracking the stiffness away. He rolled his shoulders and stretched his neck.

And then he smiled. I'd seen this grin, this gorgeous, joyous grin before in a vision. He was looking at Snapdragon as she entered a throne-like room. He forced the edges of his mouth into a thin, serious line, but the joy from his smile still lit him from within. His eyes shone with emotion. They had emotion. He was alive.

Diego was *smiling!* Truly smiling, and right at me. My heart hammered in my chest, and I was grinning back at him.

He was alive.

Finally, finally alive.

CHAPTER FOURTEEN

THROUGH THE VEIL

My errand boy hadn't contacted me in ages. The *human*. Time in my realm flowed differently from the humans' home. I twisted my magic, my words so he would listen. So pious in his worship and love for the Goddess of Judgment. He stayed by the king's side. He watched the false one. Just watching. Waiting.

And ignoring my summons.

My tower leaned more each day, pretending that it would topple with me inside. It wouldn't. It wouldn't dare. I kept a small cage full of tiny, lively pixies. They had lovely wings and lovely souls.

I grabbed two and snapped their necks between my fingers. The others cried and cursed me behind my back, but stopped once I turned. I pulled the souls from the little bodies, and instead of letting them rest, I sharpened them into arrows.

I had a message for my errand boy.

The last flurry of arrows that I sent through the links left me hazy. My staff still hovered at my side, sensing the change in me, and I leaned heavily on it. The only ones to see were the pixies, and they were canon fodder at most.

It had been too long since I scried, and something was off. The crystal wouldn't reveal what problem lay at my feet.

My tower swayed. It never used to sway; the magic that kept it upright faded as the decades came and went. I pushed that thought from my mind and delved deeper into my crystal.

Nothing.

Magic came and went so quickly here. So did the people, the Trellian guards, Deign's advisors, his mother. So many people abandoned their homeland once their king was banished, even though I remained here on his throne to guide them.

On *my* throne.

CHAPTER FIFTEEN

JACK

I filled the guys in on what happened with my shop: influx of broken and twisted souls, lots of broken glass, possible insurance fraud, and a missing in action mother. She had been gone for about seven hours now. She'd be back. I knew this. I just couldn't shake off that spell she used.

The beating had stopped, and the murderous intent had gone with it. Puddin stayed glued to my side. She wouldn't talk out loud, but sent me little thoughts, and the pressure in my chest eased. *She's okay, I can tell. He thinks he's the goddess' gift to humankind, doesn't he? Absolutely insufferable. Your sister is walking a hole in the floor. Mari has eaten four slices of pizza already. If she polishes off all of the pepperoni, I will ruin her feet.*

"So your mom can use death magic and this is the first you're hearing about it?" Falcon asked. He pushed the sleeves of his henley up to his elbows. There was a tattoo of balanced scales on his inner left forearm. His hands were greasy from the pizza, and he wiped them on his jeans. The bags under his eyes were pronounced. Maybe I was just seeing them. The tattoo was very detailed, and it reminded me of the locket. The style, the lines. I wondered if Diego had drawn it for him.

"It's not like it ever came up in conversation," I said.

"This shit keeps getting better," he mumbled.

"Why do you even care? This has nothing to do with Diego," I fired back.

"Because she's fucking with the natural order of things. Remember? Big fella over here is missing most of his ticker as a punishment for *destroying the natural order of things.* The Goddesses don't like that shit."

"They don't seem to be here. Or care," Mari shrugged. I felt her disappointment as she rummaged through the fridge, looking for a beer.

"What kind of asshole wouldn't care about someone screwing up this world!"

"Feel free to just butt out of our world," Peony said coolly.

"Not until D is stable," Falcon said. His voice changed. I don't think he even realized it. The nice guy facade slipped when Diego was involved, and I was seeing the essence of that dark green energy from my initial visions.

"Stable?" Diego said. Listening but not fully in stasis. He powered down a lot as if someone removed a battery from him. Maybe he could stay alive for longer periods now; I wanted him to be fully here. His fingers twitched. I sat on the couch next to him, and I leaned against his shoulder. After an indecent amount of time, I forced myself to give him space. He moved closer to me when I tried to move away.

"Yeah bro, I can't let you just go back into the wild all by your lonesome." He tossed a balled up napkin at Diego and it bounced off of his forehead. Diego blinked.

"All of this broetry is lovely, honestly, but once Jack helps Diego, we're done here." Mari folded her arms across her chest. I heard the nagging thought in the back of her mind that she hoped the problem wouldn't be solved quickly.

"How are these souls finding their way to me?" I asked.

"I dunno, the link is acting up. It shouldn't even be there thanks to D, but somehow there's enough of a link for Obius and Earth to interact."

"And the souls are definitely coming from Obius?" Peony asked.

"That was my thought until I learned that your Mama Bear can use *death magic* and didn't bother to tell anyone."

"She would never hurt us," I said, instantly angry.

"You? No. *Him*?" Falcon pointed at Diego. "I could see it."

"What? Why me?" For such a large man, Diego was very soft spoken.

"D, no one benefits from the links being broken. If someone found out you're responsible… it wouldn't be hard to imagine them being pissed about it."

"And you think my mother is responsible?" Peony said. She matched him tone for tone; Falcon had yet to see what a true ice queen looked like, and he was teetering on the edge of finding out.

"Prolly not. Timing doesn't really fit. I do think someone is trying to rebuild the links though," he said, looking directly at me. I didn't break eye contact. I could play ice queen too, when I wanted. More like, ice princess; Peony held the queen ranking.

"Me?"

Falcon shrugged, but I saw the conclusion already forming in his eyes. Of course it was me.

"I didn't think any being here *could* reopen the link, otherwise I would have forced them to open it centuries ago," Diego said. My attention hung on the word *forced*. It was hard to imagine this man forcing anyone to do anything. Nothing about him screamed aggressive to me, but then I remembered the look on his face in a vision, when Snapdragon was scared. The eyes of a man who would rip the world apart and did.

"Okay, well three times out to Abuela in a week is a lot, but I think it might be worth it. With everyone's magic all wonky, maybe she has some ideas," Mari said.

"Why *is* our magic acting wonky?" I asked. Mine was stronger than ever; between the fortified necklace and Diego, I was a lightning rod.

"My guess is D. He can cause power outages for alchemists," Falcon said.

"So it's temporary?" Peony asked.

"Usually. Mostly," Diego said.

"Mostly?"

"Unless I accidentally take it all," he mumbled. For such a large man, he was a *mumbler*. Falcon scrubbed a hand over his face, itching at his nonexistent beard.

"This is why I babysit," Falcon muttered.

"I don't need a babysitter!"

"Debatable, but basically Diego fucks with everyone's magic."

"What about yours?" Mari asked.

"Nah, we're compatible. It doesn't affect me anymore. At first though, I was constantly blowing chunks from his magical radiation."

"You had the stomach flu when we met."

"Oh, right. Fucking taco trucks."

"How do we get our magic stable again?" Mari asked.

"It should come back once I'm gone. I haven't been casting anything," Diego said.

Always so quiet, so soft. Diego's fingers picked at the hem of his sweater. I knew it was cashmere from when my hand brushed him, and I couldn't imagine him in anything that would better suit him. Warm, soft, subtle, classic. It hugged every muscle in his arms and shoulders. He shifted his weight forward, leaning heavily on his thighs, and I needed a moment to collect myself. Diego was a work of art. He locked eyes with me and a smile bloomed on my face.

"And you're not leaving until Jack fixes your heart," Mari grumbled.

"Yes," he said. This wasn't quiet or soft. Everything about him hardened and sharpened. He dropped the wards in his mind long enough for me to hear, *no matter how long it takes.*

PEONY

Three more texts from Sherwin. I sent back a series of kissy-face emojis and hearts. I missed him. It had been ages since I found myself smiling with someone other than the girls.

Vibes are all off, P. Already giving me a nickname? Nick-initial? Cute. *I'm fine.*

Lol sure. Pho on Saturday? 7pm? I'll pick you up at V&T. *It's a date.*

At least I hoped it would be.

Jack looked away when I saw her looking at me, looking at my phone. With that little corner smirk, she either read my mind or knew me well enough to know when I had a crush. Both were intolerable.

I felt guilty, wanting to take time away from the girls when everything felt so rocky. They needed someone to hold the reins stable, and that someone was always me. Except this time, I didn't even know where to begin with putting this shit back together. Another text from Sherwin, this time a winky face and a pink heart, and my cheeks felt warm.

"He's cute," Jack's voice played in my head.

Goddess damn it all.

MARI

Jack and I packed an overnight bag and headed out to see Abuela. Falcon decided that they needed to sit this little road trip out, and Peony was more than happy to have the night off from cleaning up Jack's mess.

Jack twirled the ends of her hair. Picked at her nails. Smoothed and smoothed the non-existent wrinkles in her jeans. Crossed and uncrossed her legs.

"Girl, do I need to drug you? Sit still."

"Sorry. I just don't love that I've left my entire livelihood in Peony's hands."

"She wouldn't let anything happen to your place, and you know that."

"With what magic? I don't know if you felt it, but she feels totally depleted." She spat the words out, but not at me. Just *to* me. To Mari, her forever confidant. Jack painted the smile on her face and played the good child, and she *was* the good child, but she deserved to shine. She deserved to rise to her true heights, and I wanted to help her do it. I wanted to rise with her.

"You think she won't grab the bat and beat some ass if she had to?"

Jack choked out a laugh at the thought of little Peony jumping up to take a swing, glasses slipping down her nose because they were comically large on her face.

"You've been cagey," Jack finally said after the giggles stopped.

"You too. Well, creepy more than cagey."

"Creepy!"

"That eye thing you do is creepy as hell. One minute you're looking at me, then you're looking at my foot and also my face? Creepy."

"Well what's with you acting all weird and quiet? You're never quiet."

"I didn't want to really advertise that my magic was gone. It's back, but I still don't wanna talk about it." I gripped the steering wheel until my knuckles turned white.

Jack waited; she wanted me to pour it all out, but there wasn't anything to say. One day I'd be standing beside her as her equal in magic, instead of in her shadow.

"But you did that fireball. It was kinda awesome."

"It was a terrifying accident."

"That too," Jack said laughing.

"Your shop really is fucked."

She groaned. "New topic. Where are we going? The OBX?"

"Yep. My dad's condo."

We drove south this time, avoiding the tunnel, heading for the Outer Banks of North Carolina; it was only about two hours from Jack's front door. My dad had a condo on the beach road. It was older and empty for the season. He rented it out from early spring until Halloween. I hadn't spoken to him in a few years, and I wanted to keep it that way. He left completely when my mother died, but by then there wasn't much left to say at that point. I had a set of keys though, and we had an understanding that the condo was mine to use whenever I wanted November through January. Come February, he'd show up to clean and pretend to update it. It was as close to a gift that Arthur Groves could muster. The updates he did were essentially swapping out my things for campy beach décor. "Life's a beach" throw pillows and seashells made in China really sold the charm of the unit.

I tried to listen for Abuela's magic, to call to her like she said. The wind didn't give me any answers, but my gut told me she would be at the beach. Water was full of magic, and Abuela liked to be close to it. She ran another little store down here that opened for the season, and if she was in town, she'd be in the back room. It was a bead store; totally normal, no magical items at all. Abuela loved anything shiny, and running the small bead store appealed to her. She hired teens and other old ladies to run the place when she wasn't there, which was often. Her little back room had a small bathroom, makeshift kitchen, and a small cot. She also had a set of keys to the condo; I'd given her a set years ago when I thought she was homeless. My dad was furious–all that *lost income*–but I didn't care; she needed a roof over her head more than he needed a paycheck.

My dad, Arthur Groves, was physically alive but dead to me. He left my mother, Daisy, when I was young, nine-ish. She died when I was a few months shy of eighteen, and Jazzy took me in. Abuela had been a babysitter. She loved my mother, and she loved me even more. Arthur didn't come back for the funeral, and only called when he needed something from me. Some magic, usually.

It took no time at all for us to cross the bridge and arrive in the Outer Banks.

"You think Abuela's in town?" Jack asked.

"Mmhmm, she told me to call her when I needed her."

"Does Abuela even have a phone?"

"Probably? I'm not sure." I unlocked the door to the condo and the faint smell of disinfectant lingered. Jack plopped her little bag on the couch, and immediately dug out my candles from the locked closet. The closet had a little sign on it marked "maintenance" and most guests took that at face value and left it alone. It was a coat closet full of all my things to make this place a home. It was my first trip down here since the season ended, so we packed up all of the "Life's a beach" crap, and pulled out my pillows, throws, and knickknacks. Every year Jack and I would come down, turn on some music, and redecorate. After we got everything unpacked, I opened up the windows to let the sea air in and the cleaning chemicals out.

Most of the stores and restaurants in the Outer Banks closed for the winter, but the locals always knew of a few favorite spots. I could already taste the fish at our favorite restaurant here, Uglie's.

The candles were doing their job, and the condo already felt warmer. Sitting under the heating vent helped too. I had plopped down on the tactful couch–tan, tufted, and utterly tasteless–and let the heat hit me.

"Tonight I just want some fried fish and a cold beer."

"You're not gonna stop by Abuela's tonight?"

"She's like a reverse vampire. The sun's going down so she'll already be in bed. Gotta get her beauty rest," I said. I used magic to light the rest of the candles, filling the air with the smell of clean linens and fresh salty air. These were the smells that always reminded me of my mother; fresh, sun-dried linen and ocean air.

"I think Uglie's is still open," I said.

"I can taste those hush puppies already."

DIEGO

The locket sat on the center of my chest. I could breathe. Really breathe.

Falcon and I had gone back to our hotel after Jack left. Her magic shop was a disaster, all because of me. The blessing of the Seer would have caught up to her eventually, but I brought it to her doorstep faster. Once I had enough magic, I'd craft her an entire cave full of enchanted items. Anything she asked for. Anything she needed.

I might have added a little magic to it. Her magic was a soft, minty green. It felt like wet grass and sunshine. She added just a touch of magic, a touch of herself to my locket and now my heart was beating. Her grassy magic surged through my veins, and I could *feel* it. My nerves were slowly coming alive.

The locket thumped on my chest, little heartbeats still out of sync with the piece in my chest. The arrhythmic beat was a little uncomfortable; my blood didn't know which way to pump, and it caused the rest of my body to be out of sync too. But still. It was beating. I was alive.

"Is that really a piece of your heart?" Falcon asked.

"Yes." Falcon's face seemed clearer. My eyes focused easier, the details of his features coming into view. How had I not noticed the wrinkles around his eyes? How much life had my friend already lived through?

"What's in the locket?"

His hair was wet and loose; the room smelled like shampoo and his fruity, coconut conditioner. Falcon showered more than any other human I've ever met, spanning nearly six centuries. The water cleansed his thoughts as much as it did his body, and my moody friend often needed a thought cleanse. The air was damp from the steam, but now I felt it on my skin. The room was humid, and I noticed how the material of my sweater clung to me.

I popped the locket open and handed it to him. A cracked sunstone came out, and Falcon held it gently.

"Your heart is a rock?"

"A cracked one, yes," I laughed. The sound came out easily, like laughter was a normal, everyday event for it. Maybe now it could be.

"How does that even work?"

"My people came from nature, from our planet. We are more elemental than meaty like humans."

"That's such a gross way to put it. Meaty."

"I'm just saying that we are different."

"So, I'm meaty, and you're a... sunstone?"

"Yes."

"You've been earthside for like five hundred years, and you still sound like an alien." He handed me the cracked sunstone so I could fit the pieces back into the locket. I sealed it again with my own magic and the locket hummed contently. Seal-making was the specialty of my family's power; crafting them, enforcing them, combining and layering magic to make a seal more potent.

And breaking them.

"Maybe you can teach me how to sound normal then," I said.

Falcon grinned, "Buddy, that'll take another hundred years and I don't have that kinda time. How long have you been holding on to that anyway?" He held out his hand for the locket, palming it tenderly. The long thin, rose-gold chain swinging back and forth. It was comically small in his larger hands. It was not made for such a hand to hold it.

"Since I've been earthside."

"And no one else has ever gotten that thing to start ticking again?"

I nodded. My heart had been shattered when I broke the link between my realm and the other two. Sanctum and Earth were cut off from the Magic Realm. Obius was the plane, the world. Trellis was my kingdom and my home. The Seer, the Judge, and the Creator decided my fate and that was that: Shatterer of Worlds, living endlessly with a shattered heart and apart from magic. Snapdragon still died. And I ruined the balance between the worlds for nothing. My eyes were wet at the memory, and I rubbed the tears away. I couldn't remember the last time I actually cried.

"Lost in thought?"

"Sorry. Yeah."

"Can I help, bro?"

"You found Jack, you've done everything I couldn't."

Falcon bumped my shoulder, returned the necklace, and laid down on his bed. "For the record, I still think involving her was a bad idea."

"It probably is, but unless I can find someone else blessed by the Seer she's my only option."

To my knowledge, there hasn't been a human with the Seer's blessing, ever. It allowed the blessed one to see the future, decode the past, look into the hearts and minds of those around them, and send souls to rest in Sanctum. The Seer's blessing was inherited: only once a priestess died, could the magic move to its next host. Those with the blessing were trained directly by the Seer herself, and then would be called Priestess. Snapdragon was the last priestess I'd known. But the Seer did not walk the Earth. She stayed in Obius, the realm that She watched over. Could She have foreseen that Her next priestess would be out of Her reach? How many before Jack died without ever knowing who they were?

My phone lit up with a message. Falcon sat up, smirking.

"It's a bad idea to get too close to her, and you know it."

"It's just a message."

"For now," he said. Falcon flopped back down, flat on his back, with his ankles crossed. He reminded me of a corpse every time he went to sleep; in Obius, that was the traditional funeral position. I prayed that someone had laid Snapdragon to rest when she died.

How's that heartache?

Gone, thanks to you.

I pictured the tinge of blush on Jack's cheeks. I remembered the prophecy from ages ago: *Fated to love are the King and the Priestess, always at arms' length, never hand in hand.* The soft magic that Jack added to the locket pulsed through it, helping that fragment of my heart remember how to beat. My phone buzzed again with a little green heart emoji. It felt like the prophecy of old was trying to fulfill itself again.

FALCON

Diego took a shower, and I stepped out for a bit. I drove out to an old park in Virginia Beach. My GPS told me it was a twenty minute drive, and with the time of night and season, it should be deserted. The online photos looked promising for that too: overgrown and well-worn. Exactly what I needed. With no traffic, I beat my navigation's timeline by seven minutes. It was dark, empty, and inundated with flora.

Perfect.

This town was nice. Being so close to the ocean had to be a magical rush. Port cities were crawling with alchemists. They'd creep into the containers, stow away on ships, and stuff magical wares into legit shipping to get them up and down a coast. Myrtle Beach was my go-to for a black market, but I'd add this place to the list for sure. The vibe here was good. I needed a place to put some roots down, and maybe one day, it'll be here.

I spent a decent amount of time in Virginia when I was a kid, but much more inland. I grew up in the mountains, practicing alchemy while standing on the edges of old, ancient mountains. I loved the mountains more than anywhere else. But when I couldn't go, I'd find a field of trees. D needed some alone time with that locket. Now that he had a living piece of himself, he'd found a little hope. I couldn't let that die.

Sigils were simple when you understood the concept. Draw carefully, pray carefully, and cast with precision. Stay focused and nothing gets summoned, opened, or killed accidentally. I pulled off my boots and socks, walking barefoot into the clearing. The ground was bitter cold, and I was keenly aware of every nerve in my feet. Still, I needed the direct connection to the earth, to the links, to other living beings. I sucked in a breath and replayed my ma's words when she taught me to work with sigils.

Start with your barriers, love. Always protect yourself.

Palm to palm, hands touching my heart. Magic swelled in me, and I let it wrap around my physical self, encasing me in a layer of magic. Energy wrapped itself around each bone; it started in my chest, around my ribs, snaked through my spine, shoulders, leg bones, down to my fingers and toes. Same process as standard issue alchemy.

Set your intention.

I pictured the Judge; the scales, ever balanced, ever watching.

Use your magic to draw your sigils, magic knows how curved a line needs to be better than your hands do.

I casted magic to my north and then south, to my west and my east.

Move through it, Falcon. Feel the sigil, write it in magic, write it with your body.

Three steps forward, sweeping my left foot through the grass to make the semi circle. Kneel. Reach forward with both hands, dragging my fingers through the dirt, down and to each side, making the main base of the scales. Up, step back, right foot sweep in another semi circle.

Exhale. Inhale. Exhale.

"Judge me fairly, though I am just a man. I balance the scales in your honor."

The sigil lit up faintly, but it surged through me. I listened as close as I could, waiting for guidance, waiting for the Judge to speak to me.

Then the words crashed through my mind, and I was left on the grass, trying to catch my breath.

Do not let the Shatterer return to Obius.

Do not let the Shatterer return to Obius.

Do not let the Shatterer return to Obius.

"But–"

Do not let the Shatterer return to Obius.

"Fuck." My knees ached, my lungs burned, and the ear-splitting headache that was forming was threatening to make me black out. I grabbed my shoes and headed back to my Jeep before the headache got too bad. That was not the message I had been waiting for.

THROUGH THE VEIL

I slaughtered the rest of the pixies. He was not *listening*. My errand boy. So I sent the message louder.

She would not stop casting. She was bringing him to life.

How was that even *possible?*

I snapped neck after neck. Their bodies were so small, so frail. Pixies were pure magic; little elemental beings that formed from ember sparks, perfect dew drops, rounded pebbles, and strong gusts of wind. As long as the realm breathed, there would be an endless supply of them.

They *will* listen.

Forging arrow after arrow, I flung them up, spelling their route straight through the veil, straight to Earth.

I fell back on the throne, utterly spent. They will listen.

JACK

Abuela was at her bead shop, just like Mari predicted. She fussed at a display, tilting and tweaking it until she was satisfied. *Oh jeez, was that what I looked like? Constantly rearranging things?* She had Mari in a hug before anyone had a chance to say hello, and had a loving death grip on my hand. Her eyes had turned to a gray-brown over the years, losing some of the vibrancy that I knew was there. I could see her as a young woman, full of fire. Now she was ancient and burned even brighter.

"Fleeing the crime scene, I see," she said. Abuela had made some snickerdoodle cookies, a coffee crumble, and had already packed us each a tiny thermos of coffee. She knew we were coming.

"*We* didn't commit any crimes," Mari said.

Abuela's eyebrow shot straight up, and she cackled. She patted Mari's cheek and winked at me. I picked up one of her business cards at the register. *Get Beady*, owner Jacinta Reyes. I laughed too.

"Jacinta?"

"Si."

"How many names do you have?" I asked as I put the card back.

"As many as I need," Abuela said. "Now, why are you in the OBX? What's happened in the three days since I sent you on your way, child?"

Mari and I gave her the unabridged version of events. Abuela nodded and tsked and hmmed while listening, not interrupting once.

"I felt the realms open a hair, but I didn't think it was possible. I knew your mama had some juice, but I woulda bet cash it was that damn cat of yours, child. Cheeky little furball, that one."

"Right?" Mari added.

"So. What can I do? I won't open the realms, if that's what you're asking," Abuela said. Mari's shoulders sagged, but she didn't say anything.

"Wait–"

"Can't or won't?" I asked. Abuela had more magic in her pinky than I did in my whole body, but I caught the hint of anger in her eyes before she got face back to neutral. Her thoughts were wild, not in English, and too fast for me to hear them. A wall of silence hit me after a couple of seconds. She knew what I was doing.

"Is there a difference when the answer is still no?"

"Yes!" we said in unison.

"But you could help him–"

"Could, but won't. He has been judged by the Goddesses. That should be enough for all of you."

"But he's suffering," Mari said.

"Oh Marigold, don't weep for the wicked."

Abuela patted Mari's hand, and tugged on one of her curls. The shop wouldn't open for another good hour. Open times were more of a suggestion down here, especially during the off season. I ran my fingers over some of the beads all in their little compartments. They were tiny artifacts.

"These have been made with alchemy? I thought you didn't sell anything with magic here?" I asked.

"Some. Not enough for a regular human to feel. An alchemist might pick up on it, but they'd need to be paying attention. Have you been paying attention, Jack?"

"I... think so? To what?"

"Everything, child. Everything."

"What do we need to do?" Mari asked.

"Child, I'm not a horoscope or a magic eight ball, why are you asking me?"

"Why won't you help me find the pieces of his heart?" The words came out as a whisper, much softer than I wanted them to be. I wanted to sound like a lion, not a mouse, and here I was squeaking nonetheless.

"Jack Hawthorne, I know everything. The fae one... He's very broken. He needs more than just some glue to put him back together, do you understand? He won't be fixed with just the act of fixing. He needs to mend. And atone. And Goddess knows he needs to *pray*. He's dangerous even if he don't wanna be. Especially 'cause he doesn't wanna be."

She smoothed the apron around her waist. It both suited her and looked ridiculous. White, frilly, frayed. There were pockets near the top seam that were worn, and threadbare. Her fingers twisted them, moving fast for arthritic hands.

"What should I do?"

"You have to help him, of course. But you already knew that, child." Abuela pulled out two bracelets; matching and made with leather and beads. She gave them to me, and as I started to hand one to Mari, she stopped me. "This is not for Mari. This is for you and him. You need a neutral link. Something to pull from that isn't your soul. You need a way to connect when you are not connected. Do you understand?"

I nodded. The magic tingled from the bracelets, and I really did understand her. I could already feel them trying to merge together, trying to stay connected to each other. The memory of Diego holding me to shield from the chaos in my store rushed back to me. Thinking of him reminded me of the smell of his skin, of sandalwood and summer rain.

"Abuela—"

"Marigold, I told you that you would be a shield. Shields are designed to protect, but not be destroyed. Protect yourself too."

"So, you aren't going to help us," I said finally. Abuela shook her head, and smiled. She grabbed a snickerdoodle from the mound of cookies.

"I'm not interfering. This is not my story, child. This is not my path to walk."

There was a pounding on a window. *Thud, thud, thud.* Mari froze. I froze. Abuela sighed. The thuds got louder, heavier. Nothing at the front windows. Mari opened the door to Abuela's back room, and then we all froze.

"What in..." Abuela started.

An entire flock of tiny, bird-like animals pecked and thudded and flung themselves at the small kitchen window.

"They're–"

"Dead," I said.

"Ish," Mari added.

"What nightmare have you raised? What have you done to those souls!" Abuela shouted, suddenly furious. Her magic wrapped around her like a cocoon, and her aura had turned from its lovely, stable forest green to red. I'd never seen red magic before.

"It's not us!" Mari said.

"Then it's the Shatterer. He's done this. *He will be punished!*" she shouted, flinging magic out the windows at the fae birds. The birds stopped pecking at the window, their bodies dropping, now fully inanimate. The bodies turned to dust, just like when Mama had used death magic, and a chill ran through me.

"They were attacking him too!" I yelled back. Abuela stopped, turning to watch me fully. I didn't have a fight or flight response; I just froze. Her rage was all consuming, much like Diego's sadness. The glimpse I saw earlier reared itself fully now. The anger pouring from her clouded my

senses, and the bracelet tightened on my wrist. The charms on it, a flower
and a crest of some kind, jingled at the clasp.

"These beasts went after the Shatterer? You're sure?"

"Yes," Mari said, "They wanted Jack too, but they really wanted him. It
was like they could only see the two of them."

"Leave. I have work to do."

"Abuela—"

"Leave, Marigold," she spat the words out and Mari flinched. "You do
not need to be here for this, and you need to be focused on getting your
magic back in shape. I've got more amber ready for you. Try not to break
them so fast this time. Now, go." Abuela stood taller; her eyes were closer
to mine now, and the years seemed to melt off of her. Just like her name,
another part of her that she changed so easily. Her hair was less silver, more
black. The lines around her eyes had lessened. Abuela marched us to the
door, her goodie bags pressing firmly into our backs. As she passed each row
of beads, some floated up behind her, shimmering green and gold. They
danced in the light, I knew they wanted us to leave too. Mari freaked a little
from all of the beads in the air, but she allowed herself to be pushed out of
the shop. She said nothing, looked at nothing.

A vision danced at the edges of my eyes. Little black dots that were
threatening to take me. I grabbed onto Mari, and she guided me down.
Abuela's rage was lost to me as the scene unfolded.

*Deign–Diego–had a sword. It was huge and golden, and sunlight glinted
off the blade. The handle was full of green stones. The sadness I knew from
him existed here too, and it sucked at me even through the centuries. I didn't
know this place; I hadn't seen this yet, but this was a memory.*

*He stood at the edge of a stone path with three arches, all covered in sigils
with their portals silvery and bright. They mirrored each other in a triangle,
and Diego stood at its center.*

Diego rolled his wrists, twirling the sword like it was weightless.

Anxious, his pulse had risen and it thundered through me. He still had a pulse here. He swung the sword a few more times, practicing. Hesitating.

"I won't let this world be destroyed. I won't let my kingdom fall. I won't let Snapdragon be the first to be martyred by the humans. Goddesses forgive me," his voice shook.

More magic than I had ever experienced flooded through me; I was burning alive. Diego had lit the sword on fire; blue and white fire. My skin cracked and peeled, I was dying, I had to be–

He swung the sword and I felt myself fracture. He swung it again, and I was destroyed. Shattered.

The glass and magic of each portal fell at his feet. He was bleeding, dying.

"What have you done!" three voices rang out. The Goddesses.

"What I must," he said. Diego stepped back through the shattered portal to Obius, and the Goddesses wailed. They raged and screamed and cursed his name.

Shatterer!

Shatterer!

Shatterer!

I cried; I was in Mari's car, and I was sobbing. She rubbed my hands, made soft, shushing noises. I sobbed. I sagged in the passenger seat, crumbling forward with my head on the dashboard. Fractured. Shattered. Everything about Mari and her car and the Earth all felt so far away now.

How could he? I saw Snapdragon's face, for once not full of rage but fear. She trembled, clinging to Diego. *"I don't want to die," she sobbed.*

"I won't let you," he said.

Chapter Sixteen

PEONY

Sherwin agreed to move up our date. I needed to drive back to NoVA and handle my caseload. It had been years since I'd been away so long, and if my inbox was any indication, I was going to be buried in work. Jack would survive three to four days without me; Mari could handle her. I wanted space to breathe too. I wanted to process and try to sort my feelings out about Falcon and Diego. Something more than just *Nope*.

Sherwin invited me to his condo for dinner. It wasn't that far from Jack's, but it was far enough. The building was nicer than I expected; newer, more modern than what his vehicle choice would suggest. I was in his elevator, riding up to the fourth floor when I got another text from him. Just a heart emoji. His apartment was at the far end of the hallway, which would mean he would have a better view of the ocean. Sherwin had soft, slow jazz playing and something heavenly on the stove. He was cooking. A man was cooking dinner for me, and I didn't even put deodorant on today.

This is why I'm single, I thought bitterly as I smiled at him. He noticed the quick shift with a coy smile.

"What did I do to deserve *that* face? Your lips smiled but the rest of you was poised for murder," he laughed. He hugged me in greeting and led me into his home. His place was darker tones, still earthy colors, but more blacks and darker woods. Clean lines and metal. Very different from the carefree surfer vibe he showed the world. It made me wonder which one was real. I sat my bag down on his counter, overly aware of his gaze. His eyes were serene, and the more I took in the tones of his home, the more relaxed I felt.

"You're cooking."

"Yea?"

"For me."

"*Yea?*"

"Like. It takes time and effort."

"I like cooking. Sorta like magic, but not as intense." He smiled so breezily, and my breath caught. It had been ages since someone cooked a meal for me. *Do not start crying, Peony. Don't be the psycho girl.*

"P?"

"I didn't even put deodorant on today."

"I bet you smell great."

"That's not the point!"

"So you *do* smell good?"

"Sherwin!"

"Look, I'm no psychic but I can see the mental gymnastics you're doing, and it's making *me* tired. We changed plans. I was going to cook, so I just made a little more. It's less romantic when I admit all that but you look like you're about to melt into the floor."

"No, that was perfect." I twisted the handle of my purse to give my hands something to do before I actually did start crying. Sherwin had a kitchen towel slung over his shoulder like he was the star of a cooking show. His house smelled like an Italian grandma's kitchen, and he had candles. The scents were all forests and flowers, mixing easily and making his house feel like a home. My heart sank again. His home felt more like a home than my place ever had. It was sterile, aside from a few gifts from Jack and Mari. I felt my lips begin to tremble–my telltale sign that I was going to utterly lose my shit–and I pinched myself. Crying on a second date was not going to happen.

"You're lost again," he said. He helped me out of my coat, his hands sliding easily down my shoulders and arms. I leaned back into him, just a little. The contact was quick, but enough for me to center myself. He hung my coat up as he went back to the stove.

"No, I'm good really." I chewed on my lip; I hated lying, even little ones.

"You wanna talk about it?" He opened two beers, handing one to me, then gave a quick stir to whatever he was cooking. Happy that dinner was back on course, he turned back to me and leaned against the kitchen island.

The words tumbled out of my mouth faster than I could process; like I had casted my own spells on myself. Sherwin listened. He didn't interrupt, and his attention only wavered when he needed to flip or stir or add something to the meal. Or when he stopped to stare at my lips. He did that a lot, actually. I felt my shoulders slumping as I finished my tale of woe. This was very much the opposite of sexy, but I didn't care. He listened, and at the least, really pretended to give a damn about what I had to say.

"I don't think we should assume the worst about your mom. Everyone has secrets, P. Still sounds traumatic though."

"There's another thing too," I said, twisting the strap of my purse even more. In for a penny, in for a pound. The dam had been opened, and my emotions flooded through me.

"What?"

"I think my magic is fading or something. It's hard to cast and…" I stopped. I didn't want to get the words out. To tell him or anyone the whole truth.

"And?"

"I hope it doesn't come back." And there it was; the truth that I had never, *ever* dared to let myself think, much less say out loud. The words could never be taken back now, and I hung my head in shame.

Sherwin turned the stove off and hugged me. I leaned into the hug and clung to him. Who was this clingy version of me? He stroked my hair, and I squeezed my arms around his neck a little tighter. There was no judgment, no shame coming from him and I dug my fingers into him. Sherwin consoled and comforted, the pressure of his embrace quieting the storm in my heart like no one had ever done before.

"You don't mean that, but, like, your magic does have more of a burden than mine. I just make plants grow well. Can you control it? When you're speaking?"

"Not… as well as everyone thinks." I fidgeted. Sherwin had gently let me out of the hug, and I wanted to crawl back into his arms.

"Practice with me then."

"Spilling all of my sad secrets isn't exactly what I'd call a sexy date night," I said laughing. My voice was shaky, and the tears were still ready to roll if anyone said anything about it.

"Really? This whole vulnerable hot chick vibe is doing it for me." I grabbed the towel from his shoulder and swatted him with it.

"Tell me your favorite color," he said, shielding himself from more towel smacks.

"Pink."

"Ahhh that's the stuff, learning about each other, having real moments," he laughed, but there was a hint of a growl in his tone. "Let's eat?" His eyes sparkled. Dinner. He meant *dinner*.

"What were you making?"

"Chicken Marsala. I'll grab some plates, can you get silverware? Second drawer from the sink." I stopped him and pulled him close again. He brushed my cheek with the pad of his thumb, so light I almost couldn't feel it. Almost. Heat rushed through my chest and further south.

I kissed him. He snaked a hand up the back of my neck, into my hair. I've been kissed before, but I'd never felt it through my whole body. His hands left my skin tingling and warm. My toes curled in my shoes. He tasted like beer, and I loved it. Sherwin wrapped his other arm around my back and held me close.

"Pea," he said.

"Hmm?"

"Dinner first. Then dessert." He kissed my nose while pulling away, and I nearly fell over. His barrel laugh and the joy sparking off of him was intoxicating.

"Oh, you're terrible!" He flashed that million dollar smile.

"Nah, just hungry."

MARI

Jack and I ate pickle chips and vanilla ice cream on the couch back at the condo. We watched reruns of our favorite crime series, about two female detective-slash-best friends. Jack had pulled the comforters off of the beds and we were snuggled into them. We didn't talk much. Jack was worn out from all the crying. She was lethargic and puffy-eyed.

"I'm going to try to align myself with these new amber stones that Abuela gave me. My magic's been off and I don't think I can really do anything to save anyone's ass at the moment."

"Marigold, I will not just sit back and let you get beat up for me because Abuela made one cryptic ass comment."

"I'm not planning on taking any punches, calm down. More like, I need to shield your magic? Maybe we need to imbue some magic in a sword? I don't know."

Jack's eyes did that creepy unfocused thing for a second, and I snapped my fingers to bring her back to me. She twitched.

"The vision I had earlier. It was um, a bad one. Another memory, I think. Diego's memory." She dug her hands deeper into the comforter–it was about twenty years old and had whales and unicorns on it–and pulled her knees up to her chest. She cradled her head on her knees, looking very much like the child that I became besties with. I remembered our handshake–high fives, locking pinkies, and kissing the backs of each other's hands–and chuckled.

"That handshake is legendary," she said.

"Were you in my head?"

"Accidentally."

"Rude." I held my hand up for a high five, and the rest of the handshake followed.

"Also, are we going to talk about your little inner monologue about Falcon? Because–"

"Oh. My. *God*. Jackie, how long have you been in my head!"

"Too long. It was an accident! I'm still adjusting to the extra magic in my necklace."

I threw a pillow at her, and she didn't even retaliate. She *was* sorry. I smacked it once more for good measure, and let the laughter die down a little. It had been too long since we laughed together.

"Tell me about Diego's memory."

"I have to stop going into his memory. I think it's too much on him, and he can feel it. Like he's letting me see it, but it also might sorta kill him? It takes a lot of his magic to let me see the past."

"Honestly, fuck that guy. We gotta get your life back to normal. Helping him is *after* that on the to-do list."

She curled back up again, trying to force herself to be as small as possible. I hated when she did that. Take up space, be loud, allow yourself to exist! I kicked her under the blankets to snap her out of whatever dark hole she tried to toss herself into. *Don't fold yourself up and hide away, not from me.*

"I saw him break the connection between the realms, Mari. I felt it. And I saw the Goddesses–well, I heard them–screaming. They were so angry. I think that's when I must have blacked out. I woke up in your car after that."

She was shaking, even through the comforter. I paused our show and got her to focus on me. I said our mantra in my head, knowing she'd pick up on it immediately. We needed to reconnect again. All the shifting had broken the link between us, too.

Be my light, my friend.
Be my guide, my heart.
Help me see through the shadows,
Walk by me and never be apart.

Jack pulled me into a hug, and we let our magic connect through our hands and arms and up through our chests settling in our hearts. It was like a magical reset or turning off the router and letting it set before rebooting it. Energy danced through my nerves, and it settled in the pit of my stomach. My magic had returned, and now I needed to learn how to harness it.

"Wanna practice some fireballs?" I asked. Jack couldn't cast any elemental magic. It was harder, but not impossible for some witches. Peony could play with water. Earth magic was my comfort, but fire burned in me, and I was ready to let it out.

"Hell, yes."

"Grab the ice cream."

DIEGO

Falcon came back to our room well after midnight, well after he thought I was asleep. I wasn't. Sleep was a human thing; and I enjoyed it, but I didn't need it like they did. My ears were sharper now too. I heard Falcon messing with the laces on his boots, tucking them into his boots. The sounds of the room—the heater, the swish of the curtains from the warm air hitting them, the clicks of the door as it opened—were fascinating to listen to. Earth was always so muted to me, but having more of my heart stitched together brought the world alive for me too.

Sleep was good for passing time, though.

I wished for sleep. Prayed for it. As enjoyable as the heater sounds were, I wanted the morning to come. Anything for the time to pass until Falcon would be awake and I could politely not ask about where he went and why he was covered in mud and smelled of ancient magic.

It stank up the room, that magic. Falcon was one of the strongest human alchemists I've even known, but he's surprisingly tight lipped about it. He rolled over in his bed and groaned. Falcon's breathing had shifted. He'd be awake soon. I sent him a text to let him know that I'd slip out for coffees and bagels.

Breakfast food was something the humans got right. If I ever made it back to Trellis, I would miss bagels. Cinnamon bagels with cream cheese. Technology was another thing. I had the human world at my fingers, and it was amazing. I'd seen humans grow and change from bloodthirsty beasts and conquerors to artists to scientists and back to beasts again. There wasn't *war* in Obius. The Seer and Her Priestesses foresaw any major conflicts and we resolved them peacefully. We had armies and warriors but fighting was for sport and soldiers were for helping our peoples. At least it was before–

I shook the memories away; even memories felt more vivid, and I didn't want to focus on breaking my heart again.

There was a coffee shop and bakery that was walkable from our hotel. I used the magic of my phone to guide me. Falcon laughed at me for calling technology magic, but it was. It was the human's own brand of magic, and I loved it.

The little map told me when and where to turn, and I let it guide me while I took in the sites. The shop was just across the street, but I wanted to see the ocean. Falcon said that magic churned in the waves, but I couldn't see at the time. I wanted to see the magic arcing through the waves, feel the life of the Earth under my feet. The air was too crisp for my liking, but I went down to the beach anyway.

The waves were calm this morning, and I was crestfallen. I sensed the magic, but it was weak. This time of year on earth was the time of dying, and even the ocean seemed to know that. Everything faded and wilted, and fell until the darkest and coldest days came. Before I met Falcon, I chased the sun. Wherever it was warmest, sunniest, that's where I would go. Obius was never cold or decaying like this. My mother always said that our realm was life itself. It seemed so garish at the time, but she was right. Death didn't hover and linger in there like it did on Earth.

The boardwalk was quiet and I'd already walked further than I intended; I had to double back to get to the cafe, and it was empty when I got there. A young girl with huge glasses and pigtails smiled and greeted me. She looked so young but it was hard to tell with humans. Her name tag read Chrissy.

"Good morning! What can I get you?"

"Hi, could I have an iced vanilla latte, a cappuccino, and two cinnamon bagels, please?" She batted her eyes, pushed up her breasts, and nodded. She was so young. I smiled–she wanted me to smile–so I did.

"Bringing breakfast to your girlfriend?"

"Best friend actually. He's intolerable before his morning coffee." She laughed, wrote her phone number on a napkin, and made my coffees.

"Call me," Chrissy said. Her bravery ended there, and she retreated back to the bakery counter.

"Oh, ah, I couldn't possibly–I am *far* too old for you, but thank you. You made my morning." I bowed my head a little, and she blushed.

"Take it anyway. You're kinda weird but old school manners can be hot. I'm only interested in a weekend, old man." She winked, the blush still staining her cheeks, and I chuckled.

"Have a good day," I said. It was practically a mantra for myself too; it *would* be a good day. A human noticed me. She smiled and wanted to spend time with me, as if I was more than just a mirage or ignored like I was a shadow. The morning sun warmed my face, and I was delighted that I could *feel* it.

I practically skipped back to the hotel. By the time I returned, Falcon had already taken another shower, casted some type of magical scent-neutralizer, and stood with just a towel wrapped around his waist while he tied his long hair back.

"Hey D," he said.

"I brought coffee."

"If the Goddesses haven't, like, blackballed you from well, everything, you'd have the best seat in heaven." I handed him his cappuccino and a bagel. He shook his head as I sipped my iced coffee. "Bro, you know it's like winter right? It's cold? You don't need *more* ice."

"Tastes better," I said, shaking the cup. The rattling ice clinked pleasantly, and I shook it a few more times just to listen to it.

Falcon laughed and grabbed some clothes. At least he closed the bathroom door this time before he dropped the towel. I've traveled with him through nine countries, and several states in this one. Falcon reminded me of my best friend in Trellis, and I loved that about him. Being his companion felt like home.

"I think I have a lead on another piece of your heart," he said.

"Another piece?"

"Didn't you say it was broken in like three pieces?"

"No," I said. Falcon paused and I saw the panic in his eyes flash before he schooled his face. His arm twitched and I could see his scales tattoo. They were unbalanced, but I was sure the scales tipped the other way now.

"Weird. Coulda sworn you said it was three pieces." He finished his routine of tying his bandanas, fastening his watch, slipping on his tennis shoes in silence. He hadn't touched the bagel or the coffee.

"What aren't you saying?"

"Huh? Nothing D, nothing. What's up?"

"You're lying, but I don't know why."

"Leave it be, dude."

"Falcon."

He turned away from me, and alarm bells went off in my mind. Falcon told me everything. Too much of everything, to be honest. He was an open book that someone read aloud and now he had closed himself off to me. My coffee was cold in my mouth, cooling me down. I was warm. My body was heating itself again.

"What're you planning?" I asked. He wouldn't look at me.

"Planning? D, no, I just need some time to think. And we need to get that locket of yours like synced with you and shit so you don't keep going all vaguely catatonic on me."

"It will just take time. It's been a dead rock for five hundred something years. I'm not in a rush." He twitched a little, and I stayed still. This was a technique I'd learned from court; stay still and watch the enemy dance themselves out, until they've shown their hands, too eager to let their plans stay secret. Except Falcon wasn't an enemy. He was my antsy best friend with a hard time expressing anything meaningful.

"You should be. You're about to be alive. Like, *really* alive again. How are you not chomping at the bit for that?"

"What's another week when you've been waiting for centuries? I'll blink and be back to normal."

"Well, if you're up for it, I've got another job for us. We've been side tracked with searching for your heart but we need to make some cash. I've got a few gigs we could start on–"

"Falcon, I can't leave yet."

"What? What do you mean? Jack did the thing. Your ticker is ticking."

"I need her to fuse the pieces back together too. I only have two pieces."

"So there are more than three pieces." Falcon flashed his trademark smile and I rolled my eyes. I tossed him the keys to his SUV and grabbed my wallet. I didn't want to just stay in this room and hibernate, even if that would pass the time the quickest. Falcon was right; I was more alive now, and I wanted to live.

"Any jobs that are local?"

"Yeah, but you aren't gonna like it."

"Falcon."

"We gotta get some wetsuits."

"Wetsuits."

"Yes."

"I hate this already." It wasn't that I hated the water, but more that the cold made everything in my body struggle to function. Wading into a wintry ocean did not remotely sound appealing, no matter how powerful the magic rolling through it would be. My phone buzzed, the generic text tone that Falcon called boring. I needed to change it. It was Jack.

Just saying hey. Hope you're feeling better.

My cheeks felt warm, and I touched my face. I was flushed. Falcon had been chattering but I didn't hear his words. I pictured Jack's face–truly hers, not Snapdragon's–and the flush deepened. I touched my face, and the heat moved through my fingers. I had enough life in me now to blush. My heart sped up and I could keep it pumping.

Yes, I am feeling better. Thank you. I hit the send button too quickly; I didn't greet her!

Hey to you, too. I sent another text message, and the warmth of my face spread down my neck to my chest. I was *alive.*

She quickly sent back a little green heart emoji. I sent one to her too.

"–so if we hurry, we prolly won't need to get fully in the water because it's gonna be cold as fuck. I'm thinking we could pull a Rio."

"A Rio?"

"Yeah, but without us blowing up the boat again. That...was less than ideal. I'm still paying that off."

"That was our first mission."

"Yep. Magic is fun and all but it doesn't pay the bills."

"You don't have any bills?"

"Just that boat I blew up." Falcon was already out the door, waiting for me to catch up. Jack didn't send another message, but I sent her another heart. Red. Not green. *I was alive.*

THROUGH THE VEIL

Deign's power pulsed through to me, and my heart ached. The power of kings was no light thing; it was ancestral, old as the world itself, and tied with blood. Before his mother passed–may she rest in eternal peace–I was careful to collect her blood. Jar after jar after jar. The power of kings did not run in my veins, but with enough blood, I could wield it. Deign couldn't return to Obius even if he stitched his heart back together. He did his part, and his family line would die with him. Deign shattered the worlds' links, and I stayed on the throne. Where I belong.

Where I've always belonged.

My staff glowed, like it did every time I let Deign filter back into my thoughts.

It glowed so often.

The forests and the mountains of Trellis had lost so much of its color since then. Every day a little duller, a few more creatures dying with no place for their spirit to go, or going into a death-like sleep. My tower swayed in the winds now; not enough soldiers left to add their magic to keep the tower upright.

The Seer was trapped in the human realm, and would not return here. It was up to my guidance for Obius to stay alive. And Deign somehow returning would only kill us all faster—nothing kills faster than false hope of a fallen king.

I searched for answers from the errand boy with him on Earth, and still nothing.

"Emerald Priestess, it's time for us to start thinking about the future of Trellis. There isn't enough magic left to sustain us," Arturo said. He was one of the only generals left from before the Shattering. Once Deign's right hand, now he was mine. He was a satyr, like a lot of the former Trellian Guard. Arturo was more beast than man.

"Thank you."

"Snapdragon, we need a plan... something. Obius is dying. We're *all* dying. How have you, of all people, not seen that?"

"You are dismissed, Arturo," I hissed, clicking my teeth.

He turned on his hoof, neighing and huffing as he left.

Blood and magic were so tightly woven together. The former queen's blood was a rarity, and I couldn't just go splashing it on the walls to revive our world. The False One was full of magic. If I could just get the link open enough to bring her here, I'd bleed her until the magic soaked back into the soil and revived Trellis. I would revive Trellis. I'd do it without fully rejoining the worlds.

JACK

Mari lit four bushes on fire and set off her fire alarm twice before I convinced her to stop. She was getting better at modulating the size of the fireball at least. Just not so much with the *aim*. This didn't shock me; Mari wasn't going to win any awards for anything sport related, and her aim at tossing a balled up receipt two feet to a trash can was awful. No injuries still made for a successful practice in my book. It was nice to see Mari smiling though. Her magic was back and stable enough for her to cast again, probably because we were away from Diego. He worked like an amp for me, but not for Mari.

My thoughts drifted to Obius, and what it would be like to cast something there. Obius felt like a made-up place; the birthplace of magic, home to thousands of mythical, beautiful creatures that I could only dream of. Home to Diego.

"You are dismissed, Arturo." Her voice rang through my mind and it shook me. Snapdragon.

"I think I need to sleep," I said. Mari cleaned up the debris from her fire and noticed my wobbling legs but I waved her off. I needed to rest, and I needed to be alone to let my thoughts sort themselves out.

"What did you just hear?" Mari stamped out the last bit of brush that smoked, and sprayed the entire back yard behind her condo with water.

"Snapdragon. She was talking to someone named Arturo? I don't know who that is. I haven't heard that name before."

"We could ask Diego."

"Yeah..."

Visions flipped through my head and I closed my eyes, trying to slow them down enough to see each one. I wobbled more, so I leaned against the cold concrete of her building. It grounded me enough so I could focus on the images I saw. The lingering fire from Mari's fire practice was perfect for scrying.

I drifted and saw threads knitting themselves together. Mama's face. Diego's smile. I saw the magic that dwelled deep in his heart, ancient and amazing. I saw the edges of a sigil–love, or maybe wholeness. It was too fast, the edges too blurred, and Mari's oddly warm hands snapped me back to the present.

"I think I know how to fix the links, Mari. Like, permanently."

"What's the plan?"

"I have to convince Diego to rebind the links first."

"Oh peachy. Lovely. That sounds *super* easy."

"It will be, once we find all of the pieces." The images held themselves in my mind. Nine pieces, three hidden by each Goddess, except the Creator, that left him with one piece to keep him alive. The binding spell. Diego and I stitching the pieces together with magic. The vibrancy of his energy as he became alive again.

Then Diego binding the realms together again. I'd be there at every step, guiding his magic until the links were alive again too. He could go home.

DIEGO

My phone buzzed its generic ringtone again. I scooped it up, my fractured heart beating at two different, equally fast, equally uncomfortable rates. Jack.

We'll be back tomorrow. Come to the shop?

I sent back a thumbs up emoji. Falcon assured me before that this was a proper acknowledgement for agreement, but it seemed silly. I sent a smiley face, then a heart—red, because that felt most honest—and then *Okay, see you then.*

The dots appeared, telling me she was reading and going to type me a message too, and then they stopped. A few moments later a little pleased smiley face appeared. No hearts. No thumbs up. My fractured heart sank a little; it was beating enough for me to feel the sinking feeling of disappointment. I didn't care for that part of being alive again.

"Come on dude, the faster we hit the waves, the faster we're out and heading back for some hot chocolate. My ass is already cold and I haven't even touched the water yet." Falcon trotted down the beach, his arms crossed, holding himself in his wetsuit to retain any heat he could. I refused the wetsuit—they looked ridiculous, and if I have to get wet, I'll be changing immediately.

Falcon and I were part time archeologists, bounty hunters, treasure hunters, and magical handymen. I never knew how people found him, but we were never without work. When we first crossed paths, in Rio de Janeiro, we were both looking for the same thing: a sunstone. He thought it was just an artifact, but it was the first piece of my heart. It was the piece that fit into the locket. After the Shattering, I begged the Goddesses to let me keep the locket. The Creator begrudgingly agreed; She was fascinated with my love for Snapdragon, but She didn't mention where on Earth She tossed that piece of sunstone.

Rio was my home before I met him. I loved that city until Falcon blew through it, and blew it up—if he ever managed to get back into Brazil, it'll be a Goddess sent mission with a fake passport—and I longed for it. Brazil felt like Trellis, people were alive there. The music and the color of the city; it was as close to Obius on earth that I had ever found.

But today, we're treasure hunters.

Falcon's client from somewhere in the midwest needed a specific type of shell. Falcon insisted that they had to be in recent contact with the ocean of their home, so here we were. He showed me a picture of the shell we needed. It looked like a snail shell.

"Moon snails, to be exact."

"What are they going to be used for?"

"No idea."

"And how many of the shells do we need?"

"Baker's dozen."

"And you're sure we can't just, *go* to a souvenir shop or order them from the internet?"

"Look at you, embracing the modern world of online shopping. They have to be in recent contact with the ocean." Falcon took a deep breath, waited for the wind gusts to pass, and waded down to the shore line.

"Can't we just... buy some from the boardwalk and then put them in a jar of ocean water?" A wave hit Falcon, and he jumped. A few long expletives later, he was jogging back up the beach to me. I zipped my hoodie–my dry, warm hoodie–up to my chin, and he swore again.

"Why didn't I think of that! If I knew you were gonna have better ideas now that you're only like one-eighth dead, I would have found your heart forever ago."

"So you've been *avoiding* helping me?" I grinned.

Falcon grinned and pulled off his beach shoes to fling them at me.

"More like not prioritizing. You're cute and all, but you don't exactly bring in the cash."

"I'm a stellar best friend. I once ripped the worlds apart for someone I loved."

"He has jokes now! Oh, man, we gotta get you back up to speed. You might actually be funny!"

"Asshole," I said under my breath, and Falcon wrapped his very wet and cold arm around me.

"Yeah, but lovable. Let's hit up some souvenir stores. I can't feel my feet. Oh, and I want a magnet too."

JACK

Thumbs up. Smiley face. Heart. Okay, see you then.

I forced Mari to take us home that night. We could have waited until the morning, but I needed to be back behind my wards. My magic was unsettled again, and the citrine was only amplifying those feelings. I didn't know what to make of Diego's text, but he said he would be at the shop and I wanted to be there when he came by.

We got back to my place around eleven that night. I tried to distract my thoughts, but they all wandered back to Diego. The shape of his shoulders, the freckles on his nose–when had I noticed those? Was it in a vision or when I saw him last? His curly, soft black hair looked like silk. I wondered if there were scars under all that hair from where his horns used to be. Mari and I had to re-cleanse the shop. Puddin had been hard at work with the barriers and the wards, and now we needed to introduce ourselves again so the magic would accept us.

It took ages honestly, and all I wanted to do was curl up on my own couch with my own blanket and pretend I didn't exist. Puddin said that was my animal brain activating, telling me to return to my own cave and smell my own scents. It was mostly because I loved my crushed velvet couch and sherpa blankets.

Mari and I danced through the wards because Puddin was from the old realm, the magic realm, and insisted we do things *properly*.

Properly was on hour two of dancing and casting. It was nearly one in the morning and I was exhausted. We were both over it.

"Puddin is there any way we can expedite this? I have to pee," I said.

"There's nothing stopping you. Y'all should have been done at least an hour ago." She flicked her tail, laying in the moonlight by my living room window. Peony crocheted her a bed for Christmas, and now she dragged it all over the house to whatever spot on the floor had the best light. My home was warmer than normal, the heat from us dancing and casting making it overly cozy.

Mari drew a circle over her head with her arms, winding down a spell, and her magic sparked off of her. Her magic flowed and jived with her, no longer broken and weak. The amber stones from Abuela were exactly what she needed.

My citrine hummed happily against my chest. No visions, no accidentally picking up everyone's—namely Mari's—private thoughts. Just the quiet, comfortable ease that came from being centered again. Binding yourself to a barrier was like tying knots; the first knot to tie the two together, then a second for strength. I focused in on the wards, on tuning them directly to me, and with each breath in and I tied myself to the barrier. With each breath out, I released a little bit of my magic to make the second knot. Mari felt it, came to me, palms up, ready to tie herself back to me, and me to her.

We laid our palms against each other. Right arm up, slow half circle to the right. Left arm up, slow half circle to the left. First knot tied. With our hands now by our sides, we released them and turned back to back and gripped each other's hands again. Second knot tied.

Puddin stretched, her fur glinting even whiter in the light, "See? You're done. You could have done all of that in twenty minutes."

"Why didn't you say anything!" I scooped her up like she was just a cat and nuzzled my face to hers.

"Because you needed the practice. You're rusty, and Mari's like a firecracker about to explode. She needed to burn some magic down without setting anything else on fire." We looked at each other for fractions of a second, then away, and Mari pretended to be fine by starting some tea.

"You haven't lit anything on fire accidentally, have you Mari?" Puddin's words purred from her mouth, a feeble, fake attempt to growl.

"Not by accident, nope."

"Mari."

"I was focused and well meaning with my minor arson."

"It wasn't like that! It was just a couple cans! We were working on her aim!"

Puddin's claws dug into my arm, and I plopped her on her kitty bed.

"Goddess save us all," she murmured.

"Who wants tea? I want tea. I need a big ass cup of hot tea." I hummed loud enough for Mari to hear and finally, finally, finally snuggled into my couch with my blanket. My phone jingled, and I saw Diego's name flash on the notifications. He was awake at one AM and thinking of me.

Are you home?

I texted back a quick *yep* and added a basic smiley. No huge grins like the one on my face. No starry eyes or heart eyes or silly smiles. Just the standard issue smile.

Diego sent back a red heart. His emoji use was deadly.

Glad you're home safe.

I sank into my couch and pulled my blanket up to my nose. *Thanks,* I sent back, mostly hidden under my blanket. I dreamt about what a smile would look like on his face.

See you in the morning.

DIEGO

Snapdragon was wilting. The season of closing was nearly here, and all of her excess flowers were drying up and falling off. She hated this time of year. Her visions had been getting bleaker; less food, less sunlight, more droughts and then floods. I worried that her visions were more nightmares than anything.

She paced around my bedroom naked. Her breasts were full, the leaves of her hips rounded and smooth, even though she was molting. Snapdragon was the most beautiful creature in Obius. She picked and plucked at every wilted leaf on her skin. The suns had darkened her to an emerald green instead of summer grass colored. I loved when she tanned. The twigs of her fingers had little sprouts too, and she ripped them away.

"My flower, you don't need to pluck those blooms."

"They're dying, Deign. I don't want death on me."

She continued her work, and as she pulled each one, it left a peach, tannish spot. She panicked when she saw the first one. Snapdragon dug at her skin, the green scrubbing off like paint with peachy, light skin in its place. The vines of her hair fell out when she touched them, and she screamed. My body was stuck, frozen. I couldn't help her as she tore herself apart. Her vines were replaced with brownish red hair. Golden hazel eyes.

Jack stood naked in front me, eyes wild and confused.

I twitched myself awake, looking around the hotel room. Falcon tugged on his boots, packing his things in his backpack. A dream. She was just a dream.

Later, Falcon and I hunted through every souvenir store at the beach until he found enough shells. We got some water from the ocean and submerged them. It would take a little while for the shells to soak up the magic of the ocean again, but that was a paycheck coming our way and Falcon seemed pleased.

He seemed distant too, not looking at me or anything in particular, but I tried not to think about that. Falcon was a man that was in constant motion, energy buzzing just under the surface, and lately he seemed... still.

We stopped at the same bakery and ordered breakfast and coffees for ourselves and the ladies. A peace offering. The barista assured me that iced coffees were quite popular, and their lavender latte was also a hit, so I ordered two of each. *Overkill, bro, overkill.* In Trellis, bringing a bounty meant you appreciated the host welcoming you to their home. Falcon said I should let go of my Trellian traditions and buy a normal amount of coffee.

My heart beat at two different rates, and I worked on slowing my breathing, trying to get them to sync up. No dice. Falcon flirted and got us an extra cupcake, then we headed for Visions and Trinkets.

"This place looks trashed," Falcon said.

I nodded. The boarded up windows, the closed sign, the silence. If Jack hadn't told me she was home, I'd assume it was abandoned. "Should we knock?"

"Just text her. It's still kinda early, she might be asleep."

Good morning Jack.

Less than ten seconds later, ***Good morning Diego.***

We're outside. We brought gifts.

Gifts?

Bagels and coffee.

Ooooooohhh!!! Come on up! It's unlocked.

Falcon nudged my shoulder, looking at my phone screen. He waggled with eyebrows. "She's awake, let's go. Bro, you good? You have that goofy smile."

"Smiling is bad?"

"It is if you're planning on sleeping with her."

"I– how could– I wouldn't–"

"I'm just saying. Arms' distance. Works out better for everyone." Falcon was already climbing the stairs, ending the conversation by knocking on the door. He let himself in, leaving it open for me.

"Good morning ladies! Err, lady. Where's the rest of the crew?" Falcon scanned Jack's home, assessing the wards, probably. They were new and strong, and not fully Jack's magic. They let us through easily, happily, the shift of acceptance from them like a whisper.

"Holy snarfballs, I'm glad I didn't make any coffee," she said. She picked up each one, reading the labels, before settling on the lavender latte. Of course Jack would choose the floral one. "Ohh, lavender! My fav. Thanks, Diego." Everything about Jack was warm: her eyes, her smile, the way she bounced from foot to foot, excited about her coffee. I'd bring her coffee everyday if she'd beam at me like that.

"Oh, um, you're welcome," I spoke too quickly, tumbling over my words, "But um, where is Mari? And Peony, for that matter." I shoved my hands in the back pockets of my jeans, just to have a place to put them.

"Home. Peony lives in NoVA. She will be back in a few days, I think. She'd been away too long." Jack's golden eyes blinked at me. They were the same color in my dream. I took in the details of her skin; she had freckles and moles. Her body was just as curved as Snapdragon's, and the memory of that body sent heat through my groin. I shifted, uncomfortable and awkward. Jump starting my heart was jump starting *everything*.

"Are you feeling alright?" I sipped at my iced coffee–vanilla, always vanilla–and avoided her eyes. She truly looked too much like Snapdragon when I looked at her eyes, and then the wave of guilt hit. Only the eyes though, now that I had been studying Jack's features, they could never be mistaken for the other, except the eyes. Watching her brows draw together, suddenly concerned for me, was like watching Snapdragon die all over again. Jack's cat teleported next to the bag of bagels and sweets on her kitchen table. She nosed it, unimpressed, and sat there staring through me. I let my wards slip a little, just enough for her to see that I meant no harm, that I'd *never* harm her. Or any of them. Puddin flipped her tail at me–a threat–and then laid down.

"As long as I don't think about things too much. Nothing dead or dead-ish has appeared since I got home, so I'm taking that as a good sign."

"Did you have another attack?" Falcon asked.

"Yeah, down in the Outer Banks. Birds. Arrow shaped birds? Lots and lots of them."

"Gross," Falcon shuddered. For a man that shared a name with other avian creatures, he hated them. Especially geese.

"I'm glad you're safe," I blurted out. I'd said that before, and my face flushed. I had enough blood pumping through me to blush, and I constantly forgot this. Falcon cut his eyes at me. He tore into a bagel, feigning distraction.

"Thanks."

"Glad we're all buddies now, but we need to talk about finding more of D's heart. He's almost a real boy now, so we need your help to work some voodoo or hoodoo or whatever you do to get it." Falcon talked with his mouth full.

Jack choked on her coffee, laughing. "Hoodoo?"

"Just covering all of my bases."

"Do we have any idea where the other pieces would be? I mean like, can you feel it?"

"No, I can't feel it," I said. This had always puzzled me; it was *my* heart but I couldn't find it. I was completely disconnected from my own heart. A nudge of magic pushed against me and I saw Jack watching me. I'd left my guard down, and she was searching my thoughts. She scanned my mind. I didn't know what she was looking for.

"The truth," she said. Falcon paused, assessing my reaction.

"I won't lie to you. I don't know where it is or how to find it."

"Where have you looked?" Jack asked.

I grinned. Where *hadn't* I looked? I spent the centuries looking at every bit of sunstone that I could get my hands on. I hoarded them. Not that it ever helped, but I still kept them all. Still have most of them too. I had a small lockbox in a bank that I moved from time to time. Once enough time had passed, I pretended to be my own son or grandson, and came to collect the stones and move them to another bank. They were in the Bahamas, currently.

"Most places, I would guess."

"What's with the smirk?" she said. Jack took another bite of her bagel to hide a smile.

"Jack, I've been alive a long time. I've been most everywhere on this planet."

"Took you a while to find me." My eyes scanned down her throat as she swallowed. I swallowed. Her neck was long and slender. She tilted her head, no doubt reading my thoughts, and I licked my lips. For a second I thought about kissing her. She would taste like lavender and she would fit so easily in my arms–

I cleared my throat, "Perhaps I was looking for the wrong prize." Her eyes glittered. The fragments of my heart beat rapidly and unevenly. I *really* wanted to kiss her.

"Or maybe you just needed someone to hone in on finding your heart. Looks like it's your lucky day," she said. Jack sipped her latte, sighing happily, and I wondered if I could get her to sigh like that for me. Her breath against my cheek, the smell of her hair. I was alive again.

"Lucky me," my words came out more as a whisper and a lot thicker than I meant.

Falcon choked on his bagel, side-eyeing me. I took a big swig of my coffee as an excuse not to look at him. I remembered all of the heart emojis she would send me, and wondered if her eyes always danced like this like when she sent them.

"Maybe we can find a spell to look for more pieces, now that we're together."

"There aren't any that I know of," I said.

"Why Diego, you act like you haven't been hanging out with the best alchemists in town." Jack beamed ear to ear. She had a plan.

FALCON

Diego and Jack were doing this weird mental standoff. Maybe flirting? I couldn't tell. Diego had never been interested in another human as long as I'd known him. He liked me, or maybe he just tolerated me. He'd become so central to my life over the years. I think he just had that effect on people; they flocked to him, flirting or chatting or making excuses to be near him. He was a fae creature, and even a broken one attracted humans.

In my gut I knew Jack was harmless, but that didn't mean she'd stay that way.

Do not let the Shatterer return to Obius.

Do not let the Shatterer return to Obius.

Do not let the Shatterer return to Obius.

The words thundered through my head. Her words deafened everything else, and I schooled my face to stay neutral.

She is dangerous. Kill her.

Kill her.

Kill her.

Kill her.

"No," I growled, low but not quietly enough. The Judge's commands were so loud in my head that I was starting to black out but Jack and Diego turned to me, confused. Diego patted his chest, looking pale. Jack's eyes didn't waiver. I forced myself to look very concerned–exaggerated eyebrows, drawn together lips, wide eyes–and patted Diego on the back.

"D?"

"It's nothing. Two heartbeats. Sometimes it's uncomfortable." He lied so easily, so fluidly, giving me an out so I took it. I patted him on the back again as if he was choking and Jack leaned back in a barstool, just studying us.

"You two are like me and Mari, huh?"

"BFFs for life, yep."

However long that life would be, anyway.

The magic that Jack had wrapped her house in made my skin itch. It was strong and durable, and it did not like me. The feeling was mutual. The Judge wanted me to kill her. *The* Judge. The Goddess of justice and balance and ruler of Sanctum was telling me to kill this girl. And sweet lord, I did not want to. I wasn't a killer. I'd never be a killer. It was wrong.

It's Justice. Her voice thundered through my head.

No, it's murder.

Death is part of life. Her death is foretold. Accept it.

And I'm supposed to just kill her?

You're supposed to obey.

Diego put his hand on mine, stroked the back of it with his thumb, easing me back into the present; he was more affectionate with me than with any woman. Jack observed every angle in my face, every line, every micro-expression. My mind felt naked in front of her and I flinched. Was this what the Seer's blessing was? Creepy and invasive mind probing?

"Falcon, are you alright?" Diego asked. He said it very softly, like Jack wasn't even there, like he did when I'd done something questionable, even for me.

"Yep. All good, just zoned out. This bagel is the bomb."

"So you don't have any starting points for Diego's last heart piece?"

"Nope. But I can do some research. Might take me a day or two. You two kids be alright if I disappear for a bit?"

"Falcon, I am several centuries older than you. I'm hardly a child."

"He's not great with expressions, hm?" Jack took another bite of her bagel, laughing through each bite.

"Not at all," I patted D's shoulder once more, assuring him that every-thing was fine, and grabbed my keys from the counter, "Keep your phone on, I'll text you later."

Kill her!

Kill her!

KILL THE FALSE PRIESTESS.

I made some smoochie faces at Diego until he rolled his eyes, and left. Jack waved, the cat ignored me–thank fuck–and I vanished. The words of the Judge left me wanting to vomit, I sat in my truck until my body stopped shaking.

Chapter Seventeen

MARI

After I got Jack home, we both wanted to be in our own spaces. My apartment was smaller, but it suited me. I didn't have any grand plans to update anything in here aside from the air fresheners.

Even in the comfort of my own home, the image of Abuela's angry face replayed in my mind. I'd never seen her so furious. She was never ruffled, never angry. But she was seething in her bead store, her rage like another living thing in the room. How had we made her so upset?

What nightmare have you raised?

She gave us our trinkets and pushed us out the door. I felt empty. No hug. No gentle touches. No tender grandma moments from her this time.

The amber stones she gave me were even stronger than the last ones. It left me feeling a little drunk. I put the smallest one in a wire cage to wear around my neck and tucked the rest of them in my little wooden jewelry box.

I pulled out some candles from my hall closet–long, plain white sticks–and set them up on my kitchen counter. House plants and favorite knickknacks safely out of the way, I took aim at the candle wicks. Magic channeled through me and the fire burned at my fingertips. It was going to work this time. Opening my hands to draw the fire there, little sparks flecked around my palms. I blew on them, and it ignited, hovering just over my hands, not burning the skin but making its presence known.

Fire!

I shot the fire at the first candle and the wick burned bright. Too high, too volatile but then settled. The candle glowed. Nothing else was on fire!

Taking aim at the next one, I fired again. Success. Then the third. The fourth. I held the fire in one hand, forcing the fifth and final candle to raise, to float up. It drifted through the air to me, wobbling like a drunk until it stopped in front of me. I blew on the fire again, this time aiming it at the candle, and it lit up too. The candle hovered, waiting for my magic to guide it.

"Hot holy damn, I *got* this!"

You are a shield, Marigold. Be a shield.

But why be a shield when I'm already forged from the fire?

JACK

Diego wandered through my home, taking in all of my photos, my things. He stopped at a picture of me with my family. He felt like a man that preferred the silence, so I stayed quiet. Before I started his heart piece, there was this sadness in him that tried to swallow me. Now there was stillness, peace. He moved without a sound, walking so reverently like he was in a church.

"It won't break if you touch it," I said.

"Hmm?"

"My house. You're acting like everything is going to break."

"Oh. Just being cautious. I've already sort of destroyed your store."

"Fair point," I said laughing. I'd been purposefully not thinking about my store. The window would be fixed by tomorrow but I'd need to stay closed for another week until all of the glass got removed and the carpets replaced. I plucked at the bracelets on my wrist. One was for Diego.

"Oh, I almost forgot, I have something for you." The bracelet came off my wrist eagerly, and the magic in it practically leapt at him. "Mari's adoptive grandmother made these. This magic is something else. She said it would keep us connected." He touched each bead, each little piece until the bracelet coiled around his wrist and tightened.

"Connected?"

"Yeah, not really sure what she meant. We have phones."

Diego lifted his wrist to his ear. I did the same, listening. It took a minute, but then I heard it. A faint beating. Just like a heartbeat. Uneven but steady. Diego's heartbeat. Each beat wove us together. I could feel Diego's touch. I could smell his hair. I felt him breathing. I felt the blood pumping through his veins, through his broken heart down all of his limbs. The bracelet even smelled like sandalwood now. Diego brought his to his mouth and kissed the clasp. The sensation of lips on skin tickled across my wrist.

"It's a heart link. If needed, we can use the magic in these to find each other."

"How does it work?" My voice was still breathy; the feel of his kiss on *his* heart link tingled against my wrist.

"It's ancient magic. They were wedding gifts ages ago, so lovers could always find their way back to each other. I didn't know anyone in this realm even knew those spells." He smelled the bracelet and the smile I thought was shy, tugged at the corners of his mouth. He wasn't shy. Diego felt all of his emotions as deeply as I did, but they didn't always make it to his face.

His smiles were an uncommon occurrence, not a rarity. *Or maybe he was just smiling for me more.*

"Are they common in your realm?"

"They were, but it's been a long time since I've been there. Might be too old fashioned now." Diego gently grabbed my hand. He flipped it over, where he had kissed his own bracelet, and examined the one on me. His fingers trailed over the charms, brushing them against my wrist.

I was brave at that moment, so I stepped closer to him. He stayed still, a hint of panic in eyes, and I placed my hand on his chest, feeling his heart. Those molten, dark brown eyes were locked on me, and the heat from them shot through me, settling low in my belly. He slowly slid his hands up my arms, settling on my shoulders. His hands held as much heat as his eyes and my skin was flushed. His nose brushed the top of my head, and I felt like he was breathing me in, like I was doing to him. Sandalwood. The stubble on his chin rubbed against my forehead, and I leaned fully into him. Everything in me was screaming *yes yes yes, stay here, stay with him.* I rested my head against his chest and his perfectly uneven heart thumped loudly.

This was a bad idea.

"I think they sound really romantic," I said. The heart link was over-heated too, my wrist pleasantly feverish as I rested my hand on him.

"They are. It can take ages to make them properly."

"Like the locket?" The sadness that I knew so well from him bubbled up for a second, before he pushed it back down. I felt his thoughts–*stay present, stay here*–and inhaled him in.

"Yes, but the locket held no magic. It was simply a gift," he said.

"For Snapdragon?"

"For the woman that I was to marry one day." His hands went straight to the locket. It was hidden under his shirt, but I could feel its presence.

"Which was–"

"Not her. I wanted it to be her, but a Priestess isn't allowed to marry in Obius."

"Why not? That sounds like bullshit to me," I said. I scratched my nails lightly on his chest, and he shivered. Even a world created by Goddesses still had patriarchal crap enshrined in it.

"The Seer was afraid that love could blind the future sight that was given to a Priestess. So no love, no marriage."

"And they... just followed that?"

"Mostly," he laughed. "'The King's Affair', as it was called, was common knowledge. Though, no one ever called it out."

"The King..." my words had trailed off. Diego was a king, but that was a life so long ago. Did I still need to bow? Should I be more polite to him?

He gazed down at me. "Jack, I'm just me. Please, don't look away from me." Diego touched the bottom of my chin, tilting my face up.

I touched his bottom lip with my thumb, and his eyes darkened. They were nearly black and so, so pretty. Braver than I should be, I reached and ran my fingers through his hair, and it was as silky as I imagined. No indicators of him ever having horns. I massaged my fingers into his hair, and he made a little noise, something close to a growl.

He threaded his fingers around my face, pulling me close, and kissed me.

I saw stars, I saw the universe, wide and unfolding forever in front of me. He started slowly, just barely touching my lips. I didn't know if it was the magic of the heart link or just the magic of Diego, but I was consumed by it. We were barely moving, our lips just brushing together like a butterfly kiss, and I sucked in a breath, shaky. Diego stopped, watching for my reaction, my approval before I parted my lips to invite him in.

It was all the invitation he needed. Diego deepened the kiss, pressing his tongue against mine. The darkness of his aura seemed to vanish, and all I felt was light. His hair fell in his face and the ends tickled my cheeks. The heart links pulsed with magic the longer we kissed, and I hoped he would never let go. I sighed into his mouth, and he deepened the kiss again. Diego held the back of my neck, his arm around my waist, and placed more featherlike kisses on my lips. He tasted like vanilla, and I wrapped my arms tighter around his neck. He nuzzled his nose against me, the heat of his breath making me shiver.

"Don't shield your eyes because you've realized who I was. Please," he murmured. Each word tickled my ear, and I pulled back enough to catch his eyes. Magic flamed through them, changing the dark, dark brown back to gold.

"Past tense? You're still–"

"Just me, just a human." He rubbed his nose against mine, and our foreheads touched.

"Tell me who you are then," I whispered. I wished I had Peony's magic, but he promised he wouldn't lie to me. Diego chuckled, and I felt the laugh though my chest.

"What do you want to know?" It was subtle, but I felt the shift of his magic, how he let the wards in his mind fall so I could scan through his thoughts, probe even deeper.

But I didn't.

"I appreciate the open book of your brain right now, but I want you to tell me who you are."

"Just Diego."

"Just Diego? No last name?"

"Ortiz. I picked it up a while ago. I like it." I saw a flash of Diego, sitting outside at a little cafe on a cobblestone street, reading a paper. His clothes were odd, even for him, and the paper was old. Another memory.

"I like it too."

He slowly let go of me, and I missed him already. His warmth seeped right out of me, leaving me cold. He noticed–of course he noticed, he saw everything about me, like it was written on my face–and reached for my hand. He tugged me into the living room, and we sat together on my couch. Diego didn't like being above anyone, he wanted to see eye to eye, and his eyes had changed back to their dark, human brown. The gold suited him.

Diego placed a delicate kiss on my hand before he served me my latte. I blushed at the simple act of his lips on my skin and the coffee in my hand.

He kept eye contact effortlessly, and I had to look away before I climbed back into his arms again.

"Who did you say made them?"

"Mari's sorta grandmother. She calls her Abuela. I have no idea what the woman's real name is. It's something different every time I see her." He slid his arms behind my back, keeping me steady and close to him. I leaned forward, resting my head on his chest. The irregular beat was fast.

"Small world," he said. He wrapped me in a hug then, a signal he was going to let go, and tears pricked my eyes. *Please don't let go, please don't let me go.*

"How so?" I rubbed my eye with the edge of my sweater, feigning to itch my nose.

"This Abuela woman is also Falcon's grandmother, except he calls her Nana. I'm not sure if they are biologically related, but Falcon spent most of his childhood with her. He doesn't talk much about his family, aside from her."

"Has he met Mari before?"

"Not that I know of, but I haven't asked. He's never mentioned her before, and you might have noticed, but Falcon likes to talk."

We sat together, quiet. I didn't know what to say, but I had to say something, anything to keep him here with me. This was right; this was aligned: Diego next me, his eyes so full of wanting and as if he were the psychic instead of me, he interlaced our fingers and squeezed. Electricity sizzled through me.

This was magic.

This was what real magic felt like.

"Want to check out the shop with me? I could use the emotional support, and some extra hands."

"My hands are here to do your bidding, Priestess." His voice dropped an octave and he raised an eyebrow, a wolfish grin spread across his face. I was about to swoon again. I swatted at him to break eye contact and hopped rather ungracefully off my couch.

"Come on loverboy, let's put those muscles to use."

FALCON

Kill her kill her kill her kill her kill her kill—

My head throbbed. I'd gotten a few blocks down the road, but had to stop. I couldn't drive like this, so I pulled my truck over into some parking garage.

I hated parking garages. They were claustrophobic at best, and I had no sense of direction once I got in one. I didn't know what the garage even was for: hotel, apartments, stores, they all looked the same.

The Judge's commands overwhelmed my senses. I finally pulled into a space that wasn't labeled reserved, and my bumper nicked the column. Why was it so damn dark in here?

Vision wonky. Head fuzzy. I've blacked out before–usually because something hit me–and I knew this feeling well. I faded and heard the horn of my car blasting, but was unable to move. My lips felt numb, and I hoped however my face had connected with the steering wheel that it didn't get blood all over the seats again.

At least when the cops came, they'd move me off of the horn. Probably also into the back of their car or in an ambulance but that was conscious Falcon's problem.

I faded.

Kill her kill her kill her kill—

MARI

Someone's car alarm rang out through my apartment complex. The walls were paper thin, and normally, I didn't care. But today, after reliving Abuela's harsh words and getting home, my nerves were also paper thin.

Pulling my hood over my head, I ducked under the blanket and turned up my TV.

Wiioouuu. Wiioouuu. Wiioouuu.

I turned the TV up three more clicks. My nerves were fried and I was skirting the line of being too overstimulated to keep acting like a person instead of a cave troll.

Wiioouuu. Wiioouuu. Wiioouuu. Wiioouuu.

"Oh for fuck's *sake*," I hissed. I looked like a hot mess, and it only fueled my rage. Sweatpants, oversized hoodie, jacked up makeup, and a completely unwashed face but it didn't matter; I was fixing for a fight.

By the time I made it down to the garage, the alarm was blaring so loud it made my skin crawl. No lights flashed in the garage. I walked closer and closer to the sound; some regular dude was about to get a dose of my fireballs. I didn't cast on the regs, but today was about to be the exception.

Someone was slumped over the steering wheel of a green SUV. I'd seen that car before, I was sure of it.

Realization, then panic, hit me. It was Falcon. He was slumped against the wheel, his weight laying on the horn enough to keep it steadily going. I smacked the glass but he didn't respond. I beat on the window some more, and still nothing.

"Falcon!" He stirred a little, but only shifted enough that he was fully pressing against the horn now.

I had to get this damn door open. A spell, I needed a spell. *Think Marigold, think!* Fire built in my hand, the heat summoning itself as soon I knew I needed it. The blast was short, fast, and concentrated. The window shattered, and the glass fell all over him. Wrenching the lock open and then the door, I put my weight against Falcon as he started to collapse out of the seat. He had to be at least two hundred pounds of dead weight. *Girl, don't you be calling him dead weight. No one is dead, dying, or crossing into the light. Wake his heavy ass up.* Falcon groaned; easing him to the asphalt was the only option because there wasn't much else I could physically do; it's not like I could carry him, or magic his ass up to the elevator.

Unless...

"Up, up, and away!"

"Did—did you just try to *pun* me awake?" Falcon said. He sounded like someone had punched him in the gut. He leaned back a little, enough to stop laying on the horn. Falcon eased out of the car, his head in his hands, supported by some shaky knees. I shrugged and offered him a hand to get up.

"Couldn't hurt. Are you okay? What happened?"

"Blacked out. Happens sometimes. What time is it? Where am I?"

"It's like five thirty, and you're in the parking garage at my apartment building."

"Five thirty? Shit, I left Jack's place at like nine? Or ten? Definitely in the AM." Falcon, to put it gently, looked like shit. Which was impressive because the man was gorgeous. He stretched, his back creaking as his shirt rode up, showing a little sliver of skin. I wondered how old he really was.

"I should get back." Falcon's weight leaned heavily on me again, and I nudged him with my shoulder.

"Can you even drive? I think you need to chill for a bit."

"I'll be fine—"

"Come inside. I'll order some pizza or something. You look like hell. I'm not gonna let you drive out of here just to see you wrap that thing around a telephone pole. Also, I sorta broke your window."

"Well shucks, Mari, I didn't know you cared."

"I care about my karma, come on."

Falcon really couldn't walk on his own, and I bore the brunt of his weight all the way to the elevator. Once inside he leaned against the wall, eyes shut, but moving under his lids.

When we got into my apartment, he didn't look around, didn't snoop. Falcon plopped on the couch, his head between his knees, and sucked in breath after breath. I sat beside him, didn't say one word about how he didn't take his dirty ass boots off, and rubbed circles on his back. The touch jolted him up, until he realized he was with me, that I wasn't whatever he thought I was, and let his head sink back between his knees.

"Pizza sounds good," he said finally.

"What's your fav? I love a good Hawaiian pizza."

"Pineapple on pizza is perfection, and anyone who thinks otherwise is insane."

"Agreed. Garlic crust?"

"Yep."

"Wings or breadsticks?"

"Yes?"

I pulled out my phone, ordered dinner, and Falcon reached for his wallet. I pushed his hand away, and the motion of it shook him. "You're a guest. Next time the pizza's on you."

"Next time?"

"It's not like we're gonna fix your boy tomorrow, and I'll be ready for more pizza by then." Falcon cracked that thousand watt smile, brilliantly charming and probably fake as hell, and I melted. It had to be magic; no man has that much natural charisma. And I don't just melt over any ol' man, either.

"Thanks," he said. I smiled back, not nearly as charming, but he relaxed a little just the same. "Do you mind if I close my eyes for a bit? Just until the pizza arrives?"

"Have at it. I'm gonna watch my shows." The streaming service had my latest favorite ready to play, *Love in the Sky*.

"K-dramas?"

"*K-classics* yes. You'll be asleep, so hush."

"Nah, I'm staying up. I haven't seen this week's episode. You got popcorn?"

"In the pantry. Two minutes and seventeen seconds."

"Yes ma'am," he nodded and was already up and wobbling over to dig through my cabinets to find the popcorn.

"Save room for the pizza."

FALCON

I stayed at Mari's place way too long. We watched two episodes of *Love in the Sky*, and ate the whole pizza. I'm a man that pays his debts, and that woman was about to get the pizza of her life in return for helping me. Mari was pretending she wasn't exhausted, but I saw the slope of her shoulders and how her eyes were blinking slower and slower.

"I'm gonna go before we both pass out on your couch. Thanks for all of your help, Mari."

"No problem, glad you didn't die in your car." She paused the start of a baking show, ready for more down time.

"I'll let myself out. Thanks again." She waved and unpaused her show. By the time I got to my truck, the Judge's voice was back.

Kill her kill her kill her kill her—

"Okay! Fuck," my voice cracked. I sat in my truck and banged my head against the headrest. "Okay," I said again, barely a whisper.

Another piece of the Shatterer's heart has already been found. You know where it is.

You know* who *it is.

"What?"

You already know her name. Jack Hawthorne.

Jack Hawthorne.

Jack Hawthorne.

Jack is his heart. And he needs it back.

DIEGO

The day had turned to evening, and the sun was setting. Falcon wasn't answering his phone and had too many protection spells and hiding spells wrapped around himself for me to find him. Jack couldn't either. I worried, but not enough to leave her company. Last night's dream was too fresh in my mind, and the memory of Jack in my arms still lingered on my skin. I tried to memorize every detail, every difference. She was different, I could see that now. Her body was so warm, her lips velvety even in the harshness of this winter chill–

Jack buzzed around, jittery from her coffee and fussing over every display, every item in the shop. Her home and shop was quiet and peaceful, and even though I wasn't sleeping again anytime soon, I felt rested.

I helped her clean, meticulously picking out glass from her carpet, using some magic to help when I could. We reorganized her shelves, the crystals, her teas that we could save, spells, and other wares.

"You have quite the array of crystals. Do you perform alchemy on them all on your own?"

"Mostly yes. Mari helps me source them, and then I usually spend a week or two layering magic. Mari and Peony and my mom add magic to them too. Each stone is different, you know? The magic it'll take, what's best for it. It takes a moment to figure it out."

"Why make them at all if your customers can't cast?"

She smiled at that, radiant and playful. It struck me then–Jack was nothing like Snapdragon. They shared a blessing, but that was it. Snapdragon was serene, graceful, and worshipful. Snapdragon was a forest fire; she burned brightly and lingered. Jack was all those things, I was sure, but she was so full of life and joy. Jack was a sunny day, and I missed the warmth.

"Diego? You look far away again." Her words were cautious. Her voice was warmer too.

"I'm sorry, I'm here."

"What were you thinking about?"

"You don't already know?" I smiled again at her, *because* of her.

"I can be respectful of a man's privacy." She curled an eyebrow, and I impulsively smoothed it down. I couldn't get over how *warm* everything about her was.

"I was thinking about Trellis."

"Do you miss it?" She knew I did; privacy or not, Jack understood my emotions. She relived my memories with me and felt how lost I was without my home. She stopped tidying her crystal stand and searched my face. No magic, just really taking everything in, everything I could offer her. What *could* I offer her? I remembered the taste of her kiss, and prayed that she used a little magic to see how much I wanted to kiss her again.

"Sometimes, but there's a lot this world has to offer too."

"You think so?" Jack's words weren't quite a whisper, but they weren't far off.

"Yes," I said simply. She smiled a little, and then I added, "Bagels are truly a treasure." She tossed a quartz at me, and I caught it.

"Can you grab the broom? I think we've gotten most of the crystals off the floor, so we can start on getting the bigger pieces of glass up now."

She answered a few calls from clients, grinning too broadly while she politely rescheduled and groaned after every call. I felt terrible about the shop.

"How long will you keep the shop closed?"

"At least for another day until the window is totally fixed. Ideally, I'd replace the carpet but who knows when that will happen. Three contractors and no one has gotten back to me."

"I'm sorry."

"For what?"

"This." I gestured to her store, and she sighed.

"I needed a break, I was just hoping it would be on my terms and because I had a beach vacay lined up."

"Where would you go? For this vacation?"

"Honestly? Anywhere, but I've wanted to go to Mexico. I've heard it's so beautiful. I'd like to see the tourist areas and then go a little further into the towns. Maybe even Mexico City instead."

"I've been. I love the energy of cities here. They feel like home."

"Really?"

"Mmm. Rio de Janeiro is my favorite place. I met Falcon there."

"How long ago was that?"

"I'm not sure, a few years? I'm not great with time in this world."

I picked up a couple of her blessed items, feeling the energy in them. Jack's magic threaded itself through each molecule of the crystal. I felt the signature of her sister and Mari too, but Jack's went the deepest. She sat at her little desk, knees tucked up to her chest and watched me.

"Tell me more about Trellis."

"Mmm, where should I start? You've seen it, in your visions."

"Is the forest really a rainbow?"

"Ha! Yes, it is. The trees change their colors depending on their mood."

"Like a mood ring?"

"A what?" Jack cackled. It was the kind of laugh that started in the gut and erupted out. She reminded me of Falcon then—he was constantly finding me hilarious.

"A mood ring. It's just to tell you how you feel, but really it's just a temperature thing. Here, I've got a rack of them. They're cute souvenirs." Jack opened the case near her register, and pulled out a tray of rings. They... looked lackluster. She pulled one out that was a solid band, just the deep blue-ish green hue across the entire thing. She slid the ring on my finger, and I was surprised that it fit. She winked at me. The band had turned a pinkish-purple.

"Hmmmmm   very   interesting,   Diego picked-up-my-last-name-from-a-newspaper-Ortiz."

"What? What does it mean?"

"You must be really infatuated with bagels."

JACK

Diego arranged and then rearranged my crystals. He felt the energies, moving them so they would be more comfortable with each other instead of by color or size or alphabet. He sniffed each of the tea bags, placing them together by scent properties. I'd switch one here or there and he would nod, agreeing to my suggestion.

He told me stories of Trellis, but this time his voice wasn't that low, somber tenor that I was getting used to. He told me how he would sneak out of the towers when he was a child to go running through the forests and how he used to jump out of the windows to scare his mother. He told me about his friends, the people in his court, and what a party really meant. He laughed between his words, and the charisma of a king shone through.

He was polished and proper in a way that couldn't be taught. The timbre even changed. Everything was lighter about him though he'd only gained one more piece of his heart. A chill ran down my spine thinking about what he would have been like before the Shattering.

My shop was back to normal now, save the window. My planner sat on the counter, and I felt guilty for all of the appointments I had canceled. Maybe I could un-cancel them? How awful would that look? The next weeks were full, mostly from all of my rescheduled ones from this week.

Diego stood just off to the side, close enough to peek at what I was doing but not close enough for me to touch him. He hovered just out of sight, just out of arm's reach. He worked so hard to take up as little space as possible, even when he was laughing with me. Now that I could sense his magic and the depth of it though, the air felt full of him. Each breath filled my lungs and I held onto every bit of his magic.

The heart links pulsed; I heard them both beating and Diego took a step closer to me. Half a step. Just shifting his weight forward a little, without pulling back. I was standing on the counter, adjusting some of the picture frames.

Diego offered his hand to help me get down. I took his hand and he pulled me in, grabbing me by the waist and lifting me easily. His hands touched the bare skin of my back and I was on fire; heat poured out of him, and it seeped into me. He held me there for a second, warm smiles, and set back on the floor. My lungs forgot how to breathe with his eyes trained on me. I trailed my fingers across his bracelet. He was inches from me. His eyes darted back and forth, like I had him cornered, but he could step away. He could be the one to break the contact.

The bracelets pulsed again, the buzz from it tickling my arm and racing through my nerves. The shop was too quiet, too easy for me to listen to his breathing and feel the double, irregular heart beat on my wrist, and–

He hugged me. He smelled like sandalwood, always like sandalwood, like when I first saw him in my visions, when all I felt was his sadness. His body pressed firmly against my back, arms wrapped around my waist and shoulders. Diego was a weighted blanket against me, and I snuggled back into him. His hands combed through my hair, taking the hair tie out to let it tumble around my shoulders. I hoped it wasn't too tangled from my bun.

He's not yours to hold!

Her voice startled me, and I twitched against him. It was so loud and so angry. She was always so angry–

Diego let go immediately, stepping back, stepping *away* and I shivered.

"I'm sorry–"

"No, no, it's not like that–"

"I should be going. Falcon has been out of touch all day. That's weird, even for him. I'll see you soon?" Diego had his hands tucked neatly behind his back, and the heart link that felt so overwhelming was so far away now. Like the galaxy in our kiss was now a galaxy between us.

"Yeah, of course." Diego reached for my hand, stopping before he took it and then waved awkwardly. I waved. He stood there, his presence now suffocating to endure, and I turned back to my planner, so he wouldn't see me cry.

"See you later, Jack."

"Yep, I'll text you." And then he was gone, and I felt lost to the stars.

CHAPTER EIGHTEEN

DIEGO

By the time I got back to our hotel, my phone was dinging constantly with messages. All from Falcon. I must have turned it off. The messages came in one after another after another.

SOS

SOF

(SAVE OUR FALCON)

ANSWER YOUR PHONE

OR NOT. I'LL JUST DIE

I called him, and he didn't answer. I called again. Then again. And once more.

No answer. Typical Falcon. Typical, pain the ass Falcon.

I tried him once more, and still nothing, so I texted back, *okay, guess you're dead.* He called immediately. "Took you long enough!"

"Are you actually dying?"

"What? No, I just wanted your attention," he said, his tone petulant and whiny. I didn't have the patience for his moods today.

"Falcon."

"I think I found it."

"Found what?"

"It! *The* IT! Your heart."

Jack's face flashed in my mind at the mention of my heart. Her own heartbeat drummed in my wrist. Each beat shot up through my arm, through my whole body. The magic of the heart link was intense and heavy. The weight of the bracelet with all of the energy surging through the links made my body a little sluggish. I'd never worn one before, but I remember my mother telling me it was the greatest gift of love you could be given. I doubted Mari's grandmother was thinking about that when she gave them to Jack.

"D, did you hear me? I think I found another piece of your heart!" Falcon's voice was loud, jarring the image of Jack's face away.

"What? Where?"

"I'll explain when I get back."

"Where did you go?"

"Doesn't matter. Get your go bag ready. I'll be there in twenty."

"Falcon, it's late–"

"See ya in twenty."

I groaned and hurried into the shower. Jack's sweet perfume was all over me, and the reminder of her was too much to process.

PUDDIN

It absolutely wasn't my place to say anything about Jack's life. I wasn't her mother or her sister. I'm her cat. Her pet. She paced through the store, pretending to straighten the now very tidy display cases. She wandered to the planner, then away, over to the non-broken window, to her phone, tirelessly in a loop.

"For chrissakes, get a hold of yourself girl. It was a *hug*. Not a friggin marriage proposal!" she scolded herself, taking out her anger on a stack of tarot decks. She knocked the stack over, huffed some more, and then went back to resorting and shelving them. I kept my mouth shut, my tail flipping with a mind of its own, and Jack came and scooped me up. I purred to calm her nerves, but it didn't work.

"Diego doesn't seem as awful as the legends make him out to be," I purred.

"Legends? There's *legends* about him?"

"He was a king that damned our world, how could there *not* be at least one legend about him? Shittiest part too is that I liked him. I mean, as much as you can like someone you've never met."

"Puddin... were you alive when Diego was king?"

"Yeah, I was a wee kitten."

"So you've always been a cat?"

"Cat-ish, yes. I was larger in my realm. More like a bipedal tiger, less house cat. My home was a neighboring country to the west. Trellis, his country, was to the south. My friends and I would go there sometimes for fun. Lots of trees to climb."

"Tell me the story," she said. Jack tucked me in one arm and locked up the shop. She was retreating again, and that meant she was going upstairs, behind her wards and under her blankets. We snuggled on her couch together. She pulled up her blanket and stroked my ears. Anything to get her out of that shop, wallowing in self-pity about not kissing that man again.

"Once upon a time–"

"Puddin."

"There isn't much to tell. You know the story. King Deign–that was his name–was a good king. He loved his people and ruled fairly, super nice, the whole nine. He fell in love with their country's priestess. Every country had one, but Snapdragon, was fucking nuts. Beautiful, but crazy, at least that's what my parents always said. She foretold her own death which was weird for a priestess. They lived a long ass time. The Seer blessed and raised them. It took years, so part of the deal was longevity. Except for her. She was gonna die, and die bloody. Her vision said the humans would invade Obius and being the bloodthirsty little cretins that they are, would slaughter us, starting with her. What better way to cripple the largest lands in Obius than cutting down their priestess?"

"So they weren't together? Was she a queen? Like, Diego's queen?"

"Oh no, they couldn't marry. Another rule for priestesses: they can't marry or have kids or anything. They can't have anything that'll distract their vision. A Priestess had nearly as much power as the King or Queen."

"But–"

"See why this was a problem? Deign lost it. He couldn't let her die. I don't know how everything went down, but he broke the links between the realms. Everyone hated him. He ruined everyone's magic. Souls were trapped on Earth or in Obius, Sanctum was closed off to protect the souls that were already at rest. It was hell. The stories about him kept changing. He's evil. He's crazy. He wanted to kill Snapdragon himself. Each generation told a different story, and now he's just a myth. Most folks probably don't even remember what it was like when the worlds were connected."

"Do you remember?"

I licked my fur, fluffing up my tail, anything to stall. Jack waited, patiently, because she was probably a fucking saint as far as humans go, and kept rubbing my ears. "No, I don't. I don't even remember the breaking. It happened so long ago." She smoothed my hair down, my hackles inadvertently raised, and guilt washed through me. I hated lying to her, but she didn't need to know that was the last time I got to swim in the lakes of

Chilijan, hug my family, or spend the day climbing through the treetops. She was already so fragile; we didn't need two broken hearts to mend.

She groaned and stretched out on the couch. "He doesn't seem evil to me."

"He's had a long time to atone," I countered. I doubted that he was ever *evil*, but he was dangerous. He was powerful, and not just because he had magic, but because of *what* magic he had. The truly ancient magic: passed down through the original bloodlines in Obius. And, he wasn't afraid to wield that power either. The stars in her eyes kept her from seeing the threat that he was.

He wouldn't stop until his heart was pieced back together fully, and he wouldn't let her go until it was. I purred louder and Jack hugged me.

"I don't see any malice in him," she said, mostly to herself.

Oh my girl, it's not malice you need to look for. It's love.

CHAPTER NINETEEN

DIEGO

Falcon said the words. He said them again. He paused. He watched my face. It must have said *what the fuck are you saying,* because he just waited for me to speak.

There was no speaking.

There were no words.

I leaned back in the weirdly vinyl chair of our hotel room until it squeaked from my weight. The coffee pot was missing its lid, and the microwave had the wrong time. Everything about this was *wrong*.

Falcon tried to hold my hand, rub my arm, touch me, bring me back to his realm and focus, really focus, on *the plan, the next step.* He kept saying that it'll be quick and everything will be okay and then it'll be over and I'll be alive–

"You can't be fucking serious." I was shaking. My hands. My chest. My feet tapped and clicked in time with each heart fragment. Falcon tried to calm me again, another too light touch on my hand, placating and patronizing, and I exploded out of the chair. I was alive enough for that. Rage bubbled through me; the last time I felt rage like this was when Snapdragon–

"It's her, D. She's the last piece of your heart. It's in her. It's probably what gives her her magic–"

"She's a *priestess!*"

"Says who? The fucking cat?" Falcon shot up too, matching anger with anger, "We don't have priestesses on Earth! The Creator made us and then peaced out, bro. Have you seen a fucking platypus? We're on our own here, D." He threw his arms up and paced.

"I don't believe–"

"Well it's the truth. I like her too, but I love you and I'm not gonna let you die."

"And killing Jack does what? You're going to cut the magic out of her? It doesn't work like that!"

"I have to."

"No, you don't. Falcon, I don't want this."

"I have orders–"

"Whose!"

"Someone higher ranking than you," he mumbled. He moved the bandana on his left arm, so it covered the scales tattoo. The Judge's symbol, a falling feather, was tattooed on his outer bicep. How had I never seen that before? His go bag was slung over his slumped shoulders, and he didn't, *couldn't*, look at me.

"Falcon–"

"I won't let you die. No matter what anyone says, you're not the villain here, D. You never were."

Falcon's fist connected with my jaw, and I saw double.

"Falcon, what're you doing!" He punched me again, squarely in the nose, and I hit the floor. My ears rang and blood dripped from my nose on the sticky, ugly carpet as he walked out the door of our hotel room. Magic laced with the blows, and it left me flat on the floor, wholly unable to move. His sudden attack had left me winded and confused. His words echoed through my head, *she's the last piece of your heart*, and I wondered how she could hold that much magic in her human body.

"Sorry, D, but I need you on the sidelines."

THROUGH THE VEIL

My crystal glowed, letting me watch the earth from my throne. The human boy finally incapacitated Deign. Not for long, but it would be long enough. Jack would welcome him, and he'd do as he was told. The humans were easy to command. They wanted someone to tell them what was the right path, the right choice. And for a human connected to the Judge, it was even easier. Any sign, any voice was a sign from the Goddess.

"My priestess," Arturo said. He stood to my left, always at attention, always ready to serve.

"Yes?"

"What are you looking at?" he asked. He didn't need to know, and frankly, he wouldn't understand. Arturo was loyal but I'd never call him the bloom of a flower. He was the thorn.

"Nothing," I lied easily, banishing the image of the humans in my crystal. Arturo huffed, bitter and low.

"Snapdragon, this has been going on for far too long. I should have done this ages ago, back when the Queen was still alive–"

"Excuse me?" I turned and found a blade to my throat.

"This is the end of your reign." Arturo said. He moved so fast, I didn't see or hear the sword being drawn. The blade pressed hard enough into me that blood prickled up. My staff hovered just out of arm's reach–both his and mine.

"How *dare* you!"

"Take her staff. Bind her." His soldiers, the few left of Deign's guard, poured into my throne room and surrounded me. I didn't need my staff to cast, so I summoned the wind. I called for fire. I drew the sigils of the elements in the air before me, and the guards didn't move, didn't falter.

Nothing happened.

How–

"Magic is dying, Snapdragon. It's been drying up for centuries. We're no better than humans now, needing artifacts to touch magic. If you paid attention to our realm you would have seen this. You are *not* the Seer. You're not even a priestess anymore! Maybe if you took your eyes off of your staff you could have seen this! All you see is whatever that staff shows you." Arturo's arm shook with rage, and the steel of his sword sliced into me. He pushed a little deeper, and I leaned into the blade. He would try to kill Trellis's Emerald Priestess? So be it. I pushed farther, and he pulled the blade back.

"Deign isn't coming back." I held my head high, chin up. My leaves and vines coiled around my arms and chest, snaking their way up to cover and protect my neck from him. The Trellian guard had seized me, and Arturo turned his back.

"It's a loss we'll never forget. You're no queen. Take her."

I shot my vines at the guards, whipping their faces and bodies, staving them off of me. Then I ran. My staff yanked free from a smaller guard's grasp and came soaring back to me. Magic gathered in the crystal, and I shot it at all of the guards. With every death, every loss of strength, that magic had to go somewhere if not to Sanctum; it came to me, to my staff. There was still some lingering magic from the pixies, but the death of one guard was enough.

I drew the sigil of the dancing flame: the Creator.

The fire came, and it danced all over the throne room. The tapestry of Deign caught fire, and sorrow caught in my chest, until the flame burned through his image.

"Don't let her leave! Go!" Arturo shouted commands, the guards now distracted with the flames and I ran. I jumped out of the window, landing on the small balcony two floors below. My knees collapsed, slamming me into the railings hard. Cutting my gown with the knife I hid within the vines of my legs, I got up and hopped over the railings to the enclave over a window. Deign's mother's old room. I leapt again and hit the castle grounds.

More spells to erase my footsteps and open the gates, I fled into the forests that used to be my home.

JACK

The moon was still mostly full, and the night was clear. Puddin slept on my bed, all curled into her nest of pillows like a princess. I snuck out of the house barefoot and went to my garden. I didn't grab my crystal ball, Harold, but I had my citrine pendant. I needed to scry. I needed to *see* again, and be back in control of my visions.

I laid the foundations for my protection spell, tying my magic to the four winds and the north star. *Eyes up, Jack. Look forward. Eyes up.* I felt strong, powerful, and connected. The citrine warmed against my chest, and I stared up at the moon. The heart link warmed too, and for a second, I imagined that Diego was standing behind me with his arms wrapped around my waist to steady me. My eyes felt heavy and my vision blurred.

Then I saw Snapdragon running from Diego's home, an army behind her. *Forward, not back,* I urged the magic. It only intensified, and I heard her breathing hard from running. I saw the sweat beading on her forehead, the leaves and vines of her hair sticking to her moss colored skin. She reminded me of a forest nymph from a fairy tale.

Snapdragon bounced easily through the trees, as if she knew each one and where its roots settled. I felt her energy. She used her vines to climb up to and then through the tree canopies. Pausing, she waited and watched. The soldiers fanned out through the forest and she smiled wickedly.

She was going to kill them all.

"No!" I shouted. She startled, head whipping around to search for my voice.

"You're here? How!"

"Don't hurt them!"

"I won't." I watched as a vine unwrapped itself from her wrist. It sprung lightning fast, around the throat of the guard nearest her. The crack of his neck was sickly and too loud in my ears. The staff that hovered constantly at her side flashed blindingly white and then the trees were on fire. The soldiers panicked and she turned and fled through the trees.

"No..." I whispered. The trees burned. The soldiers worked on casting anything that would contain the flames, but it wasn't working. The fire spread almost instantaneously, and the fae creatures cried out. Their forest would be gone in minutes.

The crystal grew brighter and brighter. It was like a small sun in her grasp.

"Jack!" Mari's voice brought me back to my body, to my garden. "What happened? Why are you scrying?"

"What are you doing here?" My head was groggy from the magic, but the image of the fire was seared in my mind.

"Couldn't sleep, and I wanted to check on you."

"Snapdragon is destroying Diego's home."

"What? Slow down." She squeezed my arms, trying to ground me back to earth, back to myself. Each compression pulled me farther from the vision.

"I saw her. She told me. She lit the forest on fire. The fae creatures are going to die." Mari rolled her neck, rocking back on her heels and sighed.

"Oh goddess," Mari sighed. There was nothing we could do. Once she let go of me, the fire brightened in my eyes again and it was all I could see. The trees screamed in agony, their cries carrying themselves through the winds. Small, beautifully peculiar creatures dropped from the trees and burned up. My lungs shut down. Why couldn't I breathe? I couldn't get *air* to the bottom of my lungs and now my chest sunk into itself–

Mama's face dashed through my thoughts, through the fire. She smiled. *You'll find the way, Jack.*

I snapped fully back, startling Mari. I had to get to Obius.

"Jackie–"

"I have to go to Obius. They need help."

Mari threw her hands up, huffing. "Girl, what are you saying? There's no way to even get there! You don't even know *where* to go."

"We can't just do nothing!"

"I can help." Falcon appeared at the back door of the shop. I had left the light on, and he stood directly in front of it. He had a hoodie on with the hood pulled up, and I couldn't see his face. Fear prickled through me as he purposely kept his face down. He stepped past the threshold and into the garden. Falcon hung back, keeping more distance than usual from us. He wobbled like he was drunk.

"Falcon? Is that you?" Mari said, but she was on alert too, next to me with her magic tightly coiled and ready to strike.

Falcon's typically walled off mind was loud. Thoughts that were not his own thundered through him and me. He didn't have the energy, the magic to fend them off and maintain his shields. He looked awful–rage-filled and bone tired. Everything about him sagged. Her voice echoed through him, through me. He shook a little, trying to withstand the sound. The tremors in his hands made my own hands shake.

Kill her

Kill her

Kill her

Kill her

Kill the false priestess!

He moved like he was wasted. Jagged. Uncontrolled. Confused. Mari inched in front of me, her arm raised protectively. I held her hand and started casting every protection I could think of. She joined, silently building a wall between us and him, strengthening my ties to the stars and to the earth. Mari worked a new spell that I'd never seen before; the sigils were new, and her amber stones were so aligned with her that they hummed with purpose and joy. Mari's magic had returned in full. Little sparks flicked off of her fingers.

"I'll be your shield," she mumbled to me. "Something's not right with him. I was just with him."

"What happened?"

"Dunno, but all he had at my place was light ass beer and most of my pizza." Falcon wobbled more before dropping to his knees. I took a step toward him and Mari stopped me. "Shields go first."

"Falcon honey, what's going on? You're looking a little deranged," she said. I elbowed her in the ribs. His mouth smiled but the rest of his face… didn't. The spells we casted to protect us did not keep the blaring noise of his mind out. His thoughts were loudspeakers, and I couldn't shut them off. My citrine couldn't stop them or ground me enough to listen for anything else.

KILL HER NOW

STRIKE NOW

KILL HER

KILL HER

KILL HER

KIIIILLL HEEERR

"Falcon, I know whose voice that is, please listen–"

I knew the timbre of that rage. I felt it in my core, and it burned. Just like the forest. Snapdragon had cut open her own link with all that death in the forest. I pictured her staff gleaming like she had captured the sun and knew it was her.

Falcon lunged at us, and Mari caught him midair with magic. Her arms trembled as she held him in place but she didn't let go. He strained and fought, but I heard his voice come out as a whisper, *"Good girl."* His body raged against her magic, desperate to get through, while Falcon clapped his eyes closed hard enough for me to see all of the lines around them. Puddin had appeared at my side, floating at eye level. She added another layer of protection, and added strength to whatever Mari had cast. Falcon couldn't push back through both of their spells and the tension lines around his eyes had ease because of it.

"I've got a mission," he choked out. He wouldn't meet my eyes.

"A mission?"

"Diego."

"But–"

"You're his heart. And I need the magic part of you to make him whole. I'll cut it out if I have to." He wouldn't look at me. His eyes were still closed and his fists were balled, with his fingers trying to open back up against his will. Mari's spell finally broke, she crumpled, and Falcon's hands were wrapped around my throat before I realized he was on the move. Puddin clawed uselessly in the air, trying to get to me, to watch over Mari.

The smell of her mossy, overgrown magic seeped out of his pores. His eyes were still closed.

"Look at me," I choked out. My voice crackled, and I clawed at his hands as he raised me in the air. Falcon's face was down, staring at my bare feet or the grass or the gardens–anything but my face.

"Look at me," I said again, a little louder. Mari stayed pinned to the ground just like how she had Falcon pinned. Puddin was gone again. Black spots danced in my eyes, my throat burned from the strength of his hands, and he still would not look at me. I reached with magic, trying to get through to him. *Falcon!*

"I'm sorry, dude."

Let go of me.

"Can't."

Let go.

"Make me. Please."

Be a sword, be a sword, be a sword–

The spell I cast I'd never tried, never heard of, but had seen before from Snapdragon. The vines that made up her body whipped and lashed at her command. I reached for my garden, where I had tied myself and my magic to the winds and the stars. I felt the roots of the trees, bushes, and flowers that I had planted and brought to life, and asked them to come to me. I felt them twisting under the ground and rising.

I pushed as much magic as I could through my body and felt the thwack of a tree branch on Falcon's back. It hit us hard enough that Falcon let go, and the brushes wrapped around me, holding me in safely.

Puddin took that moment to reappear, a tiny fury of claws and teeth, latching onto Falcon's shoulder. He yelped a little but didn't fight back. Mari encased herself in a funnel of magic, all wind and rage–fire lights blazing in her eyes, true fires, cackling and breathing through her magic–and held Falcon down in the dirt.

"I'm okay, I'm okay," I whispered to the bushes and felt the leaves retract, letting me step out from it.

"Jackie!" Mari cried. "Something's not right, that's not him. He's not like that!"

"I know." My throat was raw and my knees were weak. I touched my neck and collarbone tenderly, the bruising already coming up.

"Jackie, he's like possessed. We have to–"

"I know," I took her hands between mine, disrupting her spell, bringing her back to me.

Falcon stayed down. He didn't move, or even attempt to. He balled his fists by his side, and I saw the muscles in his arms tense. Puddin sat on his bloodied shoulder, her claws curled just enough to make the threat of them known. I reached for my plants, and they responded with little shifts in the dirt. *Check on him*, I pushed, and the roots shifted toward Falcon, wrapping around his wrists and ankles.

Alive. Secured.

"Thank you," I said. Mari glanced at me, then back to Falcon. The roots lifted him up and his eyes were finally clear. Finally Falcon.

"What the fuck were you thinking!" she shouted.

"I don't really know. I couldn't think. I just... acted. I'm sorry," Falcon said, groaning. The roots were tight against his skin. I gently urged the roots to let go of him, but they didn't. "Listen to your hash stash, girl. My brain's not right. Keep the binds on until Diego wakes up and comes flying over to play the hero and beat my ass."

"Diego can fly?" Mari asked. I shrugged. He *did* have a few feathers in Obius.

"Fuck if I know, but he's got more juice than he did before so I wouldn't be surprised." He shifted a little, just to get more comfortable. Falcon didn't bother putting his wards back up.

"That voice in your mind is not whoever you think it is," I stated flatly. Or tried to. My voice was dry, and it cracked.

His head snapped up, eyes locked straight into mine, and panicked for a millisecond.

"What do you mean?"

"It's not whoever you think it is. Your mission? It's not real."

"No offense, but I seriously doubt this is something you'd understand." We paused, waiting for him to elaborate. He shrugged his shoulders, trying to get the hoodie off, and I stepped up to help him. The falling feathers of the Judge were tattooed on his upper arm, and it clicked for me.

"Falcon, that's not the Judge speaking to you."

His heart skipped beats and thudded painfully, and it resonated through me too. The panic in his eyes no longer hidden, his breath shuddered.

"What?"

"That's not the Judge. It's Snapdragon. Diego's–"

As if by saying his name, Diego appeared, bursting through the back gate, his nose and lip swollen and bloody. The bracelets that bound us tightened and tightened, and I tugged at it to ease the pressure.

"Snapdragon is still alive," I said. He faltered then, stopping short of the hug I was so wishing for. His arms fell limply at his side.

DIEGO

"Snapdragon is still alive," she said. It stopped me midstep. Still alive. She was alive. The bracelet Jack gave me felt like a vice. My fingers turned purple. I couldn't feel them, but it didn't matter because Snapdragon was still alive.

"Diego..."

"How do you know this?"

"I had a vision."

"You only see the past."

"She burned the forest outside of the castle gates. Did that happen in the past?"

Falcon was bound too, held to the ground with Mari watching nearby. She wanted to help him. I wanted to help him. Jack stood so weakly, her hand raised to reach for me, and I backed up. Even in the low light I could see the bruises blooming on her skin.

"She would *never* harm the forest. That's our *home*," I spat the words out and she recoiled. I made her recoil from me. It stung, like I had struck her, but she was spouting lies.

"She was running from some soldiers and she set everything on fire."

"Soldiers? They must have been the human ones that were going to hunt her."

"They weren't human, Diego. They had spears like I've never seen before and they had horns or vines or fur, and a couple had wings. They were *your* people. And she tried to kill them. We need to get there before the whole forest–"

"She wouldn't do that." Jack's shoulders slumped and my heart raced. The two pieces still struggled to keep up, and each beat felt like a stab. She was so fragile. Jack stood there with her arms wrapped around herself, and I wanted so badly to pull her to me, and soothe away the nightmares she saw.

"I'm not lying to you. *I* wouldn't do that," she said softly. Her voice was so quiet and small. Jack seemed smaller too, like she wanted to fold herself away and never be seen again. She hugged the heart link to her chest, and it felt like her arms were around me again. She waved her hands, a release, and Falcon crawled to his knees. Mari dropped to his side and slapped the back of his head. She held his face to her chest and he breathed raggedly.

The scene suddenly struck me as odd; Falcon was freed but on the ground. Mari upset. Jack looking anywhere but in my direction; the heart link pulsing and pulsing against my wrist. Remembering my swollen face brought me back to the moment. I touched my tender lip, and turned to take another look at my friend.

Falcon.

He stared down at the dirt. His tattoo looked even more unbalanced, but that had to be my imagination.

"Falcon came here to kill me," Jack said, cold as stone.

JACK

No one moved or breathed, and I didn't want to be the only one to break the silence. So I didn't. Puddin blipped back in, hovering next to me, and I stroked her back. Familiar. Constant. Her purr was only loud enough for me to hear.

"Why," my voice cracked, "why did you try to kill me?" Diego's eyes tracked over me, then to Falcon.

"Because she said that you are Diego's heart."

"And you believed a random ass voice in your head?" Mari shouted. She smacked the back of his head again. He just shrugged.

"Why did you think it was the Judge?" Diego asked.

"I've been guided by the Judge my whole life. This is the first time She has ever spoken to me though. Usually it's just my scales dipping on my arm." He held his arm up to show us the scale tattoo on his forearm. The scales were balanced. I remember seeing them unbalanced before, the one closer to his body dipping down.

"What does it mean when the scales are balanced?" I asked.

"That I'm doing the right thing."

"Which is?"

"Seems like *not* killing you, but it could be me explaining, not attacking anyone else, yada yada yada. It's not exactly precise."

"Why?" Diego asked.

Everyone turned to him. Falcon had been explaining–

"Because D, I wouldn't make you hurt anyone."

"I don't–"

"And I don't want my best friend to die," he finished. Falcon's eyes were hard, and the scales started to dip on his arm. Mari watched them tip, mouth open and confused.

"What are you thinking about?" I asked, pointing at his arm. He didn't respond.

Mari stormed back into the house, slamming the door behind her. Falcon bit his lip and watched her go but didn't move. Puddin purred again, her voice in my mind, *I'll check on her*, and teleported after Mari. My neck was sore and my feet were frozen, but I didn't want Diego or Falcon behind the shields of my home right now. Diego said nothing. His face said nothing. He didn't even seem to be here, just his husk of a human body standing to watch us, and that galaxy of distance between us just seemed to be widening further and further.

"I'm not a killer," Falcon said. The truth of his words burned through me, but even still, I didn't believe him.

"Of course you aren't!" Diego yelled. He had Falcon in a fierce hug and a small, tiny part of me was jealous. Being in Diego's arms was like the stars aligning. Falcon was ready to kill for him.

KILL HER

KILL HER

KILL JACK HAWTHORNE

A voice roared around us, making everyone shudder.

"What was that?" Diego said, covering his ears. My heart link surged with energy, two painful beats stabbing in my wrist. Diego's calm facade was easy to see through when I felt the fear in his heart.

"It's the Judge," Falcon said. He resigned himself like a man on death row facing his executioner.

"No, that was definitely *not* the Judge, child." Abuela appeared in my garden now, a long walking stick in her hands like a staff with an emerald on top. "*That* is what we call a problem."

She cracked Falcon on the head with the staff, and he turned to her, reaching for a hug that she did not return. Falcon clung to her, his fingers digging into her thick wool sweater, while Abuela stood solid and unmovable like a mountain. At the sound of her voice, Mari peeked out of the back door, looking like a child. Her eyes were too wide on her face, her knuckles too white around the handle.

"I knew you'd do the right thing, Falcon. I'm just glad she was here to help you not screw things up." Abuela kissed his forehead. The staff hovered next to her. It hovered. The hair on the back of my neck stood up, and I backed away.

"Abuela?" Mari said. She padded through the garden in a pair of house slippers. They would be soaked and muddy before long.

"Come on child, we've got work to do. Someone bootlegged a link between Obius and Earth, and we need to shut that down. Now."

PEONY

I had just settled at home and felt the urge to return to Cape Margaret. I hated that town. The beach was lovely, but Cape Margaret was the seat of everyone's issues. I wanted space and freedom, and the call to come back just hours after leaving infuriated me. Sherwin had sent me a flurry of messages, all sweet nothings and well checks, and even that was suffocating. Another tie to the Cape.

When I turned twenty-five, I booked myself a hotel in Paris for a week. No phones. No connections. Just the buzz of the city and my own company. It was blissful.

Texts from Jack and Mari and Sherwin kept coming.

Ding.

Ding.

Ding.

Ding.

I grabbed my laptop, did a quick search for a flight leaving today and found tickets to Barcelona. One way. I bought one. I'd come back. Of course. I have a job and a home and a cactus to care for. A sister to protect. But for now, just for a little while–

Love you, be back soon.

MARI

I watched them through the window. Abuela held Falcon like he was her own son. She smoothed his hair, tucking it behind his ears, then would trace the outline of his ear. My mother used to do that too, but Abuela never held me that tightly, that closely. The lines around his eyes had relaxed. His shoulders weren't up to his ears. The thumping of his breathing had slowed and deepened. He was safe.

He called her Nana.

I missed most of the conversation, most of the words. I just kept hearing him say, "Nana." She was his *Nana.*

Peony wasn't responding to any texts. I thought she'd like to know that Falcon went psycho for a hot minute, but she didn't seem to care. Jack played with her phone too, waiting for Peony to chime in and save the day.

Love you, be back soon, was all she sent and now calls went straight to voicemail. Puddin hovered near me instead of Jack, and that worried me more than Peony going MIA. Puddin was Jack's shadow, not mine.

"You're shaking," she purred in my ears. Was I? I was. My arms and hands were rigid and painful now that I realized it. My body trembled, and the conversations I thought were ongoing had stopped. Everyone stared at me. I didn't even notice that the others had come back inside.

"What?"

"Mari, breathe," Jack said. I was confused, I had to be confused, because Jack had that pitiful look of concern on her face, like a puppy that got in trouble for dropping a deuce on the carpet. She only did that when something serious was happening or if she was going into vision land. Was I having a stroke?

"I'm fine–"

"You set the curtain on fire, and Diego put it out."

"What."

"And you're shaking."

"Come here my Marigold, my girl," Abuela said. My attention snapped to her but I couldn't move. I didn't want to. She waited. Everyone waited. They all watched me, probably to make sure I didn't set anything else on fire, but no one reached for me.

Not even Jack.

"Marigold," Abuela started again. Jack's magic reached for me then, and I reached back. I needed her on my side, not just *by* my side. She listened and probed my thoughts and then almost like she could teleport, Jack was across the room with her arms linked through mine, being my shield.

Something about her was off. She *smelled* different. She smelled like wet grass–

"Who are you?" Jack asked. Her voice was all ice and poison. I flinched at her tone, and she clung to me tighter. The roots and leaves and plants that had held Falcon prisoner broke through the back door of Jack's shop and snaked their way over to me. They had roared to life, growing like they were mainlining steroids. Jack raised a hand, and the roots wrapped around my feet. Then my legs. Thorny roots gripped my wrists and the stickers bore into me. Her eyes were green.

Jack had hazel eyes.

"Jackie, this hurts, stop," I said.

She cocked her head at me lazily, eyes unfocused but still staring at me. Her lips twisted up wildly.

"No, I don't think so."

DIEGO

Jack encased Mari in vines and leaves in less than a minute. By the time we all realized what she was doing, Mari was struggling to escape. She screamed, spurring us all into action. Falcon and I ripped at the plants, trying to get her out, but every leaf we ripped, another popped up in its place.

"Stop this instant, you demon," Abuela-Nana hissed. Jack's head turned around, almost fully and I leapt to urge her body with it. Her lovely face was horrible to look upon. She looked dead and reanimated. I held her arms down, pressed her against me, and the smell of moss rammed through my senses.

No.

As if summoned by the thought, the twisted souls came. They weren't humans. They weren't animals. They were fae creatures. Fae birds. Satyrs. The wood nymphs. Their bodies were warped; not fully here, not fully elsewhere.

"The links are open? How?" I asked.

"No child," Abuela-Nana said, "That demon figured out to grab ahold of the threads between us and she's opened it from her side. This nightmare is her doing."

"She's *dead!*" I shouted, holding Jack's body up. It–*she*–had gone limp. *No, no, no, no*, I pleaded, but she was dead weight in my arms, and panic clawed up my throat.

"Snapdragon is raising all kinds of hell. She shoulda died when I told her to," Abuela-Nana cursed.

Falcon cut branches to get Mari free, using the pocket knife from his boot. Mari's hands were bleeding but she yanked herself free and Falcon scooped her up and away. Jack's lifeless form flailed against her will and I tightened my grip. The fae souls swarmed her while Abuela-Nana cast a greenish, netted spell around the four of us. The netting was fine and shimmered in the light. It acted like a wall around us until it clung to our skins and seeped in. Jack sucked in a huge breath like she had been drowning, coughing and hacking until she dry-heaved and I held her face, until I was convinced that she was breathing.

"Keeps the little bastards out of your bodies. The four of you are huge power sources, like little beacons for the beasties to follow. Snapdragon has sent those poor souls from Obius here. How in the Goddesses' great names this has happened is beyond me. It's not even something I could see."

"How do we get them to Sanctum?" I asked.

"Oh, child," Abuela-Nana's eyes were red. She shook her head, her gaze fully focused on Jack. "That road does not end peacefully. They are already lost. Best not to go looking for them." She turned, held up one hand, and all of the half dead fae creatures became truly dead. Three nymphs fell against each other, their flowers and leaves all wilted. One of the girls was so young, and so familiar. I'd seen her face somewhere in Trellis, all those years ago. Their souls gathered together in the emerald on her staff. The light within it glowed brilliantly green.

"Nana, Mari is really hurt. Can you help her?" Falcon asked. Mari trembled, I think from blood loss. She shook wildly, and I could see gooseflesh on her skin raised and aching. She held onto Falcon to stay upright, and once Jack had stopped coughing, she was casting healing spells. The little cuts healed on Mari's arms, but she was pale and fragile.

"I'll help," Falcon said. He was an accomplished healer; everything Falcon casted or made was pure brilliant alchemy. Falcon cut the tip of his finger, squeezed the blood to the top, and drew a sigil on Mari's chest.

"Falcon. Do not use blood magic," Nana spat at him.

"Too late. It's just a tiny bit. Mari will be fine."

"What did you do?" Jack asked.

"Honestly, no fucking clue. Learned that spell down in Rio and it saved my ass. Figure it couldn't hurt."

Nana smacked him. "Yes it *could*! It's like I raised you in a cave."

"Well–"

"Do *not* bring up that summer in Tennessee, Falcon." Whatever retort he had at the ready fell silent. We all let out the breath we were holding when Mari could stand without leaning on someone.

"The worst is coming, child," Abuela said with magic lighting up her eyes.

Chapter Twenty

SNAPDRAGON

THROUGH THE VEIL

The forest would be gone in a few more minutes. Wildfire, the spell of the Creation Goddess, was too strong against the feeble limbs and it left everything in cinders and ashes. Cries from the fae creatures still echoed in my mind, but the castle guard was behind me and Arturo needed to learn that I would not be an easy mark. The magic was divine. How it glittered and shone in my staff reminded me of the days before the Shattering. It had been so long since the crystal had been this lovely.

It had been even longer since I left Trellis Hall. The pathways through the forests were murky in my memories now. I closed my eyes to see with magic, but all I saw were flames. The forest still raged, and they had little chance at stopping the fire. But I could stop it. I should. The lesson was for

Arturo, not the whole forest. A wall to keep the flames sealed from the rest of the trees.

The heat from the blaze was close. I'd have to act fast and use an immense amount of magic I'd collected. My staff hovered beside me, ready to work. Large magic required ceremony, even for a priestess, and especially when the natural magic of our world was so feeble. Three steps, the staff spun with me, and I called magic to each of my winds, to the moons, and down back through me. I wrote the sigil for safety in the dirt with the end of my staff, and called the wall to protect the rest of the trees and fae creatures.

A small satyr child watched me from behind a large tree. She didn't even have her horns yet. No feathers either.

"You're safe, little one." She poked head out, braver now. Her eyes were golden and so familiar. The same gold that always surrounded Deign.

"Are you a nymph?"

"Yes," I said.

"My mama said that the nymphs are crazy because that priestess made the king die. She said they all just cry now because she's so terrible."

"She didn't kill the king."

"Well he's gone and now it's just her in the castle right? She must be lonely."

"Why are you here, little one?"

"Cause the forest is burning. I'm looking for my mama. She told me to go to the Emerald Lake if we ever got separated, but without the trees to ask..." her voice trailed off.

"Follow me, little doe. I'll take you there."

"What are you doing?"

"I'm casting a spell to protect the forest."

"I'm glad you're not one of the crazy nymphs. What's your name? I'm Serra," she said, kicking at the fallen branches.

"Snaps. I'll take you to the lake so you can find your mother."

The wall continued to build itself and Serra watched each twist of the magic build and bind itself together. Once it was done, nothing would get through. The forest on this side would be safe. Serra kept distance between us, but stared openly at me. She looked at my vine-laden body, the small blooms on my arms that were singed and the fine twigs of my fingers. My braided vines were likely a disheveled mess, and my tattered gown likely added to her fear.

"Hey Snaps, you look kinda familiar."

"Most nymphs look like me."

"Have you ever been to the castle?"

"Of course."

"I haven't. My mama says that commonfolk used to go there all the time before the Shattering. I wasn't born then. She said if I had been, I mighta had real magic." Her words were so matter of fact, so simple. *Real magic.* This child was magicless? Like a human? My lips curled involuntarily. What kind of beast was her mother that had no magic in this world?

"You can do magic," Serra jogged to stay at my side.

"Yes," I said. My staff floated back to my hand, and I used it to guide my steps.

"Like a lot of magic."

"Yes."

"You must be pretty old then. It's hard to tell with you nymphs," she hopped in front me, walking backward to stare at my face.

"Can your mother cast magic?"

"She used to. She said she had a lot of magic but it's been drying up as she gets older. She always says her well is dry and this world will end because that crazy priestess wants us all to die. I think she's right. Why else wouldn't she fix the links?"

Because then I wouldn't be on the throne, I thought to myself. Serra tugged at my leaves to get my attention, but I walked silently. This child did not need me to give her answers; she asked and answered herself before I had the chance to form a response. She chattered on about how her burrow was behind my wall. How her older sister and brothers were dead now, because of the "evil" priestess. She missed them. She missed her mother. She had entirely too much to say about everything.

"The lake will be coming up soon," I said.

"I hope my mama will be there," Serra whispered.

"Why wouldn't she be?"

"I dunno. Maybe she got trapped in the fire."

"I'm sure she will come." I patted her cheek, soft with the peach fuzz of a babe.

Emerald Lake earned its name from the color of the water. The moss and vegetation of the lake shone perfect, lovely emerald green. It reminded me of the Seer's magic, so I threw a few rocks to shatter the perfect reflection. Serra laughed, thinking we were playing, and threw herself into the lake. The fish greeted her, happily swimming with her and chasing her. Perhaps leaving the tower would have been good; seeing children play was always a pleasure.

"Oh goddess, why is *she* here?"

"No, that can't be her. She never leaves the throne."

"It *looks* like her."

"Can't you smell the viciousness coming from her?"

"Oh, get the child away from her. You know she killed the king and *he* was part satyr too!" The school of fish poked their heads above the water, their beady eyes accusatory and rage-filled.

"Who're you talking about?" Serra asked. My pulse picked up; she was going to find out. But why should I care? I reached for her hand, but Serra wouldn't come to me, wouldn't budge.

"Oh little horn, get away from her! That's Snapdragon!"

"Snapdragon!" The fish all shouted. Fae birds and nymphs peeked from their homes to look at me. People gasped and spit at me. Serra turned back to me, shaking. She searched my face, looking for the insanity she spoke of. When she pulled away further, stumbling back into the water, I supposed that she found it.

"I am the Emerald Priestess, yes."

The fae creatures all came out now, attempting to surround me. They shouted insults and curses. Their collective magic was all so weak that none of their spells touched me. *False queen! Cursed woman! King killer! Why aren't you on the throne! Don't bring your destruction here too!*

I snarled, and my staff glowed. They all shouted to flee, but they were too late. Wildfire answered my call again, scorching the ground around the lake and boiling the water itself. Large, angry bubbles roiled throughout the lake, the bodies of the fish folk now floating along the top. Serra screamed, still cursing me for my reign.

The smoke from the flames soon engulfed her too. Their souls floated up slowly and weakly, and I waved my hands around the crystal. They were absorbed in a steady stream. I'd have enough magic to reach back to the earth again soon with all of this.

Once word spreads of my fire spells, I'll return graciously to my place. The guard will stand down then or face my judgment. With all of those souls collecting in my staff, one after another after another, I took aim at the threadbare link again. Death magic was cursed, vile. It was beneath my status as a Priestess, but it was effective. I needed effective. There were so many trapped, lifeless husks of a soul that were perfect to be sharpened into a weapon. My staff hummed with magic, still buzzing from the Wildfire spells, burning bright with the collected souls the fire consumed.

PEONY

My flight to Newark airport would be boarding in fifteen minutes. I bought an overpriced coffee and settled into a chair at the terminal. Even with my phone on silent, I could feel the messages tumbling in. Just a quick peak–

Seventy-eight messages.

It's been less than two hours since I muted my phone. I bought the ticket and packed up a weekend bag and was through security in ninety minutes. A new record for me.

The latest message from Sherwin sent a shiver up my spine. ***Did a drive by at Jack's place. It's locked down P. Hardcore magic. It's oldschool fae work.***

"Now boarding flight JS302, service to Newark. Now boarding flight JS302, service to Newark," blared through the intercom.

Locked down. Jack–and probably Mari, who were we kidding–were trapped by some old, complex magic. Because of course they were. Sherwin was looking for me. Chugging my iced coffee, I took my phone off of airplane mode and called Jack. She didn't pick up. She didn't immediately respond to my messages.

"For fuck's *sake*," I called her again. Nothing. The announcements called for my seat section, and I stayed parked in my chair, scrolling through message after message. I popped three antacids, and took another swig of coffee. I finished a thirty-two ounce coffee in about fifteen minutes. My head throbbed.

"Final boarding call for flight JS302, service to Newark. Final boarding call for flight JS302, service to Newark." The attendants packed up the gate just as I packed up my stuff. Barcelona would have to wait. Sherwin called as I was leaving the airport.

"I'm at Jack's place, and I can't get in. I'm supposed to have a reading with her today, not just being creepy and watching out for her because you were worried."

"Not sure I believe that, but points for being sweet instead of lurky."

"Low key lurky, I even had an appointment." The smile in his voice came through the phone, and I missed Cape Margaret so viscerally.

"Tell me about the magic."

"It's like a net. This isn't her brand, P. This is old shit."

"How can you tell? It's not like the magic has a sign on it."

"Uhh, hard to explain. It's old though, trust me. Like, pre-link breakage old." I paused, forcing myself to listen and to not force any truths from him. No more forced truths. Sherwin stayed quiet. "P?"

"Yeah, hmm?"

"Are you coming back?"

"Yeah."

"I'll wait for you then. What's your ETA?"

"About five hours. It's rush hour, and I'm coming from Dulles."

"The airport? Where were you going?"

"Nowhere, just keep me posted. Jack isn't answering her phone."

"Not to make you panic, but there's a lot of dead faeries here. Like, a horde."

"They were probably already dead when they got there. Can you still see the... bodies? Last time they faded as their souls left."

"Last time–"

"Keep your distance, I'll be there as soon as I can." I disconnected and called Mari. No answer. I left a long winded, angry message for them both and left the parking garage. I watched a plane take off, and wondered if that would have been my flight.

JACK

Abuela sealed my shop and ushered us upstairs to my home.

Diego kept his distance from me. He ran his hands through his hair repeatedly, and I wondered if he missed his horns, if it felt like he was incomplete. Seeing the curled horns against his head in visions made him feel more real, more so than the human that stood before me. I wondered how horrible the years had been without his heart. The bracelet tugged at my own heart, like someone giving it a squeeze.

Beat. Beat-beat. Beat.

He tugged at the roots of his jet black hair. It looked longer than just days before. Diego scanned over the lifeless and fading bodies of the fae creatures. The little faces of the fae birds, sort of human but definitely bird-like. Groups of nymphs lying together. Feathered dogs and winged cats. They reminded me of dead rainbows. Abuela examined Mari and fussed at Falcon and everything moved in slow motion around me.

Gathering magic from my citrine, I called to my crystal ball and detached from this realm so I could look inward. Magic hummed in my chest, and I knew that it wanted to show me something else. Harold responded immediately, showing me images of Peony at the airport, angry but returning. I saw Sherwin, her not-so-secret boo, hovering around our house on her orders.

But then Snapdragon came into view, and the vision turned HD.

The fire around the lake. More dead fae creatures; recently dead, not already decaying like the souls that landed at my doorstep. Golden, familiar eyes matched the flames and a small child screamed. The fire flashed and crackled and didn't care at all about the children that burned with it.

"Come back Jack," I heard. "Come back please." Something blood-filled and warm touched my back. It was a hand maybe? That would make sense. I was so far away from my body now that it was hard to tell.

"Jackie."

"Shit, is she dead?"

"Jack, can you hear me?"

I heard them all but didn't care. I needed to stay here in this in-between place so I could see the truth of what Snapdragon had done. I saw flashes of another land, somewhere that was different from Trellis. Was this where she was heading? The lake here was blue, not green like the one near Snapdragon. Everything was blueish here. The mermaid, the fish folk, even the land fae creatures. The landscape was different, of course, but the energy was different too. Trellis was regal, ancient. This place was homey and comfortable. It was the dandelion of the world, not the polished rose.

Heat radiated through my arms, my flesh and bone arms, and I snapped back into my body, into my true reality. Earth.

Diego. Mari. Falcon. Abuela. Puddin.

"Abuela, we have to rebuild the links between the worlds. Snapdragon is going to burn it all down. Trellis is already–"

"I know, child, I know. I can feel the flames from here. We have to start smaller than that though. First we have to rebuild him." Abuela gestured to Diego with her staff. He froze. His body went rigid, and the temperature dropped in my home. Frost clung to my living room windows. My breath was visible, but Diego was still *still*. He didn't blink or breathe. His fingers were splayed, the shock of whatever spell that hit him captured in his hands. I grabbed his face, trying to get him to move, to look at me, and he was frozen. His body hardened, and his skin turned an ashen color. He felt like stone.

"What the fuck are you doing?" I screamed. Diego was a statue now. His eyes were stony and flat. He looked like he belonged in a museum, *Died of a Broken Heart*. At that thought, his heart thumped against my wrist and I relaxed enough to breathe. His eyes were fixed and unmovable, but he was staring at me. The heart link pulsed again, reminding me that he was still alive, still with me.

"Neutralizing one threat. We have more lost souls to deal with," she said.

Mari's now signature fireball was building in her hands, and she took aim. At Abuela. Her thoughts were loud, angry, and came right through to me when I looked at her. *This is wrong*, she thought. Abuela lifted her chin, but said nothing.

"What did you do?" Mari asked. The threat of her fire heated the chilly room. Abuela's magic fought to keep the chill in, and Mari burned it away. "Abuela?"

"Falcon, you know what to do. Do the right thing," Abuela huffed. Her tone matched the temperature, and Falcon stood at attention. The light in his eyes was far away, and he marched toward us. Diego's heart beat hastened against my wrist but he couldn't help, couldn't move. Falcon closed the distance quickly, and he was back on me, hands gripped around my throat–

"No!" Mari screamed, throwing fire at him.

The first shot missed. I kicked my feet, trying to kick my way higher and further from his grip. I clawed at his fingers, scratching myself more than him. I couldn't take a full breath.

Abuela's staff swung low, near her feet, and back to her hands, sparking spells around herself.

Mari was on the floor then, face pushed into my fuzzy throw rug, held down by something I couldn't see. I tried to take it all in, but the grip on my neck was too strong and black dots started appearing in my vision. I tried to cast, tried to escape, but Falcon was much stronger than me, and I was blacking out. "Falcon, please," I thought, hoping he could hear me.

He did. He released just a bit, pretending to struggle with me, and pulled me closer to him. Falcon whispered, "Go for the crystal."

He threw me down, rubbing at his hand like I had actually done some damage, and winked. I crawled away, toward my crystal ball, and summoned it to me. Harold came sailing across the room, to me.

Abuela's blood red eyes locked onto me, to what I was doing.

"Seal her!" he screamed, and then Abuela had him airborne, tossing him across the room like he was weightless as he crashed painfully into my china hutch. My few remaining frog figurines were in there.

I had no fucking clue how to *seal* a human in anything.

Abuela had a sickly smile on her face. It looked like someone had poorly drawn a smile on her face. Her cheeks were pulled back too far, too wide, and too many of her very few teeth were visible.

Mari was up and reappeared with fire burning at her command, and she flung it at Abuela. The spell reverberated through the room, the heat of the flames making me squint. Abuela crumpled to the ground in a small, lifeless heap. Puddin had soft, warm healing spells launching at all of us, but nothing touched Diego.

Struggling to get up, I wobbled over to Diego's stony form. I ran my hands down his face, and I wanted him to respond. To tell me anything, to *breathe*. The heart link kept beating, but he was carved out of stone, and tears rolled down my cheeks. I wiped them away with the pads of my thumbs, the magic of the heart link drawing me to stay with him.

"That's not Nana. I think that bitch Snapdragon was controlling her and then me," Falcon said.

Chapter Twenty-One

DIEGO

I knew Snapdragon's magic instantly. It radiated from Abuela-Nana.
She stank with Snapdragon's mossy magic. And it did stink; her magic was
rotten. It wasn't the soft, rain kissed moss I remembered, but the dying,
sun rotted smell of the ancient forest.

Was she rotting away?

Falcon scanned the room, and I tried to cast anything I could to get his
attention. He needed to know. He would be able to handle it once he *knew*
that wasn't his grandmother.

*"Falcon. Don't react if you can hear me. Adjust the bandana covering your
Judge crest."*

Falcon tugged on the bandana, eyes fixed on Mari, on the fire she started
in her hands. My human body ached. I tried to push through the magic,
but it was stronger than mine. Snapdragon had years and years to develop
her strength and I've been living with fragments. She wielded her power

with such ease and grace that she wasn't even breaking a sweat to control a few humans in this world.

When had she gotten so lost?

Jack's heartbeat was steady on my wrist. She looked frightened but her heart told a different story. Even when Falcon was forced to attack her, she stayed calm as much as she could. Falcon's hands were at her throat and I saw the sheen of Snapdragon's magic in him too. She was alive. All this time–

"Sorry bro, I'm trying to fight it," Falcon said.

I had to get out of this spell. It had been centuries since I tried to cast anything this large: the magic of kings. A shattering, but on a much smaller scale.

Great mothers of Obius, Earth, and Sanctum,
I'm here to break the bonds of alchemy,
Shatter them,
Unbind me from this prison.

Falcon noticed what I was doing, and it broke the link Snapdragon had on him just long enough to let go of Jack before he killed her.

"Seal her!" Falcon screamed, and Mari pounced, shooting fire at her grandmother. Abuela-Nana had been neutralized.

Jack scuttled away, going for her crystal ball, and I realized I could move my fingers. She stroked my face, the tears at the edges of her eyes. The heart links buzzed in sync with each other, and repeated the spell to myself, for myself. Then my hands and arms cracked through the stone and I pulled Jack into my arms.

SNAPDRAGON

THROUGH THE VEIL

Walls had been erected to protect what was left of the forest. The lake would eventually stop burning; water had to eventually win out. I sat in prayer on a large flat rock near the lake. The fire was quite beautiful, really. All of the noise from the fae creatures and the crackling of the flames had been silenced from the walls, so I could watch it burn in peace. With small, flat rocks surrounding my larger rock, I was grounded fully. I could finally pray without all of the noise and with a layer of safety.

So I prayed.

My staff stood like a post in front of me, the crystal right at eye level. Between the hypnotic fire and the call from my crystal, I entered the Veil within seconds. Earth was, as always, a mess. I hated looking at it. I hated seeing Deign as a human. He was god-like in his beauty here, but humans were small and fleshy, and he was no exception. My little messenger boy was easy to push; so eager to please the Judge, his goddess. Any sign or noise or push in his eyes was surely from her. The humans so desperately needed something to cling to.

A whisper of Deign's true power itched in my ear, and I lost my focus on holding my messenger. The breaking spell? Then the old woman turned and stared straight through the veil, through my protections, and through my staff. I slapped at the crystal, and shoved magic through the threadlike link to inhabit her body. She was livid, but without revealing herself, she couldn't fight this much power. My staff hummed with hundreds of souls. Even she couldn't stand against it.

It was time to use the wretched death magic again.

Summoning more souls, I commanded them all to Jack's odd home. The ocean was plentiful with its dead, and even the smallest of lives still had souls. Deign breaking the tie between the realms was supposed to be the start of our reign; but the Goddesses blamed him instead of celebrating like they should have. Now with the pathways shattered, the souls stayed trapped wherever they died, instead of finding rest in Sanctum. Earth was overpopulated with souls; humans and creatures alike, and anything that lived could hear my call.

Deign hated this side of my magic. Death magic was hated by all, but especially those tied to the Judge. The power to move the dead from their rest was wicked and cruel, but if they never made it to rest peacefully in Sanctum, did it matter? What harm was done to their decaying soul that would not have visited them eventually? As a Priestess, I learned death magic as part of my studies. To learn *about* it, not to practice. But I was a dutiful student, and I learned everything that was taught to me. With enough power, I could direct the dead.

So I sent hordes upon hordes of trapped and rotting souls to Jack. It would take them days to reach her; drenched up from the oceans, rising from their graves and resting places. The soul had two manifestations: how it looked in life, and how it should have looked in life. Humans were much uglier in their soul states while the Earth creatures looked much the same.

Deign exploded from whatever had him bound, and his words echoed through my barriers.

His head was bare; no horns, no crown. The human with my blessing–*Jack, what an atrocious name*–mooned over him like a child. He was a king and she wasn't worth the moss on his boots.

Why couldn't he just do as he was *told.*

I had my grip on the old woman and spoke through her mouth. She'd hate it. She'd hate that I know her no matter what her face appeared as. The messenger boy still hadn't followed orders. He hovered by Deign, forever his shadow. Some things even time couldn't erase; Deign had a following no matter where he went.

Great mothers of Obius, Earth, and Sanctum,
I'm here to break the bonds of alchemy,

Shatter them,

Unbind me from this prison.

The power of kings, the shattering, made me gasp. He *was* casting it again! My spells crashed, I crashed, falling hard off the flat rock. Deign shattered whatever held him and any link I had to Earth. I called for my messenger, and he didn't respond. My crystal was blank and empty, just a gem instead of a portal. I'd lost my only window to seeing Deign's face, even if it was just his human one. My eyes stung, welling up from tears that I refused to let fall. I'd grieved the king like everyone else; I wouldn't grieve again.

CHAPTER TWENTY-TWO

MARI

Shit got real, real fast. Abuela came around, the fireball disorienting her more than anything, and then teleported the fuck out of Jack's living room. No clue where she went. No goodbyes either. She left so quickly that even Falcon was affected; he pretended he was fine, but I saw the tremble in his shoulders, the rigidity of his hands.

Jack's house was a wreck. In less than a week, her whole home had been trashed three times.

It was going to get a lot worse.

We felt the rift. The link had opened a little more; whatever thread Snapdragon was tugging on in her world rippled over here too.

The jacked up souls—fae creatures?—had a homing device in them to attack Jack. Or maybe Diego. The swarm of little bird girls downstairs was enough to make me gag, but the scaly lizard people would give me nightmares. Their beady, reptile eyes stared at nothing and the nothingness pulled at you. I was absolutely going to hurl on Jack's favorite rug at this rate.

They broke her windows with their dinosaur maws and the glass went everywhere. Pieces flew and one caught me in the cheek, another on my arm. Falcon scooped me up to shield me from the debris, and it was long enough for me to clear my head to start fighting back. Abuela said that I was a shield, but her words didn't mean a helluva lot right now. Fire danced in my veins and pooled in my center. I was molten; I was a sword made for war. Jack was weak, vision cloudy, and tending to Diego. Falcon and I were bloodied but battle ready. I held his hand, pushed magic into him, and he understood instantly.

Once my feet were firmly planted, we summoned the flames.

JACK

Mari and Falcon were going to burn my fucking house down. The souls of the fae creatures poured into my house. I couldn't make heads or tails from all of the heads and tails; their bodies were disfigured and missing. The light of their souls was so faint, they were nearly dust. Diego scanned the scene and sharp pains radiated from my wrist. His heart. He was in pain. I called to my garden again, pulling the roots of the plants to me and asked for a stick. My crystal ball hovered near my eyes, waiting for its post.

I was going to build a staff, just like Snapdragon's–fire with fire.

The staff built itself with the crystal shining pure, perfect gold. It was the same color of Diego's aura and now his eyes.

No longer the blackness that sucked and pulled and ripped me apart, but golden and lovely. His energy overflowed from him, the pieces of his heart finally starting to work together. My staff floated before me.

"Jack." His voice caught in his throat. Dark. Husky. The beating had synced up and a stronger pulse thrummed at my wrist. He took my hand again, turning it over in his, kissing the pulse of my wrist. His breath was warmer than his skin, with his perfect golden eyes focused right at me.

At that moment I knew three things.

One: My house was going to burn to the ground.

Two: The spell to rebind the realms unfolded in my mind as I stared into those golden, golden eyes.

And three: That I was falling in love with this beautifully broken man.

PEONY

The frantic texts from Sherwin got more frequent and less coherent. But then I realized *why* everything was on fire.

It's because there *was* an actual fire.

Everywhere.

On everything.

The trees in the front yard were burning. The house was burning. Firetrucks were everywhere. Uncomfortable to look at, dead *things* were everywhere and in varying stages of *dying*. Sherwin cast spells to make them harder to see, more like a heat mirage. I could feel his magic but I couldn't see him.

"P! Over here!" I hadn't even parked my car before Sherwin was racing down the street to me. He looked ragged. He must have been casting for ages. I jumped a curb and bumped into a tree. The impact shook me, and Sherwin picked up the pace to me.

"Peony!" He yelled my name, pulling on the door handles, and yanked me out of the car. The heat from the fire hit me, and I was parked a good block and a half away. Sherwin held me in a crushing hug.

"What's happening?"

"I don't know, the fire broke out about two or three minutes ago. It hit fast. And right before it, all of those fae creatures just started appearing en masse. I think they're souls. They don't look right to be legit alive. Some weird shit is going down," he wiped his forehead with his sleeve. Smoke and soot stained his face and clothes. How close was he when the fire broke out? Firemen sprayed the house; there was no way we could get closer without anyone seeing this magical shit show. Sherwin leaned against my car, and I felt how little energy he had left. The fire splashed shadows everywhere, and sometimes, Sherwin looked different. Less... human.

"Sher?"

"Hmm?"

"What are you?" I forced as much of my magic into my words. I promised myself no more forced truths, no more compelling my loved ones to tell me the things they wanted to keep silent. He wasn't a loved one. Yet.

"Tired, mostly." He chuckled as he said it. My magic didn't work? He held my gaze, a knowing smile on his lips–always a perfectly infuriating smile–and I realized that he wasn't lying. He just didn't share the truth I wanted to hear.

"How are we going to get in?"

"No clue, babe. The firefighters are gonna be here for a while. I haven't seen your sister or anyone else come out."

I let his words sink in. No one's come out. No one's gone in. Jack and Mari and probably both of the goons were in there. Trapped. Fire everywhere. Puddin too. Trapped. She poofed into being next to me, as if she could read my thoughts. She probably could.

"Peony Hawthorne, *where the fuck have you been!*" she hissed. Puddin's words were clear as day, no hints of purring or growling. Sherwin didn't react to her at all.

"I was going home! I have a life in NoVA!"

"You have a life *here*, you twat!"

"Hey now, no name calling!" Sherwin chimed in. Puddin hissed but then, we heard the fire roar behind us, crackling and bristling with the ferocity that only fire can. My knees buckled but Sherwin had his arm looped around my waist before I could crumble.

"Jack!" I couldn't get the words out. They were lost to the sound of the fire or just lost in me. Jack was in there. "Why didn't you take her with you!"

Puddin flinched. "Because I didn't have the energy. I've been trying to keep her from getting killed all day and then Mari sets the damn house on fire because of the trapped souls."

"Trapped souls? But aren't those fae creatures? How did they get through the veil?" Sherwin asked.

"I think someone in Obius is messing with the threads that tie the worlds. Can't maintain a link enough to do much else, but it's something I suppose." Puddin licked at her paws. They were singed.

Another explosion. The firefighters had to retreat; it was out of control, and they were losing the fight. I jumped back in my car and dug through my purse; my *in case of emergency* stones were at the bottom of my bag. A moonstone and two pearls. The moon called to me, and I had tied myself to her magic at a young, young age. Now Jack and I both can cast just about anything during a full moon. The moon was still in a gibbous phase; it was worth a shot. I put the moonstone in my mouth and held each of the pearls in my palms.

Puddin and Sherwin called my name, pulled at me, yelling for me to stop walking toward the fire, but I wasn't going to the fire. I was headed for the ocean.

JACK

My house burned. I coughed and choked at all of the smoke. Mari and Falcon had erected some intense cube-shaped barrier. It was under our feet, around us, and closed on the top. Falcon and Mari stepped together, dancing through the spells flawlessly. We couldn't *get out* but we could stay secured. It was hot as forty hells in here. Diego worked some spell, but I didn't know what. I couldn't *focus*. My eyes stung and it was so fucking hot.

A spark of energy caught my attention: Peony. She was here. Not in the inferno, but nearby. She was here! I tried to speak with her, to connect, but I was either too weak or too full of smoke. My lungs ached. Mari and Falcon didn't slow down at all. The cube held. It was bright, neon green and perfectly clear.

"Why?" I asked Mari. I pushed the thought to her head instead of trying to speak.

"Because you didn't see how many of those things there were, Jackie. I had to stop them. I'm sorry."

Mari missed a step. The cube faltered for only a fraction of a second, but the smoke came in more. I coughed and choked, my throat still raw from Falcon attacking me. Diego rubbed soft circles on my back, but the contact was too hot, too much in this fire.

"I'm coming, Jack. I'm coming. Get somewhere safe. I know you can hear me." Peony's voice rang through my mind. Mari missed another step and Falcon swore. He had to double up on whatever spell he was working just to keep the cube up.

"Peony is bringing help!"

"How long?" Falcon asked. His voice cracked from the heat too and a cough threw him off balance. Diego nudged him back into place, and started mimicking the steps, adding his magic to the spell. The cube grew brighter.

"Soon!" I lied. I had no idea, but they needed to stay focused and hold this spell before we died from smoke inhalation. The spell that felt so clear to me just moments ago was slipping; I had to rebind the realms. And it would fix Diego; I could tie his heart back together, and make him whole.

My newly formed staff was in my hand. "Hold the spell. I have to start fixing the links."

"Now! Of all times, *right fucking now?*" Falcon hissed at me.

"Yes! Before we all die and I can't do it!"

Holy Goddesses,

Creation, Judgment, and Vision.

I held my staff in front of me and the weight of it felt right. I was connecting to my magic differently. I was more rooted, more firmly planted from the staff taking up more space in my hands and against my body. With one hand, my staff floated in front of me, and the words of the spell made it spin.

Holy Goddesses,

Creation, Judgment, and Vision,

The brokenness in front of me needs to mend,

To join joyously, righteously, and with precision,

Tie together the ends that frayed,

Tie together the paths mislaid.

My staff spun furiously; so quickly I could only see the blur. I grabbed it, halting the motion and jammed the end down into the carpet of my living room. Falcon and Mari fumbled their cube spell and the heat of the fire singed my skin and hair. Diego put himself in front of everyone, turned to the fire and blew. For a second, I thought that I could see his horns, and the feathers on his arms, but it was a heat mirage. The flames went out a little with his airy magic, but not enough to fully quell it.

A vision prickled at my eyes, and I begged the Goddesses, myself, my magic, anyone, anything that could hear me to hold it off. I *needed* to be present here in this moment. I couldn't slip away while we all burned to death.

The vision got stronger, my world darkening, but I saw parts of my ceiling come down. The crash of drywall hitting the top of the cube made us all jump, and I bumped into Diego. My staff fell away, leaning against the neon wall of the cube.

"I've got you," he whispered, "I've got you."

I saw three roads, with three women at the center of the crossroads. Robes and crowns and weapons. One in gold, one in green, and the other in silver. Each color in accents on the other's robes. A sword, a gavel, and a staff. They stood facing each other, the paths still broken, and each woman unable to reach the other.

My spell was working; the breaks were healing, the paths coming back together.

But then it stopped. They searched, heads whipping back and forth, looking for the source of where the stitching together was coming from. They didn't see me. They didn't know I was there. The ground shook more, my progress with the patching instantly fading. The cracks deepened. It fractured and the women sobbed.

I'd lost control of the spell, too weak to keep it going, and the links frayed apart again.

Water hit my face, and I snapped back to my house. The fire was going out, and the smell of the ocean filled my lungs.

"Keep the spell going!" Mari shouted. She danced a little faster, Falcon upping the pace, and Diego standing steady behind me. He held me against his chest, and I felt his heart beating. One beat. One rhythm.

A wall of water pushed through the house slowly. And it was truly a *wall*. The water was squared off, slowly dousing the fire as it made its way through the walls, through the windows, the floor, the ceiling—water came through every crack and crevice it could. The ocean water was gentle. It pushed slowly, methodically. Quenching each little ember before it moved on to the next.

It was Peony.

PEONY

Well, with enough magicked-up stones, I could move an ocean. At least a portion of it. A heavy, unwieldy, wall of water that acted like a cleaning rag on a stain. I shoved at it with all of my strength. It moved colossally slow. This was why icebergs moved slowly; because they were *really fucking heavy.*

I threw myself at the spell. Everything I had. My arms ached. My back ached. Legs. Shoulders. I had a cramp in my ass that went straight up to my neck. The firemen stood back, confused, and probably a little freaked out, by the floating mass of water. I prayed that Puddin could do something about all of the spectators, but that was not the current problem. Stopping everyone from burning to death was the problem. Or dying from some other awful means. Or dying at all, really.

Stop thinking about dying, Peony. I lost some control over the water when I started to spiral, and it collapsed, drenching the sidewalk instead of the house. Sherwin ran over to the firemen, trying to distract them.

He still looked *off*. It was Sherwin, but with a little extra. They pointed at him, yelling, angry.

"Stay focused, you've almost got the fire out," Puddin flicked her tail, hissing the words out. "I'll watch the boy. Hurry up."

I had lost more control of the water, and when I stole one last glance at Sherwin, he was drenched. Whoops.

Inhale, exhale, inhale, exhale.

The water twisted at my command, listening and happy to follow my orders. Just a little more, I urged. I raised the water up higher, fully covering the roof of her house, and I released it. The water crushed the roof, the rafters, the *walls*. It went everywhere, smothering her garden and flooding the neighbors and the streets.

"Subtle, Peony. Very subtle." Puddin hopped off my car and started working recon to get things settled before we made the nightly news. Magic was *not* supposed to be on the news And giant, lumbering walls of ocean water were newsworthy.

MARI

"I am a shield. I am a shield. I am a shield," I chanted to myself. It worked–in that moment, I wanted nothing more than to be a shield and keep us all from burning to death. My magic strengthened with purpose.

The amber stones were in harmony with me and instead of cracking under the pressure of my spellwork, they glowed brighter. I had finally found the perfect piece of alchemy.

I danced. Jack and I had danced through harder spells before, but never this easily. This naturally. I moved, weaving the magic together like it was my only purpose. I was *made* to hold this cube. I was made to light fires. I was made for war.

The cube, my perfect cube, hummed with strength. It wouldn't falter again.

I was made for war.

Abuela's face replayed in my mind. The anger and betrayal. Hers and mine and Falcon's. She walked away when I needed her most, and I wanted to pretend it didn't happen, but her eyes were burned into my memory. That feeling of solitude only sharpened my focus more.

I was made for war.

Falcon tapped me on the shoulder, and I jumped. The cube didn't respond; it was solid even with another misstep.

"Mari, the fire's out. You can drop the spell," he said gently. He was all soft touches and soft eyes. Falcon had both hands on my shoulders, forcing me to still. The cube held.

"Oh." The steps kept playing in my mind, and I forced myself to stop. The magic hummed through me, and I felt tipsy. It was warm and blossomed through my chest and belly and down into my toes. The buzz rang through every cell. I was *alive*.

I was made for war.

"Jack's in bad shape," he said. Falcon's words snapped me out of the buzz. His words were still soft, still trying to ease me down the magical cliff I was standing on.

Jack was half collapsed in Diego's arms. She struggled to stand, her eyes unfocused from whatever vision she had seen. I cradled her face in my hands, then against my chest.

"Jackie, come back. Focus on me," I said. Jack's eyes slowly came back to center, both looking at me instead of goddess only knows what.

With the cube gone, our weight was too much for the floorboards of her destroyed house. They cracked and creaked, any movement set to make them crumble.

Falcon shook his head almost imperceptibly. "Girl, we gotta get out of here. The floor won't hold."

"I'm going to pick her up. I don't think she's steady on her legs," Diego said.

More of the floorboards went out. My left foot sank, going through the floor and I nearly fell. Falcon grabbed my arm, and hauled me up, everyone making a sprint for the living room balcony. The glass doors had already been blown out, and it was the only exit other than falling through the floor.

Guilt clawed up my throat; I had destroyed everything here. Jack's home. Visions and Trinkets. My home, really. I spent more time here than at my own place.

Another crack of wood cleared my thoughts and we hurled ourselves out the balcony doors. The fall was going to hurt and I curled myself up anticipating a landing that never came. Puddin was there flicking her tail back and forth, casting something and slowing our fall. We thudded against the soggy ground.

The house collapsed shortly after that.

Jack collapsed after she saw her house crumble. The house was gutted. I saw more of the inner workings of a house than I ever had before—plumbing, framing, the odd wooden skeleton of the stairs that was crumbling away too. Peony had her arms around Jack, holding her as Jack cried. I didn't cry. I turned to Falcon, who watched everything burn. Diego stood off to the side, close but always just out of frame. His eyes were glued to Jack, and after seeing how tender he was to her, I couldn't hate him even if I tried.

But my gaze was fixed on Falcon.

The enemy.

Fire built up in my chest, heating me to my core. It lit me up inside, forcing the magic to come violently alive. He raised his hands to surrender, but the knife tip of the magic dug into my chest. *Enemy.*

I was made for war.

DIEGO

The fire wiped everything out. Jack's everything was in ashes, and I could do nothing to help. There were tons of people gathered around, watching the scene. Peony and the cat and some man worked the crowd, enchanting and spelling them into believing the fire crew had put out the flames.

I'd never seen someone command the tides like Peony, but if Jack was trapped in an inferno and I could move the waves, I would have.

I would have done anything to get her out of there alive.

The heart link slowed, and I saw her standing where her front door used to be. The home had been condemned, and she wasn't allowed back inside.

Not that that would stop her; the look on her face told me she would try to salvage anything she could. Her newly made staff hovered nearby.

With the staff, she looked so much like Snapdragon it made me sick.

"Snapdragon is still alive." The words replayed through my mind but they didn't make *sense*. She died. I *saw* her die. I saw her right after I severed the ties. She died and me shattering the links did nothing.

Jack touched my arm. I hadn't realized that she was next to me. I patted her hand. This was new–touching. She touched my arm so softly, like I would shatter again if she pressed too hard. Jack touched me again, this time her hands laid on my chest. She waited, feeling my heart beat. Then I felt it–one solid, binding beat.

She had done as I had asked and tied my heart back together; at least the two pieces that I had. Jack started to let go, but I held her steady. Tipping her head back so I could see her more clearly, I kissed her. She was hesitant at first, stiff in my arms. I kissed her lips again, hoping each little peck would convey the words I couldn't seem to get out. *I'm sorry. I see you. I believe in you. I'd break my heart again if you ever asked.*

She leaned back, scanning me, looking for the truth of my feelings to be written on my face.

I caressed her cheeks, trying to take in every detail of her in case she decided to walk away now. Her warm, hazel eyes. The smattering of freckles across the bridge of her nose. Her soft, pink lips. The mess of her hair, falling from her bun.

Jack wrapped her arms around my back, her nails lightly digging into my shoulders, and she curled herself to my chest.

"Thank you," I finally choked out

"If you're going to kiss me like that every time I stitch your heart back together, we're gonna need to find some more pieces ASAP," she laughed. I laughed too, combing my hands through her tangled hair. The smell of smoke clung to her skin, but I could still smell *her.*

"What are you going to do now?" I asked. Her property was in ruins. The heart link warmed again, and her pulse was racing. She wiped at her eyes, not wanting to let the tears fall. I brushed my fingers against her cheeks, wiping away the few tears that made it out.

"I have no idea," she said. Her body was slumped, bruised, and spent. I put my arm around her shoulders, and gently pushed against her. I'd seen Mari do that to her and it made her smile. I wanted her to smile.

"I've never built a house before, but I suppose I can learn."

"Diego fake-last-name-Ortiz, are you planning to rebuild my house?"

"I'd build you a castle, but that might be a bit cliche, hmm?"

Jack's laughter barked out, and she wiped at her eyes again. Still crying. "You are so awkward."

"Jack, I'd move mountains for you, if you asked me to." The heft of the words, so similar to what I once said to Snapdragon, settled in my mended heart. It was different though. With Snapdragon, it was a dare, a promise of destruction. For Jack, it would be my life's purpose. I broke the realms once, and Jack offered me her hand to build it back again. I took it greedily.

"Let's start with all the smoldering rubble. We *just* finished arranging the crystals, too." I kissed the top of her head.

"I'll start digging for the crystals at once," I bowed my head a little, and she laughed. Goddess, her *laugh*. I was alive, alive, alive.

The fire marshal was standing with Peony and Mari now, and waved her over. The grim set of Mari's jaw made my stomach lurch, so I slipped out of sight and over to Falcon. He kneaded his shoulder, digging at his muscle. This was his tell: Falcon would pick and knead and itch at invisible ailments when he was thinking. He paced in place, his weight shifting and shifting. He kneaded harder at his shoulder, making himself wince.

"What's wrong?"

"Hm? Oh, nothing. Just. This sucks. I can't believe we burned a fucking house down."

"We didn't, technically."

Falcon laughed mirthlessly. He kneaded at his shoulder again.

"You're a terrible liar."

"I am an *expert* liar. You just know me too well."

"And we're sticking with the 'nothing's wrong,' line then?"

"Yep." He patted me on the back, all smiles but wouldn't meet my eyes. Falcon was a blank page again; he'd hidden his tells behind that smile. I felt a pain in my gut. It built and the pressure winded me. Falcon rubbed circles on my back. When he moved away, there was a bloody syringe in his hand.

"You'll be okay, D. Not like, immediately, but you will be. I'm sorry. Truth be told, I don't know what's in this shit, but she promised it wouldn't kill you, and that's all I'm really asking for."

"Wh-what?"

"The Judge. I've gotta do it, man. You don't just turn your back on a goddess."

"It's not the Judge! That's Snapdragon–"

"No, it isn't. I've been following the Judge my whole life, bro. I know my calling when I hear it." Falcon kissed my forehead. I was sweating. My guts roiled inside me, and I coughed out blood.

"I don't know how your ex is playing into all of this, but that voice in my head? It's not her. It's the Judge, and as much as I love you, I won't disobey a goddess. Don't fight it too much, bro. You'll be okay. I just. The quicker I do this, the quicker you'll be healed. I got this, D. Just trust me."

I swayed, and fell flat on my back. My body was covered by a charred bush, and I stayed there. My arms were heavy. My legs were even heavier. The pain from my stomach seeped into the rest of me and I blacked out.

"Jack..."

JACK

Time was hazy, but I'd heard Mari say once that time was fucked when you're in a crisis. And I was most certainly in crisis mode. The fire marshal didn't press; Peony sweetly guided his thoughts to understand that this was some freak accident and we're honestly just *so* relieved no one was hurt. He nodded, Peony nodded, and that was that.

Diego and Falcon were gone. They disappeared right after we got out. Diego left without a goodbye, and it hurt more than I wanted to think about. Still, something tingled at the back of my mind that this wasn't okay. Something was off, but I didn't know what. I didn't have the magic or the energy or to focus to figure it out either. I held the heart link, and it beat. Slow, steady. Diego was okay, even if he didn't say goodbye. After his declaration to build me a castle, I thought he would at least stay long enough to wave.

Peony, the blessing that she is, was already in problem solving mode. She'd ordered me some clothes and toiletries. Booked a hotel room. She promised room service would be delivered by the time I was all checked in.

Everyone's words floated in and out of my head, Mari guiding me here. Peony chatting there. Puddin trying and failing to revive some of my garden. That's what stung the most; my garden was in ashes. I ran my fingers over the ruined garden boxes and that's when the tears really hit. The flowers and bushes and trees were all dead. I reached for them, but I couldn't connect to them like I had hours before.

"Thank you for helping me," I whispered to their ashes.

The afternoon or evening, or whatever time it actually was, passed. Peony dropped me off at the hotel and was setting up *the command center* at Mari's place. The heart link was slow, and I felt like that meant Diego was resting. He needed to rest. I needed to rest.

The reality of being homeless sank in. I was homeless. Hot, painful tears gathered in my eyes. That place had been my home for ages. I got it from

Mama and made it my own. It was my everything and now it was ashes and Mama was still MIA.

I ran a bath, turned the TV on and a random cooking show was on, and zoned out. I was still in my smoky, sooty clothes and realized that only after I laid on my bed. The bed. It wasn't *my* bed. My bed was gone.

Everything was gone.

I got a text from Mari. A few heart emojis. She wanted to check in, to say sorry, but I didn't have any words for her. Peony did the same, but instead of emojis, she peppered me with questions.

Are you hurt?

Hungry?

Did you shower?

I'll get your laundry.

Already calling insurance.

Do you want me to bring you some tea?

You're prolly sleeping. Love you.

Nothing still from Diego. Which was fine. It had only been a few hours, and I needed to rest just as much as he did. I sent him a text with a few green heart emojis. The heart link throbbed slowly on my wrist, and I drifted off to the lull of it.

FALCON

Room 215. Jack was checked into room 215 at a lovely and more expensive hotel than me and D chose. It had Peony written all over it. I found it in about thirty seconds. I hated that I could already tell their preferences.

I could see that the lights were on from under the door. The drone of the TV played, but no other sounds from the room. She was probably asleep.

My stomach twisted in knots. ***Kill her, kill her, kill her—***

It was better this way. She wouldn't feel it. I'd be quick. She'd be asleep, probably, and not even wake up. The knife was sharp. Really sharp, actually. I'd cut myself with it twice already. The lights stayed on. I'd been standing by this door for too long.

Kill the false priestess!

Kill her.

Kill her.

"Alright–" I hissed. It'd probably be bad juju to curse at a goddess, but She was pushing it. This didn't *feel* right. This didn't feel like the path of justice. I checked the tattoo on my arm; it was still balanced. The scale never lied, and they told me that this was my goddess guiding me. This *was* justice, even if I hated it.

And I did hate it. I didn't kill people. Not intentionally. Not without purpose.

The sound from the TV faded. She had woken up and turned it off. *Fuck*. The walls were thin, and I heard Jack padding through the room.

Get rid of her now, Falcon. Now. The Judge's voice blasted in my ears and left them ringing. This was the power of a goddess; She could reach through broken realms and guide me. Loudly. Very, very loudly. I slipped a card into the door and let myself in. Jack was still covered in soot. Her eyes were far away, and she didn't startle when the door opened. I don't think she even heard it.

I slipped the knife out of the arm of my coat, and let the hilt slide down to my palm.

Get rid of her.

The Judge's commands were very clear: she needed to be gone. I could do *gone*. I could do that cleanly. No blood. No death. Just... *gone*.

"Falcon? What are you doing here?" Alarm bells rang in her head, and her voice was just as wary. Her staff rose and floated to her.

"I had a thought. Maybe we can... work together?" I had no thoughts; I just really didn't want to kill her.

"What's with the knife?"

"Uh. Well, the idea needs some blood," I said, still no ideas present. Jack tensed, she watched the knife, the staff crossed in front of her, and I knew I had fucked up any quiet attempt at a murder. The fight with Snapdragon had ended, but the voice in my head hadn't stopped. It thundered through me, the timbre making my organs shake. The Judge would not be patient forever. I swallowed and tried to regain some confidence. Just get it over with, and the noise will stop.

"We, um, we gotta fix the link. That's how D is gonna be healed. We–"

"You're lying," her voice was icy. Jack played at being harmless, but I saw the iron in her spine and the stance of her hips. She would kill me first, if it came down to it.

"What? No–"

"The paths between the worlds aren't going to fix Diego's heart, but I know the spell, and I already tied his heart together."

That was news to me. When had she done that? And why couldn't I tell that Diego was better?

The scales on my arm tipped a little.

Stay focused.

"Oh that's great! Then you can do the links between the realms too. I got more juice than your girlfriends and I'm way more stable."

"Now? Right now?"

"No time like the present."

"Why are you pushing this? Diego is fine."

Because it's Plan B or Plan Knifey and I like anything that doesn't end in murder better. "You don't believe me, but there's another piece of his heart out there. It's probably in the other realms. It's the only way to really heal him. It's a classic redemption arc there. Poetic justice, and all that. Link

breaker makes it better, and then bam cosmetic judgements are undone."
I smacked myself internally. Stop talking about the Judge. Stop bringing
Her into it.

"I don't think *I* have the juice for this spell, Falcon."

"I'm like an amp. Use me." I knew the spell too. I'd found it in one of
Nana's old spell books years and years ago. I copied it. Memorized it. I'd
never *tried* it but Jack seemed to have an idea, so that was encouraging.

"And you want me to reconnect the realms right now? This can't possibly wait until the morning?"

Kill her, kill her, kill her, get rid of her!

"I know D wants to go home," I whispered as I schooled my face and my
heart rate and anything else that would give away my guilt; Jack could read a
liar from fifty paces, and I was already on the shit list. She looked wounded,
that he would want to go home. It was a low blow, but I had to exploit her
affection for him. She could hate me and still be alive. I was good with that.

Her staff spun in place, like the hand of a clock going round and round.
The pace was steady and hypnotic. Jack was trying to lower my guard to dig
through my thoughts. Didn't work, but a good try. She grabbed the staff
and stamped it into the carpet. A green circle appeared at her feet, encasing
us both. She swung the staff low between us, and tossed it up, catching
it in her left hand, kneeling with her right on the floor. Three lines laced
through it, dividing the circle in uneven thirds and meeting at the center. A
delicate and complicated knot tied the three lines together. They changed
from green to gold and silver; the colors of the Goddesses.

If I hadn't seen this explicitly drawn out before, I'd be shitting my pants.
This was artful. Masterful. And she'd never even read the damn spell.

She was a damn good imposter.

Jack began the dance. She stepped lightly on each line, weaving the
magic together with her staff. The words of the spell came back to me, and
then she was speaking them.

"Holy Goddesses,
Creation, Judgment, and Vision,
The brokenness in front of me needs to mend,
To join joyously, righteously, and with precision,
Tie together the ends that frayed,
Tie together the paths mislaid."

My lips moved in time with hers, and then the ground shook. The small, delicate knot in the center of her circle trembled, cracking open. The light was golden and welcoming. It looked just how Diego described Obius in his stories. I glanced in, trying to see the rainbow treetops or find the castle spires.

She'd be okay there. I knew it. I knew it with every fiber of my being. I'd get her out of Earth, the Judge would be happy, and Jack would be too. Jack did a final spin, the portal opened wider, and I saw a field of rainbow flowers. They were more beautiful than everything I could have dreamt of.

I shoulder checked her straight into the portal.

"I'm sorry–"

She grabbed my arm and pulled me with her, the force of the portal dragging us through to the other side.

"Nice try, asshat. I'm not going alone."

We fell through and the portal closed.

DEAR READER

Thank you so much for reading *Visions of Snapdragon*! I sincerely hope that you enjoyed Jack and the rest of the crew learning the depths of their magic and what secrets are waiting for them.

If you enjoyed it, please consider leaving a review and spreading the word! This helps other readers to find this book; chatting and posting about it on social media, blogs, and forums is an absolute blessing for indie writers. This is how we connect with our readers, and every review is so appreciated!

Also, if you'd like some exclusive content and teasers for the next books in Jack's world, you can always sign up for my **NEWSLETTER** too!

Love,

Jana

Acknowledgments

There are so many people that have supported and cheered me on to making *Visions of Snapdragon* a reality. My amazing husband, Glenn, who listened and nodded *yes dear* faithfully during all of my late night writing sessions and woes. My parents, Shirley and Jim, have been steadily cheering me on since I was a young teenager to pursue my writing. My dearest friends, Emma, who whipped the plotline into a line instead of a squiggle; Emily, who saw the emotions on the page and helped me fill them out so they hit just right; Joshu, KK, and Nicolai my steadfast rocks that listened to *so much complaining* that there should be an award for it.

Then the editor that got this book to where I wanted it to be: my darling Andrea Davidson, **the Ardent Editor**, whom I can't thank enough for her skills and insights.

Thank you, thank you, thank you.

On to the next book in Jack's world!

About Jana

Writer. Wife/Mom. Servant to 4lb Chihuahua with a Napoleon complex. Avid coffee drinker. Travel junkie. Book devourer. (Not, *literally*—too much fiber.)

I've been writing most of my life, but my heart has always been drawn to magic. Urban Fantasy--mixing magic with real life--became the perfect genre for me.

Born and raised on the Southeast Coast of Virginia, when I'm not writing or momming, I'm heading for the ocean.

Come join my newsletter called **"The Magic Shop,"** where I'll send you monthly emails to tease upcoming books, provide flower, crystal, and character bios, and *of course,* pictures of His Royal Highness, Prince Babar, my chihuahua.

Feeling social? I'm on Facebook and IG, and I'd love for you to come say hello!

f

facebook.com/profile.php?id=100091558147127

instagram.com/jana_sun_books/

www.ingramcontent.com/pod-product-compliance
Lightning Source LLC
Chambersburg PA
CBHW060519160726
47991CB00001B/101